SECRETS FROM THE PAST

BLACKWOOD SECURITY VS. BALDWIN'S SHORE
BOOK 2

ELISE NOBLE

Published by Undercover Publishing Limited

Copyright © 2023 Elise Noble

v3

ISBN: 978-1-912888-74-0

Edited by Nikki Mentges, NAM Editorial

Cover design by Abigail Sins

www.undercover-publishing.com

www.elise-noble.com

For Razor, my big gangly goofball, the goodest boy ever. Hope
Janet's looking after you up there.

1

—————

HALLIE

"Can you tell me a little more about Kaylin La Rocca?" I asked.

A year ago, the thought of speaking with a billionaire would have freaked me the hell out, but so much had changed in the past twelve months. I'd been rescued from the pits of hell, otherwise known as a sex trafficker's mansion in Florida, I'd met the man of my dreams, and I'd also found that I had a knack for asking questions.

All of which had led me here on this grey day in late February—here being the Peninsula Resort and Spa in Baldwin's Shore, Oregon—for a chat with Nico Belinsky. The purpose of our conversation was twofold: firstly, I needed to glean as many details as I could about Kaylin La Rocca, the woman I'd been hired to find. Well, not hired, exactly. Emmy, one of the big bosses at Blackwood Security, had traded my services in return for Nico's help to cover up a small national-security-related incident that had happened here a month ago.

In truth, that case had shaken me. Most people managed to get through a lifetime without being abducted, but I'd had the dubious honour three times now, and the last incident had been the most terrifying, the rescue swift and dramatic. I still suffered nightmares about drowning alone in the middle of the ocean. But I'd taken a short vacation, spent some time with my not-quite-fiancé, and now I was ready to work again. A job researching a cold missing persons case was just what I needed, nothing too strenuous. Yes, Kaylin had an outstanding arrest warrant, and yes, it was for murder, but Nico assured me it was all a big mistake.

And at least there were no crazy Russian assassins involved in Kaylin's case. I'd had enough of Russian freaking assassins.

The second reason for tonight's visit? I'd been tasked with keeping Nico occupied while Emmy did a little breaking and entering, which sounds so much worse than it really was. She didn't plan to steal anything. All she needed to do was leave a note on behalf of an acquaintance, and so far, I'd managed to fulfil my role. Nico and I were hanging out together in his luxuriously appointed office, ready for a cosy chat out of the public eye. Rather than sitting behind the massive desk at the far end, he'd led me over to a quartet of leather chairs grouped around a glass coffee table in the corner and settled onto the one nearest the wall, legs crossed at the ankles. I'd taken a seat opposite as I tried to fathom him out. Emmy said he was an incorrigible flirt, but so far, he'd been nothing but professional with me.

Nico took a sip of his drink. Vodka, neat. He'd filled a shot glass for each of us without asking, but I hadn't touched mine.

"What do you want to know?" he asked.

"Let's start with some background. The basics. Details of Kaylin's family, her friends, any known addresses. Do you have a picture?"

Nico's phone had been sitting face-down on the table, but now he unlocked it and scrolled until he found what he was looking for. Not just one photo but a whole album of them. The first few were poorer in quality, as if Nico had zoomed in and cropped them from larger images, and they'd been taken when Kaylin was still a child. She'd worn her blonde hair in pigtails and favoured pink dresses. In one picture, a teenage Nico was standing next to her, an arm around her shoulders as he looked sullenly at the camera.

"How old were the two of you here?"

"I was sixteen; Kaylin was eight."

"It wasn't a happy occasion?"

"Happiness was rare in those days." He took the phone from me and studied the screen. "I think that was taken at my father's birthday celebration."

His father. Lev Belinsky had been a Moscow-based oligarch and all-around asshole who'd made a fortune in the commodities industry before his untimely death when Nico was twenty years old. Untimely because he'd been assassinated by a fake hooker who'd slipped a knife between his ribs. How did I know about the fake hooker when that detail had never been made public? Because she was one of my new colleagues, also known as Nine, former member of a Russian hit squad, aka the Bad Samaritan, Baldwin's Shore's very own deliverer of vigilante justice.

And, quite frankly, she scared the crap out of me.

Nico handed the phone back, and I scrolled through the rest of the pictures, several dozen of them in total. Kaylin had followed her mom into modelling, and these were all from professional shoots. Kaylin smiling, Kaylin pouting, Kaylin staring into the distance. Her hair was a few shades lighter compared to the earlier photos, and it bounced around her shoulders, glossy and perfect. She had a figure to die for, and her make-up was flawless. But she'd lost her smile. Young Kaylin's eyes had sparkled, while grown-up Kaylin looked polished but jaded.

Her mom had passed away by then, which must have had an impact. Was Renée La Rocca's death an accident? Maybe,

maybe not. Certainly no one had ever been arrested after she tumbled out of a window. Last month, Nico had admitted to Emmy that he didn't know whether his father had been involved in Renée's unfortunate demise, but it was possible.

Following her mom's death, Kaylin had spent her high-school years with her grandmother in Virginia. Speaking with Chelle La Rocca was at the top of my list of things to do when I returned home. I'd already tracked down her address, and it was only an hour from Blackwood's headquarters.

"Did Kaylin spend long in Russia?" I asked Nico.

"Roughly a year and a half—Renée came to Moscow for a modelling job, then stuck around after she started screwing my father."

I made a note of that. While Nico spoke fondly of Kaylin, his voice held no such affection when it came to her mom.

"What kind of relationship did Renée and Kaylin have?"

"Not a great one. Motherhood didn't suit Renée, and I'm not certain Kaylin even knew who her father was. He isn't named on her birth certificate. Whenever the two of them visited our place, Renée would bring a bag full of colouring books and pens and toys, and Kaylin was expected to amuse herself while her mother entertained my father." Nico smiled at a memory. "Penguins. She loved to draw penguins."

"Did you spend much time with Kaylin?"

"Not if I could help it." Nico sighed. "How many teenage boys want to hang out with a child half their age? But she'd follow me around to show me her drawings and the things she used to make out of beads." He hesitated for a moment, then rose to fetch something from his desk drawer. A keyring. A yellow-and-pink beaded keyring. He placed it on the coffee table and took his seat again. "This was one of her efforts. She gifted it to me on my sixteenth birthday."

And he'd kept it for all these years.

"She made an impression on you."

"I didn't have much to be cheerful about in those days. She made me smile, no matter how hard I tried to pretend that she didn't. She won everyone's hearts. The members of my father's security team weren't hired for their winning personalities, and even their masks cracked when she was around."

"What were the circumstances of her leaving?"

"I wasn't privy to that information. One day, Renée and Kaylin were there, and the next, they were gone. A few months later, I overheard the staff talking about an accident and searched the internet. That's how I knew that Renée's life had come to a premature end."

"You don't think it was an accident?"

"She was naive, but she wasn't careless. Suicidal? Possibly. She always seemed highly strung, but I'm not in a position to assess her mental state."

"Was Kaylin there at the time her mother fell?"

"Renée fell from the building she worked in, so I doubt it. But I don't know for sure. That isn't the type of thing two people discuss when they haven't seen each other for a decade."

Which brought us to the one and only time Nico had seen Kaylin after she left Russia. Emmy had given me a rundown of the details—they'd bumped into each other by chance five or six years ago and eaten lunch together.

"Tell me what happened in New York."

"There's not much to tell. I was leaving my lawyer's office, and there she was on the sidewalk."

"You recognised her right away?"

"Yes and no. At first, I was struck by the resemblance to her mother, and then she recognised me. If she hadn't smiled, I'd probably have carried on walking. I mean, she was beautiful —head-turningly beautiful—but I don't make a habit of approaching people on the street."

"Are you certain it was a chance meeting? She couldn't have known you were there?"

"Kaylin was lost, and I was behind schedule that day. If somebody hadn't jumped in front of a subway train at West 86th and Broadway, my meeting would have run to time, and I'd have missed her by ten minutes. Instead of having lunch with me, she'd have gone home after she gave up trying to find the address for her casting call."

"What did you discuss during lunch? Did she mention her personal life?"

"We studiously avoided that subject. She showed me her modelling portfolio and told me about the campaigns she'd worked on—nothing major, but she was certain she'd get her big break soon. In hindsight, I wish I'd done more. Hired her to front an ad campaign for one of my resorts or spoken to my contacts and found her more work. But seeing her was... difficult. Kaylin was the closest thing I had to a sister at one point, but she also reminded me of a past I'd rather forget."

I could understand that sentiment. There were so many events I wished I could erase from my memory—being framed for murder, being trafficked, being trapped in a basement with a serial killer, for example—but my past had made me who I was today. Instead of being almost engaged to a wonderful man and working a job I loved, I could have been waiting tables sixty hours a week at a diner in Kentucky. Over the past few years, I'd learned to take the rough with the smooth.

"Emmy said Kaylin called you again a couple of years later?"

"A little over three years ago, yes. We exchanged numbers in New York and promised we'd keep in touch. Of course, we never did. It's just what people say, isn't it?"

But Kaylin *had* tried to speak with him, and Nico had missed the call. He didn't pick up the voicemail she left until half a day later.

"And she asked you to meet her at a hotel on the outskirts of Manassas?"

"She sounded terrified. It took me another twelve hours to get there, but all I found was a crime scene."

"I've read the police file on the case."

"They gave you that?"

"Not exactly." And Ford, my boyfriend, who also happened to be a detective in the Richmond PD, didn't know I had it either. "Somehow, it just appeared on my desk."

Nico laughed. Emmy said he didn't strike her as the type of man who worried about a little law-bending, and I didn't know whether to be thankful for that or very, very nervous. According to the notes in the file, Kaylin had left her room—the Bluebird Inn was actually a motel rather than a hotel—late one evening and run down an off-duty cop who'd been walking home from a family dinner. Officer Mike Downie might have survived if he'd gotten to a hospital fast, but he'd been left to die in the gutter. Then Kaylin had disappeared, never to be seen again. Her car was found two days later on a side street in Reston, wiped clean of prints and empty of personal effects. She'd left most of her belongings in the motel, as if she'd expected to return soon. Or as if she'd never expected to leave. A small smear of blood had been found in the back seat of the vehicle, but DNA testing showed it belonged to a male other than the victim, and the database failed to throw up any hits. It could have come from the previous owner of the car—nobody had ever managed to find him—or someone else entirely.

A security camera had recorded Kaylin's Toyota leaving the motel parking lot just before the incident occurred, but the camera was old, the footage too grainy to see who was behind the wheel. But the right front tyre matched the track across the dead guy's chest, and although it was a common pattern, a minor defect in the tread removed any possibility that another vehicle had been involved.

"What are your thoughts on the incident?" Nico asked.

"The way I see it, there are two possibilities. Either Kaylin drove out of the motel parking lot with her mind on other things, hit a man, and ran, or somebody else was in the car that night."

"Yes. That was my thought process too." A long pause. "It was the second option."

"What makes you say that?"

By Nico's own account, he barely knew Kaylin. People could change a lot as they grew older. He paused for a long moment before he spoke, considering his answer, one finger tapping on the arm of the chair. When he noticed me glance at his hand, he stilled.

"When Kaylin was seven, a guard on my father's security team kicked one of the cats that ran about the place and broke its leg. I came home to find Kaylin sobbing in the living room with the thing bundled on her lap, and she'd made it a splint out of three colouring pencils and some hair ties. That's the type of person she was. Sweet and sensitive. Unless Kaylin was physically unable to call for help, she'd never have left an injured man lying at the side of the road."

"People change."

"Not Kaylin. At least, not when I saw her in New York. She didn't get ten steps from the restaurant before she emptied all the cash that was left in her wallet into a homeless man's cup."

Interesting. And I tended to agree—if she'd had a shred of decency left, she would have stopped at a gas station and made an anonymous call before she vanished. Which made my heart sink. If Kaylin hadn't been able to call for help, we might be looking for a body instead of the kind, vibrant woman Nico had described.

"What happened to the cat?" I asked, rather than putting my fears into words.

"I took it to the veterinarian, and he put a plate in its leg."

"And what happened to the guard?"

Nico shrugged and gave a tiny, sly smile.

Okay, maybe Emmy had been right about Nicolai Lvovich Belinsky. He definitely paid lip service to the law.

But was he right about Kaylin?

I glanced at the ornate gold clock on the wall—it was nearly eight o'clock. How much longer did Emmy need to do her thing? B&E was child's play for her, especially when the Bad Samaritan had provided a key, the alarm code, and access to the security system.

"I understand another private investigator already looked into the case?"

Nico nodded. "When it became apparent that the cops weren't going to find Kaylin, I hired a guy from Manassas. Figured local knowledge would be an advantage, but he hit dead end after dead end."

"Can I get access to his reports?"

"I have the entire file for you. Would you prefer a printed copy or digital?"

"Email works best."

"You'll have it by the morning."

"Do you think he'd speak with me?"

"Sadly not. He had a stroke two months ago, and his wife said he won't be working any time soon. Did Emerson explain our arrangement to you?"

"That Blackwood would perform a desktop review of the case at no charge and follow up on any missed leads we find?"

"Yes, that's what we agreed. But if you spot any new avenues of investigation, I just want to make it clear that the budget isn't an issue. If you find a thread, tug on it, and I'll pay whatever's necessary."

"I understand."

"Good. And now…" He checked his watch. "Would you like to join me for dinner?"

"Uh…"

I still hadn't heard from Emmy. She'd message me as soon as she was done, and Blackwood's comms app would tap my wrist via my smartwatch with any updates. But Nico misunderstood my hesitation.

"If you're concerned about my reputation, Emerson assured me that she'd personally remove my testicles with a rusty melon baller if I was anything but gentlemanly toward you."

"A…rusty melon baller?"

"She was very specific on that, and I suspect she's the type of woman who'd follow through."

"Yes. Yes, she is."

"Do you want to eat in the dining room, or should I ask the staff to serve the food in here? There's a wedding reception in the ballroom, so it might be busier than usual in the bar tonight."

At one time, I'd have broken out in hives at the thought of a private dinner with a man like Nico Belinsky, and the fact that I didn't start sweating at the suggestion made me oddly proud. Plus I knew Emmy would never knowingly put me in a position where I could be in danger. A melon baller… She probably kept it in her desk drawer alongside her Walther PPQ and her dick guillotine.

Nico tilted his head to one side, studying me. "We'll eat in the dining room. Yes, I think you'd be more comfortable with that."

"I—" Oh, thank goodness. I focused on the tapping against my wrist. *Taptap tap tap, taptap taptap taptap, taptap tap, tap.* Morse code for DONE. "Yes, the dining room works for me."

Nico rose gracefully to his feet and motioned toward the door with a hand. "After you, *milaya*."

Milaya? Was that Russian? I gave him a suspicious glare as I tucked my notepad, pen, and digital recorder back into my purse. "Are you still being a gentleman?"

He winked, and his polite smile turned the tiniest bit dirty. "Absolutely."

"Ladies first."

Nico's gaze dropped to Hallie's ass as she walked out of the restaurant ahead of him. *Ladies first.* It sounded so polite, so chivalrous, but he suspected some horny old fucker in the sixteenth century had come up with the concept as an excuse to check out the goods.

As asses went, Hallie's wasn't bad. Nico considered himself something of a connoisseur when it came to the female form. He'd studied women the world over, and he wore his hard-won reputation as a womaniser with pride, because better to be considered a smooth-talking playboy interested in nothing but a good time than risk curious acquaintances digging below the surface. Even now, the darkness still bubbled up on occasion.

A little gift from his late father.

And Hallie was more curious than most. Nico had seen it in her eyes, heard it in her voice as she ran through her questions. That little tilt of the head as she listened. The copious notes she took, even though she was recording the conversation. He didn't doubt that she'd run a thorough background check on him before she set foot in the hotel, but he was also certain that she didn't know his whole story. Life in Russia had been hell, but it had been a very private hell. Sure, there was speculation, but when the whispers were about Lev Belinsky, even the wildest rumours had only scratched the surface of his depravity. Nico shuddered at the memory of his father's pets—the pair of sharks and Tunguska the Siberian tiger in particular. After the old *svoloch's* death, one of Nico's first moves had been to rehome the menagerie to sanctuaries where they could be fed a more appropriate diet.

Fuck, he'd hated that life.

Hated having to kiss up to the thugs that ruled Russia, hated having to dirty his hands and do his father's bidding, hated being trapped in a cold world where all that mattered was power. Not that he'd let on at the time—back then, indifference had been a shield. A survival mechanism. Indifference mixed with a hint of arrogance. If dear old Dad hadn't believed that Nico was toeing the family line, the fragments of authority Nico had been amassing like uncut diamonds would have been crushed under the weight of his father's influence.

Instead, he'd bided his time. Waited. Strategised and formed long-term goals. *Prove his loyalty. Convince his father that the global arm of the growing Belinsky empire needed personal oversight and Nico was the man to provide it. Get the hell out of Russia.* Simply walking away hadn't been an option.

In Lev Belinsky's world, DNA only got a man so far, as Nico's older brother had found out all those years ago. Officially, the fall from the rear door of the limo had been an accident, a faulty door catch, but eight-year-old Nico had been squashed into the corner of the back seat when his father shoved Yakov out into traffic. The crime? Yakov wanted to study sociology at an American university rather than taking his place as heir. Instead, he'd spent three years in a coma before finally succumbing to the inevitable.

Something stirred in Nico's gut: guilt. Guilt and a memory of Yakov's funeral. He should have been sad, but the sadness had passed by that time, and his overriding emotion had become envy. Envy that Yakov was with their mama now while he was stuck with a cruel father and the *mudak's* second wife. In those days, Nico had spent as much time as possible in his room, watching YouTube via a VPN, learning how an eleven-year-old boy would act if he weren't being raised by a psychopath.

Waiting.

Biding his time.

In truth, he'd expected to wait a lot longer than he had.

But *she* came.

At first, he'd assumed she was just another pretty blonde from the long line of hookers who frequented his father's bedroom when the fourth Mrs. Belinksky was out doing whatever twenty-five-year-old gold-diggers did, but she'd turned out to be an angel in disguise.

Oh, sure, Nico had made all the right noises about pain and retribution, but in truth, if he ever met the woman who'd killed his father so efficiently, he'd kiss her fucking feet. But she'd disappeared as mysteriously as she'd arrived, a pale-haired ghost with a great ass, an athletic figure, and a rose tattoo on one thigh. And he'd begun dismantling the empire his father had created and building his own. Out with the darkness, in with the light.

None of that could right past wrongs, though. Renée La Rocca's death had been a tragedy. As death went, defenestration was a quick and relatively painless way to go, but Kaylin was left alive to suffer. No, Renée hadn't been the best mom in the world—her disturbing lack of judgment in getting involved with Lev Belinsky was testament to that—but she'd been all Kaylin knew.

There was that guilt again.

Guilt by association.

Guilt that half of his DNA had come from a monster.

Was Nico a monster?

The jury was still out on that question. He tried to be kind and fair, but deep down, a part of him still liked to see morally bankrupt men suffer for their sins. And a worse part of him liked to inflict the punishment.

"Dinner was delicious," Hallie said, snapping him back to the present. "Thank you."

"It was my pleasure." The steak had been sourced locally, as had the wine. "Can I interest you in a nightcap?"

There was the briefest hesitation before she shook her head. "I have an early flight back tomorrow."

She'd been pleasant company—smart, slightly nervous, not at all like her acerbic boss. Emmy Black thought nothing of breaking into Nico's villa and helping herself to his gourmet coffee. That wasn't to say that he didn't enjoy spending time with her. Mrs. Black was magnetic in a leads-men-to-their-doom kind of way, and if she hadn't been married, he might have been masochistic enough to make a move on her.

He leaned in to kiss Hallie on the cheek, politely. So politely.

"Safe travels, Ms. Chastain."

She blushed. Of course she blushed.

"I'll be in touch as soon as we've reviewed the file and worked out the next steps."

Nico watched her bypass the elevator and head for the stairs, and the guilt crept back again.

Guilt over the real reason he'd never called Kaylin after that chance meeting in New York. Guilt that after a long, lazy lunch with the woman she'd become, his thoughts about her had been anything but brotherly.

At the time, giving her space had seemed the wisest option. He'd acted in her best interests. Kaylin La Rocca was caring and kind, and the darkness that lurked within Nico had been closer to the surface in those days. Then there was the small issue that his father had murdered her mother. Nico might have claimed he didn't know the truth, but in his heart, he did. Perhaps she'd asked for money or made a misguided threat? Or maybe his father simply hadn't been fond of loose ends?

Whatever the reason, Renée was cold in the ground, just like Nico's mama and two of his stepmothers. To Lev Belinsky, women had been disposable.

And Nico had never been the type for commitment.

No, Kaylin had deserved better, and so he'd walked away.

3

HALLIE

Nico hadn't hired a slouch, that was for sure. Jacob Crumb, the Manassas-based private investigator, had meticulously followed up every lead on the trail of Kaylin's whereabouts, and he had great local connections. He'd spoken to every member of staff at the Bluebird Inn and most of the police department too, not only the cops but dispatchers and admin staff as well. I knew from experience that admin staff could be a better source of information than the officers themselves on occasion. Slowly, slowly, I was building my own network in Richmond.

I leaned back in my chair and stared at the ceiling. No water-stained tiles for Blackwood—in the past month, someone had painted a skyscape up there, complete with fluffy white clouds, birds, a rainbow, and... I squinted at the far corner of the room... Yup, a military drone. Apparently, the new decor was meant to be calming. The drone looked like an afterthought, and I suspected it was an unauthorised addition.

"Is that the Kaylin La Rocca file?" my boss asked, appearing behind me. Daniela di Grassi was a tough New

Yorker who spoke her mind and didn't take shit from anyone. "Donut?"

"Where did you get those?"

Emmy's nutritionist, Toby, took his duties *very* seriously, and although officially he only looked after Emmy and her team, he'd taken it upon himself to ensure that everyone else stayed in good shape too. After some negotiation, we'd agreed upon Fridays as the office cheat day. The rest of the week, we got veggie trays, yogurt, and bagels with low-fat cream cheese. Today was Monday. We shouldn't have donuts on a Monday.

"Emmy just happened to detour via the bakery on her morning run."

"And Alex let her?"

Alex was her personal trainer, and usually as militant as Toby when it came to her health. I wouldn't be able to stand it, having people constantly tweak my diet and exercise and monitor everything I did, but for Emmy, it was a way of life, as were her carb-related rebellions.

"Alex has mellowed since he got a girlfriend," Dan said, biting into a bear claw. "Haven't you noticed?"

I shuddered. I couldn't help it. I'd always suspected he was crazy, what with his willingness to spar with members of the Special Projects team, but he'd confirmed it when he started dating Dasha, also known as the Bad Samaritan.

"Doesn't she make you nervous?" I whispered, as if she might suddenly materialise beside me.

Dan merely shrugged. "No more than Ana."

That didn't mean much. "Yeah, well, Ana's also terrifying."

Ana was a former colleague of Dasha's. And a current colleague now that Emmy had given Dasha a job. Only part-time, but even an hour a week with her was enough to set me on edge. She was just so damn competent. At least we'd left her behind in Baldwin's Shore this week. She was probably sitting in her craft store, working out a hundred ways to kill a man with a ball of yarn and a crochet hook.

"Yeah, but Ana's on our side, so terrifying is a good thing." Dan tapped the papers I'd printed out. "What have you found so far?"

"Honestly? Not much. Crumb—the other investigator— seems to have spoken to everyone in Manassas, plus nearly all of the guests who were staying in the motel at the same time as Kaylin."

"Nearly all?"

"There were four he couldn't track down, and the cops couldn't find them either." I checked my notes. "A young couple with a baby—their accents suggested they were from Alabama, and they gave their names as Joe and Rachel Smith. Plus a guy with a large backpack and a foreign accent, possibly Italian or French, who was logged in the system as 'Alan Thingy.' Reading between the lines, the kid on the desk wasn't the brightest or the most conscientious, and the notes say he asked Alan for his name three times, and when he still couldn't understand him, he just guessed."

"This wasn't the kind of place that asked for ID?"

"At the Bluebird Inn, cash is king. They also rented rooms by the hour on occasion—our fourth missing guest is a woman named Beatrix, who Crumb believes was in the sex trade. Short skirt, twitchy, kept looking toward the parking lot. Which meant she probably had a client with her, but nobody saw him."

Beatrix had been a semi-regular at the motel, showing up for a night or two at a time and then disappearing again. Either she moved around, or she took time off. She wasn't known to the police, not under the name she gave the desk clerk, and none of the cops had recognised her from the description. Petite, blonde, great rack, not quite a ten because her nose was too big. Yes, the desk clerk was a pig.

"Why was Kaylin even in a place like that?"

"That's the sixty-four-thousand-dollar question, isn't it?"

"Crumb didn't find out?"

"He seemed more concerned with finding out where she went than where she'd been."

"It's an interesting case." Dan took another bite of donut and wiped sugar off her lips. "Is she dead, or isn't she?"

I hadn't wanted to voice my concerns in front of Nico, but I thought the chances of her being alive were slim. Disappearing without a trace wasn't easy, not in the digital age. Not if you were still breathing. Blackwood had a small team that specialised in pseudocide, and the perpetrators nearly always slipped up. They called an old friend, or accessed their money, or snuck onto social media, or got caught out by discrepancies in documentation. Kaylin's first attempt at running—and I was certain that's what she'd done, she'd been running from someone or something—had been sloppy. She'd checked into the Bluebird Inn under a false name, parked her car in the darkest corner of the lot, paid cash, and more or less hidden in her room. A couple of people noticed her using the vending machines in the lobby, but nobody saw her leave the property.

When she finally did take off, she left half of her belongings in her room, including her passport. Nobody went from panicked amateur to pro-level disappearance in a week, not unless they were cold in a grave.

"The evidence so far suggests she's dead."

"Right. So, who killed her? Did she stumble across a madman in Manassas? Or did somebody from her past catch up with her?"

"By all accounts, she didn't go out anywhere in Manassas."

"So..."

It was about her past, wasn't it? I thumbed to the notes Crumb had made on Kaylin's life in New York, but that section was thin. Real thin. She'd shared an apartment in Hell's Kitchen with two other women, and she'd left without giving notice or even cleaning out her room. The modelling agency she'd been signed with had been equal parts irritated and clueless at her disappearing act. And her former boss at the events company she used to waitress for whenever she didn't have modelling work had no idea where she'd gone either. Nobody had mentioned any sort of trouble, and there was no evidence of a boyfriend. Neither of her former roommates had been forthcoming with information. It seemed that Crumb had still been working on the New York angle at the time of his stroke, albeit half-heartedly—there was a world of difference between his comprehensive notes from Manassas and the write-up of his visit to the Big Apple. It was clear where his comfort zone lay.

What about my comfort zone?

Some days, I thought there was no such thing. I'd gone from waiting tables in Kentucky to being kidnapped and forced into the sex industry, only to be rescued and thrust into a whole new world. I was still feeling my way at Blackwood. But I loved the work, and I trusted the team to back me up. Plus I had a boyfriend now. Falling in love with a cop was the last thing I'd expected to happen in the middle of an investigation, but then Detective Ford Prestia had shown up with a dirty smile and a banana, and now we were practically hitched. The ball was in my court, he said. *When you want a ring, just let me know.*

But for the moment, I had a case to focus on.

"So... We need to follow the trail in New York. Before we can go forward in time, we have to go back."

Dan grinned at me. "Exactly. Book yourself a flight, sweetie."

"I want to speak with Chelle La Rocca first. Plus there are

four guests from the Bluebird Inn who've never been traced. Are you coming to New York?"

"Wish I could. Pay a visit to La Bella Farina for me, okay? That place makes the best cookies. I'll speak with the New York office, find you a partner who knows the city. Make sure you take things slow and steady."

"I will."

"And try not to get kidnapped again."

"That's a given."

"You know there's a pool, right? How long until Hallie's next abduction?"

"You've got to be kidding me."

"C'mon, you've managed it three times in three years. If you can wait until the first week in May, I'll win five hundred bucks."

I flipped Dan the bird. "I'm signing up for a Krav Maga class right now."

"I saw you in the gym with Dasha the other day. How did that go?"

Quite honestly? It had been both scary as hell and weirdly empowering. She'd started off with a condescending pep talk —kidnap me once, shame on you, kidnap me twice, shame on me, kidnap me three times... She'd just shaken her head in incredulity and muttered something in Russian—and then shown me how to take a man to the floor with brutal efficiency. Next, we'd headed to the indoor range, where she'd given me a long lecture-slash-lesson on point shooting, which meant a fast draw and aiming on instinct rather than relying on the sights, and then she'd made me practise over and over and over again. After two hours, I managed to get a few holes in the target. Her shots hit the centre every time.

I made a face, and Dan laughed.

"That good, huh?"

"Let's just say I'm glad she's back in Oregon."

4

HALLIE

"He said he was a private investigator, but I know a cop when I see one. And the guy who came before—Toast, or whatever his name was—was a cop."

Crumb. She meant Crumb. His notes mentioned that Chelle La Rocca had been uncooperative. But I wasn't going to admit I knew that, and boy, was I glad I'd gone in with a cover story rather than being upfront about the circumstances of my visit. Today, I was here on behalf of Nicci, a friend from New York who'd worked with Kaylin a little over three years ago and never stopped wondering what happened to her.

Chelle poured coffee into two chipped mugs and added milk and sugar to both without asking. Life hadn't been kind to her. The inside of her trailer was tidy, but the outside was weathered to within an inch of its life. Someone had patched the roof with plywood and a tarp. The odour of stale nicotine permeated throughout, and unless I was mistaken, there was a hint of weed too.

I took the mug Chelle offered and followed her to the tiny living room. She waved me toward an afghan-covered recliner, and when she moved a stack of magazines and took a seat on a side table, I figured she didn't get many visitors.

"Maybe he used to be a cop and moved into the private sector," I suggested, knowing that was exactly what had happened.

"Once a cop, always a cop. Men like that never change. Lazy and corrupt, all of them."

Okay, now definitely wasn't the time to mention that I was dating a detective. Ford wasn't corrupt, and he wasn't lazy either—the fact that he'd kept me up half the night was proof of that. My thighs clenched just from the memory.

"There are a few bad apples, no doubt about it."

Rule 101: build rapport. Whether you were talking to a witness or a suspect, you caught more flies with honey. Unless you were Emmy or Dasha, of course. I bet they knew torture techniques I couldn't even imagine.

"More than a few bad apples. My daughter was murdered, and do you know what they did? Nothing. Didn't even bother to investigate, just offered half-baked condolences and went back to arresting jaywalkers or whatever it is they do all day."

"I'm so sorry about your daughter. I didn't realise."

"Well, neither did those fools in uniform. They say she jumped out a window."

Interesting.

"And you don't think that's true?"

"Renée made mistakes, but she wasn't suicidal."

I'd read that file too. Renée La Rocca had returned from Russia, quit modelling, and gotten a job selling advertising at a local newspaper. Quite a change, but she'd met all her sales targets, and her colleagues seemed to like her—there were even rumours of a romance with one of the reporters. The night she died, she'd been working late alone when she exited the building via a fifth-floor window. The only security camera had malfunctioned. Coincidence, or something more? My curiosity burned, but that wasn't the case I was here to solve, and besides, if Renée had been given a helping hand, I already had a good idea who'd ordered it. Nico's father.

I steered the conversation back in the right direction.

"Chelle, I can only imagine the heartbreak you must have experienced losing both your daughter and your granddaughter. I understand you raised Kaylin after her mom passed?"

"That poor child. She needed stability in her life after years of gallivanting around the world." A sigh. "Renée, she was a flighty one."

"Losing her mom can't have been easy for Kaylin. Were you close?"

This place reminded me of my own teenage years, a time spent struggling to survive in a run-down neighbourhood, although on first impressions, Chelle seemed to care more about her family than my own mother had. I wasn't even sure Mom noticed when I left home for good.

Chelle shrugged. "Kaylin took after Renée." The unspoken "unfortunately" at the end of the sentence came across loud and clear. "She wasn't one for small-town life, and neither was her mama. Magpies, both of them, always attracted to shiny things. The bright lights of the city, all those pretty trinkets in the glossy magazines. Kaylin wasn't a day past eighteen when she up and left for New York."

"You wanted her to stay?"

Chelle's weighty sigh told me what her words didn't. "I wanted her to be happy."

"But you didn't think that would happen in New York?"

"I saw what the modelling industry did to Renée. All that glitz and glamour—she wanted it for herself, but it came at a cost." Chelle shook her head. "I tried to warn her. Tried to warn Kaylin too, but she wouldn't listen. Those people, they build the young girls up, they pile on the pressure, and then they tear them down. Don't even get me started on the men."

"The men?"

"The dirty old men. Two and three times her age, showering her with gifts when she was still a teenager, inviting her to parties and passing her around their friends."

"She told you that?"

"I know how things work, missy." Since I arrived, Chelle had sounded strong with a side of bitterness, but now her voice cracked. "I failed with Renée; I know I did. She took after her father. Headstrong and full of misplaced optimism."

"Was he involved in her life?"

Chelle snorted. "Not from prison, he wasn't. I saw him in Kaylin too, but heaven knows who *her* father was. He wasn't a man who paid child support, that was for sure." A sigh. "I tried to steer Kaylin along the right path, and she promised she wouldn't go down the same road as her mama. She wanted to be a singer, did your friend tell you that?"

Kaylin took after her grandma too. Despite the lines in her face and a semi-permanent scowl, Chelle La Rocca had been blessed with an old-school beauty that withstood the test of time, although she did nothing to accentuate it. Her grey hair was scraped back into a ponytail, and she didn't go in for make-up. The pile of cigarette butts in the ashtray on the table beside her no doubt contributed to her yellowed fingers and gaunt frame.

"A singer? No, Nicci didn't mention it."

"Kaylin has the voice of an angel. Won every talent contest she ever entered, once she lost her puppy fat, and she swore she'd only model until she broke into the music industry."

This was the first I'd heard of Kaylin's desire to sing professionally, so I was going to assume she hadn't gotten very far, although Crumb's notes had mentioned her winning a handful of beauty pageants. I also noted that Chelle referred to her in the present tense.

"But she was still modelling when she...uh, at the time of the incident at the Bluebird Inn?"

Chelle's expression darkened, and slightly bloodshot blue eyes zeroed in on mine.

"Whatever happened that night, it wasn't Kaylin's fault."

"That's what Nicci said too, but I can't understand why Kaylin didn't stay to tell her side of the story."

"If you grew up around here, you wouldn't stick around to talk to the cops either. They shoot first and ask questions later."

"But—"

"You think I'm lying? Look up Martell Ziegler on that fancy phone of yours." She nodded toward the smartphone I'd placed on the arm of the chair. "Go on—look it up."

I did as instructed, and there were plenty of hits. Martell Ziegler had been thirteen years old when cops shot him through the front window of his home as he played Nerf wars with his younger brother. He'd bled out before the ambulance arrived with his mother crying at his side, and the police department later admitted that they'd been at the wrong house.

As I reached the end of the article, Chelle nodded knowingly. "The Zieglers lived half a mile from here. Marty and Kaylin were in the same class."

"Was there an investigation?"

"Yes, but a few bucks and a half-assed apology can't bring back that little boy. So a cop died at the Bluebird Inn? Good riddance, I say. If Kaylin was involved, then I'm sure she had a good reason."

Yikes. Mental note: never, ever put this woman in the

same room as Ford. I had a feeling that a "not all cops" comment would shut her down, so I nodded along, even though anger was blossoming in my belly. Officer Mike Downie had been a husband. A father. A son.

"Did she give any indication as to what that reason might be? Was she in touch with you before it happened?"

"I hadn't heard from her in a month, but you mark my words—it was the cops. If you're going to carry on with this investigation of yours, then that's where you need to start, but watch your back or you'll end up in the same place as Kaylin."

Which was where? There was something off about Chelle La Rocca's answers to my questions, and I'd been struggling to put my finger on what it was, but now it hit me. She was angry and bitter and vengeful, guilt-ridden over the shortcomings in Renée's and Kaylin's lifestyles, but the devastation I'd expected was missing. Not once had she expressed sadness over Kaylin's fate or fear that she might have met a tragic end.

Did she know that she hadn't?

"I appreciate the warning." I took a deep breath and prepared for the backlash. "Ms. La Rocca, has Kaylin been in touch with you since the night she left the Bluebird Inn?"

There it was. The fear. Not fear that Kaylin might be lying in a shallow grave, but fear that I might be about to unearth truths Chelle didn't want me to find.

"It's the cops," she said stubbornly. "Look at the cops."

"What did she say?"

"That's none of your business, missy."

"If you want me to look at the cops, then I need any information Kaylin gave you. As you said, I don't want to end up in the same position."

"Nothing. She said nothing, okay? It was just a Christmas card, and she didn't even sign it."

"Then how do you know it was from her?"

"Because it had a penguin on the front, and penguins were

Kaylin's favourite animal. Plus there was money inside. Ain't nobody else gonna be sending me five hundred bucks, that's for sure."

"Do you still have the card?"

Chelle folded her arms and stood. "I threw it away." She hadn't, but nor was she going to show me. "Wherever Kaylin is, she doesn't want to be found, not while those cops are still carrying badges. If you find evidence that'll put them behind bars, then maybe she can come home."

"To do that, I need to understand what happened leading up to that night. Why did Kaylin go to the Bluebird Inn?"

"Someone probably sent her there. She was too trusting."

"Why would they send her there?"

I could guess, but I wanted Chelle to say it. Did she think Kaylin was capable of illegal activity? Working as a drug mule, for instance? She hadn't made it big as a model, and in NYC, even an apartment the size of a closet could bankrupt a person. Had she been desperate for money and made a grave error?

"She'd always help out a friend who needed a favour, and she wasn't the best judge of character, I'm sorry to say. First, there was that agency boss who charged her hundreds of bucks for portfolio pictures and never found her any work, then the idiot boyfriend who emptied her bank account, and the roommate who took her clothes to a consignment store. And those were just the ones she told me about."

Okay, that could explain why Kaylin had gone to Manassas, but not why she'd stayed in the Bluebird Inn for over a week. If she was running a shady errand, surely she'd have headed right back to New York?

"Did she have friends in Manassas?"

"Who knows? Kaylin could be cagey when it came to her new life. Too many bad influences."

Bad influences? Or she just hadn't appreciated her grandma's attitude? Chelle La Rocca cared in her own way, that much was clear, but she also came across as opinionated and judgmental. Nico had described Kaylin as sweet and sensitive. Maybe she'd gotten sick of the lectures?

Chelle moved toward the door. She wanted me to leave, and I couldn't afford to overstay my welcome, not when I might need to speak with her again in the future.

"Thank you for your help."

"If you keep on after this, watch your step around those cops."

Back at Blackwood's headquarters, I picked at a salad—okay, it was mostly pasta and fried bacon with a generous dollop of ranch dressing—while I tried to organise my thoughts. Was there any truth to Chelle's theory? Could the Manassas cops have been involved? As a former cop himself, Crumb might have been biased against following that line of enquiry. But Chelle wasn't exactly unbiased herself, and her contempt for law enforcement had shone through.

New York or Manassas? New York or Manassas? Where were the clues? I couldn't even talk it over with Dan because she'd gone somewhere with Emmy. They could be hunting for cheeseburgers, or starting World War III, or anything in between. And the office was quiet today. Folks were either getting lunch, or out in the field, or working from home. Only Kellan was in sight, munching his way through a bag of potato chips, and he was a former cop. If I asked his opinion, would his view be clouded by his former profession?

"Penny for them?" a voice asked from behind me, and I jumped out of my skin.

"Asshole," I muttered as I spun my chair around to face Slater. "Haven't you heard of footsteps?"

He gazed down at me, eyes twinkling, unrepentant. Slater was on Emmy's Special Projects team, a US Marine with an infectious grin who could flip from wisecracking to deadly in a heartbeat. Sniping was his specialty.

"According to our fearless leader, footsteps are for pussies."

I spotted the box of donuts in his hand. "Are you stealing our snacks?"

"I was sent to hunt sugar. Want one?"

"Did Toby take the secret hoard of junk food out of the third-floor stationery cupboard again?" I asked, helping myself to a bear claw. Last month, he'd replaced the post-Christmas candy selection with healthy eating posters reminding us that *to eat is a necessity, but to eat intelligently is an art*. Emmy had shrugged, told him she was dumb as fuck, and pulled out a candy bar she'd stashed in her pocket. So in revenge, he'd taken all the soda too.

"We have hummus and four kinds of cracker." Slater grimaced. "You okay? You look kinda pensive."

"Another cold case." Old mysteries were fascinating, but after the last one nearly killed me, I'd become a little more wary about working them. "A missing woman with two possible avenues of investigation."

"And you don't know which way to go?"

"Exactly."

"Would it help to talk it through?" Slater checked his watch. "I have an hour before I head to the airfield."

"Going somewhere exotic?"

"Not really. A security audit in the Hamptons."

"That sounds pretty nice to me."

"Guess it's better than downtown Kabul." He dropped into the seat next to me and took a bite out of a Boston cream. "Talk to Uncle Slater."

I paused to gather my thoughts and then laid out the facts

of the case as I knew them. Slater was smart and had no skin in the game, and I hoped he'd be able to offer an impartial opinion.

"So, you have Dan saying the key is in New York, and the victim's grandma saying the problem lies with the Manassas PD, and you don't know who to believe?"

"In a nutshell."

"And what does your gut tell you?"

"Before I spoke to Chelle La Rocca, I was ready to go to New York, but now I'm second-guessing myself. I mean, she knew Kaylin better than anyone."

"But she's not an investigator. You are."

"I'm still new at it."

"It's true you don't have much experience, but you've got good instincts. Dan wouldn't have hired you otherwise." He started on a cruller because calories weren't a thing a man like Slater needed to worry about. "Did Kaylin have a credit card?"

"Uh..." I consulted the file. "Yes, she did."

"The hotel in Manassas sounds like a shithole. A rent-by-the-hour dump. If you were a young, ambitious woman, what would make you stay there for over a week?"

"Not much," I admitted. There were dead roaches in the crime scene photos. "I'd have to be running from something even worse."

"Or someone."

"Exactly."

And knowing what I did now, that Chelle believed her granddaughter was alive, I figured there was less chance Kaylin had happened across a random psycho and more chance that her nemesis had caught up with her. She'd run again, burrowed in deeper this time, and she wasn't coming out until the coast was clear. A sigh escaped. It would actually be easier to investigate the Manassas cops—at least I'd have a starting point. But in my heart of hearts, I thought Chelle La Rocca was wrong about them.

"I'd better pack for New York."

"If you do it quickly, we can make a pit stop on the way to East Hampton. We're taking the Learjet."

Good thing I kept an overnight bag in the office.

5

HALLIE

"You must be Hallie Chastain?" The older man who'd just walked into the conference room held out a hand. "I'm Collier Dafoe."

I resisted the urge to fan myself. Collier Dafoe had to be touching fifty, but he was in better shape than a man half his age. A broad chest and muscular arms strained at a blue dress shirt. Not my type, but Peta who worked in accounting had a silver fox calendar on her desk, and she'd be licking her lips and calling him Daddy.

The smile he gave me when we shook hands was anything but fatherly, but I knew Dan wouldn't have paired me up with a pervert.

"It's good to meet you, Collier. We'll be working together?"

He nodded. "Dan said you needed someone who knew the city, and I have a light caseload this week."

"I appreciate your help."

Plus I was still training, so I'd need to work alongside a licensed PI.

"Have you visited NYC before?"

"Only for a weekend, but I didn't see much of the city." Was I blushing? My cheeks sure felt hot. Ford had surprised me with tickets for a Broadway show for our four-month anniversary, and after we'd watched *Hamilton*, we'd barely left our hotel room for the rest of the trip. I wasn't going to tell Collier that, of course, but his smirk suggested he'd guessed anyway.

"I grew up in the Bronx. Lived here my whole life, apart from a stint in the army, anyway. You got a plan?"

Kind of. I had a list. While I'd been speaking with Chelle and visiting Nico, Blackwood's data analysis program had been beavering away in the background like a digital sidekick. Providence was Google on steroids with a side of Siri. She— yes, I thought of her as female—dug out information not only from Blackwood's network but from the wider internet too, including some dusty corners she probably shouldn't have had access to. And then she joined the dots. After I'd fed in the key points from Crumb's files, she'd found current addresses and contact details for Kaylin's former roommates, her agent, and her ex-boss at the events company. We'd start there. Chelle La Rocca had held back with Nico's investigator—had others done the same?

"I'll send you a copy of the file, but in summary, we're doing a case review on a missing woman. Kaylin Marie La Rocca. She vanished after being accused of murder."

Dafoe gave a low whistle. "There an arrest warrant?"

"There is. Her vehicle was involved in a hit-and-run, but our client believes there's more to the story than meets the eye."

"How'd they get to murder from a hit-and-run?"

"The victim was a cop. He was on his way home from a get-together, but the commonwealth's attorney was up for re-election, so he said the cop could have died trying to do his duty and dressed it up as aggravated murder."

"That's a reach."

"I agree, but there were no witnesses and no camera footage, so without Kaylin's side of the story, nobody's been able to refute the allegations."

I'd had an off-the-record chat with an attorney friend, and he felt the charges wouldn't stick if the case ever went to trial, but until then, Kaylin was a wanted woman who garnered no sympathy from those who didn't know her.

"You got a starting point?" Dafoe asked, and with his neatly trimmed beard, he looked like Santa Claus's hot cousin. Any woman on the receiving end of his charming smile would think all her Christmases had come at once. Yes, I was practically engaged, but I still glanced at his left hand. No ring.

"We have four possible witnesses to visit, and then we'll see where their information takes us. Two former roommates—Anisha Kapoor and Charlotte Davison. Anisha lives in Hell's Kitchen still, and Charlotte moved to New Brunswick. Then there's Kaylin's agent at Lux Model Management on West 26th."

Dafoe nodded. "Over by Madison Square Park."

"You know it?"

"I dated a girl from there once."

"From Madison Square Park?"

"From Lux."

Dafoe had dated a model? That didn't surprise me one little bit. "The fourth person is Derek Trimmer, who runs Every Step Events. Kaylin used to waitress there when modelling work was scarce."

"So we're visiting two businesses and two individuals?"

"That's right."

He glanced at his watch. "If Lux and Every Step keep office hours, we won't make it in time, but we might catch the two roommates when they get off work. What do they do?"

"Anisha's an attorney. An associate at Perkins, Foster & Brundle."

"Big firm. Those folks work long hours."

They did. Which meant she wouldn't be home until late, if she came home at all. I'd heard stories about junior lawyers sleeping at the office during big cases. Anisha was the least hopeful candidate on my list anyway—Crumb had described her as hostile. There were a lot of "no comments" when he questioned her. Anisha had been thinking as a lawyer rather than a friend.

"How long would it take to get to New Brunswick? Do you have a car?"

Records indicated that Charlotte Davison—now Charlotte Peak—had married a chef ten years her senior and relocated when he opened an upmarket steakhouse not too far from the Rutgers campus.

"In New York traffic? A couple hours. We can take a pool car and talk on the way. You got somewhere to stay tonight?"

I'd been spoiled for choice. Blackwood staff usually booked a room at the Black Diamond Hotel near Central Park, seeing as Emmy and Black owned it, but the four members of Indigo Rain and their entourage were staying there ahead of two sold-out concerts at Madison Square Garden, and the crowds of fans outside were no joke. I didn't much feel like running the gauntlet of reporters either. When I'd called Nico from the jet with an update, he'd offered a suite at a boutique hotel he'd just invested in not too far from Hudson Square, and I'd been tempted. But then Dan offered me Emmy and Black's Upper East Side apartment, which I'd thought was a joke until Emmy texted to say the concierge's name was Alphonse, and if I wanted to get into his good books, I should pick him up a fried chicken sandwich from Rubin's Deli.

"Emmy said I could use her guest room."

"You're not at the Black Diamond?"

"Too many Indigo Rain groupies."

"Is that tonight? I think we're doing the security."

"We are. Some of the fans are getting real creative—I heard that when the band was in Berlin, a girl dressed up as a member of the housekeeping staff and tried to get into Travis Thorne's room. She even embroidered the hotel name on her dress pocket."

"How far did she get?"

"Not very far at all, seeing as she spelled the name wrong."

Collier chuckled. "When folks make mistakes like that, it sure makes our jobs easier."

Wasn't that the truth? But so far, Kaylin La Rocca didn't seem to have made many errors. I just had to hope that she'd left enough loose threads for us to unravel the truth.

6

HALLIE

"That's her," I said. "Standing by the bar."

Nobody had answered the door at the Peak residence, so we'd headed downtown to The Strip Club. "Interesting name," Collier remarked on the drive over, but I was relieved to see that everyone was fully clothed. Not a pole or pair of pasties in sight. On a Tuesday evening, the place was a quarter full, and most of the patrons looked like college students taking advantage of the "Save Before Seven" discount advertised on a board outside. According to the website, Jenson Peak ran the kitchen, and Charlotte was involved in the business too. I recognised her from her social media pictures.

"Let's go see what she has to say."

Collier led me over to the bar, past a twenty-something couple waiting at the host's station, past a group of frat boys heading for the door whose gazes oozed over me like slime. As we passed, one of them accidentally-on-purpose brushed my ass with his hand, and I flinched on instinct. A year ago, I'd have kept my mouth shut and gotten myself out of there, flight rather than fight, but I'd changed. My newfound family had given me back the confidence a series of men had stolen from me.

I wheeled around and fixed him with a glare.

"Keep your hands to yourself."

"Chill, it was an accident."

A couple of his friends sniggered.

"Oh, really? That little squeeze at the end, it was totally unintentional?"

"Bit sensitive, aren't you? Take it as a compliment."

"A compliment?" Now my blood was boiling. "How would you like it if a stranger groped your package?"

The prick actually smirked. "Why don't you try it and see?"

Collier touched my arm, and I wasn't sure whether that meant "calm down" or "I've got your back," but the first wasn't an option. I hated confrontation, but I'd hate myself more if I backed off. What would Dan do? Emmy? Dasha?

I grabbed the asshole's frat-balls and twisted.

For several oh-so-satisfying seconds, his mouth dropped open in shock, but his face quickly screwed up in pain. I leaned in closer.

"Thanks for the invitation."

He tried to push me away, but Collier got there first and wrapped one strong fist around the jerk's arm.

"She said hands off."

"You're crazy," he yelped. "She's crazy."

I released him. "And you're all words and no dick." His buddies laughed again, but this time they were laughing at him, not with him. "Get out of here."

I thought he might take a swing at me, and it took every ounce of strength to keep my feet still, to stand straight and look him in the eye without blinking. I channelled the Blackwood women who'd spent so much time helping me to believe in myself. Sky wouldn't step back. Ana wouldn't step back.

Finally, *he* stepped back, with a parting shot of, "Bitch." I couldn't stop trembling as he left the restaurant. Emmy wouldn't tremble, and Dan wouldn't tremble, but I'd used up the last of my courage when I treated his nuts like a particularly stubborn jar lid.

"Nicely handled," Collier murmured in my ear. "No pun intended."

"I swear I've never tried to castrate a man in public before."

"Just in private?"

"Uh, no. No, never."

Too late, I realised everyone in the restaurant was staring at me, and my cheeks burned. I was about to follow the jerk out the door when a girl by the window started clapping, and soon the air was filled with applause. Even a few of the men joined in.

"Boy, that was some entrance," Charlotte Peak said when the noise died down.

"I'm so sorry about that."

"Between you, me, and the big man upstairs, that guy had it coming. What can I get you folks? A glass of wine on the house, obviously, but anything else? Our second chef called in sick, so there might be a short wait for food."

I really needed the wine, but I figured it was better to be upfront. "Actually, I came to see you."

Charlotte's smile slipped a fraction. "You did? Do we know each other?"

"It's a long story, but I'm doing a favour for a friend of a friend. He's never managed to stop worrying about Kaylin La Rocca, and we're making one last attempt to find out what happened to her."

Now the smile vanished entirely. "Who are you? Are you

cops? Because I'm pretty sure cops aren't meant to grab a college boy's junk."

"We're private investigators."

"Well, you need to leave Kaylin alone. Do you want the wine or not?"

"I'd love a glass of white and a table"—my stomach grumbled on cue—"but my boss won't be happy if I don't at least ask a few questions."

Charlotte turned to Collier. "Are you her boss?"

"Nope. Just the chauffeur."

As people went, Charlotte was an open book. She looked around the restaurant, and I could practically read her thoughts. The place wasn't busy. Overheads didn't cover themselves. Should she kick us out and lose the income, or put up with our presence and hope we ordered the filet mignon? Finally, she sighed and picked up two menus.

"You can ask your questions, but I'm not going to answer them. Do you want a window seat? Or would you prefer the back?"

Once upon a time, I'd have picked the window seat so I could watch the world go by, but I'd dined out too many times with folks from work. Unless they were working surveillance, they always chose a spot near the kitchen and fought for the wall seat. Nobody liked their back to the door, and in an emergency, the kitchen offered weapons and a fast exit route. Boy, had my life changed in the past year.

I pointed to a table that fit the Blackwood criteria. "Can we have that one?"

"Sure."

"Nice choice," Collier murmured approvingly, and I was relieved not to come across as a complete amateur, even if I still felt far from being a pro.

"You used to be Kaylin's roommate, right?" I asked Charlotte.

"You already know that, or you wouldn't be here."

"That's true. Just trying to break the ice."

"You did that when you broke Kev's balls. Where did you learn to do that?"

"From my boss. She's kind of a badass."

"Your boss is a woman?"

I nodded. "Yup. Between you and me, I've had some bad experiences with men in the past." Wisely, Collier hung back and let me talk with Charlotte. I had a feeling she'd appreciate honesty. "I'm not sure I'd have taken the job working for anyone else."

Charlotte tilted her head a fraction. "And hot Santa? He's really just a driver?"

"He's a PI too, but I normally work out of Virginia, so he's shepherding me around this week."

"Right." She digested the information as she led us to the table. "Who's looking for Kaylin? I haven't heard from the cops in years."

"There are rules about client confidentiality, but he's an old friend. Not a boyfriend—more like a brother, I guess. Kaylin's mom had a brief relationship with his father."

Charlotte spun to face me, eyes wide. "Wait, you mean Nico?"

My turn to be surprised. "She mentioned him to you?"

"Yes. I mean, not a lot, but one time we were talking about our childhoods, and she said she hadn't always lived in a trailer park. And she told me about this crazy eighteen months she spent in Russia when her mom lost her mind and hooked up with some rich dude who lived in a palace, and the guy had a son who used to sneak Kaylin candy when she was miserable. Wow. Is it him?"

I had to weigh up gaining Charlotte's trust against professional discretion, but I didn't think Nico would be upset if I confirmed her suspicions. I nodded.

"She called him before she disappeared, and he's never stopped wondering what happened to her. He did hire another investigator a while back, but the guy went on long-term sick leave without finding her. Natural causes," I added hastily, just in case Charlotte thought that Crumb's illness might somehow be connected with the matter at hand.

"I think he put a card in my mailbox once, but Anisha said I shouldn't talk to anyone. Uh, so I probably shouldn't be speaking with you."

Crap. "Anisha Kapoor? You're still in touch?"

"Only on Facebook. Different lives, you know?"

I did. I hadn't kept in touch with any of my high-school friends, and now my besties were two women who'd been trafficked by the same psycho that made me work as a sex slave. The three of us had formed our own small support group. Three survivors.

We reached the table and Collier slid into a seat on the far side, back to the wall—so predictable—but I stayed standing.

"Normally, I'd agree that staying quiet was good advice, but this time, I'd be shooting myself in the foot." I conjured up what I hoped was a sympathetic expression. "Nico's just worried about Kaylin."

"Whatever the cops said she did, she didn't do it."

"That's exactly what he told me. If she's on the run, he wants to clear her name so she doesn't need to watch her back all the time."

Until now, Charlotte had veered between friendly and hostile, but now a little fear crept into her eyes.

"*If* she's on the run..." Her voice dropped to a whisper. "What if she isn't? I've tried not to think about it, but she never got in touch after she vanished, not once, and she must have known I'd try to help her."

"The two of you were close?"

"In the beginning. But we grew apart—not because of a

fight or anything; we were just so busy. She had modelling, and auditions, and those waitressing gigs, and I met Jenson." Charlotte glanced toward the kitchen. "It was love at first sight, which I know some people don't believe in, but I swear it happened. I fell head over freaking heels. Anisha told me it was too good to be true and we were moving too fast, and I guess I got sick of the negativity... Anyhow, I practically moved into his apartment within a few weeks of meeting him. Do you think that's crazy?"

"Why move slowly if things feel right? My boyfriend moved in a month after we met, and I didn't even like him in the beginning."

"Really? Whoa. Anyhow, I thought why wait? If things go wrong, they go wrong, but what's that old saying? It's better to have loved and lost than never to have loved at all." Charlotte snorted. "Anisha insisted on drafting a prenup though."

"She was only looking out for you."

"I know." A sigh. "I wish Kaylin could have been at the wedding too."

"You didn't receive any unsigned cards, did you? Maybe she was there in spirit."

"No, nothing like..." Charlotte's eyes widened. "There were flowers. Beautiful flowers in a crystal vase. I always figured the card had gotten lost, but nobody ever owned up to sending them. Pink peonies and orchids. You think that was Kaylin?"

"I think it's possible."

"Pink was her favourite colour. Wow."

Wow indeed. Yet another clue that pointed toward Kaylin being alive. Alive and staying at a distance. She still cared about her family and friends, but she didn't feel safe getting in touch with them, not even Nico. Which made sense, but also didn't. The first time she'd run—and I believed she *had* run to

Virginia rather than making the trip for money—she'd done a poor job of it. Hiding out in a run-down motel, living off vending machine snacks... But the second time, she'd vanished so completely that even the cops couldn't find her. A part of me had wondered if she was being held prisoner the way I had been, but nobody let me send cards and flowers on special occasions.

"All Nico wants to do is help her, but he can't do it alone."

"The flowers just appeared on the gift table. I don't even know who put them there."

"We believe the key to her disappearance lies in New York. Something sent her running to Virginia before the incident with the police officer."

"I don't know a thing, I swear. We barely saw each other in the weeks before she left."

"There might be some tiny snippet of information that you don't even realise is important. If we could just go over—"

"Hey, lady," a guy at the next table called. "Can we get another bucket of onion rings?"

That asshole. The moment was lost, and Charlotte backed away.

"Sorry, we're short-staffed tonight."

"Maybe we could talk later?"

There was the longest pause, and I crossed my fingers and my toes too. Charlotte had been friends with Kaylin, perhaps closer than anyone else had been in the months before the incident.

"If you can wait until we close, I'll talk with you then."

Thank goodness. "Could I get a filet mignon while we wait?"

Finally, she managed a smile. "Sure. And what'll you have, sir?"

Collier beamed at her. "I'll have the same as Hallie."

I sank onto a padded seat and let out a heavy breath. This

job didn't just teach me to follow the breadcrumbs; I was also learning how to tiptoe around the human psyche. As Emmy had once told me, everyone would talk as long as you asked the right questions.

"The drive to New Brunswick was worth it," I said, half to myself.

"If you ever get sick of Richmond, there's a job waiting for you in New York."

Guess I was doing something right.

7

HALLIE

One glass of wine turned into a bottle, and thank goodness Collier was driving. At eleven thirty, I sat at the table with Charlotte, a large glass of Chardonnay, and a leftover portion of chocolate-orange cheesecake. Collier was over at the bar, chatting with Jenson about sports or cars or whatever it was men discussed at this time in the evening. We'd decided that I should question Charlotte alone. Collier thought she'd be more likely to open up that way.

Of course, the wine she'd been drinking probably helped too, as did the generous tip. Nico wasn't the type of client who'd nitpick over expenses.

"I was such a bad friend," she said. "I should have made more time for her, you know?"

"Hey, hey, you did your best." I grabbed a napkin from the dispenser and passed it to her. "Don't cry."

Charlotte wiped her eyes. Twenty minutes in, and the interview had turned into more of a therapy session. She harboured a crap-ton of guilt that she'd spent those final weeks with Jenson instead of Kaylin.

"But us girls should stick together. Sisters before misters." She gave a slightly hysterical giggle. "Hoes before bros."

"But she didn't tell you anything was wrong, did she?"

"No, but I should have realised. She changed."

"Changed how?"

"Like, she stopped having fun. We used to pick up cheap tickets for shows every few weeks, but she started making excuses. And she used to hike on the weekends, but nuh-uh, not anymore."

"Where did she used to hike? Central Park?"

Charlotte let fly with a peal of laughter. "No, proper hiking. She used to drive to the Catskills and explore the trails. Before Anisha moved in, Juan had her room—he was an accountant at one of the big firms—and Kaylin used to go with him. I went as well, once, and yeuch...so many bugs. Anyhow, Juan had a near-death experience on the subway one night, and after that, he decided to give up all of his material possessions and go hike the Camino de Santiago. He gave Kaylin a real good deal on the car."

"I'm surprised she found anywhere to park it."

Emmy had a parking garage—of course she did—but two women had almost come to blows over a metered parking space on the street outside this morning. Plus the drivers here were terrifying. If I lived in NYC, I wouldn't have a car.

"She left it at Mrs. Farquarson's place."

"Who's Mrs. Farquarson?"

"She lived two blocks away. And she was, like, ninety years old. Kaylin saved Mrs. F's dog from being run over when it slipped out of its collar, and Mrs. F let her use the garage as a thank you. I think Mrs. F's husband was some big shot on Wall Street, and when he passed, she stayed in their brownstone alone. Oh, yeah! There was a note. Kaylin left her a note."

This was new. "What did the note say?"

"Not much, only that she'd be away for a few weeks. Kaylin got real quiet. Secretive, you know? I should have asked more questions or...or given her more hugs. Both. I should have done both."

"What do you mean by 'secretive'?"

"I don't know, just not as chatty as she used to be. Before, I'd ask her where she was going in the evening, and she'd tell me all about her modelling job or the party she was staffing or the audition she had or her next date, but in those later months, she'd just shrug and say 'work.' I mean—and you're gonna think this is crazy—I began to wonder if she'd gotten involved in something shady."

Interviewing suspects under the influence was definitely the way to go. Who needed truth serum when a bottle of good vino would do the job perfectly?

"Shady? Can you expand on that?"

"Like, working for an escort agency? Or, uh, running drugs? When I said that to Anisha, she just put on her lawyer voice and told me I didn't hear anything and I didn't see anything." A giggle. "Anisha has a stick up her ass, but don't tell her I said that."

I mimed zipping up my mouth and throwing away the key. "My lips are sealed."

"The drugs thing is probably kinda farfetched because Kaylin wouldn't even smoke weed, but the escort thing? She changed the way she dressed, now that I think about it. She always used to be pink and girly, but there were all these designer bags in her room, and her closet was full of boring black shift dresses and those shoes with the red bottoms. Christian Louis...Louba..."

"Louboutin?" I supplied as Charlotte drank more wine.

"Yes, those. Kaylin always used to like fancy stuff, but she was real careful with her money. Most of the time, she bought consignment store clothes and knockoff designer purses, and if she couldn't afford something, she used to make it. That trend for the purses with the giant flowers? She made one for each of us—her, me, and Anisha. Although Anisha wasn't always a fan of the arts and crafts. One time, Kaylin made this costume for an audition, a corset and a mask with feathers and jewels, and there were bits of feather floating around everywhere. I had to buy Anisha a six-pack of lint rollers because she was giving Mrs. Grumpy Pants a run for her money."

"Mrs. Grumpy Pants?"

"Our upstairs neighbour."

I was so grateful the apartment building I lived in had great soundproofing. That was important when you had a parrot who loved to curse—loudly—and rehash a murder he'd once overheard. No kidding. Emmy had tracked down the culprit, though, so it was all good.

"So Kaylin liked to live a champagne lifestyle on a Prosecco budget?"

Charlotte snort-laughed and quickly clapped a hand over her mouth. "Yup, and she always volunteered to work the fancy parties so she could hang out with the rich folks. But the shoes were real, the Louba-whatsits. I pawned some of them to pay the rent after Kaylin disappeared, and honestly, I still feel so guilty about that, but I couldn't afford to cover her share and I figured we could un-pawn them when she came back, but she never did."

Fancy parties? Now, that was interesting. Very interesting. Money and secrecy went hand in hand, and if Kaylin had found herself a sugar daddy, it might explain why the cops hadn't been able to follow her trail. What it didn't explain was why she'd been hiding at a motel in Virginia.

"In those final weeks, she always said she was working? Did she go on any dates?"

"Uh..." Charlotte pressed her hands to her temples, thinking. "No? At least I'm almost sure she didn't."

"What about auditions?"

"Nuh-uh. She used to practise her songs in the bathroom before auditions—good acoustics, she said—and Mrs. Grumpy Pants always complained to the landlord. And because the lease was in my name, he'd call me, and then I'd have to call Kaylin and remind her to keep the volume down because Mrs. G was moaning again."

"And your neighbour didn't complain in the weeks prior to Kaylin's disappearance?"

"Radio silence. The apartment was a dump, but the landlord lived out of state and he mostly left us alone unless Mrs. G whined about some dumb thing."

So, no dates and no auditions. Charlotte was right—there had definitely been a change in Kaylin's lifestyle, and now I had a new theory to work on. A mystery man we had to identify.

"How did Kaylin arrange dates? Did she hook up with men she met in bars? Or through work? Or did she use apps?"

"Oh, she used apps. Swipe left, swipe left, swipe left. Ninety percent of those assholes lie, did you know that? Say they're thirty, and they're fifty. Say they work in medicine, and they're a janitor at the hospital. Say they're single, and they have a wife and three kids."

She sounded as if she spoke from experience. "You used to use apps as well?"

"Yup, but I met Jenson on the subway. The train broke down, and he gave me his bottle of water." Charlotte turned toward the bar and blew him a kiss. He formed his fingers into a heart shape and grinned at her. "Isn't he the sweetest?"

"He seems like a good guy."

"And he can cook so well too. That's what sealed the deal. One time, I went home with a guy who had scorch marks on the wall in his kitchen, and he offered to make me breakfast, but I was like, 'Nope, gotta go.' Kaylin could cook okay, though. She didn't need a chef. Or a somma...sommlee...the wine guy." Charlotte waved at her husband. "Honey, we need more wine."

Jenson Peak left his spot behind the bar and strolled over to us. Everything I'd seen of him tonight suggested that he was indeed sweet. When the two of them were in the same room, he kept looking over at Charlotte with the tenderest of glances, almost as if he couldn't quite believe his luck.

"Nah, babe. You don't need more wine."

She craned her neck up to look at him and nearly fell off her chair. Oops.

"Just a small glass?"

"We need to get you home."

"What about the clean-up? The kitchen?"

"All done."

"Aww, you're the bestest hubby in the world."

He bent to kiss her hair, then scooped her up in his arms. "If Charlie doesn't get some sleep, she'll be good for nothing in the morning, so if you have any more questions, they'll have to wait."

Ah, the downside of using alcohol as an interview aid. But I didn't argue. Charlotte was struggling to keep her eyes open, and as with Chelle, I couldn't risk outstaying my welcome, not if I wanted her to cooperate in the future.

"I appreciate your time. And if I'm around these parts again, I'll be back for dinner because that steak was delicious."

"Don't forget to tell your friends about us."

"You got a flyer?" Collier asked. "I'll put it on the noticeboard at work."

As I climbed into the car, the adrenaline wave I'd been

riding began to wear off, and I realised I was as tired as Charlotte. It had been a productive evening, but the case was only just beginning. A sugar daddy? Was it possible that Kaylin was being protected by a rich boyfriend?

And if she was, how would Nico feel about it?

8

———

HALLIE

"She was a nice girl. Two inches too short and a cup size too big for the runway, but she had a good smile. Great teeth. I always found her work, but it was usually at the lower end of the pay scale. Not every model can make millions."

Martina D'Angelo was a former model herself, according to the bio on the Lux website, and even in her fifties, she was painfully thin. Her corner office had views into two other buildings, and across the street, a nervous guy in a suit was giving a presentation to a dozen bored executives on the sixth floor. Martina had decorated her wall space with portfolio shots, a couple of her and more of her models. I recognised one or two of them. Her words were directed to Collier, as was her flirting.

On this occasion, I deferred to him. This was what teamwork was all about. Figuring out the best strategy to meet your goals and supporting each other in its implementation.

"She was working steadily until her disappearance?" he asked.

"Nothing's ever 'steady' in this business, Mr. Dafoe."

"Call me Collier."

Martina twirled a lock of auburn hair around a finger. She wore it in a chin-length bob, sleek and straight.

"Collier. The fashion industry is full of highs and lows, and we're either rushed off our feet or waiting for the phone to ring. We have fashion weeks and seasonal collections to work around, and there's a constant search for fresh faces."

"If Kaylin wasn't a runway model, what sort of work did she do?"

We already had a reasonable idea from the information we'd found online, but it was good to get witnesses talking with easy questions.

"Ad campaigns, some catalogue shoots, occasional in-person work." Martina tapped a few keys on her iMac. The glass desk was piled high with papers, and I had to sit up straight to see over them. A mug of coffee balanced precariously on one stack. She hadn't offered us drinks, but she had agreed to squeeze us in between appointments, so I couldn't complain. "She was the face of Samba Jewelry—that's a local brand—and she got a lot of foot work. Kaylin had good toes." More scrolling. "There were web ads, plenty of those, and she handed out samples at the Supercar Expo two years running. Some swimwear work... One of the swimwear companies wanted to book her for another campaign, but she turned it down."

"Why was that?"

"She didn't give a reason, just said she didn't want to do swimwear anymore. She modelled for Samba after that, only one shoot, but then she was booked for a canine couture campaign in Central Park a week later, and she didn't show up." Martina shook her head and tutted. "At first, I was worried she'd had some kind of accident because she'd always acted professional, but then she didn't return any of my calls. And two weeks later, the police showed up and said she'd murdered an officer in Virginia. You know, Collier, I have plenty of work for a man with your looks. The silver fox aesthetic is so hot right now. How do you feel about a test shoot?"

Oh, she didn't... Was she seriously trying to poach my partner in the middle of a missing persons investigation? Talk about brazen.

"Well, ma'am, I'm flattered, but I already have a job."

"It's never too late for a career change."

"I like what I do." Collier's muscular thigh tensed as he shifted in his seat. Those jeans were probably meant to be a relaxed fit, but there wasn't much room in them. "Apart from refusing a swimwear shoot, did Kaylin do anything else that seemed out of character?"

"Not that I heard about. For the most part, I don't spend much one-on-one time with the models, although I've been known to make exceptions. Let me give you a card." Before Martina handed her contact details over, printed on thick cream cardstock, she wrote a second number on the back with a sleek silver pen. "Here you go, sugar."

Sheesh. It was as if I weren't even there.

"Thank you for your time, ma'am. We appreciate it."

"Call me if you change your mind. Or just...call me."

Collier managed to keep a straight face until the elevator doors closed behind us, then he sagged against the wall and chuckled. I mean, I understood what Martina saw in him, but I wasn't about to admit that.

"Not very subtle, was she?" he muttered.

I raised my voice an octave. "Just...call me, sugar. Do women hit on you often?"

"Occupational hazard." He straightened. "So, what do you think?"

"That's two people who say Kaylin wasn't quite herself before she disappeared. For someone so dedicated to her career, who waitressed when she couldn't get enough modelling work, turning down a shoot is weird."

"Maybe not, if she was involved with a man, and that man was the jealous type. Say he told her that he didn't want her showing flesh anymore?"

I considered that. If I wanted to model swimwear, would Ford be happy about it? Honestly? He probably wouldn't, but he also wouldn't stop me if it was something I really wanted to do. He accepted that I was my own person, and he trusted me. Not that I did want to model swimwear. The thought of strangers staring at my half-naked body made my skin crawl.

"We're back to the mystery-man theory."

"Yup."

"But we have no clue who he is."

"Said I liked my job. Didn't say it was easy."

The elevator reached the lobby, and Collier touched the small of my back, indicating that I should exit first. A gentleman. Had Kaylin's mystery man been a gentleman? From the picture Charlotte had built up, I imagined Kaylin's type was wealthy and well-connected. A man who could offer her something besides a quick roll in the sack. Chelle La Rocca had mentioned dirty old men showering her with gifts—had one of them charmed her into a date? A relationship? I shouldn't judge people by the sins of their parents, and I sure hoped I was nothing like my own mom, but Renée La Rocca had been involved with Nico's father for over a year. A married man. How much had Renée's behaviour influenced Kaylin? I had a feeling this case was a hand grenade just waiting to explode.

"Let's go see if Derek Trimmer will speak with us. If she met someone, maybe it was at one of those parties she worked?"

"It's possible. And we should look into dating apps. There's more than one that specialises in sugar daddies."

"Would her profile still be active?"

"Unlikely, but there must be an archive. Fifty bucks says the geek squad can find her if she's in there."

Mack could; I was certain of it. "No way I'm taking that bet."

"No, no, no, no, no. Fraternisation between staff and clients is strictly forbidden. A fireable offence."

Kaylin had been a casual employee, not salaried, but I wasn't going to get into the semantics. Derek Trimmer had granted us five minutes of his precious time, and the conversation wasn't particularly private, seeing as he kept barking instructions into a headset in between answering our questions. Right now, we were following him around an empty hotel ballroom as he supervised arrangements for an upcoming gala.

"How about guests of the clients?"

"Same difference. Every Step has an excellent reputation, Ms. Chastain, and I'm not going to risk that by having a waitress doing the unmentionable with a client or future client. Every employee signs a contract agreeing to abide by our code of conduct."

"Nobody ever breaks the rules?"

"Occasionally they—" Trimmer put a hand to his ear. "No, Deborah, the cake needs to come to us in the ballroom, not the kitchen. Have them put it on the table next to the stage." A pause. "Good. As I was saying, Ms. Chastain, occasionally a team member does something stupid, and their contract is terminated immediately. Regular memos are sent reminding team members of the need to remain professional at all times."

"Right, I understand, and it sounds as if you run a tight ship."

"We do, and that's exactly what I told the police. I honestly don't see how this conversation is relevant. I haven't spoken with Ms. La Rocca in over three years, not since she was a no-show at the Grumann Investments Christmas party."

"We really appreciate you talking to us, Mr. Trimmer. I used to waitress myself, but nothing as fancy as this. How many events do you run each year?"

"Usually around four hundred. We get many more enquiries, but reliable staff are hard to find, and we don't want to overstretch ourselves. Quality is more important than quantity."

"What kind of events did Kaylin work in the months before she disappeared?"

"The usual—weddings, parties, corporate gigs. Although she started turning down more work than she took. Disappointing, but not unusual with girls like her. I figured her modelling career was taking off, and she lost interest in hospitality work. Even after she cut her hours, she began calling in sick, and then she didn't show up at all. No phone call, no email, nothing." He shook his head and tutted. "So disrespectful. Although of course, I was shocked when I found out what she'd done. Murdering that poor police officer? A tragedy, and such bad judgment on her part."

"You believe she was capable of murder?"

"If you'd asked me before she disappeared, I'd have said no, but the police told me they had a strong case. At least Every Step didn't get any blowback from her actions. A couple of clients mentioned the incident, but I was very clear that she was a casual, part-time worker."

"Do you keep guest lists for events?"

"Yes, we do. Am I handing them over without a warrant? No."

Another job for Mack and her team. She was going to love me.

"How many events would you say—"

"Deborah, what do you mean, the ice sculptures are here already? They're not due for almost two hours." Trimmer pinched the bridge of his nose. "Those *fools*. Ms. Chastain, you'll have to excuse me. I have a crisis to deal with."

He marched off without another word, leaving Collier and me standing in a sea of half-decorated tables. Trimmer hadn't given us much, but he'd given us something.

"Kaylin had another source of income," I said. "She must have if she was turning down modelling work *and* events. Charlotte would have told me if she was late paying the rent before she left, plus she was either buying or being gifted designer clothes."

"Agreed, but she sure kept her source of funds quiet."

"We still have Anisha to try."

Collier huffed out his frustration. "I read Crumb's file, and I gotta say, I'm not filled with hope."

"Three years have passed. Maybe she'll have softened a little?"

"Maybe she will."

But Collier didn't sound convinced, and neither was I.

9

HALLIE

Anisha Kapoor hadn't softened. If anything, she'd gotten harder in the years since her roommate disappeared. Harder to track down, harder to crack. If I'd whacked her with a hammer—which was tempting the way she sneered at me— she'd probably have shattered. Even Collier's charms didn't work.

"We're just concerned about Ms. La Rocca," he said.

"Mr. Dafoe, if you think stalking me and then ambushing me in a deli is going to get me to talk to you, you've got another think coming."

Okay, so our approach was a little unorthodox, but we'd tried her apartment twice last night with no answer, and her assistant at work wouldn't do more than take a message. In the end, we'd resorted to staking out the building where Perkins, Foster & Brundle occupied floors thirty-two through thirty-eight and following her when she left to get lunch. At least she didn't eat at her desk. We'd figured there would be a fifty-fifty chance she'd want some fresh air, seeing as she didn't seem to get out much otherwise.

The café approach had the potential to work—it was how

I'd met Ford—but Anisha didn't seem to appreciate our ingenuity. In fact, I was beginning to suspect that Charlotte had been right when she said her former roommate had a stick up her ass.

I had a try. "If Kaylin was my friend, I'd want to protect her too."

"That being the case, why bother interrupting my lunch?"

Anisha took a step toward the counter, and I had to admit the sandwiches looked tempting. Maybe I should buy one for Alphonse? He'd saluted me as I left Emmy's apartment building this morning.

"Because we have the same goal. I don't want to see Kaylin in prison any more than you do."

"Ms. Chastain, I guarantee I've spent more time wrangling the US legal system than you have, and if Kaylin reappears, that's exactly where she's going."

"So you think she's guilty?"

"I think the justice system isn't always just."

"Whatever happened that night, there was someone else involved." I took a shot in the dark. "She had a boyfriend, but we haven't been able to find him."

"Yes, well, I can't help you. I only saw him once, and she never mentioned his name."

Wait a second... "You *saw* him?"

She realised she'd said too much. "I need to get back to the office."

How had Kaylin and Anisha been friends? Nico described Kaylin as sweet, and I'd figured she came out of the same mould as Charlotte Peak, albeit several inches taller and slightly more ambitious. True, Anisha was an attorney, which meant she'd spent at least three years in law school learning how to argue, but she'd lost her empathy along the way. Possibly her objectivity too, seeing as she refused to hear what we had to say. Dan said that I'd learn as much from listening to my enemies as to my friends, and I should always let them talk. As long as they weren't actively trying to kill me, anyway.

"Okay, go back to the office. Hide behind your legalese. We're going to find Kaylin whether you help us or not, and if she's innocent, we'll prove that. And we'll also tell her that you hindered rather than helped us."

Now Anisha really bristled, and I noticed a couple of the folks waiting for service were eavesdropping on our conversation. Oh, they were pretending not to, but when the line moved forward without them, it gave the game away.

"Are you threatening me?"

"Nope. Not at all. I'm just saying that we're not giving up, even though you want us to."

"I could be fired if I got caught aiding and abetting a criminal," she hissed, lowering her voice. Had she noticed the eavesdroppers too? "Kaylin isn't the only one with something to lose."

"A criminal? So you *do* think she's guilty?"

Anisha snatched a package of organic pita chips from the nearest shelf and hugged them to her chest like a shield. As if that would help. I loved pita chips.

"He was approximately thirty," she said in a barely audible whisper that still managed to sound angry. "Dark hair, Caucasian, and handsome with an arrogant expression that said he knew it." She closed her eyes for a moment as if remembering. "Average build, and not much taller than her. Well-dressed in a suit and a wool overcoat. I saw them outside the Museum at FIT as I was leaving a client's office one lunchtime, and he had his arm around her waist. That's my final word on the subject."

She pushed past me and stood in the deli line, still clutching the chips as she blanked us. I blew out a long breath. Whew. Questioning people was an art, Dan said, but I still felt as if I were flinging paint at the canvas, Jackson Pollock style, and hoping the result was better than that of a toddler let loose with crayons.

"Sure you don't want to move to New York?" Collier asked.

"Virginia is my home." I was shaking. Actually shaking, and my chest felt tight. Did this ever get any easier? New case, new partner, new city, and I was way outside of my comfort zone.

"Shame. What's next, kemo sabe?"

"Uh…" My mind was blank. We'd questioned our four potential witnesses, and while we had a bunch of information, there were still no concrete clues. "I'll update everything we have into Providence and see whether the cyber team has made any breakthroughs."

The hackers. Between them, Mack, Agatha, Mouse, and Ziggy could ferret out almost any piece of digital information we needed, not necessarily legally. Which might have been awkward with me dating a cop, but we operated a "don't ask, don't tell" policy. And it wasn't as if Ford never requested favours.

"Okay."

"What would you do?" I asked Collier. This was my case, and so far, he'd let me run it, but he had years more experience than I did, and it would be dumb not to take advantage of that.

"What would I do? I'd get lunch."

"I suppose we do need to eat."

"Always think better when I'm eating. Calories fuel ideas."

They did? Perhaps that was why Emmy ate so many cheeseburgers?

"That sounds like a great excuse to order pizza."

"You want pizza?"

"Is there a good place nearby?"

"In Midtown?" He shook his head and offered me his arm. "Little Italy's better."

I looped my arm through his, which I wouldn't have been able to do six months ago. The healing process was long, but I was getting there, one step at a time. The cab we took to Little Italy was probably slower than the subway, but this was my first proper trip to the city, and I wanted to get the full New York experience. See the hustle and bustle, view the sights, and choke on traffic fumes while our driver yelled at a cyclist who clipped his wing mirror. And as horns honked around me, I mulled over the case. The answer lay here, somewhere among the skyscrapers and eight million strangers. We were hunting for a needle in a haystack, but I'd meant what I said to Anisha: we *would* find Kaylin.

"How about that place?" I suggested as we climbed out of the cab. The smells wafting out of Mamma Mia's Pizza Parlor made my mouth water.

"Only if you like putting money in the Mafia's pockets."

"Are you serious? The Mafia runs a pizza restaurant?"

"Gotta launder their money somehow. They run plenty of restaurants, but that's one of the better establishments."

"Uh, no thanks."

Collier laughed and steered me across the street. Uncle Gino's Pizzeria looked every bit as nice as Mamma Mia's, but Collier assured me that the owner—Gino's nephew—wasn't involved in organised crime. We took a seat at the back, and Collier poured me a glass of water from the carafe on the table. This wasn't the kind of sleek, fancy place that Ford liked to take me, but the worn wood and checked tablecloths felt welcoming in a homey way, and when I eyeballed the food on the next table, I decided that Collier had chosen well.

"If you like seafood, try the lobster ravioli," he suggested. "You won't get better."

"Thanks for the recommendation."

Once we'd ordered and taken the edge off our hunger with a basket of breadsticks, it was time to return to the problem at hand. Kaylin La Rocca. More specifically, her mystery man. I thought back to my relationship with Ford. That had stayed secret for about three seconds around the office, and it hadn't been long before he was staying over in the apartment I shared with Mercy.

"She was seeing a guy, yet she didn't mention it to her two closest friends?"

"Maybe she figured they'd disapprove?" Collier said. "Anisha seems like the judgmental type."

"Why would she disapprove of a wealthy, handsome thirty-year-old? If he was wearing a suit at lunchtime, then it's likely he had a good job. What's FIT?"

"The Fashion Institute of Technology, over by Madison Square Garden."

If only we'd been tackling this case three years ago, there might have been camera footage available.

"I wonder if he worked there? Kaylin could have met him through her modelling work. Do you think Martina D'Angelo would tell us if she ever did a job there?"

Collier grimaced. "I could try calling her, but I don't want to do that more than once, so let's list all the follow-up questions we have first."

I made a note in the case file. Blackwood's investigations app let us keep track of our thoughts, and our files automatically backed up to a central server so if a device got stolen, we didn't lose any work. The data could be wiped remotely in an emergency. Plus Providence worked away in the background, adding extra information that might be relevant to the case. There was a memo telling me that Derek Trimmer had once been arrested for public indecency, for example. I scanned the details. When he was eighteen, he and three other boys had mooned their high-school principal on the eve of graduation. That fact probably wasn't useful, but it did show that Trimmer hadn't always been quite so uptight.

"Or maybe the guy was a model?" I said. "If he was handsome and he knew it? If we manage to get a list of talent, we could filter on age, hair colour, and height."

"We'd still have at least a hundred possibles."

"We could discount those with a lower net worth."

"That might work. We'll have to head back to the office—nobody's running that kind of analysis on a phone."

"I only hope Lux still has the records from four years ago. Martina D'Angelo didn't strike me as the most organised person in the world, and if her hard drive is as messy as her desk…" A message flashed up on the screen, and I skimmed through it. Freaking heck, Agatha was a genius. "Hey, we have the event schedule and guest lists from Every Step already."

"Fast work."

"Agatha mocked up a website for an ice sculpture artist." She'd called it Freeze the Moment, and it looked surprisingly professional for something she'd created in an hour. "Trimmer clicked to download the price list, and now we have access to everything." Dammit, if only I had my laptop. I was gonna give myself eye strain by squinting at the phone. The waitress slid a plate of ravioli in front of me as I tried to make sense of the data, and there was a pattern, sort of. "For nearly two years, Kaylin worked four or five events a week with the occasional gap—presumably when she had to travel for modelling jobs—but in the months before she vanished, that dropped to two a week, then one."

"There was a catalyst."

"I think we're looking at the end of June or the beginning of July."

Which was further back than we'd thought. There was a build-up.

"What events did she work before that?"

"Weddings. Summer is wedding season." Weddings were probably more fun than Christmas parties. Better weather, families and older guests rather than hundreds of drunk executives. "Plus a birthday party, but that was for a six-year-old, the notes say. You think she could have met a guy at a wedding?"

"Oh, yeah. Got four sisters and fourteen cousins, so I've been to a lot of weddings." Collier smirked. "Hooked up at every single one of them."

"With the waitstaff?"

The smirk grew bigger. "Once or twice. Single women watch another gal getting hitched, it does something to their hormones."

I rolled my eyes. I'd never attended a wedding as a guest before, but back when I lived in Kentucky, I used to wait tables at Jack's Roadhouse, and when Sindy Delvecchio had married Rowdy Carlson in front of the bar—so classy—I'd spent most of the night cleaning up broken glass and vomit. The idea of hooking up with one of Rowdy's buddies made me want to puke.

But a fancy New York affair held by folks who could afford to hire Every Step? Maybe Kaylin *had* met an eligible bachelor at one of the receptions.

"Okay, we'll need to go through the guest lists, working backward from early July. We have the Musson-Voyce wedding, the Janes-Lopez wedding, the Calder-Gibb wedding, the Bender-Theobald wedding, the Anderson-Moss wedding, the Cavallaro-Bucci wedding, the Gutiérrez-Tremblay wedding, the—"

"Did you say Cavallaro-Bucci?"

"She worked that one the last week in June. Why?"

Collier tipped his head toward the front window. "See Mamma Mia's over there?"

"Yes?"

"The Cavallaro family owns it."

I choked on a piece of pasta. "Are you saying Kaylin worked at a Mafia wedding?"

"Seems that way. Even criminals get married, and they got the cash to pay for a flashy ceremony."

"Yikes. Do you think that's a coincidence? That she was there, I mean."

Collier shrugged and forked another piece of ravioli into his mouth. "Objectively speaking, 'tall, dark, and handsome' would fit half the Cavallaro boys. And they sure aren't the type of man you'd want to take home to meet the family."

Could it be possible? Had Kaylin gotten involved with the New York Mafia? I began to get a bad, bad feeling in the pit of my stomach, and suddenly, I wasn't so hungry anymore.

"Tell me more about the Cavallaros."

"You heard of the five families?"

I was a true-crime aficionado; of course I had.

"Yes."

"Unofficially, there's a sixth one, and that's headed by Vito Cavallaro. They're dirty as fuck, but as well as the money laundering, the drug- and people-trafficking, the counterfeiting, the corruption, the loan-sharking, the extortion, and the illegal gambling, they have an empire of legit businesses that give them a veneer of respectability." How could Collier keep eating? "Heard Renzo Bucci's papa is into arms deals, so maybe they're expanding their horizons."

"How do you know so much about them?"

"It's my job, same as Dan di Grassi knows half the assholes in Richmond by sight. The Cavallaros keep a lower profile than, say, the Gambinos or the Genoveses, but they're like rats in a sewer. Never far away."

The thought made me shudder. Next time, I'd suggest we visit Wonder Burger for lunch. Prices around Times Square might be criminal, but at least we'd be farther from the Mafia's heartland.

"Do you think we could get pictures of the men in the Cavallaro family? Anisha might be able to pick out the guy she saw with Kaylin."

"Bet there were a few reporters at the wedding, plus we can go through the police mugshots, but good luck in getting Kapoor to cooperate."

If we managed to put together a photo line-up, I'd try anyway. She could only say no, right? And we might be able to narrow down the suspect list beforehand—how many thirty-year-old Cavallaro men could there be?

I set Providence to work and picked up my fork again. We were getting closer; I could feel it.

10

DASHA

ost people only live one life. They spend early childhood with their family, followed by some sort of education, and then they work a humdrum job until they die. Perhaps they fall in love along the way. Get married, have kids, start the whole miserable cycle again.

Programmed to endure mundanity, my former mentor used to say. To accept the status quo.

Me?

I was programmed to disrupt.

So far, I'd lived three lives, or at least that's how it felt, and I was in the process of embarking on a fourth.

"Do you think our luggage made it?" Paulo asked, checking his hot-pink wristwatch. "We left the plane nearly an hour ago. What if my clothes got left behind in Newark? I hate layovers."

"They have systems in place, hun. I'm sure it's just a little delay."

Actually, I knew for certain that our cases were halfway between the plane and the terminal. The tracking app on my phone told me so. But I couldn't divulge that to Paulo because firstly, Darla wasn't the type of woman to put a tracker in her luggage, and secondly, it was mildly entertaining watching him freak out about a potential lack of clean underwear. Second rule of travel—always pack a change of clothes in your cabin bag. The first rule was obviously to carry as many weapons as possible. I'd gone one better and sent anything important to Virginia aboard Emmy Black's private jet last weekend.

Darla was my third incarnation, a laid-back caregiver turned craft store owner with a disturbing love of muumuus. I'd adopted the persona four years ago out of necessity, and at first, living like an everyday American had been a novelty. A relief, even. Darla had given me breathing space, but in the past year, the tedium of small-town life had started to grate. I'd even begun to hanker after my second life, the years when I'd travelled the world as a top-tier assassin, doing my master's bidding. Which was why, when Emmy had offered me a part-time job on her Special Projects team, I'd grudgingly accepted. That and the fact that I was fucking her personal trainer, and Alex had a weird loyalty to the crazy English bitch.

Which was why I was currently at Richmond International, ready to build another layer on my cover story. My excuse to spend more time in Virginia. Emmy had offered whatever resources I required to set up a new branch of the Craft Cabin, including assistance with staff recruitment so I'd be able to step back from the place and focus on my real job.

But first, we needed to get the place up and running.

Hence my trip with Paulo. And I'd also need to fake a meet-cute with Alex because admitting that we'd first met on a military helicopter in Russia almost two decades prior wasn't an option. Paulo would be a useful witness, an unwitting participant in the story we were writing.

I grabbed a luggage cart while Paulo flitted around the

conveyor like an over-caffeinated toddler, and I guess I could understand the sentiment. Luggage theft was always a possibility, although any two-bit criminal would be disappointed when they got past Paulo's woefully inadequate padlock and found a collection of hand-knitted cardigans, assorted thong underwear, and six types of hair product. Ten years ago, give or take, I'd caught a woman my age wheeling my Louis Vuitton suitcase toward the exit at Khrabrovo, and once I'd explained the error of her ways, I'd gifted her boyfriend—the airport security guard who'd put her up to the task—a first-class ticket to the hospital. I never bothered to find out whether they'd managed to reattach his finger, but I doubted it.

My phone buzzed.

ALEX

What time will you get to the store?

ME

Should be there by eleven.

My heart leapt at the thought of seeing him, although it was irritating that I'd have to share him with Paulo. Still, this was better than the alternative of not having him at all. Short-term pain for long-term gain. Once Alex's presence in my life was established, I wouldn't have to sneak around so much; I'd be able to make phone calls and go on dates like a normal person. Well, kind of. Alex had invited me climbing at Seneca Rocks, and I couldn't imagine most people found scaling a cliff romantic.

Good thing I wasn't most people.

"That's one of my bags," Paulo announced. "See? The pink one with the rainbow strap."

"You want me to grab it, hun?"

"No, I can do it."

I swallowed a laugh as he dragged it off the conveyor and dropped it on his foot, then I grabbed his other two suitcases and my duffel while he hopped around cursing.

"Maybe you should wear steel-toed boots next time?" I suggested.

"That's a fabulous idea." Of course, he couldn't wait. He pulled out his phone and tapped at the screen, then pulled a face. "Urgh, they're all so ugly."

"Why don't you customise them? You did a terrific job with Sara's shoes."

On Tuesday, he'd stayed up most of the night sticking thousands of crystals onto her Cinderella-inspired pumps. The final product was blinding when the light caught it, but his efforts meant he'd slept like the dead on the flight from Oregon, so as far as I was concerned, he could customise anything he wanted to.

"I suppose I could do that."

Thanks to a cab driver with a death wish, we made it to the Craft Cabin by half past ten, and I hauled the bags inside while Paulo hobbled on ahead, oohing and aahing over the work so far. And I had to concede that Bradley's team had done a reasonable job. And a fast job. When I opened the first Craft Cabin in Baldwin's Shore, it had just been me, working all hours on a shoestring budget. Emmy and her husband apparently had numerous property-related investments, which necessitated having their own maintenance team, and Bradley had thrown them at the problem. The fabric of the building was in a good state. The plumbing, the drywall, the floor tiles, all done. The bathrooms were functional. The walls had been painted white, a blank canvas, and the kitchen was half-complete. Bradley assured me the kitchen installers would be finished by the end of the week. We just had a fuck-ton of furniture to assemble, plus Bradley and Paulo's favourite part: the decorating.

One p.m., and it was time for a murder. Paulo was the wannabe victim, attempting to sing "Here Come the Girls" when he couldn't hold a note. Except he replaced the "Girls" with "Boys," an inaccuracy because our visitors were definitely men. Bradley led them inside, half a dozen admittedly handsome specimens, and I realised from the way they moved that Emmy had sent a selection of her Special Projects team to assemble flat-pack furniture. My head said "what a waste," but my eyes were reasonably happy with the situation.

There were women as well, two of our new employees. Isabella was a Blackwood acquaintance with a love of handicrafts who'd been left in a fragile state after she was trafficked into the US. This would be her first job since the ordeal ended, and Emmy's mother-in-law had offered to support her. I'd met the woman once before. The wheelchair had surprised me; the look in her eyes, not so much. Marisol was one of us.

Bradley ran past them with an iPad in his hand, tripped over a chair leg, and nearly ended up in Marisol's lap. She shot out an arm and shoved him upright with a roll of her eyes.

"Thank you, my lovely," he said. "Okay, guys and gals! I have the layout. We need shelving units here, here, and here..." He gestured like a flight attendant demonstrating the safety procedures. "And the tables go over there."

"Where did you get those hotties?" Paulo whispered to

him as six deadly operators began carrying boxes inside. "This is better than Christmas."

Bradley gasped. "*Nothing* is better than Christmas. But Alex is my boss's personal trainer, and he offered a bunch of gym rats fifty bucks each if they'd help out. And voila! Eye candy, and not the low-calorie version."

"Are you folks going to help or just stare?" I asked.

Paulo's mouth was still hanging open. "Can we take option two?"

"Aren't you seeing that fellow from New York?"

"You're right—I should send him pictures."

Alex approached from behind. I didn't need to turn and look to know it was him; I could tell from the rush of heat between my legs. This was a relatively new phenomenon for me, and apparently not a medical issue. I'd researched to check.

"Where should I put this unit, ma'am? It looks like a checkout counter."

Ma'am? That was a nice touch.

"Right over there by the window. Here, let me give you a hand. I really appreciate your coming by to help."

The corner of Alex's lips twitched because he wasn't accustomed to me wasting time on pleasantries. He'd better not get used to it. Darla's personality was an unfortunate necessity, and whenever I spent too much time being fake-nice, I wanted to stick pins through my tongue.

"Makes a change from wrangling Emmy and Sky," he said, too quietly for anyone else to hear.

"How is the bitch today?"

Another smirk. "Tired."

"Good."

"Soon, you'll be tired too."

"Also good."

I found the assembly instructions in the box and

scanned them. Seemed straightforward. A reasonably competent child could put this furniture together, or possibly a trained monkey. But Darla? No, she was going to struggle.

"Boy, there sure are a lot of parts here. We need to find these doohickeys first."

"What doohickeys?" Alex leaned in close to read the booklet over my shoulder, and his hand landed on my ass. "Careful," I warned under my breath.

"Irresistible," he murmured back.

I stepped to the side. "That's an interesting accent. Where are you from? No, wait, let me guess... Poland? I had a Polish neighbour once, and he used to make those little dumplings with the onion and potato."

"I'm Russian."

"Oh, boy. I hear it's real cold there."

"That depends on which part you go to. Northern Siberia has arctic temperatures, but Sochi's climate is more like France, just windier."

We made inane small talk, all the time keeping an eye on Paulo. In return, he was glancing at me, thinking he was being subtle but failing entirely. I understood why—Darla didn't make a habit of chatting to men, and Paulo had a good heart. He wanted me to be happy. He just didn't understand that I was more likely to find joy on a firing range than in a fancy restaurant.

Finally, he sidled over.

"Building shelves is faster than I thought." Said the man who'd yet to pick up a screwdriver. "But that counter's way too plain. Can we paint it?"

"Yes, but go easy on the glitter. Nobody wants it stuck to their clothes."

Alex finished tightening the last screw and straightened. If we'd been alone, I would have tested his construction skills by having him fuck me on his handiwork, but we had an audience. Teamwork had its cons as well as its pros.

I held out a hand. "Well, thank you, Alex. You and your friends sure did speed things up."

"It was a pleasure. If you're in town for a week, do you want to get lunch sometime?"

"Lunch?"

"I know a good burger place near here."

Paulo was standing to the side of my dearly beloved, mouth open and hands pressed to his cheeks. "Say yes!" he mouthed, then pointed at Alex's ass. "OMG."

"I'll have to check my schedule, but maybe you could give me your number?"

Now Paulo was waving his arms like an Italian grandma, but Alex just smiled.

"Sure."

Once Team Blackwood had disappeared back to the firing range, or the assault course, or the drop zone, or wherever they usually spent a Thursday afternoon, Paulo found his tongue again.

"Are you crazy?" he asked. "Do you have a fever? That Adonis was asking you out on a date, and you have to check your schedule?"

"A date? Do you really think so?"

"Duh, yes."

"I figured he was just being friendly because I'm new to the area. Well, I have staff to interview and suppliers to speak with."

"Hello, priorities? He has buns of titanium."

"You shouldn't objectify people like that, hun."

"Oh, don't be such a party pooper. I'm sure he has a nice personality too."

"He seems pleasant."

"So you're going to call him?"

"Possibly."

"Possibly?"

"Probably."

He trotted off, singing, "Darla's going on a date, Darla's going on a date," and Marisol shot me a look of sympathy. I decided I liked her. My phone buzzed a moment later.

> **ALEX**
>
> What time are you planning to finish at the store tonight?

> **ME**
>
> As soon as Paulo runs out of energy.

Which could be hours, since he'd been the Energizer Bunny in a previous life. The last time I'd suggested knocking off early, he'd stared at me in shock, gripped his glue gun tighter, and informed me there was no rest for the wicked. Did he think I wasn't already aware of that? I was as wicked as they came, which was why I'd brought tranquillisers with me—only mild ones, enough to make him sleepy.

> **ALEX**
>
> Need a ride?

Of course I did. That was the whole reason I'd come to Virginia. Although my relationship with Alex was about more than sex. I'd worked out that the weird lightheadedness I felt around him wasn't a problem with my blood pressure; it was love. Friendship and fate were involved too, and even though I hated the way he unsettled me, he was an addiction I couldn't quit. Ana—whose life had been twined with mine thanks to the monster who created us—said I deserved happiness. But I had a secret fear that karma was just playing a sick joke, giving me a glimpse of heaven before she drop-kicked me back into hell where I belonged.

ME

I'll meet you in the hotel parking lot no later than 20:00.

I did have access to transport in Virginia—I could borrow a Blackwood pool car or use one of Ana's vehicles—but that would lead to questions from Paulo. Which meant taking a cab to the Black Diamond Hotel, where Emmy had provided us with two standard rooms, and letting Alex play chauffeur.

ALEX

Can't you ditch Paulo any earlier?

I would certainly try. It all depended on whether the kitchen fitters Emmy had provided decided to work late. I didn't need them asking questions if Paulo went from hyper to hibernation in the time it took him to drink a mug of coffee.

ME

As long as there are no witnesses.

ALEX

Need a hand?

Coming from anyone else, the question would have been insulting and the answer easy. But Alex wasn't trying for one-upmanship. He simply wanted me naked and in his bed, which meant that in at least one respect, our goals were perfectly aligned.

ME

Sure.

"Ohmigosh!"

"What?" I asked Paulo, trying to sound vaguely interested. "Ohmigosh" could mean anything from a missing diamanté on his purse to a nuclear explosion off the coast of California.

"Bradley just texted, and did you know it's National Pancake Day?"

Pancakes had a fucking day? Was he serious? "Can't say I did, hun."

"He knows this fabulous pancake restaurant, and he's inviting us to go with him and some friends." Paulo glanced up from his phone, eyes pleading. "How late are we working tonight? He says the strawberry daiquiris are to die for."

This was Alex's plan? Enlisting Bradley to stuff Paulo with cocktails and carbs? Hmm, it had potential—Paulo was incapable of stopping at just one drink.

"I want to check through the inventory that's arrived so far, but why don't you go for pancakes with Bradley?"

"You shouldn't miss out on the fun. That wouldn't be fair."

"I'd just cramp your style, hun, and you know I don't touch alcohol."

Darla was a gosh-darned saint. Me? I had a taste for top-shelf horilka and the self-control not to overdo it.

"Oh, I couldn't..." But Paulo really, really wanted to. "Are you sure you don't mind?"

"I've always been fond of my own company. We can put in a longer day tomorrow if we fall behind."

"When are we interviewing for staff?"

"Bradley sent me over a stack of résumés to read through."

Not that I needed to—Emmy had already hand-picked the key team members who would assist with my cover story. Samya was married to a Blackwood employee, and she'd managed a café downtown before Emmy poached her, plus Isabella would work four days a week. Dan had recruited three more women from a domestic violence shelter she was involved with, and they'd undergone their initial training while I was in Baldwin's Shore. But pretending to interview candidates would allow me to spend another day or two at Blackwood's training facility. Ana had been raving about their new kill-house simulator. Back in Russia, we'd used real bullets and been expected to bleed for our sins—I couldn't help feeling that using VR was cheating.

"I can't wait to meet all the new people. Can any of them crochet? Crochet is *sooo* in right now after that new Armand Taylor movie. You know, the one where he carries yarn and a crochet hook alongside his AK-47?"

I hadn't seen it, but it sounded ridiculous. Ana had once killed a man with a knitting needle, but a crochet hook? It wasn't nearly sharp enough. Unless you could ram it through an eye socket, and then it might—

"Holy cannoli, Bradley just got a new car, and he says he'll pick me up at five." Paulo thrust his phone into my face. "Look, it's pink!"

Bradley's lime-green Lamborghini had come to a sad end last week when Dan borrowed it to go on a donut run and ended up chasing a carjacker. The suspension was somewhere along I-95, and the remaining parts had gone to car heaven along with the carjacker's left nut.

"That's the exact shade of the new La Coutoura limited edition yarn we got in last week. Maybe you could knit him a matching sweater?"

"Ooh, that's such an excellent idea. You're sure I can go out tonight?"

I wasn't his fucking mother. "Just don't stay out too late. You know you get cranky if you don't get enough sleep."

Paulo threw his arms around me in a hug, and I shifted so he didn't notice the shiv in my bra. Old habits died hard. So did terrorists, if there happened to be one on the airplane.

Who cared about TSA agents when you could assemble a weapon after security with a roll of tape and a shard of broken glass? If Paulo hadn't been waiting outside the bathroom with a croissant, I could have built an IED with items I bought from the gift store.

I sent a message to Alex.

ME

Pick me up at 17:15.

HALLIE

Eleven.

So far, we'd identified eleven Cavallaro men who fit the description given by Anisha Kapoor, and Collier hadn't been kidding about the family's business interests.

As well as Mamma Mia's Pizza Parlor, they owned a dozen more restaurants and cafés, bars, a billiard hall, a cabaret club, and a concert venue. Rumour said some of the businesses sold drugs as well as food, but convictions were thin on the ground, no doubt due to healthy donations made to key political figures.

They were active in traditional Mafia industries such as trash-hauling and construction, but they'd modernised too. The Cavallaros ran illegal online gambling sites, and they were major players in the porn industry. Cam girls made them millions, and I shuddered to think that Kaylin might have gotten mixed up in that. What if one of the men had coerced her into appearing on camera? I'd have to ask Agatha to take a look.

Real estate was another money spinner for the sixth family, and they rented out overpriced slums to desperate tenants, exploited immigrant workers in the agriculture industry, and bribed public officials to grant licences for wind farms. One or two of the peripheral family members had even run for office. Cavallaro thugs extorted local businesses—although that had become harder to do now that corporate chains had taken over downtown America—and as well as running street prostitutes, the family allegedly controlled a high-class brothel somewhere on the Upper West Side. Their ties to the entertainment industry didn't end there. Aldo Cavallaro owned a beauty pageant, Carmine Cavallaro had invested in a vacation resort, and Otello Cavallaro ran a record label. Hmm... A record label... What if he'd reeled Kaylin in with promises of stardom?

"Who's Otello Cavallaro?" I asked Collier. "Could he be our guy?"

We'd asked the server at Gino's to pack up dessert, left a healthy tip, and then walked past the bakery Dan had told me to visit. When Collier assured me it wasn't linked to organised crime, I picked out half a dozen cookies for myself, plus another two dozen to take to the office. Then I bought extra boxes to ship to Dan and Emmy because even though they drove me crazy, I loved them really. Collier carried the bags as we took the subway back to Blackwood's office. The hot-desk area was only half-full, so we snagged two spots together, made coffee, and returned to brainstorming.

"Otello? Nope. He's one of Cesare's brothers, but he weighs at least three hundred pounds."

"Are any of the other Cavallaros involved with that business?"

"I can put some feelers out."

There had indeed been reporters present at the Cavallaro-Bucci wedding, like rubberneckers at a car crash, all waiting to critique Lia Cavallaro's designer gown while secretly hoping for a confrontation between the guests and the small crowd of

Mafia victims who'd bravely gathered outside to protest. Pictures showed a pretty brunette in a bejewelled fishtail dress leaving the church on the groom's arm amid a shower of confetti. Several police officers milled around to prevent any trouble, and they'd succeeded, although there were reports of a later scuffle between several guests at the reception. The bride had been given away by her uncle, Vito "The Duck" Cavallaro, boss of the family and all-around thug.

Crime definitely paid.

I counted at least six dark-haired, handsome-in-an-arrogant-way men in the photos, and I copied those pictures to a separate file for further investigation. Then my phone rang. A video call.

"How's it going?" Dan asked. "Did you find La Rocca yet?"

She didn't really expect me to say yes. Her tone was light, and she had a cupcake in her hand. I recognised the kitchen behind her—she was over at Emmy's place. Riverley Hall was a Gothic-style mansion nestled among the trees and pastures of a sprawling estate to the west of Richmond. And Mrs. Fairfax, Emmy and Black's housekeeper, made the best cakes and pastries, although La Bella Farina in Little Italy gave her a run for her money.

"Not yet, but we have several new leads."

"Good job, sister. Did you update Nico?"

"I'm planning to call him tomorrow. Things moved quickly, and we've spent most of the time since I arrived talking with potential witnesses."

Emmy strolled into view and reached forward to grab a pink-frosted cupcake.

"Hey, honey," she said. "How's the Big Apple?"

"I understand the 'big' part, but where does the 'apple' come from?"

"Buggered if I know."

"Something to do with horse racing," Dan said. "You found the roommates?"

"Both of them, plus Kaylin's agent and her boss at the events company. We think there was a man involved, a boyfriend, and we've narrowed the time period down to—"

"What the fuck?" That was Emmy, and the sound of retching followed.

Dan reached over to thump her on the back. "You okay, sweetie?"

"I just swallowed a damn feather."

"That was a dumb thing to do."

"It was on the freaking cupcake. I thought it was a decoration."

"Oh, dear. It must have floated on there." Mrs. Fairfax appeared in the background. "Bradley was making his wings in here earlier."

"Wings? What the hell are you talking about?"

"They weren't wings; they were fans," Dan told her.

Another cough. "The question still stands. He has a craft room, so why was he messing around in the kitchen?"

"He spilled a bottle of neroli oil in the craft room when he was making scented candles, and he can't get the smell out of the carpet."

Emmy walked past again, this time with a red face and a phone clamped to her ear. "Bradley, you can't do crafts in the kitchen." A pause. "I don't care. Get a new carpet. ... A what? No fucking way. I'm not doing a burlesque workshop. I run a security firm, not a cabaret club."

Dan started laughing, and I covered my mouth with my hands so I didn't do the same.

"I don't need to unleash my inner goddess. Tisiphone's already in residence, and there's no room at the inn. ... No. Just no." Emmy hung up and glared at Dan. "I don't know why you're sniggering, tassel tits. He expects you to join in too." She turned to the camera. "And you."

But my mind was far away. Feathers... Who else had mentioned feathers recently? Charlotte. Charlotte said Kaylin had been making a costume for an audition. Jewels and feathers...

"Collier, the Cavallaros own a cabaret club. Which of them runs it?"

"That I don't know, but I'll see if I can find out."

"The Cavallaro family?" Dan asked. "One of your leads involves the Italian Mafia?"

"Uh, maybe?"

She paused for a moment, considering. "That's a fun development. I guess it fits—if Kaylin's alive, then whoever helped her to hide has money and connections, and if she isn't...well, they have experience with that too."

"I think she's alive."

"Just watch your back, okay? You have Collier with you?"

"He's right here."

"Is he behaving?"

"Impeccably."

"Hmm." She sounded a little surprised. "Good. Take care, and if anything feels off, step away. The Cavallaros aren't people you want to mess with."

"I promise I'll tread carefully."

Emmy smushed her face into shot again, and her colour looked more normal now. "Although if you are gonna get abducted again, could you hold off for a fortnight? That's the week I've got in the pool."

"Thanks for the show of confidence."

"Hey, it happens to the best of us."

"*You* got abducted?"

"It was on purpose," Dan said. "It doesn't count."

"What about the time when I was hiding in the back of a truck and someone stole it?"

"Nothing was stopping you from jumping out."

"Apart from a bunch of asphalt and the desire to avoid road rash and broken bones. Yeuch, half of these cakes have got bloody feathers on them."

I left Emmy and Dan to their baked goods and bitching, and returned to more important matters: finding my quarry. Collier was looking at me expectantly.

"Why the cabaret club? Was Kaylin a dancer?"

"Not that I'm aware of, but don't they have singers too? She was making a fancy corset for an audition, feathers and gems. That's the kind of thing a woman would wear in a cabaret club."

"Oh yeah?" Collier raised an eyebrow, and I wasn't certain his interest was purely professional. "Maybe we should pay a visit?"

"To a seedy Mafia haunt?"

"It'll be safe enough. Doubt they'll start capping people with an audience."

"You doubt? That means there's a chance?"

"I'm almost certain there haven't been any murders there, not in public anyway. If I thought there was a risk, I wouldn't suggest it."

I'd never dare to set foot in the place alone, but along with my new Blackwood family came confidence. I trusted Collier to keep me safe. And if we paid a visit to the cabaret club, we might be able to narrow down the suspect list further, perhaps even get a picture of any Cavallaro men present to show to Anisha. I could ask Charlotte to act as the middleman—or rather, the middlewoman.

I wasn't sure I'd ever live dangerously the way Emmy did, but I was hella curious, and a night at a club with a tough PI might even be fun.

12

HALLIE

"Another drink, ma'am?"

At twenty bucks a pop? Thank goodness I had an expense account. The Starlight Lounge was classier than I'd imagined, dark but not dirty, no hint of the shadiness I knew lay beneath the sparkly veneer. The waitresses wore satin corsets, tiny shorts, and impossibly high heels, and the waiters looked as if they'd walked out of a strip club and into the vests and black tuxedo pants that appeared to be their uniform.

On the semicircular stage, a group of silver-spangled dancers were high-kicking their way through a song, complete with glittery ostrich-feather fans and an oversized disco ball. Tonight was burlesque night. The Starlight Lounge also offered a comedy club, circus shows, and jazz evenings, all accompanied by overpriced drinks, gourmet food, and access to an after-party when the entertainment had finished. Judging by the variety of accents around us, ninety percent of the audience were tourists.

"Just water, thanks." Which probably cost ten dollars a glass.

"Sir?"

"I'll have a beer."

We'd booked the gold package, which included a complimentary themed cocktail and a souvenir feather boa. Did I need a feather boa? No, but the gold tables were closer to the stage than those in the silver package, and the platinum seats were sold out. We'd arrived early, and after Collier hinted to the hostess that I had a bladder problem—thanks, buddy— she'd seated us at the side near the bathrooms and the kitchen. Our table for two came with velvet tub chairs and a cute beaded lamp. While I watched the show, Collier had been focusing on the staff and performers coming and going, filming all of them with a hidden camera. So far, we hadn't seen anyone who looked like a Cavallaro, but the night was still young. Next up was Coco Delite, according to the program.

"Sounds like a dessert," Collier remarked, and maybe that was intentional because ten minutes later, she popped out of a giant cake amid a cloud of confetti, just as the appetisers were served. Okay, the food *was* pretty good. I wasn't sure if it was two-hundred-bucks-a-ticket good, but definitely better than a Wonder Burger. I speared a piece of grilled asparagus while Collier tucked into seared scallops. No buckets of onion rings here, and sheesh...that woman was flexible. I'd be in the hospital for a week if I tried any of those moves. How did she get her leg behind her head like that?

We had a good view because the table in front of us stayed empty. A "Reserved" sign stopped anyone who might be tempted to move closer to the stage. Those were platinum seats, three hundred bucks a pop, so someone clearly had money to burn.

"Damn, I love my job," Collier said as a trio of scantily clad women shook their asses at him.

"I've had worse evenings," I admitted. I'd been expecting a tacky show one step up from a strip club, but the performances were surprisingly good. Kind of like a Broadway musical, but with lip-syncing and fewer clothes. Short stories rather than a novel. If it hadn't been for the whole Mafia thing, I might have suggested swapping Bradley's burlesque workshop for a girls' night out at the Starlight Lounge. "How long do you think they spend rehearsing?"

"Hours every day. My ex-wife was a dancer."

Collier had been married? "I'm sorry things didn't work out."

"Don't be. We're both happier without each other." Collier glanced at his phone and leaned closer. "This place belongs to Vito Cavallaro, but his youngest son runs it day-to-day. Cesare. A slippery motherfucker."

"You've come across him before?"

"Not personally." Another glance, and Collier nodded toward the screen. "Used to share an apartment with a couple of cops, and they'll still help me out off the record. Word on the street says Cesare formed a strategic partnership with Renzo Bucci."

Renzo Bucci. The groom. "Arms dealing?"

"The NYPD hasn't managed to pin anything on him yet."

A chill ran through me, and Dan's words echoed in my ears. *Watch your back.* I took comfort in the fact that I was in a room full of people and the Cavallaro family had no idea who I was. The thought that Kaylin La Rocca might have gotten tangled up with these people was beyond terrifying, and I knew that from experience. When I'd crossed paths with a gang loosely affiliated with the Mafia—the man in charge had been their banker—I'd found myself trapped in a luxury prison, expected to fuck dozens of men in return for not dying. Not every girl had made it out, but I had, thanks to Blackwood. The logical explanation was that Kaylin had suffered a similar fate, but if she'd been able to send a card to her grandma and flowers to an old roommate... Something didn't add up.

"A friend of a friend got arrested for murder just for taking photos in a public park, and folks like the Cavallaros can sell illegal weapons without consequence? Sometimes, the justice system makes me sick."

"Easy, tiger. Why do you think I never applied to join the NYPD? My uncle was a cop, and when I was a kid, he'd come over for dinner and rant about the unfairness of it all. And then his ex-partner—" Collier cut off and turned his attention to his last morsel of pan-fried sea bass. What had he been about to say? I never found out because once he'd chewed and swallowed, he nuzzled my ear with his nose. "Don't turn around. Vito just walked in."

Holy crap. It took an effort not to spin my head like a stuntwoman on *The Exorcist*. A moment later, four men came into view, all wearing suits, heading for the empty table. The thing that surprised me most about Vito was his size. I'd only seen headshots, and in person, he was shorter than me. The man beside him was four inches taller, and the pair of them were sandwiched between two hulking giants who made no attempt to hide the bulges under their jackets. Bodyguards.

"Just in time for the headline act," Collier murmured.

Daisy de Ville and the Divas would be appearing at nine p.m., followed by the Vixens at ten. Marlena the Magician would be circulating among the gold and platinum tables for a more personal touch. We hadn't decided whether to stay for the after-party—if Vito stuck around, I'd probably succumb to morbid curiosity, but otherwise my thousand-thread-count sheets were calling.

"Is that Cesare with Vito?" I whispered to Collier.

"I think so."

Cesare Cavallaro. A dangerously attractive fledgling arms dealer who may or may not be the key to my case. The more I watched him from the corner of my eye, the more convinced I became that he could be the man Anisha saw. *Handsome and he knew it.* Even leaning back in his seat with a drink in his hand, he exuded power. And arrogance. He ordered the servers around as if they were trash.

The lights dimmed, and a hush fell across the club. Even the Cavallaros stopped talking and looked toward the stage. Someone had brought out a microphone, and a figure moved toward it, then stilled as the band struck up the opening bars to "Diamonds Are a Girl's Best Friend." A spotlight hit Daisy de Ville, and Bradley would have turned green with envy if he'd been there. The effect was blinding. She sparkled from the crystal feathers on her ornate eye mask to the tips of her bejewelled pumps. Her long chestnut hair was styled into vintage pin curls, and a corset bodysuit accentuated her curves and pulled in her tiny waist. When she opened her mouth, I changed my mind about the ticket prices. Maybe they were actually too cheap? The Divas danced behind her in an elaborate routine involving a champagne glass and an oversized pearl necklace, and nobody in the audience uttered a word. I couldn't take my eyes off her.

Then she sashayed across the stage toward us, microphone in hand, and a synapse fired in my brain. The mask hid the top half of her face, and a curtain of hair covered the left side. But when she lowered the mic for a second, there was something familiar about the mouth. The plump bottom lip, the deep Cupid's bow, the momentary pout. Then there were the high cheekbones, the straight, narrow nose, and the delicate line of her jaw.

Could it be...?

No, no way.

But when I turned to Collier, he was watching her with the same curiosity, his gaze fixed on her face rather than her cleavage. He raised an eyebrow.

Fuck.

This was a tourist haunt, and other patrons had their camera phones out, so I grabbed mine and shot a few stills followed by a video. Had Kaylin La Rocca been in New York the whole time? Hiding in plain sight? Performing on stage to enthralled audiences?

I couldn't be certain.

But I believed there was a possibility.

She moved on to "Fever," her voice strong and throaty with an impressive range. I consulted Google. Daisy de Ville might have been headlining at the Starlight Lounge, but her online presence was limited. Several carefully staged pictures on the club's website, plus the occasional mention on Trip Advisor. Five stars, fantastic singer, a great end to our vacation. Even Providence didn't find much from a basic search.

"Enjoying the show, ma'am?" our server asked as she placed a dark chocolate and clementine torte in front of me.

"Oh, I love it!" I slipped into tourist mode. "You don't get this kind of food on Broadway. Isn't it great, honey?"

Collier played his part as the long-suffering husband and grunted non-committally.

"How often does Daisy de Ville sing? Maybe we can catch another show before we go home."

"She performs every Thursday. On Fridays, we have Kiki Luna, and on Saturdays, Honey Sweet headlines, but this weekend's shows are already sold out."

My disappointment was real. That meant we wouldn't be able to come back tomorrow with a better camera.

"Aw, we fly out on Wednesday. I probably shouldn't ask, but does she sing at any other venues?"

"No, only here. She's the boss's wife."

The server might as well have jabbed me with a cattle prod. A jolt ran through me. Maybe-Kaylin had married into the

Mafia? But who to? Vito or Cesare? It had to be Cesare, right? Kaylin was twenty-six, and Vito was forty years older. Cesare would make more sense.

Words deserted me, but Collier covered.

"Lucky man. We'll catch the show next time we're in New York, babe."

"Really?"

"If that's what you want." He gave my shoulders a squeeze. "Can I get a whisky on the rocks?"

"Sure, sir. I'll be right back."

After her set, Daisy de Ville disappeared backstage with the rest of the Divas, and a few minutes later, Cesare Cavallaro rose from his seat and pushed through the "Staff Only" door that led to the kitchen. Neither of them came back. We stayed until the end of the show, but when Vito left with his henchmen before the after-party started, we made our exit too.

"Gotta say, that wasn't how I expected tonight to turn out," Collier said as he stepped to the kerb to wave down a cab. "First time I've ever been serenaded by a misper."

"You truly think it's her?"

"If I was a betting man, which I am, I'd put ten bucks on it. Better than a fifty percent chance, I'd say, but it's hard to be sure when we can only see a quarter of her face."

"I was trying to get a good look at her eyes. I think Kaylin's were blue rather than brown, but Daisy de Ville could have been wearing lenses."

"Lenses, a wig, that shit women inject into their lips... Plus Cavallaro Junior would have the cash for hush-hush cosmetic surgery. I'll work my contacts, see if anyone knows when the wife came onto the scene."

"Providence didn't find any evidence of Cesare Cavallaro being married in public records."

"Maybe she's a common-law wife? Or they got hitched overseas? My baby sister had one of those destination weddings. We all spent a fucking fortune flying out to Grenada, and she divorced the prick a year later."

"I'm sorry to hear that."

"At least I didn't have to pretend to like him anymore." A cab pulled up, and Collier opened the door for me. "Let's get some sleep, and we can regroup in the morning. Start thinking about how we can get a look at Daisy de Ville without her mask on."

In theory, that sounded like a great idea, but inside, I was buzzing. I wouldn't be getting much sleep tonight.

13

DASHA

"Stop stressing, Dashenka," Alex murmured in my ear. "This is meant to be fun."

He rolled his hips lazily, and his cock hit *that* spot deep inside me. A ripple of pleasure made me gasp, but no matter how much I wanted to stay here in Alex's bed forever, naked and slightly sweaty, he'd still have to hurry this up.

"I *am* having fun. Aren't you having fun?"

"You just checked your watch."

"I'm meeting Paulo for breakfast at eight."

"Text him and say you're not going."

"For what reason? Darla never cancels plans."

"Tell him..." Alex twisted my head and played dirty with a searing kiss. "Tell him you're with me."

"Darla isn't a 'sex on the first date' kind of woman." I glanced at my watch again. "Which means you have eighteen minutes to finish."

Because I needed seventeen to shower and dress and thirty-four to drive back to the hotel. Well, Darla needed thirty-four. She didn't speed either. In fact, she was the most boring person on the planet. What was life without a little sin?

"Paulo will be late."

"Paulo has many, many faults, but tardiness isn't one of them."

"He went out with Bradley last night. Five bucks says he's late."

I wanted to lose that bet, but at the same time, I didn't. On the one hand, losing wasn't a favourite pastime of mine, but on the other hand, I'd become addicted to Alex-induced orgasms. If I used dry shampoo rather than washing my hair and made dubious calls at stoplights, I could shave off five minutes, which meant... Alex's hand found its way between my legs, and fuck, the man knew precisely what to do with his fingers. He didn't just play dirty, he played filthy.

"I'll tell Paulo I got lost on the way to the dining room," I blurted.

"Good idea."

"Don't think this is a sign of weakness."

"I would never think that."

"Because I'm not—"

Alex's arm banded around my waist, and a second later, he flipped me onto my knees and thrust into me *hard*. Motherfucker. I hated being caught off guard like that, and if anyone but Alex tried that shit, he'd wave goodbye to body parts. But this *was* Alex. I bit my lip, stretched the kinks out of my back, and let him fuck me into the damn mattress.

Darla was twenty minutes late. I hurried toward the hotel dining room with excuses on the tip of my tongue—the elevator took an age to arrive, all the corridors looked the same, some fool directed me the wrong way—only to find my magenta-haired assistant conspicuous by his absence. Had he been and gone? Unlikely. The last time we'd eaten breakfast at the Black Diamond, Paulo had piled his plate high with everything from the buffet except scrambled eggs—he complained that they reminded him of brains, although they didn't look like any brains I'd ever seen—and then he'd troughed down just over half of it and spent the rest of the morning complaining that he felt sick. It was possible he'd learned from past mistakes, but I doubted it.

And now I owed Alex five bucks.

"Can I get you coffee, ma'am? Or tea?" a server asked after I'd taken a seat. Back to the wall, facing the door, next to the emergency exit. "Toast or an omelette?"

"Just a black coffee."

"Americano, espresso, lungo, ristretto, red eye, or regular?"

"Regular."

"Arabica or robusta?"

Did I look like the type of person who cared? The difference was negligible anyway, but I gave a dumb giggle.

"Oh, I'll have the arabica, thank you for asking."

Where the hell was Paulo? I typed out a text.

ME

Everything okay, hun? Catching up on your beauty sleep?

If I hadn't been well and truly sated by Alex, I might have felt irritated by Paulo's no-show. At least he'd promised to work through lunch. My time with Alex was precious, and I wanted to finish on time today so we could go out for dinner.

My coffee arrived, but Paulo didn't. I helped myself to a bowl of fresh fruit, added a generous dollop of live yogurt, and was about to check the tracking app I'd installed on his cell phone when he finally broke radio silence. FaceTime. Why couldn't he just call like a normal person? Why did he need video?

I shoved earbuds into my ears and answered. Then swallowed a laugh. Damn, Paulo looked as if he'd been dragged through a nightclub backward and then shot out of a glitter cannon. Dark circles under his eyes, hair mussed, a smudged painting of a butterfly on one cheek. I tried for a sympathetic expression. Darla would do sympathy.

"Rough night, hun?"

"Ohmigosh, I'm sooooo sorry! Am I late?"

The camera panned around a hotel suite—which wasn't Paulo's hotel suite—and I spotted three sleeping drag queens on a couch behind him. At least, I hoped they were only sleeping. Disposing of bodies was so tedious, especially at this time in the morning.

"How were the daiquiris?"

"They were— You know, I don't really remember. My head hurts."

"Where's your purse? Did you remember your Tylenol?"

"I..." He looked around the room, and his eyes widened when he spotted the drag queens. His voice dropped to a whisper. "Who are those people? Where am I?"

An excellent question.

"Why don't you try waking one of them and asking?"

"Uh, I guess I could do that."

The camera wobbled as he picked his way across the room. At least he was still wearing clothes.

"Excuse me?" A pause. "Excuse me?"

"Huh?"

"Do you know where we are?"

"Wha... Oh, sure, the Black Diamond."

"Thank goodness." Paulo's worry turned to relief. "Darla, can you come get me? I can't find my pants."

Okay, make that half-wearing clothes. "Which floor are you on? Borrow a bathrobe, and then we can go to the lobby and get you a spare room key."

"Uh, which floor? Do you know which floor?"

Another pause. "Presidential Suite. Twenty-third floor."

Paulo repeated the information with a note of hope in his voice. False hope, as it turned out.

"Hun, this hotel only has six floors, seven if you include the basement."

I focused on the sliver of view behind him and tried to keep a straight face. Fuck me, I owed Alex considerably more than five bucks, and Bradley too, that crazy, overly exuberant genius. Yes, he was the human equivalent of a stone in your boot, but I was beginning to see why Emmy kept him around. Paulo's confusion was more entertaining than Netflix.

"I...I don't understand."

"Do you think that maybe you could have ended up in a different hotel?"

In, say, New York? I'd only been there a handful of times, but I still recognised that skyline.

"Uh, I don't know how—"

"Good morning!" A door slammed against a wall, and I recognised Bradley's voice. Either he'd indulged in considerably fewer daiquiris than Paulo had, or he'd overdosed on Tylenol and amphetamines. "Who wants to go roller-skating in Central Park? My friend Ishmael invited us." He gave a dazed Paulo a side hug. "How's my favourite daiquiri-drinking, unicorn-riding, Macarena-dancing bestie? The concierge is having your pants repaired right now, so they should be fixed by the time we finish our Bloody Marys. Oh, Lady Ramona, you lost one side of your eyelashes!"

Paulo had finally met his match, and it was glorious.

"Wh-what happened?" he asked.

"To your pants? You split the seam doing a cartwheel right before you passed out. Don't worry, Cherry Divine carried your trophy back."

"My t-t-trophy?"

"For winning the rodeo unicorn contest. You don't remember?"

Paulo shook his head and then winced.

"Chill, I videoed it," one of the drag queens said from off camera. "We can watch the replay before our tap-dancing class."

I caught a brief glance of Paulo's ashen face before the phone bounced around and finally focused on the ceiling. The sound of distant retching followed. Lightweight.

Bradley's face came into view.

"You owe Alex five bucks."

"Thank you, I already know that. How did you get Paulo to New York?"

"In a helicopter." What did Bradley do, roofie him? Emmy had trained him well. "When should I bring him back?"

I considered the question for a moment. Paulo was only meant to be in Richmond for five days before he travelled to New York to visit his not-so-secret boyfriend anyway. Without him here, I could spend more time with Alex while Samya, Isabella, and Marisol handled the Craft Cabin. I wouldn't need to run red lights on the way to breakfast, and I could ditch the damn muumuus for one blessed week.

"Don't bring him back." He was somebody else's problem now. "Drop him off at Davis French's apartment and tell him to enjoy his extended vacation."

I'd sure enjoy mine.

14

DASHA

The four of us flitted through the lingerie department like wraiths, guns drawn—me, Ana, Emmy, and Sky. Sky was the baby of the team, Emmy's protégé, just eighteen years old. Her inexperience showed, but that was hardly surprising. When I was her age, I'd already had four years of active combat experience under my belt. Plus one trip to a juvenile colony—think barracks, a uniform, forced labour— and five years of psychological trauma. I'd lost count of how many men I'd killed by then.

Movement beside a scantily clad mannequin caught my eye, and I lined up a shot, only to hold back as a terrified civilian raised her hands. An employee wearing a department store uniform. I motioned her to stay down, and she shrank back behind a rack of panties. Perhaps I should invest in some less utilitarian underwear? Not that it would stay on for long around Alex, but those dumb magazines Paulo kept leaving in the break room at the Craft Cabin suggested I should make the effort. Maybe something in silk, definitely not pink, but—

"Three o'clock, behind the mannequin in the see-through...thing," Sky whispered, and then she sniggered.

A simple trip to the mall had turned into an active shooter situation when a disgruntled employee decided to express his displeasure to his boss in the least subtle of ways. Now the four of us had been tasked with stopping him, using only our concealed-carry weapons plus whatever we could improvise as we went along.

"See-through thing?" Ana said. "Who programmed this sim?"

"Logan," Emmy told her. "The size of the tits gives it away."

I'd been dubious about training in a simulation at first, sceptical that it could be anywhere near realistic, but I had to concede that it wasn't terrible. I reached out to a rack of crotchless panties and fingered the lace. Real. The Blackwood sim was set up in a cavernous building that allowed the training team to overlay real-world props with virtual reality. Some items were genuine. Others were not. The carpet, for example. It looked like maroon pile, but beneath my feet, I felt concrete. Something to bear in mind if I tucked and rolled.

"Ah, shit." That was Sky again. "Hostage."

The target came into view, briefly, his face hidden behind the voluminous curls and tear-streaked face of a terrified blonde as he backed toward a door marked "Staff" and disappeared through it. The four of us stacked up outside the doorway, two on the left, two on the right, listening carefully as we planned our next move. Emmy looped the tie from a silk robe through the handle and used it to slowly, quietly pull the door open without putting herself in harm's way. The blonde's sobs grew fainter as footsteps faded into the distance.

Emmy nodded to Sky, and Sky stepped back and sliced the pie. First, she established her reference point—the left-hand doorjamb—then she inched forward on an imaginary circle, using the doorjamb as the pivot. With each step she took, she was able to see another small slice of the room beyond, all while revealing as little of herself as possible. Tactics 101.

"Clear."

The perfumed air turned musty as we moved into a mess, and I was talking literally, not metaphorically. The customer-facing areas might have been tidy and spotless, but behind the scenes, Willard's Department Store was an homage to poor discipline. Boxes of stock were stacked haphazardly, armless mannequins stared from the shadows, and dust coated everything. A cork board held a picture of the employee of the month—a thin-faced blond guy named Chris P Bacon—a reminder of the staff dress code, and a discount voucher for Moe's Diner. Blackwood sure paid attention to detail. As they should.

The sobs became quieter as we headed in their direction. The hostage was travelling faster than us, which always presented an interesting dilemma. What if there was a second hostile? Should we push on or move more cautiously? Where did this hallway lead? Where were the exits? What if the hostile doubled back and flanked us? I glanced upward, noting the suspended ceiling. If I were alone, I'd be in there by now, watching. Waiting. Something didn't feel quite right.

Ahead of me, Sky stilled at the sound of a falling box, and I followed suit, signalling to Ana and Emmy behind to do the same with a raised hand.

"D-d-don't shoot!" A brown-haired man stumbled out of an office, hands above his head. An employee? He wore black trousers and a pale blue shirt, a name badge pinned to the pocket.

Sky waved him past. "Keep your hands up and exit the store."

"O-o-okay."

As he approached me, his right hand dropped an inch, and

I shot him. The bullet entered through his philtrum, and he crumpled without a word.

Sky's eyes bugged out. "What the…?"

Emmy checked her watch. "Nice, we'll make it back for lunch. Good shot."

"She just killed a civilian."

"He was the hostile," Ana told Sky.

"But—"

"Look at the shoes."

White sneakers with red laces and the logo of a well-known sportswear brand on the side.

"They're not in line with the dress code," I explained.

"Last time I checked, that wasn't a capital offence."

"But murder is." The name badge on the hostile's pocket read "Chris Bacon, Supervisor" in block capitals. "Ten bucks says you'll find the real Chris Bacon dead in that office."

And the hostage would be stumbling out of the store by now, released by the hostile on the condition that she kept quiet and didn't turn back. If we'd carried on after her, we'd have been the ones with bullet holes. I flipped the hostile over and removed the semi-automatic from his waistband. Who was playing the bad guy? A member of the training staff? Not one of Emmy's core team, that was for sure—this man felt pudgy around the middle.

"We'll probably lose marks for using lethal force," Emmy said. "At least you didn't shoot him in the back."

"I'm not an amateur." And Chris P Bacon wouldn't have thanked me for the bruises if I'd slammed him into the concrete floor. "Plus I saved the taxpayers money. Twenty thousand bucks a year for incarceration plus the cost of the trial."

In Russia, it was cheaper. Trials were rigged, and prisoners were shipped off as cheap labour or cannon fodder. Life sentences were common, whether by accident or design. The sim flashed a message, an imitation of a retro video game: *Game Over! You Win :)* The four of us traipsed back through the lingerie department and homeware, down the stairs, and around the make-up counters. When we reached the main doors, I removed my headset, and the fancy store became a drab grey building once again. My stomach grumbled. After Paulo's call, I'd abandoned breakfast and headed straight to Blackwood's headquarters with the intention of using the range and then grabbing a granola bar, only to find myself co-opted onto Ana's sim team after Carmen's kid puked at school.

"Anyone else fancy a bacon double cheeseburger?" Emmy asked. "Sky, we can debrief on the way to the diner. You did good for a regular active shooter situation, but on rare occasions, we'll encounter a hostile with a brain, and we need to be prepared for those."

Ana snorted. "If you sneak out to the diner again, the next hostile will be called Kale P Lettuce. Toby will make sure of it."

"How many guys named Kale do you know?"

"I went to school with a guy called Kale," Sky said. "His sister was in my class."

"Go on, what was the sister called?"

"Quinoa. She shortened it to Quin."

"I thought it was pronounced 'keen-wah'?"

"Yeah, well, that's not how she said it. I don't think her mum shopped at Whole Foods."

"Can't blame her for that." Emmy shuddered. "So many lentils, so few E numbers. Are you peeps joining us?"

Ana shook her head. "I have a PTO meeting."

"Yikes. Try not to murder anyone. It's the best preschool in the area, plus I'm too busy to bury a body. Dasha?"

"I'm having lunch with Alex."

"Nice. Enjoy your grilled chicken."

Why the sarcasm? There was nothing wrong with grilled chicken. It was healthier than a cheeseburger, at any rate.

"At least I won't die from blocked arteries."

"Eh, I doubt I'll live long enough for that to happen. Why do you think I don't do Botox? Every wrinkle is a reminder that I've made it through another year."

The door opened, and Dan walked in with a man I didn't recognise. She made the introductions.

"Nick, this is Dasha. Dasha, meet Nick. He's one of the head honchos at this circus." Then that would make him a ringmaster, not a honcho. "Did somebody mention blocked arteries?"

"I'm going to the diner with Sky," Emmy said. "Wanna come?"

"I'll have to meet you there. Gotta go through the sim first, and then I need to juggle the workloads in the New York office because we picked up six new cases this morning, and we didn't close any of the old ones yet."

"Anything looking hopeful?"

"Maybe. Hallie thinks she might've found Kaylin La Rocca, which would free up a chunk of Collier's time."

"Oh yeah? Being honest, I thought that was a lost cause."

"Me too, but she just briefed me, and there's a lot of circumstantial evidence on their side."

"Are we talking alive or dead?"

"Alive and married to a wise guy from Tribeca."

"When you say 'wise guy,' are we talking about a stand-up comedian or a Mafioso?"

"The second one. I told her to watch her back. She hasn't managed to get a good look at the woman yet, so that's the next step."

Emmy groaned. "Fuck my life, she's gonna get kidnapped again, isn't she? I'd better get Sloane to clear my schedule."

"She'll have Collier with her."

"The same Collier who blew a month-long surveillance operation when he decided to break cover and chase a mugger six city blocks?"

"At least he caught the guy."

"It would've been cheaper to buy the woman a new damn handbag."

"He learned from that mistake."

"I bloody well hope he did. Hallie's been through enough shit in the last year, and if he does something dumb around the Mafia, they're gonna start shooting, not leg it through the back alleys of Brooklyn."

"You want me to assign somebody else?"

"*Is* there somebody else?"

"I'd have to pull them off another case."

"We can't let paying clients down." Emmy muttered a curse and turned to me. I also muttered a curse. "Dasha, how do you feel about a trip to New York?"

Blyat. "I just offloaded Paulo in New York."

"So? Can't you manage to avoid one dude who'll spend the whole time either fucking his boyfriend or abusing the poor guy's credit card in Bloomingdale's? Haven't you put a tracking app on his phone?"

"I can avoid him."

"Then what's the problem?"

The problem was that I'd only spent one night with Alex, and I liked waking up next to him more than I ever thought possible. But Emmy would be paying me ten thousand bucks a day if I babysat Hallie in New York, and I wanted a new rifle. And a new motorcycle. And a new solar array for the cabin I used as a bolt-hole.

"There's no problem. I'll go to New York."

At least stalking a member of the Mob would make a change from hunting the Bratva.

"Excellent. Just keep Hallie safe and do your facial-recognition voodoo. If she really has found Kaylin La Rocca, we can write a report for Nico so he can lament her poor taste in men and move on with his life."

Fantastika.

One day, if I managed to build up a nice nest egg and gain a full complement of wrinkles, maybe I'd be able to move on with mine.

15

HALLIE

"Did it work?" I said softly into the phone.

"Nope." Dammit. "Other hosts may allow you to meander freely through their hallways," Collier mimicked in a high-pitched voice. "But that's not how we operate at Belgravia Place. Our residents value their privacy and security. You'll leave your package here at the desk, or you won't leave it at all."

"He sounds as if he'd be a hoot at parties."

"You'll serve those appetisers on silver trays with your nose in the air, or you won't serve them, period."

Cesare Cavallaro lived in the penthouse at Belgravia Place, a thirty-three-storey pillar of glass and steel that rose into the sky near the Hudson River. The building had been constructed by Seco Developments, a Cavallaro company run by Cesare's older brother Alonzo. Generous balconies cut into the sides of the building, the railings overflowing with greenery and a sea of yellow flowers. According to the Seco website, the building was carbon neutral and featured a rainwater-harvesting system and solar panels on the roof.

I'd taken a position in a café opposite, laptop open,

headphones on, just one more remote worker looking for excellent coffee and a change of scene. The privacy filter on my laptop kept my real purpose hidden from prying eyes as I waited for any sign of Maria Cavallaro.

That was her name.

Maria.

And Kaylin's middle name was Marie, which seemed like a mighty big coincidence.

One of Collier's NYPD buddies had come through with a few snippets of information—Maria had first been spotted with Cesare almost four years ago, at a gala dinner in aid of victims of domestic violence, before Kaylin appeared at the hotel in Manassas, before she called Nico begging for help. A blurry picture showed a blonde who could have been Kaylin. Since then, she'd dropped out of sight apart from going to the occasional party with Cesare and her turns at the club. Daisy de Ville had made her first appearance two years ago.

"Maybe the evening shift won't be so uppity?"

"Unlikely. Plus there was a guard standing near the elevators. Not a rent-a-cop; probably one of Cavallaro's men."

"You gonna come join me for coffee?"

"Once I've changed into regular clothes."

Collier had gone in dressed as a bike messenger, and let's just say that if the concierge had been a woman, she'd have let him go anywhere he wanted. One lady outside had tripped over a kerb because she couldn't keep her gaze off his package, and I didn't mean the box he was carrying.

I went back to watching the front entrance. There was a parking garage too, but that would be harder to stake out. The roller door opened into a narrow service road alongside a neighbouring apartment building, and there was a camera monitoring the area.

I picked out a handful of likely residents—a grey-haired couple, a blond guy in a suit with a trophy girlfriend on his arm, and a perfectly coiffed lady in yoga gear who might have been thirty or forty or fifty depending on how much surgery she'd had. Most of the activity came from the worker bees wealthy folks surrounded themselves with. Maids, masseuses, personal trainers, shoppers, stylists, even what looked like a psychic dressed in a flowing purple robe. A dog walker departed with a fluffy white pooch. A guy with long hair and a backpack sporting a logo from the Houseplant Hub jogged up the steps and hovered by the desk as the concierge checked him off against a list. A limousine pulled up outside, waited as the jobsworth of a concierge helped an elderly Chinese woman into the back seat, and glided smoothly into traffic.

My phone rang. Dan.

"Did you get a good look at her yet?"

"She doesn't seem to go out much, but I got to see Collier in Spandex shorts, so that's something."

"Thighs like tree trunks, right?"

"How long does he spend in the gym?"

"There's one in his building, and I'm pretty sure he spends more time there than in his apartment."

Belgravia Place had a gym too. And a spa, a pool, a movie theatre, a residents' lounge, and a virtual golf simulator. No wonder Mrs. Cavallaro didn't feel the need to leave the building.

"When does he sleep? He's been working from dawn till dusk."

"Yeah, about that. The New York office is slammed right now, so we're gonna need to borrow him back for a while."

My heart sank. I'd grown to like having Collier as a partner, and working surveillance alone sucked.

"So I'm on my own?"

"I didn't say that." What was with the fake cheer? "Now that this has moved from an investigation into more of a logistical, how-can-we-get-a-photo-of-the-Mob-boss's-wife kind of job, we figured you'd be okay with a less experienced partner."

"Like an intern?"

"Not exactly."

"Then what?"

"Dasha will be with you later this afternoon. Save her a seat."

"Dasha? Are you joking? I can't work with her, no way."

"Relax, sweetie. She's great with faces. Just don't let her shoot anyone. Gotta go—I'm meeting Emmy and Sky for lunch. Ciao."

I couldn't argue, not in the middle of a café, and besides, Dan had hung up anyway. Just don't let Dasha shoot anyone? I was almost sure Dan was joking because nobody could stop Dasha from doing anything she wanted to do.

Collier showed up an hour later, minus his bicycle and dressed more appropriately in jeans and a T-shirt. Both too tight, of course. Maria-slash-Daisy hadn't made an appearance yet, but I was learning plenty about the residents of Belgravia Place. These people did literally nothing for themselves. One woman even had an assistant to carry her purse, and I'd seen not one, not two, but three catering services arrive at the building. Did any of the wealthy layabouts know their neighbour was an arms dealer?

"Have you heard the news?" I asked Collier.

"That I'm being bumped? Yeah, I heard. Sorry to leave you in the lurch. More cases came in, and Jake's on paternity leave. Fuckin' twins. I hear he wants to come back to the office for a break, but his wife won't let him."

"She did the hard work. It's only fair that he takes a turn."

"True enough. Look, if you need backup, call me. I'll help out off the clock if I can."

"They're sending a colleague from Richmond to assist."

"Someone I know?"

"She's new."

"Any experience with surveillance?"

"I believe so."

"Well, don't let her do anything stupid."

Easier said than done. "I'll do my best."

"A pizza?" Dasha managed to look equal parts offended and scornful. "Why would I want to order a pizza?"

"Uh, so we don't have to cook?"

"I'm not here to cook *or* eat pizza; I'm here to work."

"But it's seven p.m."

"Precisely. No self-respecting investigator would be eating fast food at seven thirty."

"Is it the time you're taking issue with? Or my choice of menu?"

"Both. Why aren't you wearing shoes?"

"Because we're in Emmy's apartment and it's really fancy?"

"You should always wear shoes; you never know when you'll have to run. We'll leave in five minutes. Where do I find the building schematics for Belgravia Place?"

"The what?"

"The architectural drawings? The blueprints?" She stared expectantly. "You don't have them?"

"Why...why would I need them?"

"To work out possible methods of ingress and egress? What, you plan to sit around outside with your thumb up your ass?"

"Collier already tried to get in. There's a concierge and a security guard in the lobby."

"What did he do, try to get past with good looks and charm?"

"No, he had a package."

Dasha rolled her eyes. "How original."

Today, she was a brunette, a businesswoman dressed in a pantsuit and sensible shoes. I hadn't even recognised her when I passed her in the lobby downstairs. Only when I was waiting for the elevator to Emmy and Black's penthouse did I hear the soft voice behind me, the accent pure New York.

"Boom. You're dead. You need to learn to watch your back, Hallie Chastain."

She'd contoured her face with make-up, making it appear thinner, and her eyes were brown rather than blue. And unless I was mistaken, she'd added padding around her hips and chest because she wasn't normally that curvy.

"So what would you have done?"

"I'll know the answer to that after I've assessed the building, its occupants, and the surroundings."

"We could just wait until Thursday. Daisy de Ville has a show at the Starlight Lounge, and she'll have to leave the building then."

"Thursday? You want to waste six whole days?"

"I mean, we might see her sooner."

"Why aren't you wearing appropriate footwear yet?"

This was going to be a long, long night.

Nine a.m. on Saturday saw me back in the café, and today, I needed the caffeine more than ever. Dasha had spent five hours in Tribeca last night, meandering through the streets, occasionally stopping to talk with people, studying the buildings, all while going through three changes of clothes and four different accents. A little after midnight, she'd looped her arm through mine and stumbled down the service road that led to Belgravia Place's parking garage in a pink sequinned party dress, then retched into a dumpster. A security guard had arrived within sixty seconds and politely but firmly asked us to take a hike. Dasha's reaction? A wrinkle of the nose, followed by a "Hmm, they're vaguely competent."

This morning, she was out on the street again, apparently waiting for a bus while I picked at a triple chocolate muffin in the café. I knew who'd gotten the better end of the deal.

"Who's the blonde?" she asked quietly through my hidden earpiece.

I'd been researching the building's occupants, but I'd only identified a quarter of them so far.

"I'm not sure."

Luckily, the café was busy, full of tourists and office workers, and half a dozen of them were on the phone. My murmured words drew no attention.

"And the dog walker? Was she here yesterday?"

Finally, a question I could answer. "Yes, at the same time."

"Hmm."

I watched as Dasha left her spot and bent to pet the mutt. Was it a Shih Tzu? A Bichon Frisé? Whatever, it had been primped to within an inch of its life, and it desperately needed some anti-frizz serum. Dasha chatted with the walker for a minute or two, then wandered off along the street, not a care in the world.

"Where are you going?" I asked.

"To the park. The sun's out. Want to come?"

"Hello? We're working?"

"I know this."

Good thing I didn't leave because fifteen minutes later, Cesare Cavallaro strode out of the building. The concierge rushed to open the door for him, and why didn't he lick

Cesare's boots while he was at it? Yes, yes, I understood that opening the door was his job, but the man was obsequious to the max with the residents, and then he treated the staff and delivery drivers like dirt. I saw him through the huge windows, wagging his finger and crossing his arms. Jackass.

When Dasha came back from the park, she was wearing a sundress instead of skinny jeans. How many outfits did she have in that shoulder bag of hers? And how did she change so quickly? Practice. It had to be practice. Did she stand in front of the mirror every night, timing how long it took to put on pants? She moseyed along the sidewalk, past Belgravia Place, and an hour passed before she slid onto the seat beside me with a salmon Niçoise salad and a bottle of sparkling water.

"Who is that?"

She didn't need to point. The concierge helped a pretty redhead to wheel a stroller down the ramp at the side of the steps, and I squinted as she came closer.

"I think it's Grace Fields, sixth floor. Her husband's an investment banker."

"You *think*?"

I angled my laptop so Dasha could see the screen. "The hair's different."

She only needed one glance. "It's her."

Dasha never forgot a face, so Emmy said, which I figured was both a blessing and a curse. Why was it that the people I wished I could erase from my mind formed my most vivid memories?

"This food is surprisingly edible," Dasha said. "I didn't have high hopes."

"There's still no sign of Daisy."

"No matter. We'll see her tomorrow."

"How can you be so sure?"

"Because I have a plan now."

I kind of expected her to give me a clue what it was, but

she just forked an anchovy into her mouth and checked her phone. Alex. I saw the name flash up on the screen, and the first line of the message said he wanted to... Yikes, was that physically possible? My cheeks burned.

"Do you want to read my emails too?" Dasha asked.

"Sorry. I'm sorry, I didn't mean to...uh..."

"Yes, you did, and you *should* be reading people's messages. What you shouldn't be doing is getting caught. Don't stay still; people sense it. Move naturally."

"Uh...okay."

She fell silent as she replied to the message, and this time, I kept my eyes averted. Dasha was one strange woman.

"Tomorrow, you'll dress like a tourist," she said. "Jeans, casual jacket, sneakers, expensive camera. Make sure the battery is fully charged and test the memory card before you leave the apartment. And don't get mugged because I won't be rescuing you the way your friend Collier would."

"Aren't you going to brief me on the plan?"

"No. I need a natural reaction from you."

"But—"

"I'll see you in the morning. Enjoy your pizza."

"I... Where are you going?"

"SoHo. This is New York, yes? Shopping is mandatory. Be ready to leave at oh-eight-hundred tomorrow."

She disappeared out the door, leaving me with half a muffin and a whole lot of confusion.

16

HALLIE

*A*ct natural, Dasha said. Just be ready when the time came.

When the time came for what? She still hadn't told me, and nor had I seen her since she headed off in the direction of the Hudson. Delivery drivers came and went from Belgravia Place, and Grace Fields departed with her baby. I spotted a town car registered to Cesare Cavallaro pull up outside, and he left the driver to idle at the kerb, getting honked at and shouted at until his boss emerged from the building ten minutes later. Alone. No sign of Maria.

The dog walker set off with the fluffy white furball, then ambled back ten minutes later, pausing on each step as the dog climbed its way to the lobby. She said a few words to the concierge, then vanished into an elevator.

The houseplant dude showed up again. How much care did plants need? We had a couple of potted plants in the living room at home, but I only watered them when the leaves looked droopy, which turned out to be once a month in the winter and more often in the summer. Pinchy the parrot loved the trees. Whenever we let him loose in the apartment, he'd perch on the ficus and curse us out.

Five minutes passed. Ten, and I was beginning to understand why most of my colleagues hated surveillance detail with a passion. Sure, the cakes were good, but I was bored and a little bloated. Too many carbs. Maybe I should take a leaf out of Dasha's book and try a salad?

Or...maybe I should get the hell out of there.

An alarm sounded from Belgravia Place, and I could tell from the concierge's agitated movements that he hadn't been expecting it. Was this Dasha's doing? My camera was ready to go, and I hastily shoved my laptop into my bag and tossed ten bucks into the tip jar.

"What's going on over there?" I asked the barista.

He shrugged. "Beats me."

The residents were beginning to spill onto the sidewalk, many in casual clothes and one in a dressing gown. Was that a whiff of smoke? A fire? A building like Belgravia Place would have a sprinkler system, surely? Sirens sounded in the distance as I scanned the faces of the evacuees. Passers-by had stopped to gawk, making the task more difficult, and I elbowed myself to the front of the crowd. Several people shot dirty looks in my direction when they noticed the camera, but I ignored them.

Just doing my job.

And then I saw her.

Kaylin La Rocca.

The brown hair must have been a wig because she was blonde now, and holy fuck, she wasn't alone. A small boy sat on her hip, two years old at a guess, one small hand clutching at her sweater and the other holding a blue-and-white striped snail in a death grip. Kaylin had a son? She wasn't only a wife but a mother too?

I snapped as many pictures as I dared, then quickly checked the screen. They were good.

Kaylin had done what you're always told not to do in a fire —she'd grabbed personal belongings on the way out of the building. Now she was trying to juggle not only the toddler but a purse and what looked like a bag full of kid stuff as well. Before I had time to think things through properly, I stepped forward.

"Hey, let me give you a hand."

I grabbed the changing bag as the strap slid down her arm, and she flashed me a half-smile. But no fake expression could hide the fact that without her stage make-up, Kaylin La Rocca looked utterly miserable.

"Thanks. I just... I can't..." The boy's face creased into the beginnings of a wail. "Matty, shhh. It's okay."

"What happened? I was getting a coffee when an alarm went off."

"It's the fire alarm." Kaylin glanced back toward the building. "I smelled smoke in the stairwell."

"It sounds as if the emergency services are on the way, so I'm sure they'll soon have everything under control."

Fear flashed in her eyes. "Right. That's good, I guess."

"Why don't you come sit down? There's a bench right over there. Your son looks heavy. Sorry, I shouldn't make assumptions—is he your son? Or are you his nanny?"

"Yes, he's my son, but—"

"I'll take that."

The bag was lifted from my arm, and I whirled to find one of Cavallaro's henchmen glowering at me.

"It's okay." Kaylin's tone turned placating. "Dino, it's okay. She was just trying to help."

I held up both hands. "Sorry, I didn't mean to upset anyone. This is your husband?"

"No, no, just a...friend," she said, but her expression told a different story. She wasn't fond of Dino at all, and I wasn't certain whether the flash of fear I'd seen was due to my mention of the emergency services or because Dino was headed in our direction.

"We're leaving," he told her. "Car's over here."

She shot me an apologetic glance but didn't say another word. Instead, she followed Dino to a waiting limo and climbed into the back seat with her son, and a moment later, the three of them were gone.

My phone rang. No surprise who it was.

"Did you get the photos?"

"Yes, but how—"

"Good. I'll see you back at the apartment."

Then Dasha was gone as well.

My mind was working overtime when I stepped off the elevator and into Emmy's sumptuous marble hallway, but I was stopped in my tracks by the sight of a small fluffy dog staggering across the polished tile.

"What the hell? Where did the dog come from?"

Dasha sauntered into view, now dressed in sportswear. "I picked it up at the dog park."

Huh? "I don't understand."

"It's simple. All you need is a cocktail wiener, a tranquilliser, and a large purse."

"Wait, you *stole* a dog?"

"Relax, I only borrowed it. There's a phone number on the tag. Once the tranquilliser's worn off, I'll give it back."

"You can't just go around taking dogs."

"Actually, I can."

I crouched to steady the poor thing as it stumbled sideways. "Easy, little one, I've got you." I checked the tag attached to the shiny blue collar. Bertie. His name was Bertie.

"Fine, you *shouldn't* go around taking dogs. His owner must be worried sick."

"Not his owner, his walker. And maybe she should spend more time watching the dog and less time chatting."

Dealing with this woman was *impossible*.

"Why would you even want to take Bertie?"

"So I could get into the building." Dasha spoke slowly, enunciating each word as if I were a small child. "It's difficult to pose as a dog walker without a dog."

"*You* were the dog walker?"

"If you're going to keep asking dumb questions, this will be a very long day. Think, Hallie. Use that detective brain."

I wanted to throttle her, but I shut up and thought. I'd watched the dog walker leave Belgravia Place a few minutes after eleven, and she'd returned ten minutes later. Yesterday, she'd been gone for longer, and today, the dog had been slow getting up the steps. That had been Dasha, hadn't it? Dasha and a sleepy Bertie.

"Where's the real dog walker?"

Tell me she wasn't lying in a dumpster somewhere.

"Probably on her way back from Battery Park by now."

"You spoke with her yesterday. She told you she walks the dog every day, didn't she?"

Dasha gave me a slow clap. "Well done."

"What did you do, tell the concierge the dog was sick, so you'd come back early?"

"See? You're not a lost cause, after all." Dasha gave a self-satisfied smile. "The concierge doesn't like dogs. He gave Cricket Cavallaro a wide berth yesterday, so he wasn't going to notice if I showed up with a different mutt today."

"Cricket Cavallaro? The other dog belongs to Kaylin?"

"She never walks it herself. The dog walker assumes that's because she's busy with the child, but if my prints were on file and I was wanted for murder, I'd keep a low profile too."

"How are you *not* wanted for murder?"

She gave me another of those "Are you dumb?" looks. "Because I'm careful."

"I can't believe you found out Kaylin had a son, and you didn't tell me."

"What would have changed if you'd known?"

"Nothing," I admitted. "But we're meant to be a team. Holding back information feels, well, sleazy."

"Where I come from, the less information a civilian has, the less the enemy can extract from them under duress."

"Firstly, I work for the same people you do, and secondly, who's going to be torturing me?"

"You've never been in the military, and concern was expressed that you might be abducted again."

Expressed by who? By Dan? By Emmy? Okay, so I didn't have a great track record, but their lack of faith in me still stung. And Emmy had never been in the military either, or Sky, or Dan, so what did that have to do with anything?

"You were sent to babysit me?"

"Those are your words, not mine."

"I'm not planning on getting abducted again."

"I'm sure you weren't planning on it the first or second or third time either."

That was a low blow, but unfortunately, one I couldn't deflect. And Dasha had been responsible for freeing me from my captors in the third incident, so while she had the personality of a cheese grater and a knack for making me feel like an amoeba, I still owed her a debt of thanks. She'd also flushed Kaylin out of the building today, even if I disagreed with her methods.

I sucked in a calming breath. "So after you got into the building, you set off the fire alarm?"

"Precisely."

"With an actual fire?"

"Only a small one."

"You could have burned the whole freaking building down."

"Unlikely. I only dropped a lit cigarette into a metal trash can. The flames were reasonably well-contained. If you think about it, I actually did the residents a favour."

"Oh? How do you figure that?"

"That building was constructed by the Mob, yes? And they're notorious for low-balling their contractors, which means the crews tend to cut corners. I figured the sprinkler system only had a fifty-fifty chance of working, and it didn't. Better for the residents to find out now than in a more serious fire."

"Don't sprinkler systems need to be inspected?"

"Yes, theoretically, but a contractor has the option to self-certify." Bertie tried a few more steps, his nails clicking on the marble. "Don't you have a report to write? I need to return the dog before it shits on the floor."

Yes, I had a report to write, plus I needed to review the pictures I'd taken and the footage from the backup lapel camera I'd been wearing. At least I had good news for Nico. We'd found Kaylin and she was alive, even if the unbearable sadness in her eyes haunted me. The case was solved, and it was out of my hands now.

17

NICO

S he was alive.

Kaylin was alive.

Nico had been plagued with doubts about Hallie Chastain at first—she was young, inexperienced—but he should have realised that a woman like Emmy Black wouldn't have hired her unless she was competent. Lesson learned.

Kaylin was alive, but she was living in a gilded prison. Nico clicked through the photos Hallie had taken, and then played the video again. Again. *Again.* This wasn't the girl he'd known in Moscow, or the woman he'd met in New York. The light had gone from her eyes.

"It sounds as if the emergency services are on the way, so I'm sure they'll soon have everything under control," Hallie told her on screen.

"Right. That's good, I guess."

Nico played the clip over and over. What did that mean? *That's good, I guess.* The normal reaction would have been relief that the fire department was on the way, not ambivalence. Kaylin wanted the building to burn down?

Logic said he should walk away and leave her to her new life, but his conscience wouldn't let him.

His conscience.

Some said he didn't have one, and a decade ago, he'd believed they were right. But Nico had changed in the years since he left Russia. It turned out his father hadn't been quite as successful as he'd hoped in beating the morals out of a son who'd disappointed him in so many ways.

Which left Nico with a problem.

On the surface, Kaylin had everything. A husband, a child, even a dog. A luxurious lifestyle and the singing career she'd always wanted. So why did she look so unhappy? Yes, there was the small matter of an outstanding arrest warrant, but surely a man like Cesare Cavallaro had the resources to take care of that? Why hadn't he?

Nico thought he knew the answer.

Feared he knew the answer.

If there was one thing he knew well, it was mafia bosses. His father had been a pakhan in the Bratva, his godfather was currently one, and most of the kids he'd been friends with growing up were still involved in organised crime in some form or another. It was the oligarch way. Oh, sure, they dressed their transgressions up with a veneer of respectability, but they were all crooks. Shady businessmen working hand in hand with shadier politicians to keep their grip on power in a country where the gap between rich and poor was a chasm few could leap.

Cavallaro might have been American, but he shared the same mentality as his Russian brothers. Control. It was all about control. He hadn't tried to clear his wife's name because he could use the outstanding warrant to keep her in line, and what kind of life was that?

Kaylin, Kaylin, Kaylin... Why didn't you learn from the past?

She'd probably been too young to understand how badly Nico's father treated her mother. All she remembered was the trappings of wealth, the illusion.

Nico? He remembered the screams that came from his father's bedroom as he roughed up Renée La Rocca. He remembered watching movies with eight-year-old Kaylin and turning up the volume so she wouldn't have to listen. Back then, he'd been a weedy sixteen-year-old, still developing, and he remembered the helplessness, the frustration of being unable to stop his father from treating women as throwaway items. His mother, in her way, had been complicit. She came from a good family, and she was happy for him to use her name and connections as long as she got money out of it. Hadn't cared about the mistresses as long as he left her alone. While Nico had lived in Moscow with a succession of nannies, she'd lunched in Paris and shopped in Milan before being found dead in a Sardinian hotel suite a week before his twelfth birthday. She'd tripped and fallen, the autopsy report said. Any mention of blood alcohol content had been erased from the official record.

And now the cycle continued. Kaylin followed in her mother's footsteps while the boy, Matty, walked in Nico's.

Would he spend sleepless nights plotting his father's demise? Would he get as far as loading a gun, only to back away at the last moment? Nico had chickened out a dozen times before the angel of death visited. Viktoria, she'd called herself, although he doubted that was her real name. As his father lay dying, he'd watched her flit across the lawn and into the trees, carefully avoiding the security patrols. A ghost. At twenty, he'd have stood a better chance of identifying her ass than her face, so he'd been no help to the police in that respect, not that he'd tried hard to describe her.

Some things were better left alone.

But Kaylin's fate wasn't one of them.

This time, Nico had been blessed with the good fortune to cross paths with Emmy Black, and if she was the person he suspected she was, then perhaps he wouldn't have to spend another decade waiting for the nightmare to unfold.

He picked up the phone and dialled.

18

———

EMMY

I tamped down a smile as Nico Belinsky walked across the rooftop pool deck at the Black Diamond Hotel in NYC. I'd told him to wear Speedos—partly to check he wasn't wearing a wire and partly for my own amusement—and he'd complied. Yeah, yeah, I was married, but that didn't mean I couldn't appreciate a fine specimen of a man when he was right in front of me.

"Drink?" I asked.

"Belvedere, straight up."

Must be serious if he was diving right into the liquor. I waved over a waiter and relayed the order, plus requested another orange juice for myself. I needed to stay sober for the discussion I suspected we were about to have.

"We can take a swim while the bartender pours."

It was a little chilly to hang out poolside, which made the location perfect for my purposes. There were only two other couples present, and I'd made sure they were assigned cabanas far away from ours.

Nico gave a one-shouldered shrug. "I'm not wearing a wire."

"I didn't think for a minute that you would be, but it's so much fun to check."

He looked me up and down slowly, and my bikini didn't cover much more than his teeny-weeny trunks. Finally, he grinned, but there was tension in it.

"Okay, I'll play the game."

A member of my team would be checking his luggage while we talked, including the contents of his phone and laptop. I'd told Nico to leave any electronics in his suite. Even if he'd locked his shit in the safe, that wouldn't cause us a problem. Hotel safes were a joke. There was always an override because so many guests forgot their code. And my tech team was the best in the business, so bypassing passwords wouldn't be a problem either, although I'd be disappointed if Nico used his birthday or the name of his cat, both of which I knew.

I dove cleanly into the pool and ended up at the far end in four strokes. It wasn't a big pool, more of a gimmick than anything else, but the bar was top notch. Nico followed suit and quickly caught up with me.

"*Blyat*, that's freezing."

"Oh, poor diddums. Have your nuts shrivelled?"

"Not as much as your nipples."

"Touché. I thought you'd be used to the cold."

"I lived in Moscow, not Siberia, and when it snowed, we flew somewhere warmer."

"Sometimes, I wish I could do that."

"You married a billionaire. Don't you have a beach house?"

"Several, but whenever we try to take a holiday, something goes wrong."

"Such as?"

"Dead bodies in awkward places, for example."

Nico raised an eyebrow. "I got the impression you might be used to that."

Instead of answering, I ducked underwater and swam to the other end of the pool, then headed for the cabana. I'd left a white-noise generator underneath the double lounger, and now I flipped it on.

Nico followed suit when I shrugged into a fluffy white robe, then settled next to me, his head propped up on one hand.

"Your impression isn't wrong. Why am I here, Nico? I already told you I don't get out of bed for less than twenty-five thousand bucks, so if you just wanted to stare at a pair of tits, there were far cheaper options."

"I'll always pay more for quality, but in this instance, it's your professional services I'm interested in rather than your physical attributes."

"You're worried about Kaylin La Rocca."

"I am. In truth, I didn't think you'd find her, but now that you have, my concerns for her well-being have only grown. I guess I thought she'd have tucked herself into the shadows. Taken an under-the-table job in a quiet town in Buttfuck, Nowhere, to stay off the cops' radar. We could have worked quietly to clear her name, and then I'd have set her up for a fresh start. Bought her an apartment, found her a job, that kind of thing."

"But now you've found out she's shacked up with a Mob boss, and there's a child involved."

"It does add a layer of complication I hadn't anticipated."

The bartender was hovering in my peripheral vision, and I motioned him forward. He knew better than to interrupt our conversation. Good man. Nico downed his shot in one and asked for another. On the surface, he was smooth as fuck, but there was uneasiness simmering beneath the calm exterior.

"Lighting a fire under a cold case could ruin her new life, and I doubt her hubby would be too happy either."

"Hallie sent me a video," he said. "Did you see it?"

"Yeah."

"What are your thoughts?"

"About Kaylin? She wasn't exactly brimming with joy, and I don't think it was because the sprinkler system failed."

"That was my impression too, but it's hard to make a solid assessment based on such a brief conversation. I wish I could just call her. Ask if she's okay."

"If she has a phone, it isn't registered in her name."

"You checked?"

"All part of the service."

Why had I held this meeting on the fucking roof? The outdoor heater was working overtime, but my feet were still bloody freezing. I wasn't about to admit that, though.

"I have tickets for her show tonight," Nico admitted. "But I still haven't decided whether or not to go. What if my presence upsets her?"

"That could happen, but it's also possible she sees you as a white knight. Don't forget who she called for help after she ran to Manassas."

"She never called me again, and it's been over three years."

"Last time she reached out, someone died. Maybe she's trying to avoid a repeat?"

"Do you think Cesare Cavallaro knows who I am?"

"I'd say no. You were one of Kaylin's allies, and she would have wanted to protect you. If I had to guess what went down that night? I'd say Kaylin called for help, but Cavallaro and/or his men arrived before you did. Either she panicked and ran the cop over while she was trying to escape, or she was incapacitated and the driver wasn't looking where he was going. And don't forget the timing—her kid's a toddler, and I'd put money on the fact that she ran because she found out she was pregnant."

I'd brainstormed with Dan before I left Virginia, and the

pregnancy angle also fit with Kaylin dipping out of swimwear modelling. Or perhaps Cavallaro had put his foot down at the thought of other men ogling her? She'd run, her psycho of a boyfriend had caught up with her, and now she had the choice between staying in her gilded prison, being arrested for murder, or doing another runner with Satan's little bro on her heels. I'd probably stick around too.

Actually, scratch that. I'd introduce Cesare Cavallaro's skull to a frying pan, skewer his balls on an ice pick, and then get the hell out of Dodge. And if I got caught? Well, if I was going to go down for one murder, I might as well go down for two.

Nico rolled onto his back and groaned, the heels of his hands pressed against his eyes.

"If I'd only picked up that message sooner…"

"Can't turn back time, dude. No point in wasting brainpower on what-ifs."

"What would you do in my position?"

"Ah, now I get it. You dragged me all the way here so I could act as a really expensive agony aunt."

"The other option was setting up a throwaway account on Reddit."

"You just know that someone would suggest punching out the Mob boss."

"Much as I'd enjoy doing that, I believe a subtle approach would be more appropriate."

"Agreed." I took a sip of my juice. "Would I go to the club tonight? Yeah, I would. It's the quickest way to get answers. Even if Kaylin can't talk, she can react. If she blanks you, or has one of Cavallaro's foot soldiers throw you out, or, hell, if she invites you for drinks with her hubby afterward, it's a fair bet that she's happy where she is. But if she still needs help, she's going to signal that somehow."

"Makes sense." Nico took one long breath. "If she does want to leave, I'm going to need assistance in getting her out of there."

I'd thought as much. "It won't be cheap, but my team can do it. No problem. But I'll tell you now, we'll have to bring the kid too, and probably the dog. If Cavallaro's the bastard we think he is, she won't let them stay with him."

Nico nodded slowly. "You're right. Of course you're right. Does twenty-five thousand bucks get me company this evening?"

"As long as we're talking company in a professional capacity."

"Of course."

"Just checking. You have a reputation, Mr. Belinsky."

"And if you weren't in a committed relationship, Mrs. Black, I'd be living up to it."

I laughed. Nico was harmless; at least, he was when it came to flirting. A dark undercurrent still ran through his veins, but he was no Cesare Cavallaro. Nico had ethics, but if the need arose, he'd step from the grey side and into the black to protect the people he cared about. That included himself. Nico was a survivor—he'd had to be with a father like Lev Belinsky.

"What time does the show start?"

"Seven. Wear something slinky."

"Does that mean you'll be in a tux?"

"Sadly not. The dress code is actually casual to cocktail."

"Guess they like to hoover up those all-important tourist bucks. Not everyone travels with a posh dress."

"But you do?"

I gave him a mock salute. "Girl Scouts are always prepared."

"Were you a Girl Scout? I can't imagine you participating in that type of organised group activity."

"Nah, I was too busy boosting cars and picking pockets." I finished my juice and stood. Before we headed to the Starlight Lounge, I needed to do a bit of recon, check my weapons, and get a blowout. "See you at six."

Just another day in the life of a globetrotting mercenary.

19

EMMY

Tonight, we were Rico and Emily, out to celebrate Rico's fake birthday with good food, copious amounts of alcohol, and the best seats in town. Were we planning to keep a low profile? Hell no. If we skulked around at the rear, Kaylin would be able to ignore us if she chose. And if she wanted to, say, slip Nico a note, it would be harder if we were at the back of the room. No, I wanted to see her reaction when we were up close and in her face, and given that I was wearing a shimmery gold cocktail dress that barely contained my boobs, she could hardly miss me.

Emily was a brash Texan with fluffed-up hair, a love of heavy eyeshadow, and a beauty mark on her chin. Blue eyes peered out beneath clumps of mascara. The ring on her finger doubled as a handcuff key, her bra held a switchblade, and there were enough illegal substances hidden in her oversized necklace to either tranquillise or kill everyone in the place. Her handbag contained a stun gun disguised as a lipstick, a box of breath mints that transformed into a single-shot pistol, and an emergency packet of Skittles. As I said, it was just another day in the life of a globetrotting mercenary.

A hostess led us to our table while I kept up a stream of inane chatter befitting of a half-sloshed bimbo with an overblown sense of self-importance.

"I've been dying to visit this place for months. *Months.* Our friends Jim and Laurie came last summer for the *Alice in Wonderland* show, and they said that the next time we were in New York, we absolutely had to see Daisy de Ville and her Divas. Are they sisters?"

"No, ma'am."

"My sister used to sing, but me, I can't hold a note. Isn't that right, honey?"

Nico smiled and nodded. "That's right. She sang karaoke on our last anniversary, and I had a headache for three days straight."

"Aw, don't exaggerate."

"Okay, it was two days."

That raised a smile from the hostess, and when we reached the table, Nico pulled out a chair for me, ever the gentleman. The decor was old, but fake old. Velvet seats, fleur-de-lis wallpaper, a wood-panelled bar. Starched white tablecloths meant nobody could see my hands in my lap, but I couldn't see theirs either. Fifty years ago, tobacco smoke would have hung heavy in the air, but now, quiet AC units worked unobtrusively near the ceiling, filtering out fifty kinds of cologne. Glasses clinked, and the hum of conversation rose above the jazz playing in the background.

I checked the exits. As well as the door we'd come in through, there was a fire exit stage left and doors to the loos and kitchen stage right. Hallie's notes said the Cavallaros came in through the kitchen, which meant that if they were present, there'd be a car and security in the alley that ran down the north side of the building. The fire exit would bring me out on a cross street where I could blend into the crowd rather than hiding behind a dumpster while Mafia goons shot at me.

Our table was front and centre, so if I had to leave in a hurry, I'd either go for the fire exit or head out the main entrance.

"A server will bring your complimentary cocktails in just a moment. Can we get you any other drinks?"

"A bottle of your best champagne," I said.

"Better get some water too, baby."

"Still or sparkling?" the server asked.

"Still. Sparkling tastes like TV static. Who even drinks that stuff?"

"One bottle of still?"

Nico beamed at her, and she blushed.

"One large bottle."

We'd drink more water than alcohol, but we needed to maintain our cover. Asking inappropriate questions was easier to get away with if people thought you were slightly drunk. I checked the program. The running order was the same as last week, so we had a couple of hours to kill before Kaylin made her appearance. Okay, that was a poor choice of words. I wouldn't be killing anyone, not tonight anyway.

Nico draped an arm over my shoulders, and we settled in to wait. Even though he looked relaxed, I could feel the stress in him, and I suspected that, like me, he'd had plenty of practice at hiding his true feelings.

"You okay?" I asked quietly after the server had brought our drinks.

"I've been waiting for years to see her, and now the last couple of hours are going interminably slowly."

"Father Time's a stubborn asshole. And why is it Father Time? Why not Mother Time? Women are arguably more pig-headed than men, or so my husband always tells me."

"I don't know the answer, but I'm sure Google does."

"Okay, another question... Why do you spell Nicolai with a C and not a K? Isn't Nikolai more common?"

He cracked a smile. "It's a nod to Niccolò Machiavelli. My father was a big fan."

"I'm not sure whether to say 'Yikes' or 'I'm sorry for your loss.'"

"Let's go with the first option."

"You didn't get along?"

Although we were meant to be staying relatively sober, Nico drained his glass of champagne. A long moment of silence followed, then he leaned in and whispered so close that his lips brushed my ear.

"When I saw the woman who killed him leave via the balcony, I could have alerted the guards. I could have checked on his health. Instead, I poured myself a drink and managed to watch nearly two episodes of *Detektivy* before the shouting started."

So Nico had sat back and let his father die? That was... interesting. And good news for Dasha, although she'd be annoyed that her escape hadn't been quite as clean as she thought.

"Didn't you vow retribution?"

"Yes, but I lied, so I guess there's a touch of Machiavelli in me, after all. My father would be proud."

"Did you ever find out his killer's identity?"

"I only knew her as Viktoria. Could I pick her out of a line-up? Maybe, if it was a rear view."

"Didn't spend much time looking at her face, huh?"

"I was twenty years old, Mrs. Black, and I'd been raised to appreciate the finer things in life. But it was more than that. It was the way she moved. I couldn't take my eyes off her as she crossed the grounds—walking, not running, pausing on the edge of the motion arc as the security cameras scanned. She was poetry in motion. My dream, and my father's nightmare. A succubus."

"If she paid you a nocturnal visit, you'd probably wake up screaming."

Nico cracked a smile. "Yes, I probably would. Mrs. Black, you're the only person besides me who knows the truth about that night, and I'd like to keep it that way."

"I know how to keep my mouth shut."

"I didn't mean any offence."

"None taken. We both lead lives where trust doesn't come easily."

The first course arrived—steak tartare with truffles and a quail's egg—and we watched the opening act. Bradley wanted us to try burlesque? Good luck... I'd be out of the country that year. I'd rather take my chances in a war zone than shimmy around the stage wearing frilly knickers and tassels on my tits. Okay, fine, I'd been a stripper once, but if my old boss had mentioned tassels, I'd have stuffed them up his pasty white arse.

"Shut your mouth, dear," I said to Nico.

"I'm just getting into character."

Yeah, right. Nico might be in his mid-thirties now, but he still appreciated a good backside. As did I. Some of those women must spend hours in the gym. Emily whooped and giggled, and by the time Coco Delite had danced off the stage hidden behind a giant fan that looked like a slice of watermelon, everyone in the Starlight Lounge knew it was Rico's birthday, and I was on first-name terms with the guests at the surrounding tables. No doubt because I'd bought them all drinks. People would put up with a lot of crap for a free glass of bubbly.

At a quarter to nine, the Cavallaros' table was still unoccupied as it had been last week, but there was a "Reserved" sign in the centre. Was that permanent? They'd leave the table empty rather than sell it to anyone else? Or did they always show up at the last minute? Nico kept checking his watch until I touched his wrist, and then he started tapping his foot instead. For the love of fuck. I gave him a kick, and he stopped.

"Just relax."

When he reached for his champagne glass, I switched it for water. Funny how a bunch of folks in Baldwin's Shore thought he could be the Bad Samaritan when he had zero chill and barely any tradecraft. Now I understood why he wanted to hire Blackwood instead of attempting the job himself. At least he knew his limitations, and I had to respect him for that.

Finally, Vito Cavallaro strode in at five to nine, along with a bunch of other wise guys, none of whom were Cesare. I recognised Alonzo—he was the gym rat with the goatee—and Otello and a dude who could have been Fausto if Fausto had put on forty pounds since his last mugshot. Maybe-Fausto had a blonde on his arm, the kind of woman who looked as if she'd get along well with Emily. Loud and a little bit trashy.

The lights dimmed. The band struck up.

Show time.

Kaylin La Rocca was a decent singer, I'd give her that, assuming she wasn't lip-syncing, and I didn't think she was. No...she definitely wasn't, because when she looked down and saw Nico staring up at her, her eyes saucered and she fumbled a line of "Candyman," although she covered it well. I saw her glance at him half a dozen times during that song alone, as if she couldn't quite believe he was real and sitting right there. I also saw her gaze dart over to the Cavallaros, checking they hadn't caught on.

They hadn't. Vito was already on his second glass of Scotch, and the blonde had been slurring her words from the moment she walked in the door.

C'mon, Kaylin, give us a sign...

She made it through another two energetic numbers with barely a stumble, then settled under the spotlight to sing "At

Last." It took me a few moments, but then I realised she was doing something weird with her left hand, the one the Cavallaros couldn't see. It was upside down, but was that... American Sign Language? She was fingerspelling?

It was slow and clunky, and Kaylin definitely wasn't proficient, but I sounded out the letters in my head.

Why you here?

I leaned close to Nico. "Do you know ASL?"

"Not really. Why?"

"Watch her left hand. Do it subtly."

He did so, then cursed under his breath. "I've forgotten most of it."

"ASL?"

"Kaylin went to the international school in Moscow. There was a deaf kid in her class, and she wanted to be able to speak to him, so she learned the alphabet. I used to practise with her. She was only eight. How can she remember so much?"

Because she was smart. Book smart, not street smart, seeing as she'd got mixed up with a motherfucker like Cesare Cavallaro, but not totally dumb.

"She's asking why you're here."

"*You* understand ASL?"

"Nah, dude, I'm just making shit up." At Blackwood, we had a CPD program that focused on more than simply shooting at things. Since we had several deaf team members, we'd added ASL classes to the curriculum, and anyone could show up on a Thursday lunchtime to learn. Yeah, the program cost a fair bit, but we ended up with well-educated employees and an excellent staff-retention rate. "I know the basics."

"Tell her she's a hard woman to find."

I angled my body so the Cavallaros couldn't see, my hand hidden between my chest and Nico's. Kaylin sang on autopilot, watching as I slowly spelled out Nico's response.

"She says she didn't do it." Presumably referring to the dead cop. "She's stuck here now."

"Does she want out?"

"She can't. She has a kid. A dog."

It was as I'd thought. She'd landed up in a situation she disliked, but she couldn't see a way to escape.

"Tell her that if she wants us to get her out of there, we will. The kid and the dog too."

I relayed the message, but out of the corner of my eye, I saw Alonzo Cavallaro leaning forward. He was watching Kaylin closely. *Too* closely. Had he noticed her hand? Or was her demeanour off? She seemed stiff, a bit wooden, and when she first walked out on stage, she'd been far looser.

Whatever, she'd noticed him too, and she turned on the style again, cradling the mic with both hands as she let her gaze roam the room. Then the Divas moved on to another dance number, and we still didn't have an answer.

Dammit.

Dessert was served during the interval, and Emily leaned across to introduce herself to the trashy blonde.

"Hey, hun, I love your nails. Did you get them done around here?"

She looked to Fausto, who nodded. Sheesh, she needed permission to answer a question?

"At Paintbox in SoHo, but they don't take walk-ins."

"Maybe I'll give them a call, see if they can fit me in before we go home."

"You're on vacation?"

"It's my hubby's birthday." I waved at the waitress hovering behind the big boss. "Hey, can we get some drinks for these folks?"

"Uh, sure, but—"

I gave Vito a wink. "Order the good stuff, honey. We're celebrating."

Luckily, Vito seemed to be more amused than annoyed by the vapid idiot in front of him, probably because she had good cleavage, which he kept eyeing up.

"Bring a cake too," he told the server. "Put candles on it."

"Aw, that's sweet of you, sir. The folks back home said that New Yorkers weren't so friendly, but everyone's been real good to us so far."

"A cake?" the poor girl asked. "I'm not sure we have—"

"Bring a cake," he repeated, then turned to Alonzo. "Is she new?"

"Who the fuck knows?" he muttered.

One valuable snippet of information gained: the Cavallaros weren't overly familiar with their waitstaff, and that was a fact I could turn to my advantage if the need arose.

There must have been a late-night bakery nearby because a three-tier chocolate cake appeared before Kaylin returned to the stage, and the whole damn audience applauded when Nico blew out the candles, Vito included. If it weren't for the fact that he exploited women, defrauded people out of millions, and terrorised New York, I might even have liked the guy.

The lights dimmed again, and a handful of people who'd been sitting at the bar returned to their seats. Nico had only eaten half his slice of cake, so I picked up a fork and finished it off. Why waste a good dessert?

My phone buzzed. My actual husband was asking for an update.

BLACK

Managed to start a war with the Mob yet?

ME

The night is still young.

BLACK

Will further services be needed?

ME

Ask me again in half an hour.

Which was the same amount of time we'd allowed Kaylin to consider her future. What would she decide? Would she risk everything and ask Nico for help? Or stick with the status quo? There was also a third possibility: that she'd ask for a rain check.

I rested my head on Nico's shoulder and waited.

20

KAYLIN

B reathe.
   Just breathe.

My pulse was racing, and my heart threatened to hammer its way through my ribcage. Nico was here. Here! Not only in New York but at the Starlight Lounge, and now he realised what I'd become. He'd seen through the flashy facade to the wretched woman beneath.

He understood how stupid I'd been.

Every night, I lay awake, regretting my poor life choices and wishing I was brave enough to run again. Wishing I was smart enough not to get caught this time. But even as I imagined holding my son tight against me, stealing down the stairs, and vanishing into the night, I knew I never would.

Last time, a man had died, and now I was a wanted woman. Cesare had shown me the news stories, the ones that said there was a warrant out for my arrest. Nobody would believe I'd been in a different vehicle, he said. It was my Toyota that had done the damage. I'd been the one staying at the motel. Alonzo, who *had* been driving, was one of my husband's brothers, and the family's code of loyalty meant he'd rather go to the grave than talk.

But now Nico was here, and that changed everything. Was his presence an accident? He'd dropped by to watch the show, only to witness my spectacular fall from grace? Or had he come to see me on purpose? To help? He had resources that I could only dream of, and I was eighty percent sure he wasn't a psycho. Once, that percentage would have been higher, but I didn't trust my own judgment anymore. Not after my colossal mistake with Cesare.

He'd been so kind at first. So sweet. I'd been serving drinks at his cousin's wedding when several of the guests began fighting, and long story short, I'd ended up with a black eye and a liberal coating of red wine. Cesare had been the one to find me fresh clothes and an ice pack.

Did I know who he was at the time? Yes, I'd had an idea. I'd heard the whispers among my colleagues, and of course I'd googled the Cavallaro family. But I'd also read way too many romance novels, and fictional capos loved and protected their women. They fought for them. You know, the whole "touch her and die" vibe? They didn't borderline rape them, take away their choices, and threaten them with prison if they stepped out of line.

As I said, I'd been stupid. I knew that. Boy, did I know it.

But I'd been in a bad place. Struggling to make ends meet, miserable after a series of truly awful first dates and a handful of equally useless boyfriends. Cesare sold me the dream. Plus it wasn't my first foray into the world of organised crime. The Cavallaro family wasn't the only one I'd googled—back in the days when I still had access to the internet, I'd researched the Belinskys too. The year and a half I'd spent in Russia had been the best time of my life. Mom hadn't been stressing about money, I'd made friends at school, and we'd lived in a beautiful apartment.

Sometimes I got lonely when Mom spent time with Lev Belinsky, but there was a huge house to explore, and Nico had always been kind. Looking back, I realised he'd only spent time with me out of pity, but he'd never made me feel like a nuisance. No, he'd spoken Russian slowly and carefully so I could learn, helped me with my homework, and made cookies with me when the housekeeper grumbled about mess in the kitchen. Hell, he'd even let me paint his face with make-up once. Just once. The memory made me smile, and few things did that these days.

So I guess when I'd accepted Cesare's dinner invitation, I'd been trying to find joy again. To get back a little of the old magic. Even Mom had been happy with the Belinskys, found light among the dark days. So many dark days. We'd travelled the world, hopping from modelling job to modelling job, and she'd smiled for the cameras and then cried behind closed doors. I'd always tried to comfort her, but in the end, I hadn't been enough.

"Ten minutes, Maria," someone said.

Ten minutes. Ten minutes to decide on my future.

Should I take the risk? If I stayed, Matteo would be moulded into a clone of his father, and I'd forever be trapped. Cut off from the world, kept on a short leash, yanked back into line if I put a foot wrong. Cricket would suffer too.

Should I trust Nico? Unlike Cesare, he'd never been cruel. And he was here. Over three years ago, I'd called him for help, and he'd never given up trying to find me. That had to count for something, right?

I took a deep breath. Let it out a fraction at a time.

If Cesare caught me trying to escape, he'd kill me. I didn't doubt that. But if I stayed, I'd die a slow death, forced to watch as he turned our son into a monster in his own image.

The risk was one I had to take.

I waved the Divas over. Each had been hand-selected for dancing ability, looks, and compliance.

"I want to change a few things around in the second act," I told them. "The crowd's buzzing tonight, full of energy."

"Probably because of all the alcohol," Kizzy giggled. "That blonde lady in the front row is buying drinks for everyone."

Nico's wife? I'd seen rings on both of their fingers. I'd always imagined he'd end up with someone more...polished, but she wasn't the airhead she first appeared to be. No, she understood ASL, and she'd realised right away what I was trying to say.

I smiled back. "She'll have everyone up and dancing by the end of the show."

"Vito told Lindy to bring a birthday cake," Amber said. "And Lindy was freaking out, but I told her to go to Reggie's Diner and see if they have one of those chocolate fudge gateaus."

"Maybe I should sing 'Happy Birthday' to the lady?"

"I think it's the husband's birthday, not hers."

Now I knew for certain that Nico's presence wasn't a coincidence. His birthday was in August, not February—I remembered that because he'd had an outdoor party on the terrace.

"Do you know his name?"

"Rico, I think."

Rico? Seriously? I swallowed a laugh. He'd chosen the acronym for the Racketeer Influenced and Corrupt Organizations Act as his fake name? With Vito, Alonzo, Fausto, and Otello in the audience? The man had balls.

"Listen, we need to switch out the slow numbers. Swap Etta James for Journey and Nina Simone for Fontella Bass."

This show was the only part of my life where I had any control. A choreographer assisted with the dance routines, and a singing coach helped me to master my voice, but Cesare and Vito left the set list up to me. Of course, the rehearsals were always monitored, just in case I—gasp—tried to make a friend or—shock—attempted to communicate with the outside world. I'd only managed it twice, when our old cleaner agreed to send a card and some cash to Nana and flowers to Charlotte —I'd been so thrilled to see the wedding announcement in the *New York Times*—but then Angela had quit and her replacement was a real dragon.

"So we're closing with Fontella?" Kizzy asked.

"That's right."

Over the past two years, I'd learned how to read an audience, and last-minute changes weren't entirely unknown. I was almost certain I'd get away with it. And after a couple of stumbles in the first act when I'd been trying to finger-spell and remember lyrics at the same time, Alonzo had started to watch me more closely, so I couldn't risk another silent conversation. Alonzo was dangerous. Perhaps even more dangerous than Cesare, and the two of them were close.

Tonight, I'd sing my heart out and hope Nico and his wife got the message.

Then I'd go home, hold back the tears while the man I hated fucked me in any way he pleased, and pray.

21

NICO

The woman was crazy. Not that Nico hadn't suspected it before he asked Emmy to accompany him to the Starlight Lounge, but now that she was snacking on birthday cake and a selection of canapés with Vito Cavallaro, he had no doubt.

Had he made a mistake in hiring her? The jury was still out on that. Her team *had* found Kaylin, and Blackwood had an excellent reputation. Plus Emmy's ethics were firmly in the grey zone, which was what Nico needed for this task. Attempting to rescue Kaylin alone would be a recipe for disaster. Maybe he could get her to safety, but the child and the dog as well? That added a whole other layer of difficulty.

Years had passed since Nico had undertaken that kind of work, and even then, he'd done it grudgingly for the most part because it hadn't been his fight. The last man he'd killed had been a thug, a petty criminal who'd been sent to murder Nico's father. Nico had put a bullet through the man's head, and then done the same to the former business acquaintance who hired him. They'd been too clumsy to succeed. He'd briefly considered taking them aside and giving them tips, but in the end, disposal had been the only option. Fortunately, Viktoria had made her appearance soon afterward.

Emmy returned to her seat. "Show time."

"You've finished consorting with the opposition?"

"Haven't you heard the old saying? Keep your friends close, but your enemies closer."

When Kaylin walked onto the stage, Nico's breath hitched. She'd been a cute kid with an infectious smile who hadn't cared about her puppy fat. Now? Now, she was beautiful. An angel under the thumb of a devil who didn't appreciate her.

The question was, did she want to stay with him?

Kaylin had changed into a short sequinned dress that glittered in shades of purple under the lights. She clasped the mic with both hands, her knuckles white.

"Before we start, I hear we have a *very* generous guest in the house tonight. Won't you all join me in singing 'Happy Birthday' to Rico?"

She wasn't shying away from him. That was good. Did Kaylin remember that his birthday was in August? She'd sung "Happy Birthday" to him when he turned sixteen, he recalled, and his father's friends had applauded before they returned to discussing their underhanded deals. One of them had made a lewd comment about her—a fucking eight-year-old—and his was one of the few deaths Nico had taken pleasure in causing. Business was business, but kids were off limits.

Emmy angled herself so her right hand was hidden from the audience and began signing, as they'd discussed during the intermission. *Do you want out?*

But Kaylin didn't sign back. Instead, she cut her gaze toward Vito's table, and Nico noticed one of the men focused on her. Alonzo. Damn. Had he spotted their earlier communication? Or was he naturally the suspicious type? Perhaps he just had the hots for his brother's wife?

"There's a problem," Nico murmured to Emmy. "Alonzo's watching."

"Then we wait. Kaylin's clever. If she wants out, she'll send a message somehow."

"You'd better be right."

"I'm always right, dude."

"And modest. You forgot to mention modest."

Emmy just laughed and leaned into his side. Meanwhile, Nico's stress levels rose sky-high, and when ten o'clock came and went, the ever-increasing tightness in his chest had him considering a trip to the ER.

"Relax," Emmy told him.

"How can I fucking relax?"

"Try breathing exercises?"

The only breathing exercise that would help right now would be putting his hands around Cesare Cavallaro's throat and choking the life out of him. At least Alonzo had stopped watching quite so intently. He was deep in conversation with Fausto now, his gaze only flicking in Kaylin's direction every so often.

Give us a sign, zollotse.

"Thank you, New York! I'm going to finish with one of my favourites, but first, can you all put your hands together for the Divas?"

The audience broke into applause, and Emmy whooped and hollered for good measure. She was acting drunk, but in reality, she'd barely touched her champagne. By ordering enough drinks for everyone, she'd managed to pour most of the alcohol into other people's glasses instead of her own.

But sober or not, she'd been wrong about Kaylin, who hadn't tried using ASL again, or semaphore, or Morse code, or asking a server to slip them a note. Nico was ready to tell Emmy that in this instance, she'd misjudged, but then the sign came.

Kaylin launched into the opening line of "Rescue Me."

"Are you choking on them?" Emmy asked.

"Huh?"

"Those words you were about to say. Are you choking on them?"

"Yes. Yes, I am, and I'm taking great pleasure in it."

Because he was getting Kaylin out of NYC, and then he was going to make sure she got her life back.

"Dude, no. That's not how it works."

"You said you'd help."

Now Emmy was drinking properly. They'd retired to her Upper East Side apartment, where she'd kicked off her shoes and poured herself a gin and tonic, but unfortunately, alcohol hadn't mellowed her at all.

"Yeah, and by 'help,' I mean that you'll fly back to Oregon while my team extracts Kaylin, her kid, and her dog from Rapunzel's tower, and then you thank us by paying my extremely large invoice promptly."

"I need to be there for her."

"And you will be. Once she arrives on the West Coast."

"I'm not a complete novice at this sort of thing."

"You might have done your father's dirty work in Russia, but there's a world of difference between slotting some dipshit whose family won't retaliate because of who your daddy is, and walking onto Mafia turf and stealing a capo's fucking wife. You can't do it by force."

"So how *will* you do it?"

"I have a few ideas, and none of them involve a shoot-out in the streets of New York."

"She'll be scared."

"Do you have any idea how many hostages we've rescued?"

"How many?"

"Okay, so I don't know either, but only because I've lost count. Definitely over a thousand."

"And how many have you lost?"

"Four."

If Nico were in Vegas, he'd play those odds, but he wasn't, and this was Kaylin's life they were talking about. But what kind of life would it be if they didn't act? If Cesare Cavallaro was anything like Lev Belinsky, then Kaylin's life expectancy would be considerably shorter than average.

He'd have to play the hand, and like it or not, he'd have to play by Emmy's rules. Once, he'd had the weight of the Belinsky name behind him, but it didn't mean much outside of Russia. And even inside Russia, he'd mostly left the game. True, he hadn't entirely divested from his father's business interests, and he still had some favours owing, but he had no desire to start a war.

"One condition. I'll stay out of the way, but I want to fly with her."

"You'll wait on the plane."

She was telling him, not asking him, but Nico nodded anyway.

"Yes."

"I'll leave a man with you, and if you so much as breathe funny, he'll shoot you up with enough ketamine to knock out a horse."

"Agreed."

"We're talking seven figures for this, plus expenses."

Nico had expected nothing less, but fortunately, he'd inherited over a billion dollars from his father, most of which was as dirty as the back streets of Volokolamsk. Spending a million or two fighting everything his father had stood for would be a nice "fuck you" for the old man.

"Kaylin's worth it."

"What about Cesare? How do you want that handled?"

A good question, and a tricky one. "My first instinct is to remove him from the picture entirely, but I'm not certain that's the right approach."

"Because you're worried Kaylin might not want that?"

"Precisely. She's not happy, but she still married the asshole. He's still the father of her child."

"He'll want revenge."

"So will the rest of his family if we kill him."

"True. Plus the kid might need a kidney someday, and matches aren't easy to find." Emmy took a swallow from her glass. "Fun fact: that's the only reason my mother's still alive today."

"In case you need a kidney?"

"Yup."

"What if she's not a match?"

"She is." Cold. That was cold, but Nico would have expected nothing else from Emmy Black. "But if you want blood typing, tissue typing, and a serum crossmatch for Cesare Cavallaro, that's gonna cost you a hell of a lot more."

"How about we just stick with the standard rescue mission? If we need to carry out a side project later, we'll call that a separate contract."

Emmy clinked her glass against his. "Deal."

22

EMMY

We had a green light, a blank cheque, and the brief from hell. Extricate a wife, a child, and a fucking dog from a Mafia man's clutches. And not just any old Mafia man. Rumour said that Cesare Cavallaro was tipped to leapfrog his one surviving uncle and become boss of the family if anything happened to Vito. Which it probably would, and sooner rather than later. Rumour also said that Vito had a dodgy ticker, a rumour we'd confirmed when Agatha took a gander through his preferred hospital's billing system.

"Belgravia Place is still a problem," Ana said over dinner in our New York apartment. Sushi for Dasha, pizza for everyone else. My core team for this job was female because I knew, based on what I'd observed so far, that the Cavallaros would underestimate us. To them, women were good for entertainment and keeping house, not special ops and assassination. We'd bring in others as necessary, but for now, I had Dasha, Ana, Sky, Hallie, Dan, and Sofia with me, although I couldn't take Dan away from the Investigations team for long. But she was a New Yorker, and she knew the city better than I did.

And yes, Ana was right. Belgravia Place *was* a problem. Not only had the sprinkler system been fixed, but the dog walker came in the mornings when Cesare was usually home. Kaylin's hubby was too lazy to walk the mutt himself, and he was also a late riser. All that criming was tiring for a man.

We'd been watching the apartment building for over six weeks, testing, probing, assessing. Thanks to Bradley and his pal Ferdinand, we'd even been inside a handful of times. Ferdinand was a make-up artist who specialised in latex and special effects, but well-paid work was getting harder to come by with Hollywood's current fondness for CGI, and he'd spent the past three months waiting tables. CGI couldn't help you to break into a building, though. I was tempted to offer Ferdinand a permanent job. He'd already shown interest in a barista position in the café at Craft Cabin 2.0, so we could provide him with a steady paycheck and time off for other projects.

When applying for a role as concierge at Belgravia Place, it seemed there was only one question on the form: are you a condescending twat? If the answer was "yes," then congratulations, the job was yours. Four supercilious pricks shared the role, staffing the desk twenty-four-seven between them.

Dasha had gone brunette and donned yoga wear plus a new face to become Loranne Brookhurst from the fourth floor. Once inside, she'd spent an hour mapping out key infrastructure before the real Loranne returned from her spa appointment. I'd morphed into Luella Haas from the eighth floor and taken the stairs to the parking garage, where I'd installed a camera to watch the comings and goings. Doing the same for the penthouse was a no-go since the elevator opened directly into the foyer, but Agatha had gone one better and hacked the Cavallaros' nanny cam. Now we had eyes and ears inside, but mainly in the nursery.

"Why couldn't they have purchased a two-way baby monitor like normal people?" Dasha grumbled.

"Maybe Cesare's a cheapskate," Sky suggested.

Ana shrugged. "Or maybe he worried that his wife-slash-prisoner would use it to contact the outside world."

"Yeah, or maybe he just didn't want some creepy dude talking to his kid in the middle of the night," I said. Baby monitors were notoriously insecure, hence us turning one into our secret spy cam. "This is why I have birth-control shots. I don't have to worry about nursery security."

"Mack's already designed a custom baby monitor," Dan told me. "It's hack-proof, and it speaks in her voice."

I only hoped she'd have the opportunity to use her creation. Mack didn't much like to talk about it, but fertility problems were making her miserable, and she was about to start her first round of IVF. I found it hard to know what to say to make her feel better. I mean, I'd offered to donate eggs if she needed them, but Luke, who was her husband and my ex —awkward—had looked so freaking horrified by the suggestion that I'd garbled an excuse and left.

Anyhow, back to a problem that was more up my alley, and easier to solve too. Namely, how to get the kid out of the apartment. Aside from that one day with the fire alarm, we hadn't seen him outside. What kind of existence was that for a child?

The baby monitor had given us certain useful pieces of information, such as the fact that there were two guards on duty inside the apartment whenever Kaylin was home alone. There appeared to be a security office off the foyer, but when Kaylin carried the monitor around, we saw the men in the kitchen, in the living room, even in the nursery. She didn't seem comfortable near them.

When Cesare was home, the two upstairs guards left, confirming that they weren't there to keep intruders out; they were there to keep Kaylin in. A man stayed in the downstairs lobby twenty-four-seven.

Another fun snippet: when Kaylin went to the Starlight Lounge, Cesare rarely accompanied her. He preferred to stay home. Did he look after his son? Oh, no, he'd hired a babysitter for that, although she didn't spend much time with the kid either. No, she was too busy sucking Cesare's cock and, on one memorable evening, riding him like a low-budget cowgirl. Ana had watched the show from the roof of the building next door. When Matteo began crying, Cesare just muted him. Father of the year, right there.

So, we had a logistical challenge.

Option one involved sneaking past the guard in the lobby, incapacitating the two guards in the penthouse, and getting Kaylin, Matteo, and Cricket out of the building before anyone raised merry hell. Issues? The fire door that led to the street was alarmed, and the parking garage was monitored by cameras. We could attempt to bypass them, but following the sprinkler malfunction, several residents had kicked up a fuss, and the maintenance company was running regular system checks in an attempt to placate them. The alarms were tested every Thursday afternoon, which added a spanner to the works if we wanted to go with option two.

Option two was similar to option one, except we'd create a distraction at the Starlight Lounge and pick Kaylin up there. We'd have two fewer guards to take out at Belgravia Place, but we'd still have to deal with Cesare and the babysitter.

Option three was a variant of option two, but we'd wait for an evening when Cesare went to the cabaret or, better still, somewhere else, and left Matteo alone with the babysitter. But we might be waiting a long time, seeing as Cesare seemed quite taken with the girl's oral abilities. His dynamic with Kaylin was very different. More of a master/slave relationship.

Option four would be riskier, both for us and for Kaylin.

That would involve more force—storming the building and silencing anyone who got in our way. I wanted to avoid that if possible.

Sofia was studying the building's schematics. "What if we put something in the water?"

"Wouldn't work. I bet most of the folks who live in Belgravia Place only drink the bottled stuff."

"From the wilds of Scotland with the cap screwed on by a genuine mermaid," Sky added.

"And then flown three thousand miles to be served by a regular maid who gets paid a couple of bucks an hour."

"Okay, what about gassing them?" Fia suggested.

"Takes too long. Someone would call 911 while they were woozy."

"Is that a bad thing? We could dress up as EMTs. Nobody's gonna question a first responder on an emergency call."

"Where would we get an ambulance?" Sky asked.

Dasha paused before she bit into a maki roll. "Easy. You just call 911 and they send one for you to borrow."

I knew she was kidding—it was a reference to the day we'd tangled with a group of terrorists who'd done exactly that. But her delivery was deadpan, and deep down, I suspected that Dasha in her pre-Blackwood days might well have made the call. Her morals were even shakier than mine.

Sky fixed her with a hard gaze. It was like an antelope trying to stare down a lion.

"Are you serious?"

Dasha gave me a sideways glance. "No."

Then she bit into her maki roll and half the filling fell out. When I laughed, the glance turned into a glare, but the conversation had sparked a thought. Getting into the apartment would be our biggest challenge. We'd considered having Ferdinand work his magic on one of us—probably

Dasha because she was the tallest—but the dog was a sticking point. Even if Dasha could pass a cursory inspection by the concierge and the guard, Cricket would know she wasn't Kaylin, and little dogs could be every bit as protective of their homes as bigger ones. Plus the kid might sense there was something wrong. I mean, I'd be upset if Dasha picked me up, so I couldn't blame him, but a chorus of crying and barking wasn't conducive to a stealthy escape.

We needed a more subtle approach.

And now I had a new idea. One that would require teamwork and audacity, but which also had the potential to sow confusion in the aftermath.

"Hey, what do you think of this plan...?"

23

DASHA

It was a reasonable plan. I could grudgingly admit it. And different from the jobs I used to do, but in a good way. The General had been focused on speed and budget—get in, do the job, and get out, all as cheaply as possible—but Emmy placed a greater emphasis on doing the job well. If that took slightly longer, then so be it, although I knew from experience that her people could move fast when they needed to. Blackwood's Special Projects team catered to the luxury end of the market, a master tailor versus fast fashion.

Plus she took a refreshing approach to staff well-being. The guys with guns weren't our biggest enemy, she said. Burnout was. If we enjoyed our work—not the actual assassination parts, clearly—then we'd be able to do it for longer. People over profits, that was her approach, although I imagined she was charging Nico handsomely for our services. A team of eighteen didn't come cheap.

Better yet, putting the team together had been a collaborative affair based on skills and strengths, not a directive from the top. We'd all had input. Which was why I was currently sitting in the Starlight Lounge with Alex. My arm candy, Emmy had told me with a wink, although Alex was a seasoned operator himself. Sky had brought Rafael, who appeared to be a younger clone of Emmy's husband, and Dan was cosied up at a table in the back corner with Evan, whom I hadn't previously met. Sofia and Alaric were sitting at the bar while we waited for Daisy de Ville to take to the stage. According to Ana, Emmy had dated both Sofia and Alaric in the past, which again reinforced my view that Emmy walked her own path in life.

"Vito just pulled up," Logan said in my ear. He was in a car across the street, a spot that had taken him over an hour to secure.

The ball of tension in my gut expanded, but I'd long since learned to let the rush fuel me rather than unbalance me. Alex's arm tightened almost imperceptibly around my shoulders. The situation in the cabaret club tonight was fluid, eight of us involved in a deadly dance with one finale in mind. Ultimately, it didn't matter which of us spiked Vito, only that one of us did. There was no glory, only a common goal. Another welcome change. In my old team, Ilya, Pav, Vik, and I would have been in competition while Rad tried to keep the peace, and if Ilya or Pav had lost the game, they would have been angry and sulky, respectively. Perhaps Vik would have been annoyed too, but he'd always been so fucking cold it was hard to tell.

Anyhow, Sofia had supplied us all with an appropriate drug, explained the dosage, and warned us to scrub our hands fast if it touched our skin. I noticed she was fond of gloves. Now we were watching, waiting, ready to move. Vito drank Scotch or whisky, Talisker Single Malt or Cutty Sark, and he usually ate an appetiser and entrée but rarely dessert. Everyone on the team had visited the Starlight Lounge several times, and Vito came in three or four nights a week. He hadn't missed any of Kaylin's shows. Supporting his daughter-in-law, or just ogling the Divas?

Speaking of which... Kaylin's six backing dancers trooped out onto the stage, and now Bradley's fun started. He was watching the feeds from our covert cameras, and now he had a quarter of an hour to make any last-minute tweaks to Emmy's costume. She didn't have to pass a close inspection, but from a cursory glance, she needed to look like a Diva. This evening, they were shimmering under the spotlights in the same halter-neck swing dresses they'd been wearing the week before last—think fifties vibes—but they'd added white headbands. Ah, well, Bradley liked a challenge, didn't he?

And there she was.

Daisy de Ville.

Also known as Kaylin La Rocca.

She had no idea what was going to happen tonight. No idea that Nico was waiting for her on a jet at Farmingdale Airport. No idea that there were eight trained killers watching her sing an Etta James number with another five waiting outside. No idea that her father-in-law was about to suffer a tragic cardiac arrest.

"Having fun?" Alex whispered.

"The New York Mob has better taste in music than the Bratva."

Vito settled into a seat at the next table along with Otello and Salvatore—Salvatore was one of Cesare's cousins—plus Salvatore's wife and another blonde who might have been a friend or a hooker for Otello. He didn't have a girlfriend. He also ate Vito's unwanted desserts and invariably managed to drop blobs of whatever onto his shirt. I slid the syringe into my hand, ready in case a suitable moment arose. Eight pairs of eyes watched as two goons stood in their designated places behind the Cavallaros, looking bored, and a waitress took everyone's orders, starting with Vito. They all wanted liquor. Good. In my peripheral vision, I saw Sofia move toward the bar with Alaric, and Sky headed for the restrooms, ready to intercept any food that might leave the kitchen. The tray would be easy to identify—the servers always brought a stack of extra napkins for Otello. The tricky part would be working out which appetiser was destined for Vito, but so far, he was the only member of the family who'd eaten scallops, and he'd done so on every visit but one.

If Sofia and Sky failed, then I'd step in with a little social engineering. Meanwhile, Dan would be watching Kaylin, ready to act when the time was right.

"Package delivered," Sofia said softly, and the tension loosened a fraction. This was how a well-planned operation should go. No surprises, no drama, at least not yet. Give it ten minutes, maybe fifteen, Sofia had told us.

I sat back to enjoy the show.

24

———

KAYLIN

Six weeks had passed, and I hadn't heard from Nico. Not a word. There had been no sign of him or his wife, and I began to lose hope. Maybe he'd done a little digging and realised just what an impossible task it would be to free me from Cesare's clutches? Honestly, there were times I wished I'd taken my chances in jail. At least prisoners were permitted to make the occasional phone call.

Matty and I hadn't been allowed out in months, not since Lucia told Cesare that I'd asked her to send a letter to my grandma. She'd seemed so sweet at first, and I'd made a huge mistake in trying to recruit her. Now she tormented me five days a week, Cesare's eyes and ears as she vacuumed and dusted and threw me pitying glances. Loyalty was the only reason Cesare kept her around; I knew that because she was a terrible cleaner.

And thanks to my error, Matty was suffering too. Before, we'd been able to walk in the park during quieter times, always under supervision, of course, but I missed the sound of the wind in the trees and the gentle lap of water as we ambled around the lake. These days, I was only allowed as far as the roof terrace, and if it hadn't been for Matty and Cricket, I would have thrown myself off it.

Like mother, like daughter.

The crowd was quieter tonight, mostly couples and a large group of Japanese tourists who kept taking pictures. Did that worry me? Not really. In the two years I'd been performing, only Nico had recognised me as Kaylin, and I never sang in public without a wig and heavy make-up. Cesare had once told me that the best place to hide was in plain sight, and he'd been right. A group of cops had even booked out the club one night for a bigwig's retirement celebration, and I'd thrown up in the dressing room before I went on stage, but there hadn't been so much as a glimmer of recognition.

Get out there and own the place, Cesare always said, and that attitude was how he got away with as much as he did. He believed nobody would challenge him, and they didn't. Me? I wasn't so brave. No matter what people thought of me, I didn't fit into his world.

Vito held up a glass toward me, toasting my choice of song. He was an Etta fan. When I first met the big boss, he'd seemed kind and convivial, everyone's favourite uncle, but it was all an act. He was as hard-hearted as the rest of them. After the Virginia incident, I'd begged him for help, told him what Cesare was doing to me, but he'd coldly informed me that I was carrying his grandson and heir, and from now on, I'd better do as I was told if I wanted to see Matty grow up.

I forced a smile as the band played the opening bars of "Midnight Train to Georgia" and wished I were on it. I'd been to Georgia once, when Mom had a modelling job in Atlanta. She'd left me in a hotel room all day, quiet as a mouse, hiding behind a *Do Not Disturb* sign, but after she'd finished her shoot, we'd gone out for pizza. Well, pizza for me and salad for her. Back in those days, I hadn't worried about my weight.

"Ain't No Sunshine" came next, and wasn't that the truth? I'd seen the faintest glimmer when Nico showed up, but now the storm clouds were back. Matty had been cranky today, bored from being cooped up inside, and there wasn't a damn thing I could do about it. I'd asked Cesare to take him to the park, but childcare was a woman's work, so of course he'd refused. Oh, he liked the idea of having a son, just not the practicalities. But someday, when Matty was older, things would change. Cesare would want to train him to follow in the Cavallaro men's footsteps. By rights, those footsteps should lead to jail or an early grave, but there was no justice in the—

Wait, what was wrong with Vito? Out of the corner of my eye, I saw him swallow the last of his Scotch, and he looked... odd. As I watched, the glass slipped out of his hand, hit the polished table, and shattered along with my last nerve. He clutched at his chest. Was he having a heart attack or merely suffering from indigestion? When he straightened, I thought I was imagining things, but the expression of horror on Salvatore's face when he finally turned to glance at his uncle didn't lie.

Was it too late to add "Hallelujah" to the set list?

I kept singing, but Sal was yelling for someone to call an ambulance. He had a phone—he was addicted to Candy Crush and never went anywhere without it—but he wasn't used to doing things for himself. One of the bodyguards did the honours, and now the band had stopped playing, so I figured it would be bad form to carry on singing, even if this was the most joy I'd felt in months.

"Can I help?" a tallish blonde asked. "I'm a nurse."

Darn it, could she save him? Vito was gasping for breath now, and what a beautiful sight that was.

"I think he's having a heart attack," Otello said, sounding more puzzled than anything else, probably confused that his furred-up arteries had outlasted his father's. "Do you know CPR?"

"Of course I know CPR. Do you have an AED here?"

"A what?"

"A defibrillator. Try any public buildings nearby, gyms, health clubs, fitness studios. If the ambulance doesn't get here soon, we might need one."

Sal started yelling at people again—he was an expert at that —and Otello lumbered toward the front door. For a moment, I wondered if I could slip away in the confusion, but I had no money, no phone, no way of getting to Matty before someone noticed I was missing, as they inevitably would. Then Cesare would—

"Hey!" I blurted as a stranger lifted me from the stage. A giant, but not one of Vito's men. He was dressed too casually. "What are—"

Someone wrapped a coat around me, cape-style, and I found myself being half carried toward the fire exit. Was this a kidnapping? I mean, if they asked me nicely, I'd just go with them because nothing could possibly be worse than spending yet another night as Cesare's sex doll. There was no need for all the manhandling.

"Nico sent us." The voice belonged to a woman, and my misery turned to elation in a heartbeat. He'd kept his promise? He hadn't abandoned me? "We're leaving."

I wanted to ask about Matty, about Cricket, but I could barely breathe as they bundled me down the steps and into the back of a waiting cab. I landed hard, gasped as I found myself next to one of the Divas, then realised she wasn't a Diva at all; she was just dressed like one. The purple dress, the big hair, the white headband.

"Who are you?" But I already knew the answer. "You're Nico's wife?"

Her laughter was unexpected. "Hell no. But he's kind of

cute, don't you think?" The driver coughed, and the blonde gave an unladylike snort. "Nico's waiting at the airport. Once we've picked up your kid and the dog, we'll head over there and say bon voyage."

"How?" I blurted. "How will we get Matty and Cricket? Cesare's at home."

"Right now, Cesare is roughly halfway between Belgravia Place and the Starlight Lounge. If he decides to turn around, my team will let me know, and we can deal with it."

"Louie's in the lobby, Serge too."

"Louie's the guard? Cesare promoted him to chauffeur. When we get to Belgravia Place, the car will pull up outside the front door, and we'll go inside. You're going to tell Serge that there's a medical emergency and the whole family needs to get to the hospital. Cesare sent you to get Matteo so he can be with both his parents."

"What if he tries to check with Cesare?"

"There's no landline at the front desk, only a cell, and we'll be jamming it."

"Lyndsey's upstairs with Matty."

"Tell her the same thing. Cricket's coming to stay with me for a few days until the Vito situation resolves itself."

"Will Vito be okay?"

"Is it a problem if he isn't?"

"My only regret would be that if I'm leaving the city, I won't be able to dance on his grave." I forced myself to breathe. To take stock of the scene. "Where will I go? Cesare's going to come after me."

"Your first destination will be Oregon. After that, who knows? That'll be for you and Nico to decide. I'm just the delivery girl. But Cesare won't find it easy to track you, and with all the hoo-ha tonight, he's going to think you took advantage of the confusion to slip away. He won't realise immediately that you had outside help, so you'll have time to consider your next move."

Whoever this woman was, this delivery girl, she shared Cesare's confidence. I only wished I could. Serge was an obnoxious little prick, and I wasn't sure where Lyndsey's loyalties lay. I got along okay with her, but she'd been hired by Cesare, and look what had happened with Lucia.

"I feel sick."

"Well, you'll have to hold it. This isn't an airplane. We don't have puke bags in the seat pockets."

"What if something goes wrong?"

"Then we'll deal with it. Relax—this time tomorrow, you'll be freezing your ass off beside Nico's swimming pool."

I only hoped she was right. If she wasn't, I'd be dead, and Matty would be one step closer to a future in hell.

25

EMMY

So far, so good. Vito was in cardiac arrest, Dasha was trying to crack his ribs under the guise of CPR, and his minions were running around Tribeca in search of an AED. The nearest one was in a hot-yoga studio five blocks away— we'd already checked.

Ryder was babysitting Nico at the airport, and he reported that our client was behaving himself. The smaller of Blackwood's two jets was fuelled and ready to go. Hallie and Collier were outside Belgravia Place, watching for any unwelcome developments, while Slater and Gage tailed Cesare on motorcycles. Ana was following in an SUV she'd "borrowed" from a jackass who'd cut up two other drivers and then stolen a parking spot from a lady who'd been waiting politely.

Now Kaylin had to play her part, and she was the weakest link.

I put a hand on her back and half guided, half pushed her through the sliding door into the lobby at Belgravia Place. Serge looked up, a sneer fixed in place, and his double take was understandable. He'd probably never seen Kaylin without a meathead escort before.

"Ma'am?" His question asked nothing and everything.

"There...there's been a family emergency. Cesare's father collapsed, and...and..."

For once, her nerves actually helped. She came across as overwrought due to Vito's condition rather than shitting herself because she was about to flee the state. I helped her out.

"Vito's real sick, and Cesare wants all the family together. Benny's gonna drive Maria and Matty to the hospital."

"Nobody told me about this."

"Why would they? You're, like, the doorman."

Serge bristled, as I'd suspected he would. He really did have an overinflated sense of self-importance.

"I'm responsible for the security of the building, and that includes monitoring the residents' movements."

"Yeah, well, we just told you what's happening." I increased the pressure on Kaylin's back, moving her toward the elevator.

"I should call Mr. Cavallaro."

"Do whatever you feel you have to do, but I doubt he'll be happy if you interrupt his father's last rites."

The elevator doors opened painfully slowly, and I kept my head down so the camera in the corner didn't get a good look at my face. We could have cut the feed, but if Serge's screens went blank, he'd have been even more suspicious than he was already.

"Hey, you can't go upstairs. You haven't signed the visitor log."

"I live here," Kaylin shot back. "And which part of 'family emergency' didn't you understand?"

Then the doors were closing, and I smiled to myself. So, Kaylin did have a backbone; it had just been crushed under the weight of Cesare's spite for years.

"Do you know the elevator code, or do I need to bypass it?"

"Yes, I know it."

"In and out," I told her once the elevator had begun its ascent. "There won't be time to grab clothes, jewellery, or anything like that."

"What about documents? Matteo's birth certificate? My passport?"

Bringing those things would reinforce the idea that she'd run alone, but we didn't have time to waste looking for them.

"Where are they?"

"In Cesare's safe. He thinks I don't know where the key is, but he has a fake wine bottle in—"

"Forget it. You'll get new ones."

"I don't have any money."

"Nico will fund your living expenses until you get back on your feet. Hurry." I pulled the collapsible dog carrier out of my oversized handbag and pushed out the sides. Bradley had found one that I could wear as a backpack, which let me keep my hands free. "Is Cricket friendly?"

"Mostly. He doesn't much like Cesare."

"Smart dog."

"Yes, he is."

"Put him in the carrier and pass him over to me. You can bring Matteo."

"What if Lyndsey tries to call Cesare?"

Would the jammer work on the thirty-third floor? No, the signal wouldn't reach that far, and nor did we want it to. A localised issue in the lobby wouldn't raise too many eyebrows, but if everyone in the building lost cell service, that would lead to more questions than we wanted to answer.

"I'll deal with Lyndsey."

As always, I had a plan for that. And I needed it because when we walked into the apartment, Lyndsey Austin—age twenty-three, an aspiring actress originally from Redboro, Alabama, population 407 and a stone's throw from Montgomery—was walking around the cavernous living room with Matty on her hip. She was trying to get him to stop crying, but unsuccessfully, probably because her technique involved jiggling him around while snapping, "Shaddup, you noisy brat." I didn't know much about kids, but I was fairly sure there were better courses of action.

"I'll take him," Kaylin said.

Lyndsey spun around, which only made the kid wail louder.

"What are you doing here?"

"This is my home. I live here."

The line might have worked on Serge, but it didn't work on Ms. Ooh-Harder-More-More-More.

"You're meant to be at the club. Cesare said so."

"He told me to pick up Matty and take him to the hospital."

"No, no, he said I should take care of Matty until you both got home."

"That was before he realised how sick Vito is. We'll be at the hospital all night, and I expect the whole day tomorrow too."

"Then I'll stay here and look after the little man. Honestly, it's no problem."

"I'm his mom. We don't need a babysitter when I'm with him."

"Cesare said you shouldn't be left alone with him, okay?" Lyndsey turned to me. "I don't know who you are, but she has problems." She mimed drinking from a bottle. "Matty deserves better."

Uh-oh. This one had drunk all the Kool-Aid.

"He said what? I am *not* an alcoholic!"

And this was fast turning into a shitshow.

"Go and get Cricket," I instructed.

"But—"

"Go. And. Get. Cricket."

Kaylin's bottom lip quivered, but wisely, she decided to obey. She grabbed the carrier and ran farther into the apartment just as the radio blipped in my ear.

"Cesare's car is turning around," Slater said. "Heading back to Belgravia Place."

Black spoke up from the driver's seat of the cab. "Wasn't Serge. He's tried turning his phone off and on, and now he's whacking it on the desk."

"Someone probably noticed Kaylin was missing from the club," Fia put in. "Otello disappeared out back on the phone."

Wonderful. That left me with Lyndsey, and fuck, we didn't have time for this.

"First, I'm going to start by telling you that you're damn lucky because I'm here to explain what you're getting into. See Maria? If you keep fucking around with her husband, that could be you in ten years. Isolated, miserable, being lied about by the man who manipulated you into a relationship. You still have time to get out. And that's exactly what you're going to do."

"Who the hell do you think—"

Oh, this one had backbone too. Cesare hadn't broken her yet, so that job fell to me.

"Lyndsey, Lyndsey, Lyndsey. You love your family, don't you? Your mom, your dad, your Grandma Reba. Tucker, Kenny, little Julia. You send them money every month. Take the bus back to visit whenever you have a few days off. How do you think your daddy would feel if he saw the video of you sucking a man's cock? What would his congregation say? Redboro's kinda conservative, isn't it?"

Her jaw had dropped, and alarmingly, her grip on the child had loosened too. I grabbed him before he ended up on the floor, and hopefully, Nico had remembered to bring diapers because something didn't smell so good.

"You can't..."

"I can, and I will."

"How...?"

"Ever heard of a nanny cam? Let this be a lesson: don't fuck around with married men. He's still wearing his wedding ring in the video, by the way, which is a nice touch. What's your daddy's view on sex out of wedlock? Isn't 'no adultery' one of the Ten Commandments?"

Slater spoke in my ear. "Incoming, two minutes."

"He told me they were only together because of Matty."

Meh. That might even have been the truth.

"That's what they all say, honey. Now, you're going to wait two minutes, and then you're going to call Cesare and tell him Maria picked up her son. And after that, you're going to leave New York and find a new job. Babysitting isn't a good career for you."

"But...but..."

"Do I make myself clear?"

The fight went out of her. "Yes."

Kaylin hurried back with a yipping Cricket securely zipped into the carrier, and I swapped the dog for the child. Four legs, I could handle. Two legs, not so much. I gave the mutt a little taste of Fia's special medicine, and it flopped onto its side.

"Two minutes," I reminded Lyndsey. "A second sooner, and Granny's gonna need popcorn."

And we were gonna need a miracle to get out of the building in time. Stairs or elevator... Stairs or elevator... The stairs would give us more options, but the elevator would get us out faster. I jabbed at the button.

"Gonna need help here," I told my team.

"Understood."

Kaylin seemed to understand the urgency of the situation, and she leapt into the elevator the second the doors opened. A moment later, we were heading for the lobby, and Serge had better not try my patience because I didn't have much of it left.

"One minute," Slater said.

And then I heard the glorious *crunch* of metal, followed by an opening door and my beautiful sister's voice. *Thanks, Ana.*

"Oh my gosh, I'm so sorry. You just came from nowhere, and— Hey, where are you going?"

Slater provided an update. "They're on foot now. Cesare and the bodyguard, but Cesare's faster."

The elevator opened into the lobby, and we ran outside. Black already had the rear door of the fake cab open, waiting. Serge only made it halfway out of his seat before Kaylin and I spilled onto the sidewalk.

"Into the car, now."

We had mere seconds before Cesare appeared around the corner. Kaylin dove into the back seat head first after me, and I slammed the door behind us. Then I reached across and shoved open the door on the other side, relieved that Black had thought ahead as usual and sourced a vehicle with tinted rear windows.

"Out. Stay down."

"Huh? Why—"

I snatched the kid from her and ran in a crouch, and thank fuck she had half a brain and duck-walked after me.

"Into the alley." At least the kid had shut up, probably out of fear, but I didn't much care why at that moment. "Get behind the dumpster and keep Matty quiet. Whatever it takes."

Kaylin nodded, her eyes wide, and I watched from the shadows as Black pulled smoothly away in the cab. A moment later, Cesare sprinted into view, huffing and puffing because fitness wasn't high on his list of priorities. Serge jogged outside, and there was much gesticulating. Slater rode past on his motorcycle, staying below the speed limit, right before a white Mercedes drove up and Cesare jumped inside. The Merc sped away, and it was clear the driver didn't much care for traffic laws.

"What if they catch up with the cab?" Kaylin whispered.

"The driver can take care of himself."

Cesare and a steroid-addicted buffoon versus Black and Slater? I knew who my money would be on, and they'd have to find Black first. The magnetic sign from the car's door would be long gone, and he'd be lost in traffic by now.

A dented white panel van trundled down the road and stopped in front of us. The rusted side door slid open, and inside, the van was far from grungy. It was filled with state-of-the-art surveillance equipment, bags of kit, Bradley, and Hallie.

"Go," I told Kaylin.

She ran, and I brought up the rear. Only once the door closed did I begin to relax. Thank fuck that was over. Okay, so the ending had been slightly hairy, but another successful operation was almost complete, another hostage rescued. Collier took the next left, then circled back past the wreckage of the SUV to collect Ana. The others would take surveillance-detection routes, and we'd meet at the apartment later. By then, Kaylin and Nico would be somewhere over Illinois or maybe Iowa. I reversed the dog's sedative and began to breathe again.

"You okay?" I asked Kaylin.

"For the first time in years, I think I might be."

"I brought champagne," Bradley announced, because of course he had. "We can toast your new life."

For crying out loud, we were in the middle of a job.

Kaylin shook her head. "No, thank you. But I don't have an alcohol problem, I swear."

"Couldn't blame you if you did, honey."

"Cesare only let me have wine on the weekends. Two glasses per week."

"We believe you."

"I tried to be a good mom."

I put an arm around her shoulders. "We're not here to judge. You set your own rules now. If you want a glass of champagne, have a glass of champagne. If you don't, then don't."

The dog began yipping, no doubt thrilled about the idea of walks on the beach. Nico would need to buy earplugs.

"I think maybe I'll wait until we're out of New York. Nico's really at the airport?"

"Wearing a hole in the hangar floor, by all accounts."

"Does he know I'm with you?"

"He's been updated."

And my debt to him was settled. I collected favours like currency, but when I owed one, I always paid up.

26

KAYLIN

There he was. Nico Belinsky. A man I barely knew, but one who had moved heaven and earth to find me and then sent a band of rather terrifying angels to do the impossible.

I was free.

Okay, not free, because I still had a murder charge hanging over my head and a furious husband who'd hunt me to the ends of the earth, but for now, I could breathe forbidden air and dream. This time yesterday, I'd had nothing. Now, I had a chance.

Nico opened his arms, and I walked into them. For years, I'd saved my tears for the privacy of my bathroom, but when he wrapped Matty and me up in a hug, I couldn't hold back.

"Th-th-thank you. I-I-I don't know what else to say."

"Then don't say anything." He leaned back to look at me. "You're really all right?"

Physically? Apart from a twisted ankle and a skinned knee, I was fine. Matty needed a clean diaper, though. Mentally? I was a mess. When we'd ridden down in the elevator, I thought I'd be following Vito to the hospital, my heart had been hammering so hard. Even though the blonde woman stayed ice cool, I'd expected Cesare to be waiting when the doors opened, and he always carried a gun. Dying in a hail of bullets definitely hadn't been on my bucket list when I moved to New York.

"I'm good." A lie, but Nico didn't need to know that. I'd already caused him enough problems. "Just a little tired."

"You can sleep on the plane."

"We're going to Oregon?"

"Yes."

"Is that where you live?"

"Mostly. I have other properties, but that one feels like home."

"Is there anywhere I could get a diaper before we go? Matty's been potty training, but he's not quite there yet, and I couldn't bring anything. No changing bag, no clothes, no—" I clapped a hand over my mouth as Matty began to fuss. "We forgot Shelley."

"Who's Shelley?" the blonde asked. Nobody had told me her name, and I didn't dare to ask either. She scared me.

"Matty's favourite toy. He can't sleep without her."

"Well, we're not going back."

"We can get him new toys," Nico promised. "Whatever he wants."

A sweet gesture, but I knew Matty would only want Shelley the snail. He had a hundred other toys, but they rarely held his attention for longer than a few minutes. Shelley was the only one that had stood the test of time, nearly a year so far. But the blonde was right; we couldn't go back. Matty and I would both be starting from scratch, and we'd just have to get used to it.

"Thank you."

"And we have diapers. I consulted with people who know more about children than I do and picked up the basics."

"The dog could use a potty break as well," the blonde said. Her accent had changed from American to English. Which one was real? Or were they both fake? "I'd rather it didn't shit on my jet."

The plane was hers? Perhaps I should have been surprised, but since I'd spent a couple of hours in her company, I really wasn't. She probably owned a rocket and a submarine too. She struck me as that sort of woman.

Nico crooked a finger, and a uniformed lady appeared with a leash.

"Ma'am, we have a secure area for the dog to relieve itself."

The dark-haired woman we'd stopped to pick up in the van—before we'd switched to a town car—reached out for Matty.

"I'll change him."

Instinctively, I clung to my son tighter, but Nico nodded to let me know it was okay. A wave of tiredness washed over me as I handed Matty over. Tiredness and relief. For so long, I'd been alone, but now that others were sharing the burden, the feeling was almost overwhelming.

"Take a bathroom break and then get Kaylin on board," the blonde ordered. "It's gonna be a long flight."

Most of the night, if my math was correct. And for the first time in forever, I was looking forward to the morning.

This...wasn't what I'd expected. Nico lived in a hotel. Well, not actually in a hotel, but he owned the hotel—the Peninsula Resort and Spa—and he lived in a villa on the grounds. I'd woken to a view of the ocean, to the sound of waves crashing against the shore.

Most of the journey had passed in a blur. Matty cried

when the plane's engines rumbled into life, and the pressure changes had made him howl. He'd finally passed out from sheer exhaustion two hours into the flight, and I'd followed suit. After we landed, Nico had helped me to strap Matty into a car seat, and we'd woken up in Baldwin's Shore.

Now? Now Nico and I would have to talk. I'd have to explain what an utter mess I'd made of my life, from thinking I could make it in the cutthroat entertainment business, to getting involved with Cesare, to ending up pregnant, to getting my ass hauled back to NYC when I tried to escape the first time.

But where *was* Nico? When I stumbled out of the guest suite wearing a fluffy bathrobe over the pyjamas I'd found on my bed, he was nowhere to be seen. I spotted a note on the kitchen counter in his painfully precise writing, telling me that one of his staff had taken Cricket for a walk and to make myself at home.

Matty was still sleeping soundly, thank goodness, so I tiptoed around downstairs, feeling like a voyeur. Cesare had been fond of all things ostentatious—gilded furniture, chandeliers in every room, expensive paintings, a grand piano he couldn't play. Think Versailles meets the Marble Palace. Nico's tastes were far simpler, and his favourite colour seemed to be white. I recalled his old bedroom in the Moscow mansion—he'd been a neat freak even then.

The only cluttered space was the living room, and that was filled with shopping bags and stacks of boxes. Toys, clothes, a booster seat, a potty, a first-aid kit, sippy cups, faucet extenders, diapers, wipes, a flat-packed playhouse... Wow.

The front door was locked when I tried it, the same with the back door, but the sliding door that led to the terrace opened smoothly. I stepped outside and breathed. Just breathed. Nobody stopped me, no asshole in a suit appeared to order me back inside. There was a yard. An actual yard that

Cricket would love. A pool too, and the metal fence around it looked hastily erected and out of place. Beyond the pool, palm trees and other greenery gave Nico's space privacy. The cabana would be beautiful in the summer. Would I still be here then? Or would I spend the rest of my life on the move, constantly trying to stay one step ahead of Cesare and the cops?

"Did you sleep well?"

I jumped when Nico spoke from behind me, then turned to face him. He hadn't shaved this morning, and his hair was tousled, probably by the wind. If I stayed out here for long, I'd need to find a ponytail holder.

"I guess it's relative, but I slept better than I have in a while."

"Matty's okay?"

"He's exhausted, but he'll want breakfast soon."

"I have cereal, eggs, fruit, toast, and milk." Nico checked his watch. "Breakfast service is almost finished, but the hotel kitchen can whip up anything else you want."

"Matty usually has a scrambled egg with toast and mashed banana."

"What about you?"

"Just coffee. I have to watch my weight."

Nico looked me up and down, a slow perusal that set butterflies fluttering in my belly. Guilt quickly squashed them. Nico was like a brother to me, and his gaze definitely shouldn't make my thighs clench the way they did.

"Why?" he asked.

"Why? Why do I have to watch my weight? Because I have costumes to fit—" No. No, I didn't. I didn't have costumes anymore. I didn't have an image to maintain, and I didn't have to sing at the Starlight Lounge. I didn't have Cesare criticising my diet and telling me that if I got fat, I was more likely to suffer another miscarriage. "Okay, I guess I could have a slice of toast."

"Are you up to talking as well?"

Was "no" an acceptable answer? "Yes."

For years, my head had been filled with memories of Nico the boy. The long-suffering teenager who'd helped me with my homework and let me win at chess. The day we'd met in New York, I'd gotten a glimpse of Nico the man, cool, detached, and unattainable. I'd thought about him more than was healthy, but I'd never called him, not until I ran out of money and options in Manassas. Now I remembered why.

Nico-the-man was magnetic.

Deep down, I had to admit what I tried to deny. That I'd dated Cesare because over the course of one stupid lunch, I'd developed a crush on Nico, and I knew I'd never be able to have him. When he left, he'd patted me on the shoulder, for Pete's sake. Cesare had offered the same dark, dangerous energy, but—so I thought—none of the risk to my heart. I figured we'd go out for dinner once or twice, share a few wild nights, and then go our separate ways, no damage done.

A rejection from Nico, on the other hand? That would have hurt like hell.

I took a seat at the counter as he fiddled with the coffee machine, dumping beans into a hopper on the top. No instant for Nico. How had he ended up here in Oregon? If he'd inherited his father's billions, he should be on a yacht in the Med.

"Sugar? Cream?" he asked, and I shook my head.

"Just the caffeine."

He set a mug on the counter in front of me, plain white with a twisted handle.

"We have a lot to discuss, but let's get the important points out of the way first. I realise you've just got out of one luxury prison and the last thing you want is to end up in another, but I think it would be a good idea if you keep a low profile for the moment."

That, we could agree on. "I'm planning to."

"Baldwin's Shore is a small town, and fortunately or unfortunately, depending on how you look at it, my friends here include two sheriff's deputies, a lawyer, and a Scandinavian princess whose head of security is fond of running background checks."

I swallowed hard. "Background checks?"

"Don't worry, your new identity will hold up. There's also a vigilante in town, and nobody's quite sure where his loyalties lie."

"A princess? A vigilante?" What sort of a place was this?

"Brie's a sweetheart. She's overseas at the moment, but you'll meet her soon. As for the Bad Samaritan, I'm sure he's nothing to worry about, but he likes to help out the sheriff's department, so it's best if we keep the Manassas incident quiet."

"I won't go out anywhere, I swear."

"Hopefully, this situation is only temporary." Ouch. But at least he'd made his feelings clear. "After breakfast, I need to take your photo for a new passport."

"You can do that? Get me a new passport? With a different name?"

I knew it was possible because Cesare had managed it, but Cesare owned people in one of the New York passport offices.

"Can I do it myself? No. But I know somebody who's able to."

"A forger?"

"I'm not sure whether it'll be a good forgery or a real one obtained through dubious channels, but my contact assures me it'll pass inspection at any border."

"You trust him?"

"Her. And she's delivered so far."

The pieces clicked into place. "Your fake wife?"

Nico cracked a smile. "She's quite a woman."

Of course she was. And that was the kind of girl Nico would be interested in—a modern-day superhero with the power to evade the Cavallaros and conjure up passports. But I had him as a friend, and that was the only thing that mattered right now.

"Yes, she *is* quite a woman."

NICO

Practicalities. Nico had to focus on the practicalities, and definitely not on Kaylin's perfect ass.

He was an ass man and he made no apologies for it, unless the ass in question belonged to Kaylin La Rocca, and then he was very sorry indeed. She'd just escaped from one heir to a crime empire; she didn't need to become inappropriately entangled with another.

At least she was sitting down now.

"We need to come up with a story. A reason for you being here. Emmy recommends sticking close to the truth because then we're less likely to slip up."

"Emmy?"

"My fake wife." Her ass wasn't bad either. Charles Black was a lucky man, Emmy's homicidal tendencies excepted. "If anyone asks"—which they would, because Baldwin's Shore was full of busybodies—"we'll tell them that you're an old friend who's escaped a difficult relationship, and you're here to lie low for a while."

"That isn't revealing too much?"

"In a small town like this one, everybody gets into

everybody else's business, but they're also protective of their own. If the women know there's an unpleasant ex-partner involved, we'll get an early warning if any strangers begin poking around. That'll buy us time while we establish your new identity and find you someplace to live long-term. Do you have anywhere in mind?"

Kaylin shook her head. "I dreamed of so many places. Of moving to a desert island, of getting lost in Paris, of hiding in the Australian outback because Cesare's scared of spiders, especially the big ones." She rolled her eyes, and Nico recalled Sasha, the spider who'd lived in the blue bathroom in Moscow, the eight-legged freak Kaylin wouldn't let anyone kill. The day Timofey had accidentally stepped on him, she'd cried all afternoon. "But I never made actual plans."

"Well, now you can start considering your options."

"I don't have a job, not anymore."

As if that mattered. "I'll fund a fresh start wherever you want to go."

Don't cry. That sniffle was alarming, and Nico produced a clean handkerchief from his pocket. Kaylin began twisting it in her hands.

"I'll pay you back, I swear. It might take me a while, but I'll do it. And for the rescue."

Unlikely. Emmy was nothing if not efficient, and even with a "friends and family" discount and the initial favour taken into account, the invoice that landed this morning had been over a million bucks. Worth every cent, but still not a sum Kaylin would be repaying any time soon.

"Let's not think about that at the moment."

Nico wanted Kaylin's stay at the Peninsula to be a pleasant one. He could worry about the future while she relaxed in the spa and walked on the beach with her son. Because they were only fifty percent of the way to freedom. There was still that pesky murder charge to deal with, and the small matter of the

Mob lurking in the background. Blackwood was quietly—very quietly—working to trace the missing witnesses from the Bluebird Inn, and Emmy had given Nico two tasks before they went their separate ways last night: first, find out what really happened that night, and second, learn whether Kaylin had any information to trade. She'd spent nearly four years with Cesare Cavallaro—what did she know about his business, if anything? Proving Kaylin innocent was the goal, but if that was impossible, an immunity deal was the next best option.

But that would have to wait because a wail came from upstairs.

"Mama!"

Kaylin was on her feet in an instant.

"I shouldn't have left him for so long."

"I'll set up the baby monitor while you do...whatever it is toddlers need."

Emmy had handed the monitor over yesterday. It had come with a warning that the store-bought versions contained a multitude of security flaws. Had Blackwood made use of them in the Cavallaro apartment? Nico considered that a reasonable possibility. He also considered it likely that Emmy had built a backdoor of her own into her parting gift, but on balance, he'd rather have her watching Matteo than an ill-intentioned stranger.

"He needs to go potty. Then I'll make his breakfast—do you have any plastic utensils?"

Nico glanced toward the mountain of baby products in the living room. Three of the housekeeping staff—all of them mothers—had spent yesterday in Coos Bay, buying everything Matteo might need. They'd earned every dollar of their overtime pay.

"I should imagine so. What do you need? A plate and cutlery?"

"And a sippy cup. I think I saw one of those near the top of the pile."

Who knew such a small person could need so many accessories? A Baby Shark Swim 'n' Play bath toy? A Rockin' Unicorn? An Under the Sea Activity Gym? The only toys Nico could remember from his childhood were a selection of plastic guns and an electric Ferrari.

By the time Kaylin reappeared with Matteo, Nico had dug out two sets of dinnerware and three sippy cups, plus some kind of fleecy all-in-one suit in fetching tiger stripes, a Magna Doodle board, and a bag of dried apple slices.

"Is there a website where I can learn what all this stuff is for?" he asked. "Or a book? What's this thing with the straps? It looks like something from a fetish club."

Kaylin studied the packaging for the Hip Sling 3000. "I think it's a carrier." Then, "You've been to a fetish club?"

Time to change the subject. "I was curious. Let's get breakfast."

"Want Shelley," Matteo said, reaching out a hand.

"Are there any toys in that pile?"

"Undoubtedly. What does Shelley look like?"

"She's a snail. Knitted, not furry."

Nico began rooting through. "We have...a mouse?"

The kid shook his head.

"A giraffe?"

Negative.

"How about a penguin?" Kaylin had always loved penguins. "Or a clown?" Actually, that one appeared somewhat demonic. No wonder the child looked concerned. "A bumblebee?"

"Cat! Cat!"

"I don't think we have a—"

"Cat!"

Nico's fluffy white cat stalked into the room, her tail held high in the air. She'd met Cricket when they arrived home last night, and she hadn't been impressed. No, she'd hissed, then screeched, then finally jumped on top of a bookshelf in the library and sat there, glaring. The dog seemed more bemused than anything else.

"Matty, shush." Kaylin turned so the boy could get a better look. "He's never seen a real cat before. Is she friendly?"

"She doesn't see many children. I suspect she'll run if he tries to touch her."

"What's her name?"

"Snezhinka."

"Snowflake?"

So she still remembered some Russian. "That's right. You're more of a dog person?"

"You mean Cricket? I just...I just wanted a friend. He was left in a box by the dumpster one night when he was a puppy. Cesare told Serge to put him in a bucket of water, but I begged to keep him, and he said I could." Her lip quivered. "I was real surprised, but I guess I shouldn't have been."

"Why?"

"Cesare was all about control, and Cricket was another bargaining chip. Step out of line, and the dog gets it, that sort of thing. One time..." A sniffle. "One time, Cesare threatened to throw him off the roof terrace."

"You have no idea how sorry I am that I didn't find you sooner. The first investigator I hired came highly recommended, and he certainly put in the hours, but he was looking in the wrong place. He tried to track you forward from Manassas."

"That was the worst night of my life."

Kaylin shuddered, and her grip on Matteo loosened. Nico leapt forward to help and found himself holding the boy. First time for everything. He looked at Matty, and Matty looked at him.

"Dada?"

"Hell no. Heck. I meant heck. Can you say 'heck' around a two-year-old?"

"Cesare said a lot worse. Matty's third word was f-u-c-k."

"I'll try to watch my mouth." Nico looked down at the boy. "I'm not your dada."

Kaylin gave a nervous laugh. "I guess you both have that tall, dark, and dangerous vibe. Here, I can take him back. Sorry about...you know. I just hate thinking of it."

"I need to hear the truth about what happened that night, Kaylin."

She cast her gaze to the floor. "I didn't kill that officer."

"I never suspected for a moment that you did, but unfortunately, the authorities think otherwise."

"Cat?" Matteo asked again, just as there was a knock on the front door. Kaylin jumped out of her skin.

"Relax. It's probably the staff with Cricket."

"In my world, a knock at the door is never a good thing."

"Want me to get a bell installed?"

That earned him a hint of a smile. "I don't think I'll ever stop looking behind me."

Join the club. Nico had tried not to burn bridges as he extricated himself from his father's more unsavoury business dealings, but when tiptoeing around the who's who of Russian organised crime, it was impossible not to step on a few feet.

"We have a security team on site. Kaylin, I promise I won't let anything happen to you."

It was a promise Nico meant to keep, but the road to hell was paved with good intentions. And broken promises, like shattered trust, were hard to repair.

28

KAYLIN

I owed Nico. I owed him an explanation. But producing the words to account for all that had happened since we crossed paths on that fateful day in New York was like unravelling my insides piece by slimy piece.

But I owed him, and I had to pay up.

I owed him everything.

Nico was keeping his promises, and today had been my best day in years. We'd gone for a walk. A walk! Outside with the wind on our faces, not on a treadmill staring down, down, down at people scurrying like ants below. And the air was so fresh here. A car had taken us to one of the hiking trails on the edge of town, and Nico pushed Matty's stroller because I was so busy taking in the scenery that I kept tripping over rocks and tree roots. I could have kept walking forever, but when the temperature dropped and a deer ran past and startled Matty, I knew it was time to come home.

Home.

I'd only spent a day in Nico's villa, but I already felt more comfortable there than I had in Cesare's gilded penthouse, other than this discussion, obviously. Matty was asleep, and I was on my third glass of red. If any conversation called for alcohol, it was this one.

"I did know who Cesare was before I accepted his invitation to dinner," I admitted. "Everyone working that wedding was whispering about the Cavallaros." I appreciated that Nico was giving me the space to speak. Telling this story would be hard enough without constant questions. "I was at a low point. I'd just been dumped by a guy who told me I was too pretty to be smart, and the slimeball before him had borrowed nine hundred bucks for an acting course and then moved to LA without paying me back." He'd "borrowed" my credit card too. It had taken me months to pay off the debt. "The one before that? His ex-wife interrupted us over dinner at Le Jardin, demanding to know why he hadn't paid child support for six months. Which was a surprise because he hadn't mentioned he'd been married or that he had three kids. Cesare was kind to me at the wedding. Courteous. Polite. I thought there wouldn't be any harm in going on one date, plus he promised to get me an audition at the Starlight Lounge."

"But you didn't tell your roommates about him?"

"Did you meet Anisha?"

"Not in person."

"She would have put on her 'mom' voice and given me a lecture. Illegal activities, RICO Act, blah blah blah. And if I'd told Charlotte, she would have let it slip, even if she didn't mean to. It was only meant to be a bit of fun. And at first, it was." I took a deep breath. "But I messed up."

"From what I've heard, you weren't the one at fault."

It was sweet of Nico to try to make me feel better. "Cesare spoiled me. Fancy clothes, expensive restaurants, flashy parties. I felt like...I felt like my mom, back when she was happy. Like in Russia, with your dad. Sure, she was miserable after things ended and we came back to the US, but I told myself I wouldn't get in that deep."

"My father wasn't a good man, Kaylin."

"He was always nice to me."

"Underneath the charm, he was an asshole."

"Well, *you're* a good man."

"I have a number of exes who would disagree with that statement."

Those poor, dumb women. They'd had Nico Belinsky and let him go? Fools. He *was* a good man, a good man who'd left his father's world despite being heir to an oligarchy. A man who'd kept searching until he rescued a woman he owed nothing. Cesare had always been colder, more controlling. I just hadn't realised how much of a monster he was until it was too late. I'd been blinded by shiny things, seduced by money and power.

"Maybe you never let them see the real Nico."

He seemed to ponder that for a moment. "Maybe I didn't."

"I didn't see the real Cesare to start with, and you know what? I didn't care. The relationship was supposed to be temporary. I thought I'd be old news after a month, and I was fine with it. But one night..." This was the hard part. The part I struggled to put into words. "One night, I had too much to drink, and that was my first encounter with the devil. Worse, I ended up pregnant."

Until that moment, Nico's expression had been sympathetic, but now his eyes turned into two glittering black diamonds. And I realised that there was a side of *him* I'd never seen before either.

"Are you saying what I think you're saying?" he asked.

The memories were still fuzzy. I recalled my weak protests, but perhaps I hadn't been firm enough? Hadn't made my feelings clear? I remembered stumbling to the bathroom afterward to be sick, and there was a vague recollection of wiping sticky white cum from my inner thighs, but then in the morning, Cesare had brought me coffee and a croissant on a little gold tray as if there were nothing wrong, and I'd begun to think that maybe the worst parts had been a dream.

"I'm saying that night was a mess." *Had* he raped me? I'd thought so at the time, but when I confronted him the next day, he'd told me that I'd wanted it just as much as him. That had been the beginning of the three-year mind fuck. Sometimes, it had been hard to tell which way was up with Cesare, but over the course of our time together, the charming side of him had made fewer and fewer and fewer appearances, replaced by anger and indifference. I preferred the indifference. "And a month later, I began to feel sick, so he sent me to the doctor."

I hadn't realised the kindly, grey-haired man was on the Cavallaros' payroll. That he'd informed Cesare of my "condition." If I'd been thinking logically, I'd have taken Plan B with that damn coffee and croissant, but I'd never managed to think straight around my then-boyfriend. So after I got the terrifying news, I'd gone home, tossed a few belongings into my car, and taken off.

"And the doctor reported back to Cesare?"

"How did you know?"

"Because that's the way my father would have handled the situation."

"I thought doctors took an oath to do no harm?"

"Money speaks louder than morals to some people. That's when you went to Manassas?"

I nodded. "I needed space to decide what to do. Whether to keep the baby or not. I...I hated the idea of a termination, but the thought of spending the rest of my life tied to Cesare was worse. I knew he wouldn't let me walk away, not if I was carrying his child."

Matty was a joy, a treasure, but I couldn't deny there were times when I'd resented his presence. Resented the chain he'd put around my neck. And every time I had one of those evil thoughts, the guilt ate away at me.

"I tried to get to you," Nico said. "I was in Europe when you called, but as soon as I picked up the message, I came right away."

I squeezed his hand, and the damn tears came back. "That means a lot. Really, it does. But Cesare got there first. I think he tracked my phone when I turned it on to call you." I'd ignored all the voicemails from him, the hundreds of text messages, and turned it off again, but it had been too late. "He was with Alonzo. They grabbed me as I was walking to the convenience store along the street and bundled me into the back of a vehicle. Cesare told Alonzo to get my car so it looked as if I'd left on my own."

"Alonzo Cavallaro ran over the police officer?"

"Yes? I mean, I didn't witness it, but he was the one in my car."

He would have wiped away any fingerprints; I was confident of that. Perhaps he'd paid off the cops too? It wouldn't have surprised me—the Cavallaros owned several dozen members of the NYPD, including at least two bureau chiefs. I'd heard Cesare bragging about it on the phone.

"What happened after that? Did they take you back to New York?"

"Cesare was furious. One of his men drove us to Belgravia Place, and he laid out the rules." That was the day I'd become a possession. At first, he'd been so angry that I'd feared for my life, and if I'd gone through with the abortion, I was quite sure he would have killed me. "I was his, and if I disobeyed him again, I'd regret it. Guards watched over me twenty-four-seven, and when I saw the reports about the police officer's death on the TV, I realised I couldn't leave even if I had the opportunity. It was a strange existence—I never wanted for material things, and Cesare would still take me out to expensive restaurants and act nice, especially if there were people around. But if I made one mistake—didn't smile enough, or disagreed with him, or took too long to do something—then he'd snap."

"He hit you?"

"Not often, and never when I was pregnant. Mostly, he just restricted my freedom. So I tried to fit in. To *conform*. After a year, he finally let me have my audition."

A year where I'd become the mother of a beautiful little boy. I loved Matty with all my heart, no matter who his father was or what Cesare had done to me. A year where I'd gone from possession to vessel. It turned out that Cesare didn't find postpartum bleeding attractive, or mommy pooch, or stretch marks. I'd spent several blessed months sleeping in the nursery before he'd decided that Matty should have a little brother or sister.

But Nico was still focused on the first part of my answer.

"Not often? *Not often?*" If dark vibes could kill, Cesare would have been dead. "That motherfucker."

"You're scaring me," I whispered, and Nico's expression turned to horror.

"I'm sorry, *zolottse*. That's the last thing I meant to do." His smile was tight as he reined in the darkness. "The Starlight Lounge was lucky to have you. You're a natural-born performer."

"I didn't have much choice." When it came to acting, I was the queen of faking orgasms. "It was the only freedom I got. Cesare let me choose the songs and help with the costumes and choreography."

"You should have been on Broadway, not in a club that serves watered-down drinks."

"That dream's over. Right now, I'm just happy to be out

of New York. All I want is a quiet life, no fame, no fortune, only a happy, healthy son and enough money to survive. It's funny how you miss the small things when they get taken away from you. I used to dream of going to the grocery store and buying pizza and candy and bottles of rosé. Just meandering up and down the aisles and pretending to grumble when Matty wanted to buy some crappy plastic toy."

"Then tomorrow, we'll go to the grocery store."

"Really?"

"I'll even push the cart."

Another tear threatened to escape, but this time, it was a tear of relief. Nico, my big not-brother, my secret crush, my knight in shining Armani, was doing his best to make things right, even though I knew I was unfixable.

When Mom had first announced that we were staying in Russia, I'd cried. My friends were in the US, I didn't understand the language, and it was always so damn cold. But now? Now I was grateful for that time in Moscow because without it, I'd never have met the man beside me.

He wrapped an arm around my shoulders, and I leaned into him as he kissed my hair. After three years with Cesare, the thought of being touched by a man had repulsed me, but this was different. This was Nico, and his arms were my safe place.

29

NICO

"Katy Lord?" Kaylin turned the passport over in her hands. "That's my new name?"

Katy Lynn Lord, and Matteo had become Matthew. Matthew Nicolas Lord. Was that Emmy's idea of a joke? Nico had thumbed through the passport before he handed it over, noting stamps for Canada, the UK, and Thailand.

"Emmy said it's better to use a name similar to your real one. Answering feels natural that way."

"This looks real, and the driver's licence."

"They probably are."

"Probably?"

"Emmy assures me the licence won't raise any red flags if you get pulled over, but she recommends sticking to the speed limit."

Which made her the world's biggest hypocrite if the rubber she'd burned leaving the Peninsula the last time she was there was any indication.

"I don't even have a car. It's hard to get pulled over while pushing a stroller."

"I have several vehicles that you're welcome to borrow. Just let me know if you're planning to take a drive so I don't send out a search party."

"You'd let me go out alone?"

Cesare Cavallaro really had done a number on her, hadn't he?

"I'm not your keeper, *zolottse*." Nico shouldn't keep calling her "darling," but it rolled so easily off his tongue. "I'd suggest trying the Audi SUV. It has an excellent safety rating."

"Will you come with me at first? I don't know my way around and..." Kaylin blew out a breath. "Damn, I sound so needy."

No, she sounded like a woman who'd been virtually imprisoned by a madman for three years. A woman whose confidence had been shaken, whose psyche had been damaged.

"My weekend is yours." Plus Nico had cleared his schedule for the next week, but he didn't want to smother her. "We can buy as much pizza and candy and rosé as you want." He slid a cell phone and bank card across the counter. "These are yours too."

"You bought me a phone?"

"In the interest of full disclosure, there's tracking software installed on it." Courtesy of Emmy Black, of course. He'd debated not telling Kaylin, but enough men had breached her trust already without him adding to the list. "If you want to disable it, you can, but I'd prefer you didn't. There's also a panic button. If you activate it, I'll get an alert with your location."

"You're worried about Cesare." A statement, not a question.

"It pays to be cautious."

She studied the phone. "I won't disable it. And I don't want to use the card, but..."

"He didn't deserve you," Nico blurted, breaking the cardinal rule of remembering to think before he spoke.

There was a long pause. "I wish I could believe that. I was foolish enough to play with fire, and I should have realised I'd get burned."

"Don't make excuses for him."

"Dada?" a small voice said from behind.

No, still not guilty. Nico wasn't sure whether to be horrified or flattered or take Matteo for an eye test. Kaylin scooped him up as he toddled across the room and brought him over.

"Not Dada. Nico."

The kid attempted to smush a toy giraffe into her face, and she ducked with practised ease.

"You're a good mom."

"You think? I had to learn everything from books and TV and Cesare's mom." A roll of the eyes told Nico what she thought of her mother-in-law. "As if I wanted my son to grow up like hers. Matty, you want a banana?"

The boy nodded.

"Toast and banana?"

Matteo nodded. "Toats and nana."

"My mama left the parenting to my father," Nico said. "Although I'm genuinely not sure whether it would have been any better if she hadn't."

"You turned out pretty good."

"I had to learn everything from books, American movies, and internet forums. Hollywood's idea of organised crime and the reality are very different."

"Tell me about it. Same with assholes in romance novels and assholes in real life."

"Ah, romance novels... I once granted an interview to a student newspaper in the hope of meeting my future submissive, but they sent a football player named Bart."

He'd hobbled in with his ankle bandaged and explained that it was important to have a backup career in case sports didn't work out.

"*You* read romance novels?" Kaylin asked.

"I was curious about women's expectations, especially after an ex-girlfriend informed me I was a selfish jackass."

"Why? You're anything but selfish."

"Because I flew to London for a business meeting instead of attending an album launch for a rapper named Bling Boi."

"Bling Boi? You're serious?"

"He'd replaced his teeth with diamonds, or so he claimed. I listened to one of his tracks, and his talent level suggested they were more likely to be cubic zirconia." Cubic zirconia combined with stunningly bad taste. "But the launch party was on a yacht in Cancun, which made me a jackass for refusing to change my plans."

"I bet the romance novels disagreed."

"According to the romance novels, I should be hiring a maid who's one paycheck away from losing her apartment and waiting for her to accidentally walk in on me in the shower."

"Really? I thought you should be catching a penniless student after she trips on the sidewalk and nearly nosedives in front of a speeding SUV."

"So that's where I'm going wrong."

"Of course, if you'd rather stay in Oregon, you could always try cutting down several hectares of forest and falling in love with the eco-warrior who's determined to stop you."

"I fought with the eco-warriors when I built this hotel, but it didn't work out. The closest I got to being propositioned was when Elmira Fairbanks threatened to castrate me if I didn't install a wind turbine."

"And did you install a wind turbine?"

"It was already part of the plans. I was tempted to eliminate it out of sheer bloody-mindedness, but it provides the power to heat the pools and I quite like my testicles where they are."

Kaylin got Matteo settled onto a booster seat she'd retrieved from the pile and mashed banana into a bowl. Having her around felt comfortable. Nico still wasn't sure about the child—he'd never spent time with a toddler before—but how much trouble could a two-year-old be?

The answer? Big trouble. Matteo used the spoon as a catapult and caught Nico in the face with a lump of banana while Kaylin was busy wiping goo off the refrigerator door and apologising. Then, when she put a plate of toast triangles in front of him, he threw the spoon on the floor and began sobbing.

"Scare, scare."

"Fudging heck," she muttered under her breath.

"What's wrong?"

"He wants the toast cut into squares. Last week, he'd only eat triangles."

"But it's basically the same."

"You try explaining that."

Nico looked at the plate, and then he looked at the screeching two-year-old. "I'll make more toast."

"You're my hero."

Kaylin tried placating Matteo with the cuddly giraffe, but to no avail. Rationality and toddlers did not good bedfellows make. Nico made a note to purchase an express toaster, if such a thing existed. Every second counted when ruptured eardrums were a very real possibility. Finally, the toast was buttered, and Nico sagged onto a stool as Matteo nibbled on a square. This was like sharing a home with a tiny dictator.

"If we go out today, can we look for a toy store?" Kaylin asked. "Shelley the snail always calmed Matty down, and I need to find something similar."

"If it stops him from crying, I'll take you to any toy store in the world."

"Even if you did, we wouldn't find a new Shelley. Lyndsey bought her last year, one of those seasonal specials from the grocery store. I'm kicking myself for not grabbing Shelley when I went to get Cricket."

"There wasn't a moment to spare, from what I heard."

Kaylin bit her lip and Nico reached for his handkerchief, just in case tears followed.

"No, there really wasn't. Lyndsey had Matty, and she didn't want to let him go, and I thought...I thought..."

Kaylin took a handful of gulping breaths, and Nico rubbed her back. In a brotherly way, he hoped, and not like a horny prick in a billionaire romance novel.

"You did get out, all of you, and Lyndsey isn't a concern anymore."

"I only hope Cesare didn't punish her for letting Matty go. Do you know if she's okay?"

"I know Emmy told her to leave town. Lyndsey wasn't your friend, Kaylin. Don't waste too much sympathy on her."

"We might not have been friends, exactly, but I still don't want Cesare to hurt her."

Nico debated telling Kaylin about the affair, but he hated the thought of upsetting her further. At least Cesare had used a condom when he was fucking the help. Emmy had helpfully included that snippet in her report, along with the results of Cesare's latest health screen. As of a month ago, he'd been clear of STDs, so it was unlikely he'd passed any nasty surprises on to Kaylin.

"I'll try to find out how Lyndsey is."

"And Vito? Did he survive?"

"He's still breathing."

Although the urgency had gone out of the investigation now, Emmy was still providing regular updates, which included news of Vito Cavallaro's medical condition. And Hallie was ready to follow any leads that came in regarding the missing potential witnesses from the Manassas incident.

"What does that mean? He's okay?"

"It means Vito made it through Thursday night and then had a stroke on Friday morning. The extent of his recovery is still uncertain, but I'd say he won't be taking an active role in family affairs for the foreseeable future." The term Emmy had used was "overcooked vegetable," but Nico liked to think he had a little more tact. "Don't worry about New York. We'll go out and find Matteo a new snail, and then we can take another walk. I heard you enjoyed hiking in the Catskills?"

"I did. And it's kind of weird that you know so much about my adult life when I barely know a thing about yours."

"I'd much rather have learned these things the old-fashioned way, believe me, but the research was a necessary evil. That changes from today, though. We can walk and talk."

"Matty can't walk very far, so we'll have to take a route that's okay for the stroller."

"Or I could carry him. I'll even use the sex swing sling."

Kaylin choked out a laugh, and it was good to see her smiling again.

"Did you really go to a fetish club?"

"I suppose it depends on your definition of 'fetish.'" Nyx catered to all tastes. "But none of the women there called me a selfish jackass, so there's that."

"I realise I've never met your ex-girlfriend, but I know I don't like her." Kaylin wiped up a stray lump of banana. "Want me to cook dinner tonight? I only learned from books and the TV, but I make an edible chicken parmesan."

"I don't think anyone's ever cooked for me in this kitchen before."

Although Emmy had made him coffee once. Right after she picked his lock and showed up in his bedroom with an amused smile on her face. She'd been completely unrepentant, as he recalled.

"Do you have breadcrumbs? Garlic powder?" Kaylin asked.

"I'd say that's highly unlikely."

"Then I'd better make a shopping list."

30

KAYLIN

Living with Cesare had been hard, but in some ways, staying with Nico was harder. With Cesare, there had been no heat sizzling through my veins, no temptation to keep sneaking forbidden glances. Only a vague attraction that turned to cold hate and finally to resignation.

Nico was head-turningly handsome. No kidding, a woman had twisted her ankle when we were walking in the forest and she'd been looking at him rather than at where she was going. Her husband had caught her before she caused herself a serious injury, thank goodness, and Nico had remained oblivious as he pointed out a squirrel to Matty. We'd found a better carrier before we left, and now Matty was riding around the toy store on Nico's back, pointing at everything and chattering excitedly to anyone who would listen. And also calling Nico "Dada" again. Super awkward.

"Nico," I reminded Matty. "Neeeee-co."

"Dada Nico?"

Nico smothered a chuckle.

"It's nothing personal," I explained. "Cesare never spent

much time with him, and we didn't get out often, so he started calling any man with dark hair 'Dada.'"

"I bet that irked Cesare."

"Oh, it did. Hell hath no fury like a self-proclaimed alpha male whose son gets him confused with the chauffeur."

"A fragile ego is a dangerous thing." Nico picked up a furry red-and-yellow caterpillar from the shelf. "How about this one? Is it similar to the snail?"

"Shelley was blue and white and twice the size."

"They both eat plants."

"I don't think Matty cares about his plushie's diet." I pulled something fluffy and blue out of the bargain basket. "Maybe this one?"

"It looks like an Ebola virus. Let's not give the boy nightmares."

"Well, do you have a better idea?"

Nico thought for a moment, and a woman nearly pushed her cart into me.

"Sorry," she mumbled. "He's just...so...so..."

"I know," I whispered back.

Nico tossed the Ebola toy back into the bargain basket. "Actually, I *do* have a better idea. Let's head to the grocery store, and then we'll make another stop on the way home."

"Ladies—and Paulo—this is Katy. Katy, meet Brooke, Darla, and Paulo."

Three faces stared back at me with undisguised curiosity, then their gazes moved to Matty, who was desperately trying to reach a ball of yarn from his perch on Nico's back.

"Hi," I said, feeling like a kid on the first day of school—and I'd had a lot of those days, thanks to my mom's wanderlust. "We're staying with Nico for a few weeks. Me and my son. He's, uh, Matthew. Matty for short."

Could I sound like any more of a dork?

"Is this your first trip to Baldwin's Shore?" Brooke asked, and I knew she was Brooke because they were all wearing name badges. Brooke was the petite brunette with the ready smile, and Darla was the older, more reserved lady in the muumuu. She'd decorated her badge with two rainbows and an ostrich feather.

"It's my first visit to Oregon."

"Where are you from?"

"Uh..."

"Maryland," Nico said firmly. "And there was some unpleasantness with her ex, so I'd appreciate if you'd keep her presence here quiet."

Darla rolled her eyes. "We've all been there, hun."

I sincerely doubted it, not in quite such a spectacular fashion, but I managed a weak smile.

"Men suck." Crap. "Apart from the ones here, I mean."

Paulo gave a shimmy. "Because we're awesome. So, how did you meet this hottie?"

"You mean Nico?"

Dammit, that was an admission I hadn't meant to make.

"We already know how you met *moi*. C'mon, spill the beans... Did you pick him up at a fetish club?"

I turned to the hottie in question. "Does *everyone* know about the fetish club?"

"What?" Paulo gasped. "I was making a joke. Did you really go to a fetish club, hot stuff? Tell me everything."

"I'm afraid the membership agreement precludes me from doing that."

"Wait, there's a membership?" Paulo elbowed me in the side. His badge said "World's Best Craft Store Assistant," and he'd stuck a gold crown in one corner. "He's a dark horse, isn't he?"

"I honestly wouldn't know."

"You wouldn't?" He waved at Nico, game-show assistant style. "How can anyone resist this package?"

"We're just old friends."

"Can we stop discussing my sex life?" Nico asked.

"Well, Brooke won't discuss hers, and Darla doesn't have one, so we're limited on options. Well, probably. Darla went out for burgers with a stud named Alex, and they're taking things slow, whatever that means."

Brooke and Darla both put their heads in their hands.

"How about we don't discuss anyone's sex life?" Nico suggested. "There's a child present."

"Aw, how old is he?"

Darla opened the register and waved twenty bucks at Paulo. "Why don't you shoot next door and pick up cookies for everyone?"

"The sandwich ones with the marshmallow in the middle?"

"Make sure you get something a three-year-old can eat as well."

I liked Darla. She was an island of sanity in a turbulent sea.

"Matty won't be three for another few months; he's just big for his age."

"Does he like fruit?"

"Melon and strawberries are his favourites. Do you have kids?"

"Only a cat, hun."

"Pickle lives here in the store," Paulo said. "She was around five minutes ago, but she's probably gone into the break room. Do you have pets?"

Darla interrupted before I managed to answer. "I'm sure Mr. Belinsky didn't bring you in here so Paulo could start the

Spanish Inquisition. Is there anything we can help you with? We have a new range of cross-stitch kits that are good for beginners. Do you paint? If you'd like to learn a new skill, we run classes every week."

"I've never tried painting, but I used to love sewing. Customising clothes, mainly, but sometimes I made skirts and bags from scratch."

"Do you have a sewing machine?"

"I don't have much stuff at all."

"If Katy wants a sewing machine, then we'll purchase a sewing machine," Nico said, and that was perfectly normal for him, wasn't it? Buying whatever he wanted, never having to budget. When I first moved to New York, I'd kept track of every cent. At the time, I'd hated being poor, but after three years with Cesare, years when money hadn't been a problem but I'd had to justify every request, I'd begun to miss my spreadsheet.

"Oh, I don't need a sewing machine, but maybe I could try a cross-stitch kit?"

I didn't mind staying indoors, not with Nico, not when it was for my own good rather than at somebody else's command. But a hobby would help me to pass the time. There was only so much cooking I could do, and Matty liked to take a nap in the afternoons. Always for two hours at least, usually two and a half. Sometimes, I could swear he was part sloth, but other times, he behaved like the love child of a Tasmanian devil and an octopus.

"I'll show you the kits," Brooke offered. "We have a unicorn, a butterfly, a tiger... On second thought, I have another idea—what about stitching an alphabet for Matty? Each project has a letter and an object. A is for apple, B is for ball, C is for cat, you know?"

"I love that idea."

"We're missing the C at the moment," Darla said. "Some

folks over in Coos Bay named their daughter Cashmere, and her grandma loves to craft while she's watching TV."

"Can you order the C?" Nico asked.

"We sure can."

One step at a time. "Maybe I'll just try the A to start with."

Nico took a step to the side to let Brooke and me pass, a big mistake because that put Matty a step closer to the yarn. He made a grab for his favourite colour—blue—and a second later, it was raining yarn balls. Then a cat leapt into the melee.

"Pickle!" Paulo shrieked, right before he ended up on the floor, covered from head to foot in silver glitter.

Oh. My. Gosh.

I was beginning to see that being confined to an apartment did come with some benefits. Matty's ability to wreak havoc had been limited.

"I'm so sorry. Here, let me..."

Our skulls cracked together when Paulo moved to get up at the same time as I bent down to help, and I staggered backward into Nico's arms.

"I've got you."

He always had me.

"I should—"

"Oh, don't worry about the yarn," Darla said. "It's just a mishap. Brooke, can you fetch the A? Katy, is there anything else we can help you with today?"

Nico spoke first. "We were wondering if anyone local takes knitting commissions?"

"What do you need knitted? A sweater?"

"A snail. Matthew lost his favourite toy in the move, and it's proving difficult to replace."

"Do you have a pattern?"

I shook my head. "I don't even have a photo. It was about ten inches long, blue and white."

"Have you tried the internet?" Brooke asked.

"It's been discontinued," I told her. "It was one of those summer specials from the grocery store."

"Have a look on eBay. Or those secondhand clothing apps—they have plenty of children's items. Some people buy up all the discounted seasonal lines and sell them for a profit. But if you can't find what you want, Darla's a great knitter."

"Darla's the knitting queen," Paulo announced. "She can knit anything."

"It might have been crocheted."

"I can crochet as well," Darla said. "If you draw a picture of what the snail needs to look like, I can surely have a try. Paulo, did you forget about the cookies? See if you can find melon and strawberries too."

There was a table at the back of the store, and Brooke made coffee and picked up yarn while I sat down to draw Matty's snail in between eating the most delicious marshmallow cookies I'd ever tasted. How many calories did those things have? I banished the thought as soon as it reared its ugly head because my diet didn't matter anymore. Nobody was judging me here. Nico hadn't said one word when I'd bought whole milk and two bags of candy in the grocery store. Nobody was giving me condescending looks. No, Darla was helping a customer, Brooke was asking Nico about the summer menu at the Peninsula, and Paulo thought it would be a great idea to try finger-painting with Matty. Red, blue, and yellow. I only hoped Nico had a good stain remover in the laundry room.

Darla studied my drawing with a critical eye. "It might take me a week or two because my evenings are a little busy right now."

"She's totally sexting with Alex," Paulo said in a mock whisper.

"You have a dirty mind, hun. I'm actually visiting with a

friend in Roseburg. She just had surgery, and she's not getting around so well as she usually does."

Darla seemed like a real sweetheart. "I'd appreciate any help you can give."

"Are you free on Monday?" Brooke asked. "A group of us are going out to Applejack's for dinner."

Nico groaned. "Let me guess: you, Addy, Romi, Blue, Brie, and possibly Sara?"

"Not Sara—she has a new boyfriend—and Brie isn't sure whether she'll be back from Valetia in time."

"It'll be carnage," he warned me. "But I can drive you there and pick you up."

My heart leapt. Years had passed since I'd been on a girls' night out, but I had a son now.

"What about Matty?"

"We offer a babysitting service at the Peninsula. One of the ladies can come to the house, and I'll be there to keep an eye on them."

Those damn tears threatened again. Not only had Nico spent more time with Matty in two days than Cesare had spent in two months, but now he was also offering to supervise so I could have a night out?

"I think...I think Monday might be a bit soon."

Brooke wasn't to be deterred. "Okay, then how about the two of you come over to our place next Saturday? There's a basketball game on—the details aren't my strong point, but it's a great excuse for a get-together. Everyone's bringing a plate, and Matthew's welcome too. If he gets tired, he can sleep in a guest room until it's time to leave."

I looked to Nico, but he shrugged. "It's your decision."

Cesare wouldn't be looking for me in Brooke's home, would he? And Matty needed to get out and see the world. We'd both missed so much.

"I'd love to come."

31

NICO

"Nico?"

"*Da, zolottse*?" Barely awake, he answered in his mother tongue out of habit. "What's wrong?"

"There are sirens."

"Sirens?" The covers slipped down to his waist as he sat up in bed. "An alarm?"

He strained his ears, but all he could hear was the waves breaking against the shore. The sound lulled him to sleep every night, a sedative, and it was one of the reasons he'd decided to build a hotel here. Back in Russia, he'd been restless in bed, but now he slept like the dead.

"More like the police. I've heard them go past three times, and I thought... I don't know what I thought. Cesare couldn't have found me so fast, could he? I wouldn't put it past him to wreak havoc as a distraction. One time when he torched a building that belonged to a guy who'd upset him in some way, he staged a car crash to block the street so the fire trucks couldn't get through."

Now Nico heard a siren too. Not close, but definitely in Baldwin's Shore and heading north away from Main Street, which ruled out an incident at one of the two bars. Baldwin's Shore was a sleepy little town, or at least, it had been until a year ago. Since then, Brooke had been plagued by a stalker, Brie had brought her own drama, and two members of the Baldwin family had gone to prison. Yes, *those* Baldwins. Their estate lay to the north, but there were only five of them left, and three of them seemed relatively normal. Could the twins be causing trouble again? There was a reason Nico had banned Kayleigh and Lillian from the Peninsula.

"Let me make a couple of calls."

Without thinking things through, he rolled out of bed, lifting his phone off the nightstand and turning on the light as he went. He only realised there was a problem when he saw Kaylin's face. The shock.

"What—" He glanced down. Oh. *Blyat.* "If you just... Uh, let me put on a pair of pants."

Mental note: sleeping naked wasn't the best idea when you had a female houseguest. Kaylin spun around, and at first, he thought she was crying, which wasn't ideal. But...hold on...

"Are you...laughing?"

"Sorry. Shit, I'm sorry."

"What's so funny about my dick?"

"Nothing! I swear, there's nothing funny about it."

"Then why are you giggling?"

None of his exes had voiced any complaints. One brunette, a woman who'd had a strange fondness for historical re-enactments, had even nicknamed it "broadsword."

"No reason, it's just that when you looked down..." She snorted, then clapped a hand over her mouth. "Your expression when you saw it swinging there in the breeze."

"What breeze?"

"Uh, that was a figure of speech. Do you have pants on now?"

"Give me a second."

Nico grabbed a pair of sweatpants from his walk-in closet and pulled them on. Kaylin was still facing the window, and although she was silent now, her shoulders were shaking. She, of course, had clothes on. A T-shirt and... Hold on a moment.

"Are you wearing my boxers?"

Oh, now she stopped laughing, and when she turned, her cheeks were quite pink.

"Uh, maybe? I forgot to buy sleepwear, and they're comfortable, and... I'll launder them in the morning."

"Keep them." It came out as a growl, and Nico realised that he really fucking liked seeing Kaylin in his clothes. And also in his bedroom. Damn, he was an asshole. "Let me make those calls."

Luca wasn't answering, but Colt picked up for long enough to tell Nico there had been a shooting at The Lookout, that the situation was still unfolding, and to stay inside. So, it *was* about the Baldwins again, but that didn't stop Nico from unclipping the hastily installed child-safety lock on his nightstand drawer, removing the semi-automatic that lay inside, and tucking it into his waistband.

"You have a gun?" Kaylin asked, her eyes wide.

"Old habits die hard."

"What's going on?"

"There's been a shooting. On the edge of town, not close by, but we need to stay inside and stay alert."

"You think it could be Cesare?"

"I doubt it. It's far more likely to be a local disagreement— the family in question has been somewhat volatile lately. Why don't we make coffee, order something sweet from room service, and wait to see what develops? Don't forget we have twenty-four-hour security here."

Finally, Kaylin nodded. "Okay."

One more siren sped past while Nico was making lattes, and a waiter brought over a selection of petite fours, nothing heavy seeing as it was past midnight. And after the caffeine kicked in, Nico realised that Kaylin had divulged a rather interesting snippet of information earlier.

"You said that Cesare blocked off a street with a deliberate accident?"

Which was something of an oxymoron, when Nico thought about it.

"He was a psycho. You don't need to tell me that."

"Do you know the specifics? The building in question, the date, the people involved?"

"Some of it? It happened over a year ago, and he did so many bad things that I can't remember the exact date. Why? Does it matter?"

"It might. Emmy's team is still quietly investigating the Manassas incident, but if they can't find enough evidence to prove your innocence, she mentioned making a deal with the authorities—information in exchange for immunity."

"I...uh..." Kaylin lost focus, and her gaze wandered downward. "Uh, could you put a shirt on? Your chest is distracting."

Distracting? What was that supposed to mean? Nico obliged and tugged on a plain white T-shirt, and he decided to take the comment as a compliment.

Distracting.

Kaylin had begun pacing now. "I know things. Of course I know things. Cesare had a phone voice, and that voice was *loud*. I could hear him talking in his office, even if the door was closed. And he used to invite his brothers over to watch baseball, and his cousins, and his friends, and I was meant to keep Matty quiet and serve chips and beer and stay out of the way. And they talked too. More like bragged, really. *You shoulda been there—when Eddie Locatelli's head hit the sidewalk, it cracked like a fuckin' egg.* But if I took a deal, then wouldn't that mean admitting guilt? I didn't run that officer down."

"I know you didn't, *zolottse*. But knowing it and proving it are two different beasts."

"And if I spoke to the police, or the FBI, or whoever, that would mean coming out of hiding. If things went wrong, then I'd end up in jail. Or worse, Cesare's men could get to me. He owns cops, Nico. High-up cops."

Nico caught her hand as she passed. "Don't be upset. It was only an idea."

"I hate it. I just want to live quietly under the radar and hope they forget me."

The chances of that happening were slim, in Nico's opinion. About as likely as finding the evidence that proved her innocence. Forgetting Kaylin La Rocca was impossible, but he wasn't dumb enough to say so.

"Then we'll focus on building your new life. You just need to decide what you want the future to look like, okay?"

"Okay."

She wrapped her arms around him and laid her head against his shoulder, and heaven help him, but he wanted that new life to be right here in Baldwin's Shore.

"Do I look okay?" Kaylin asked.

"You look perfect."

It was no lie. They'd made another trip to Coquille yesterday, and Kaylin had added to her wardrobe. Tonight, she'd picked out dark blue jeans, fur-lined boots, a tight pale-pink top, and a chunky cardigan. It wasn't the kind of outfit she'd worn in New York, but she seemed more comfortable in it.

"How long will it take to get to Brooke's place?"

"Ten minutes? Possibly fifteen?"

Dinner was going ahead, despite the dramas of the past week, which thankfully hadn't been anything to do with Kaylin. An unfortunate fool had tried to break into The Lookout, and it hadn't ended well for him. So far, his motives were unclear, but rumour said he was a stranger in town, probably an addict looking to steal money for a fix. If Nico found a moment to have a quiet chat with Colt or Luca tonight, he could learn more.

But the priority was making sure Kaylin—Katy, he had to remember to call her Katy—had a good time. She'd been quiet this week, content to walk Cricket on the beach in the mornings and then hang out at the house with Matty, plus indulge in the occasional spa treatment while the boy was sleeping. That she trusted Nico to watch her son during those times meant a lot.

"Is it weird that I'm nervous?" she asked.

"Not at all."

"Can you put Matty's bag in the car?"

"Already done."

"And the cake?"

"It's in the back seat."

Brooke and Luca lived on the second floor of a former car dealership, a vast industrial-looking building that Brooke's brother, Aaron, had picked up for a song. Aaron lived with his girlfriend, Romi, on the first floor, and the dinner-slash-party was being held in his apartment because it had more space. It wasn't a formal affair. People could drop in and out as they chose, and Darla was leaving as they arrived.

"Oh, excuse me, hun. I just came to drop off a few snacks, but I can't stay. How are you getting on with the cross-stitch?"

Kaylin's hold on Nico's arm loosened infinitesimally. He was carrying the cake in his other hand while Kaylin kept a firm grasp on Matty to stop him from running somewhere he shouldn't. The boy was surprisingly fast for someone with such short legs.

"I've finished A and B and started on D. It's really relaxing."

"The C should be here early next week. The supplier dispatched it yesterday." A whoop came from inside, and Darla glanced behind her. "Paulo's already started on the daiquiris. If he gets too loud, don't be afraid to tell him to quiet down."

Inside, dishes of food were laid out on the kitchen counter along with plates, napkins, and cutlery, and everyone was helping themselves. Kaylin added her strawberries-and-cream cake to the mix while Nico braced as half a dozen women made a beeline in their direction. But for once, they weren't interested in flirting.

In fact, they weren't interested in him at all.

"Aw, so this is Matthew?" Addy cooed. She'd been Brooke's best friend since their school days, a whirlwind to Brooke's quiet calm. "Isn't he the cutest?"

Matty looked more scared than anything else, and he hung onto Kaylin's leg in a death grip.

"He's not used to big groups," she explained.

Colt's eight-year-old daughter elbowed her way to the front. "Hi, I'm Kiki. Do you want ice cream?"

Matty hesitated for a moment, then nodded. He and Kaylin were quickly swallowed up by the crowd, and Nico found himself standing alone for the first time in a week. But not for long.

"Relax, buddy," Luca said. "They'll look after your girl. Want a beer?"

"A beer sounds good, but Katy isn't my girl."

Luca's expression said "yeah, right," but he popped the cap on a bottle of beer and handed it over.

"So, how'd the two of you meet?"

It was always easier to stick close to the truth. "Her mother had an affair with my father."

Luca searched Nico's face, presumably looking for a sign that he was joking but eventually coming to the conclusion that he wasn't.

"That's...different."

"Dear old Dad didn't make much effort to hide his indiscretions. Katy and I stayed in touch, and she knew I'd always offer her a place to stay if she needed one."

"So you're just playing the overprotective friend while she gets back on her feet?"

"That's right. She's quite jumpy at the moment."

"Brooke said her last relationship didn't end well?"

"The douche belongs in a dumpster. Speaking of ending well, did you resolve the situation at The Lookout earlier in the week? Baldwin's Shore seems to be attracting a disproportionate amount of trouble for such a small town. It's not good for business."

"Understood. And the situation is...partially resolved."

"Oh?"

Luca glanced around, and when he started the story, Nico was glad Luca had checked the women were out of earshot. Sara Baldwin—quiet, mousy Sara Baldwin—had apparently made a dangerous enemy, and her circumstances weren't entirely dissimilar from Kaylin's. A powerful man against a young woman. Evidence that could go either way in court. A future curtailed because she'd always be looking over her shoulder. It was also clear that Luca hoped the Bad Samaritan would step in and make things right, although he didn't say as much in words.

Which left Nico with a dilemma.

This wasn't the first time Luca had hinted about vigilante justice. It had been mentioned during the last Baldwin debacle. The Bad Samaritan *had* gotten involved, which meant one of two things: either the Bad Samaritan was Deck, Luca's other suspect for the role, or the Bad Samaritan was half-psychic and had acted of his own accord.

Two things were clear in Nico's mind—firstly, the men terrorising Sara had to pay for their sins, and secondly, he wasn't the man for the job. A simple bullet to the head, and maybe he could handle it, but this plan would require someone with significantly more experience in liquidations than he'd managed to gain.

Which meant he had a phone call to make when he got home.

But for now, he just smiled and nodded. "It's a tricky problem. Let's hope it resolves itself, but in the meantime, do you have another beer?"

"Game's about to start," Aaron yelled.

Luca took two bottles of Bud out of the refrigerator and handed one over.

"Yeah, let's hope."

"How's Kaylin doing?" Emmy asked.

"She's sleeping."

And tipsy too. She'd probably had one more drink than she should have, but Nico had been glad to see her laughing tonight. Between the two of them, they'd gotten Matty into bed, and Nico had judged it to be too late to speak with Emmy Black, so he'd sent a message instead. Seemed she suffered from insomnia because she'd called two minutes later.

"Lucky her."

"You couldn't sleep?"

A pause. "I get nightmares sometimes." Barking sounded

in the background. "Excuse the dogs; we're playing football. Soccer over here, I guess. Anyhow, I take it this isn't a social call?"

"So perceptive, Mrs. Black."

"Problems with Cesare? He's been trying to find Kaylin. Calling in favours left, right, and centre, by all accounts, but so far, he's been focusing on New York and Virginia."

"It's not Cesare. No, there's a different issue." Nico laid out the story Luca had told, including the hints he'd dropped about possible action and the fact that Decker Langdon was also a candidate for the role of Bad Samaritan. "I feel that Sara deserves a future as much as Kaylin does, but if Deck isn't the Bad Samaritan, I have no way of passing the message to the intended recipient."

"What do you think? Is it Deck?"

"Honestly? I don't know. I was hoping for some advice. Either that or... What are the chances of you unmasking the Bad Samaritan? I'd pay you for the work, of course."

"I'll level with you—I'm not taking that job. If the Bad Samaritan's hanging out in a place like Baldwin's Shore, it's probably because they want to enjoy their retirement. Do you have a picture of Deck? I'd be interested to see one, just for my own curiosity."

"I don't have one, but I could get one."

Nico had first met Deck when he enquired about selling his sculptures in the Peninsula's boutique, which had been a no-brainer because he was a talented artist. But he also worked locally as a carpenter. If Matty was going to be around for a while—and Nico sincerely hoped that would be the case— then the temporary fence around Nico's private pool would need to be replaced with a more permanent construction. If Deck was interested in taking the job, then Nico could invite him over to measure up.

"Cheers," Emmy said. Then, "Do you believe in fate?"

Wasn't it a little late for a philosophical discussion?

"It's not something I've given a lot of consideration. How about you? Do *you* believe in fate?"

"I think there are things we don't yet understand about the world. But don't worry your handsome little head about the Bad Samaritan—a hundred bucks says that justice will be done."

"I'm not sure I should take that bet."

"Oh, go on. I like winning."

Nico had heard enough about the Bad Samaritan's handiwork to suspect that Emmy would indeed win. And if she did, it would be the best hundred bucks he'd ever spent.

"Why don't I just send you the money right now?"

"That would also be acceptable. Did you mention the possibility of an immunity deal to Kaylin? I'm meeting with a pair of FBI agents about another matter tomorrow—yawn—and I could start feeling them out."

"She isn't keen on the idea of admitting guilt for something she didn't do."

"Yeah, I can understand that. We've got a few possibilities for the missing guests at the Bluebird Inn, but we're having to track them down one by one. Some travel will be involved."

"The cost doesn't matter."

"Then we'll keep digging."

"I hope you manage to get some sleep, Mrs. Black."

"And I hope Kaylin and Sara find the peace they deserve."

32

DASHA

"Can you talk?" Emmy asked, and I instantly regretted answering the phone.

Le sigh.

I dumped another bundle of cedar shingles on the scaffold platform and glanced at the treeline. If I got one more row finished before dark, I planned to go for a ride on my new motorcycle, which meant I didn't have time to shoot the breeze with the British bitch.

"What do you want? Is there an issue with the La Rocca girl? She seems to be getting cosy with Belinsky."

"I thought she might be. Do you see much of them?"

"I've run into them a couple of times. Could you send me a tracker? One of the small ones that uses kinetic energy to recharge."

"Dare I ask why?"

"I need it for a craft project."

Emmy just laughed. "I'll see what I can do. And I'm actually calling to dish the dirt on Sara Baldwin."

Okay, that was vaguely interesting. And also irritating. If anyone had dirt on a resident of Baldwin's Shore, it should be me. This was my home, and if I hadn't spent every spare moment for the last two weeks replacing the ancient roof on my cabin, then I'd be the one with the gossip. Not that I gossiped. I preferred to hold my cards close to my chest.

"Tell me."

There had been a shooting last week, but for once, I hadn't pulled the trigger. And I liked Sara. When I used to work for the Baldwins, she was the only one of the kids with a heart. I might not have one myself, but I was capable of recognising the trait in others.

Emmy detailed the events that had unfolded over the past week, and even as the sun dropped, I found myself more interested in the details than in firing nails into the roof and pretending it was my former mentor's genitals. The man had ceased breathing several years ago, but hate never died.

"I might have guessed a politician was involved," I said. "Nobody enters a life of public service to serve the public. They only serve themselves."

"Are you interested in playing the Bad Samaritan again?"

"I'll do some groundwork. See what's possible."

"If you need resources, let me know. I don't much like politicians either. One or two of them are okay, but Congress is ninety-five percent cuntwaffles."

For years, all I'd wanted to do was work alone, but now I understood the difference between a competent team and a good team. My former colleagues had been competent, but half of them had suffered from severe personality defects. Emmy's team was...better.

"Can you get the file from the investigation in question? Details always help." Although I did have a certain amount of inside information in this instance, thanks to my former employer—an old man who loved to talk—and an idea was already forming at the back of my mind. A way to kill two birds with one stone by leveraging one culprit's guilt to frame another…

"No problem."

"And I'll need to build up a picture of the targets' lives. Their regular movements."

"We can cover the Virginia end. Incidentally, you might want to watch your back in Baldwin's Shore. There's another allegedly retired operator in town."

"Decker Langdon?"

"Right." She seemed disappointed that I was already aware. "I suppose I shouldn't be surprised that you know."

"I see it in him."

"He's ex-Delta. Had a disagreement with a commanding officer and went AWOL. Would've been court-martialled, but they couldn't find him."

I wasn't sure how I felt about that. Desertion was unprofessional, the worst crime for a soldier, sailor, or airman, but those who lived in glass houses shouldn't throw stones. It was only thanks to my untimely "death" that I had a cosy little cottage on Valley Drive and my hideaway cabin in the forest. If I'd stayed, I'd most likely have joined my mentor in hell by now.

"What were the circumstances?"

"I'm still looking into that. Everything's buried deep. I only know his name and the basics because one of my circle recognised his photo."

I wasn't about to ask where she'd obtained the picture. Deck didn't use social media, I knew that much.

"I'll watch my back."

"How's the new motorbike?"

"Fun. And it would be more fun if you'd get off the phone so I could ride it."

"Hint taken. Enjoy scaring the local wildlife."

"Enjoy eating junk food and driving your husband insane."

"Thanks, honey. See you soon."

"Whatever."

I shoved the phone back into my pocket and picked up my nail gun. Emmy was an acquired taste, that was for sure, but I didn't find her as unpalatable as I once had. Plus she'd brought Alex into my life and ensured he could stay there, which meant I was in her debt, even if I'd never admit as much.

For now, I had to focus on the Sara Baldwin conundrum. Taking out a politician was nothing new for me, but these things always took planning, patience, and a certain amount of creativity.

The Bad Samaritan had another game to play.

33

KAYLIN

*T*his isn't a date.
   This isn't a date.
So why did it feel like a date?

We were in a Mexican restaurant in North Bend, La Cantina, just Nico and me. I'd agonised all day over whether to leave Matty behind, but the babysitter Nico arranged had set my mind at ease. Meli Snyder was one of Colt's neighbours, or at least, she had been until he built a huge new house with Brie. I hadn't been there yet, but Colt said they'd have a housewarming party as soon as they got furniture. Anyhow, Meli used to care for Kiki while Colt was at work, and he trusted her completely, plus she'd worked for Nico for over a year, one of five or six certified babysitters who offered their services on an ad hoc basis. The Peninsula catered mainly to adults—couples, corporate clients, and groups—so there wasn't a dedicated kids' club. For extra insurance, Nico had asked Emmy to run a background check, and she'd concurred with Colt. Meli was a safe person to leave my son with.

Just for one evening a week, just a few hours. I still felt guilty for going out and enjoying myself, but for so long, I'd existed only as a mother and an accessory. Now I was a woman too. A friend. A part of the community.

A friend.

Sometimes, the way Nico looked at me felt anything but platonic. Did he feel it too? The spark? That day in New York, I'd tried to deny it, but it was getting harder and harder to do so. But I had to stay strong. Without Nico, I'd be up shit creek again, so if he said we were friends, then that's all we were.

Perhaps the rush I felt was just a natural reaction to the many years I'd spent starved of affection? A rebound? Until Charlotte met Jenson, she'd pinballed from man to man, rebounds of rebounds of rebounds. Yes, that must be it. These feelings were perfectly normal. All I had to do was resist them until they went away. But damn, Nico was handsome when he smiled.

"Do I have something on my face?" he asked.

And I was staring. Crap.

"Sorry, I was miles away. What's good here?"

"Everything, but you won't beat the tacos."

"Okay, great! I'll have those."

"What do you want to drink? A margarita?"

"Sure, why not?"

"He'll be okay, I promise," Nico said, and thankfully he interpreted the mixed-up mess in my head as mom nerves. "Meli won't mind if you call for an update."

"Maybe I could text her?"

"That's a good compromise."

A perky waitress sashayed over as I typed out a message. I couldn't honestly blame her for fawning over Nico, even if it made me want to poke her eyes out.

"What can I get you folks?" she asked. "We have a Wednesday special—free nachos with a pitcher of margaritas."

"Sure, we can start with that, and then we'll have two orders of the beef tacos," Nico said.

A pitcher of margaritas? Thank goodness neither one of us was driving.

"Could we get a bowl of churros too?"

"Sure, ma'am."

Nico didn't watch her ass as she walked away, which was a refreshing change from what I was used to. Cesare had suffered from wandering eyes, probably wandering hands and a wandering cock too. At first, it had bothered me, but later, I'd learned to be grateful because if he was screwing some other poor fool, then at least he wasn't screwing me. I closed my eyes, thinking once more about the consequences, namely adding "get checked for STDs" to my to-do list. I hadn't had any symptoms, but...

"You okay, *zolottse*?"

"Just thinking about the future."

"And?"

"I need to do things right this time. When I was younger, I had so many plans. I wanted to be rich and famous. I wanted to see the world. But now I'm thinking that the simple life might not be so bad after all. That it might be better to put down roots and have one place to call home."

"Do you have anywhere in mind?"

"Maybe Oregon? Everyone in Baldwin's Shore has been so kind, although I'm not going to lie—the shooting the other night shook me up."

"Steer clear of the Baldwin family, and you'll be fine."

"I hope so. Brooke asked if I wanted to go hiking with her and her dog someday, an easy trail so I can take Matty, and Addy offered to help with Cricket."

Vega, Brooke's German shepherd pit bull mix, certainly looked intimidating, even if he was more likely to lick a bad guy than bite a person. I'd met him at Saturday's party, along with Romi's pug, Chunky Monkey. Romi said she might join us, but Monkey couldn't go hiking because his short nose and flat face meant strenuous exercise disagreed with him.

"You should go," Nico said. "The trails to the east of town are meant to be very scenic."

"Meant to be? You haven't hiked them yourself?"

"I'm guilty of spending more time in the gym than outside. Maybe we both need to make some changes to our lifestyle?"

"What made you move to Baldwin's Shore?"

"I never intended to stay here. But I accepted the land at the Peninsula as payment for a debt, and when I visited, I thought it would make a good spot for a hotel, although not all of the locals agreed with me. And the longer I spent there, the more comfortable I became. It seemed right to make it my main home."

"You have others?"

"I have an apartment and a hotel in London. Plus other hotels in Paris, Dubrovnik, and New York."

"Nowhere in Russia?"

"I lease my father's estate to a charity for a few roubles a year. They use it as a refuge for the homeless, so hopefully someone will have good memories of the place. Plus Daddy dearest will be turning in his grave at the thought of poor people using his pool and tennis court, which is another win."

Just when I thought I couldn't love this man any more... Love? Did I love Nico? Yes, I guess I did. It had started as a sisterly love with perhaps a little hero worship because teenage Nico had been like a demigod to childhood me. In New York, I'd felt the first flickers of heat between us, and I'd been... shocked. Shocked that the man I'd thought of as a brother stirred up those forbidden feelings. Now? Now, I still loved him, as a friend and...maybe more.

And I had no idea what to do about that.

"Do you ever go back to Moscow?" I asked.

"Not if I can help it. I've been a handful of times in the past decade. Occasionally, I have dinner with my godfather if we happen to be in London at the same time, but I don't go out of my way to keep up with old acquaintances."

"Baldwin's Shore has a nice feel about it. My grandma's neighbourhood in Virginia was real insular. They weren't fond of outsiders, and even though my mom grew up there, I never felt entirely welcome."

"There's a permanent population in Baldwin's Shore, and some families—like the Baldwins—have been there for generations, but a lot of people come and go. Plus tourists pass through depending on the season."

"What are the schools in the area like?"

"Truthfully, I have no idea. It's not something I've ever needed to worry about, but we can find out."

"You've never wanted children?"

"I've never *not* wanted kids, but in order to consider fatherhood, I'd need to meet the right woman. And that's proven difficult."

"Dating is a minefield." Although I'd managed to step on a freaking nuke, hadn't I? "Even before I met Cesare, my attempts to find The One were just one disaster after another."

"If it's any consolation, a Spanish model threw a shrimp salad over me in one of the most exclusive restaurants in Miami."

"Are you serious?"

"Apparently, when a woman asks if you like her hair, the answer is always 'yes,' even if she reminds you of a Shetland pony. It turned out the photographer on that day's shoot liked volume."

"Do you know trolls? Those toys with the bright-coloured hair that sticks straight up?"

"Tell me you didn't..."

"The stylist promised it was temporary. I had to work an event with bubblegum-pink hair, and my boss was *not* amused."

"I dated a hairstylist once. When I told her I didn't think we were compatible, she replaced my shampoo with bleach."

Oh my gosh.

"You went blond?"

"I went ginger."

The server arrived with drinks and nachos, and I made a respectable dent in my margarita as I imagined Nico as a redhead. Nope...tall, orange, and handsome didn't have quite the same ring to it.

"Are there pictures?"

"I sincerely hope not."

"One time, I matched with a guy who said he was six feet, and when I got to the bar, he was barely five-seven and ditched me for being too tall."

"My last girlfriend wanted me to wear lifts in my shoes."

"But you actually are six feet tall? Was she a basketball player?"

"She was six feet one when she wore her favourite stilettos, and she said it was weird looking down at me. She also wanted a cat, so I bought her a cat. Then she decided she didn't like cats and told me to take it to the shelter."

Was that Snezhinka? Nico treated her like a queen.

"Let me guess—you kept the cat?"

"Snezh's claws aren't as sharp as my ex's."

"I would have gladly swapped Cesare for a cat. Or a spider, or a scorpion, or even a bedbug. Do you think..." I drained the glass and picked up a nacho. "Do you think we could mail Cesare a package of bedbugs?"

Let him see what it was like to share a bed with an unwelcome predator for once.

"Where would we get the bedbugs? The Peninsula isn't that kind of establishment."

"Is the Bluebird Inn still open? I itched for weeks after I stayed there."

"It is." Nico screwed up his face in distaste. "I hear it hasn't improved."

"So, whaddya think? You, me, a couple of hazmat suits...?"

"Unfortunately, I have to fly to LA the day after tomorrow."

"Anything to get out of manual labour."

He reached across the table and took my hand. "No, really. It's only for a few days, and the team at the Peninsula will take care of you."

"I..." Until that moment, I'd been having fun. Nico was so easy to talk to. But the thought of him abandoning me, even though I knew he had to work, even though logic said I'd be safe... I hated it. "It's okay. We'll be fine."

"Will you?"

"Sure, sure. We'll stay inside."

"You can come with me if you'd prefer. I just wasn't sure you'd want to travel with Matty."

"Uh... I don't want to be a burden."

"You could never be a burden. Look, I have three meetings to attend and there's a party I need to show my face at. The remainder of the time, I'm yours."

"How would we get there?"

"I'll charter a jet. Nobody's going to ask questions." He gave my hand a gentle squeeze, and a shiver ran through me. A good shiver. A dangerous shiver. "I'd like you to come, but the days of a man making decisions on your behalf are done. The ball's in your court."

When he put it that way, there was only one decision I could make.

"I'll come to LA."

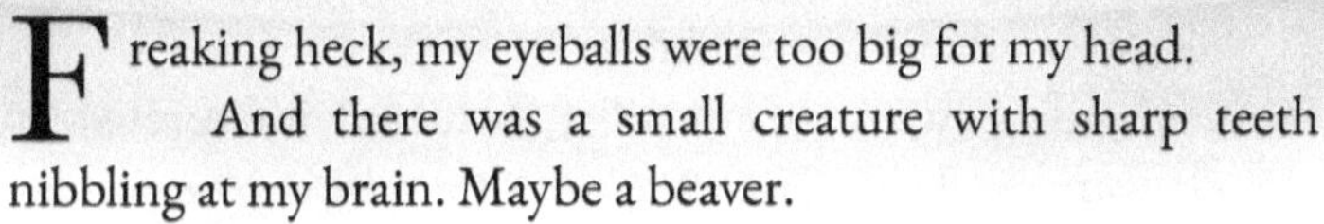

34

———

KAYLIN

Freaking heck, my eyeballs were too big for my head.

And there was a small creature with sharp teeth nibbling at my brain. Maybe a beaver.

I tried lifting an eyelid and quickly rethought the decision. So much sun. So bright.

What was wrong with me?

Try as I might, I couldn't remember a thing after the second pitcher of margaritas. Cesare had always told me I was a lightweight, and you know what? He was right. But only about that one tiny thing. The rest of the time he was so, so wrong.

What time was it? I stared at my watch until the hands came into focus, which took longer than it should have. Holy crap! It was nearly nine o'clock. *Matty.* I had to go see to Matty. He never slept past seven thirty, and his potty training was still hit-and-miss, mainly because Cesare kept yelling every time he had an accident, which only made the situation worse. I rolled out of bed and realised I was still wearing yesterday's clothes, but someone had taken off my socks and shoes. Nico? Had Nico put me to bed?

I ran into the third-bedroom-slash-nursery, but the bed was empty. That was the moment panic hit. Where was Matty? Where was my son? Heart hammering, I ran into the hallway with worst-case scenarios making my headache even worse. Had he climbed out of bed and fallen somewhere? Gotten lost within the hotel grounds? What if Cesare had—

"Mama!"

I stopped short. Matty was sitting on his booster seat at the kitchen counter, wearing a pair of bib overalls and a faceful of chocolate spread. Nico was also wearing chocolate, but it was on his T-shirt, and when I didn't come over right away, Matty threw a square of toast in my direction.

"Shit." Nico's eyes widened. "I mean darn. Matty, you shouldn't throw food at your mom."

"You...you made him breakfast?"

"He said he wanted 'nut seller,' which I interpreted as Nutella, but we don't have that, so I found a recipe on the internet and got the kitchen to whip up a batch. They had plenty of hazelnuts for the praline in the Paris-Brest."

"But...you got him dressed?"

"That was an interesting challenge. And yes, he's used the bathroom."

"How did you know what to do?"

"I've been watching you for the past two weeks. I'm sure I've done something wrong, but I managed to keep him alive." Nico raised an eyebrow, expectant.

"Uh, he usually wears a shirt with the overalls."

"Well, I guess that's one less thing to wash chocolate out of. How's your head?"

"Sore. How much did I have to drink?"

"Not an excessive amount, but one minute you were giggling, and the next..." He mimed his head hitting the counter. "Lights out."

"Sorry, I'm so sorry."

"For what? Enjoying yourself a little too much on a night out?"

"For being irresponsible."

"Irresponsible would have been leaving Matty home alone while you drank the bar dry and then attempted to drive back. But you engaged a fully vetted babysitter, you made sure a driver was on standby, and you have a *highly* competent roommate who's almost capable of dressing a toddler."

"Highly competent and modest. Don't forget modest."

"When the shoe fits." Nico stood and took a bow. "I'll get you some Tylenol. Are you up to taking over? I could do with attending the operations meeting at nine."

"Of course."

"What else do you need to do today? One of the staff will bring suitcases so you can pack for the trip."

What trip? I screwed my eyes shut, trying desperately to remember.

"We're going to LA," Nico prompted.

"Right."

"It's not too late to back out."

Give up a weekend in California with Nico? No way.

"Matty and I are coming." He always wailed when his ears popped on the plane, but I had a feeling that Nico would be a lot more understanding about his distress than Cesare had been. "Darla messaged to say that she's finished Matty's snail, and the C from the cross-stitch alphabet is in too."

"We can pick those up this afternoon."

"Everything okay?" Nico asked.

I eyed up the sleek white jet sitting on the tarmac. A porter had taken our bags to load, and I just had Matty to carry.

Cricket was back at the Peninsula, being spoiled by Leona the yoga teacher, who'd agreed to dogsit over the weekend. Cricket adored her.

"When I was a teenager living in Virginia, I used to dream about flying on a private jet. I thought it would be a sign I'd made it, you know? But Cesare used to fly private, and that kind of took the shine off things."

"Did you travel with him often?"

"His family has a compound in the Bahamas." Three villas on the beach, and since Vito wasn't a fan of the cold, the whole clan used to head there every Christmas. "Our first trip was to Europe though, and I was terrified of being arrested at the airport. I was literally shaking. But you're right—if you're rich enough, nobody pays much attention to the paperwork."

"Whereabouts in Europe?"

"Sicily. Cesare has family there, and since his great-grandma was about a hundred years old and couldn't travel, he decided that was where we'd get married."

He hadn't asked me; he'd told me. I'd spent the whole journey hoping the plane would crash.

"We wondered where the ceremony took place. Emmy couldn't find any record in the US."

"I was six months pregnant, still puking my guts up every day, and Cesare's great-grandma called me a dirty whore for having sex out of wedlock."

"Did Cesare take his share of the blame?"

I snorted. "Of course not. But Great-Grandma Lucrezia choked on an olive at the reception, so I suppose there was an element of poetic justice. We had to stay an extra week for the funeral."

"The more I hear about the Cavallaro family, the more they make mine seem almost normal."

"In your research, did you come across Cesare's cousin Aldo?"

"The name doesn't ring a bell."

"Probably because Cesare likes to pretend Aldo doesn't exist. I mean, he's so dumb that he managed to run over his own leg in a strip club parking lot. And two years ago, he decided to get some of those indoor fireworks to celebrate the Fourth of July and set fire to his apartment. Except he couldn't even get the date right, and it was the third of July."

"I hate to say it, but I can understand where Cesare's coming from."

"Me too. And last summer, Aldo broke into a hospital and assaulted his ex-girlfriend's new husband in the delivery room. Cesare wanted to leave him in jail, but Vito bailed him out."

"Seems jealousy runs in the family."

"It does. The Cavallaros are a genetic nightmare. I only hope Matty doesn't grow up to be like his father."

At least he stood a chance of a normal life now, or as normal as it could be with Nico Belinsky involved. Not every toddler got to ride on a private jet. Matty was fascinated by airplanes, and he'd barely said a word since we arrived in the VIP area. No, he was too busy staring out the window at the runway. For a moment, I considered buying an apartment near an airport because the peace was glorious, jet engines excepted.

"I didn't turn out like my father," Nico said softly.

"You're a hundred times the man he was."

A hostess walked over, all smiles. "Sir, ma'am, are you ready to board?"

Nico touched a hand to the small of my back, and I fought to keep from melting.

"I'm ready."

"Not Shelley!"

Matty was usually well-behaved, for a toddler anyway, but on the rare occasions he acted out, those meltdowns were spectacular. And today, he'd decided that forty thousand feet in the air was the perfect place to throw a tantrum.

Not-Shelley flew across the jet and bounced off the flight attendant's shoulder. She was an older lady, not one of the young bimbos Cesare had favoured. We'd both known he hadn't hired them for their safety skills.

The flight attendant scooped up the snail and offered it back, but Matty shook his head.

"Want Shelley."

"I'm so sorry," I said to the poor lady.

"Ma'am, it's okay. When my son was little, he always used to get cranky on airplanes. It's the pressure changes."

I'd given Matty acetaminophen a half hour before takeoff, but he'd still wailed at the top of his lungs, and so far, he'd hurled several crayons and a package of raisins as well as Not-Shelley. I hadn't dared to get out the tub of Play-Doh. Thank goodness it was only a two-hour flight.

"How long did it take for him to grow out of it?"

"I'd say maybe five or six years. He's eighteen now and getting ready to spend the summer backpacking around Australia."

Nico crouched down in front of Matty and stuck out his tongue, then blew a raspberry. The sight was so unexpected, it made me giggle, and it surprised Matty too. Cesare had never helped. No, he'd just made snide comments about my parenting skills and blocked out the noise with earplugs. Matty paused mid-shriek and studied the man in front of him, more curious than anything else. Then he stuck out his tongue too. Nico puffed his cheeks and pulled on his ears. Matty tried to copy him, but he ended up laughing instead. The breath I'd been holding slowly escaped.

"Looks as if Daddy's got this," the flight attendant

whispered, and I didn't correct her. Nico had said it would invite fewer questions if we let people assume. "Can I get you a glass of wine?"

"Maybe a very small one?"

"I'll be right back."

I settled in the plush leather seat, holding Not-Shelley and feeling guilty that Matty didn't like her as much as Shelley 1.0. Darla had obviously put hours of work into the toy, but it wasn't quite the same. The eyes were bigger, the wool softer.

With Matty occupied, I connected to the in-flight Wi-Fi and checked eBay again, hoping for a miracle. And it seemed that today was my lucky day. There were two listings for Shelley 1.0—one looked a bit grubby in the pictures, but the other was "as new, unwanted gift, my daughter never played with it." I bought the toy in a heartbeat. If Darla asked, I'd tell her that Matty loved Not-Shelley, but we left her at home for safekeeping. A little white lie wouldn't hurt anyone, right?

"Here's your wine, ma'am."

Nico and Matty were colouring now. I took a sip and relaxed for the first time all day.

35

NICO

Hand on heart, Nico hadn't been thrilled at the idea of a child moving into his home. The villa in Baldwin's Shore had been his quiet sanctuary, an escape from all the ills in the world. Kaylin's arrival had upset that balance but, it turned out, in a good way.

Yesterday, he'd sat through an investor presentation, then excused himself to go to Wonder World. Lev Belinsky hadn't been keen on frivolities, so Nico hadn't been allowed to visit amusement parks as a child, and it was surprisingly entertaining. First time on a roller coaster? Check. Dressing up as Prince Pleasant and Princess Peony? Oddly fun. Matty had become Wilbur the Wonder Hound, and now he refused to take the costume off, even to go to bed.

Nico would never have visited Wonder World without the two of them. Ride the spiral slide alone? Suspicious looks. Ride the spiral slide with an almost-three-year-old? Socially acceptable. Dig up "treasure" on Pirate Island without a child? Get arrested. Help Matty to hold the shovel? Three women told him what a good dad he was, and he'd overheard one comment about exploding ovaries.

"Is Matty still asleep?" Nico asked, checking his watch. It was eight a.m.

He'd booked a two-bedroom suite at the Black Diamond Hotel, and of course Emmy Black had known about it. Not only did she ensure he received a discount, but there had been a bottle of champagne on ice in the room when they arrived. And the coffee was excellent.

Kaylin nodded, mug in hand. "You really tired him out yesterday."

"I tired myself out too. How do you do it every day?"

"Caffeine and a lack of other options."

Her words gave him pause. "Do you need more help? Should I find a nanny?"

Did he feel guilty about taking over the care of another man's son? Probably he should have, but it seemed there was a little of the old man in him after all. And Cesare hadn't been a great father. Yes, he'd provided material things, and there was no shortage of money, but the boy hadn't been allowed to interact with anyone outside his own family and the hired help. What life was that for a child?

"No, no, no, I didn't mean... Things are much better now. Cesare never used to lift a finger to help because in the Cavallaro family, childcare is a woman's work. Along with cooking, cleaning up, maintaining her figure, and being charming at parties. At least I only have Matty. Francesco and Bambi have six kids, and she always looks as if she's about to drop."

"Bambi?"

"She was a stripper, but it turned out that's actually her real name."

"I'm surprised you didn't have more children. Cesare struck me as a man who'd want to pass on his genes."

"Oh, he tried." Kaylin's tone froze the blood in Nico's veins. "The doctor said that stress on its own couldn't cause a miscarriage, but every time I got pregnant, I wanted to throw myself off the roof terrace. That couldn't be healthy, right?"

A tear rolled down her cheek, and Nico cursed himself for saying the wrong thing. Fuck. A hug couldn't fix this, but when he wrapped his arms around her, she leaned her cheek against his shoulder.

"I had three miscarriages. Well, one stillbirth at six months. A girl. We named her Cosetta, and giving birth to her was the most horrible thing I've ever done. I was devastated to lose her, but at the same time, I felt...relief. And guilt. Guilt that I felt that way."

Her shoulders shook as she sobbed, and Nico kissed her hair.

"I can't tell you things are okay now because they aren't, but I hate that you went through that." Hated that *he* had put her through it. Cesare. Not for the first time, Nico considered hiring Emmy again. "I'll do everything within my power to ensure you and Matty never have another dark day."

"I wish I'd called you after we had lunch in New York," she mumbled. "Right after, I mean."

"You're not the only one with regrets about that."

"Really? Then why didn't you call?"

What had Kaylin said before about minefields? Nico was on tiptoes now.

"I experienced some feelings that weren't necessarily compatible with our history."

"I see."

"Do you?"

Slowly, Kaylin nodded. "I know what I looked like. Your big head saw a girl you'd treated as a kid sister, and your little head saw the kind of woman you'd pick up at a party."

"That's a succinct way of putting it, yes." She hadn't kicked him in the balls, which he had to view as a good thing. "Does that upset you?"

She choked out a strangled laugh. "How can it? I mean, that's why I didn't call you either. It would've felt weird."

"And now?"

"Now, it's still weird, but I don't care anymore."

Kaylin looked up at him, and their gazes locked as Nico slowly, slowly lowered his head and brushed his lips against hers. The breathy little sigh that escaped her lips made him hard in an instant. Fuck.

Definitely inappropriate.

"Sorry," he whispered.

"Kiss me again."

She didn't wait. Before he could oblige, she stood on her toes and nibbled his bottom lip, which did nothing to help with the dick situation. This was a side of Kaylin he hadn't seen before, and damn, he liked it. Her arms twined around his neck as her lips parted, and suddenly, nothing mattered but her. Kaylin tasted of coffee, and she was definitely keeping him up.

Why hadn't he called her five years ago? Of all the mistakes he'd made in his life, that was the biggest.

"I'll cancel my meeting," he said when they finally broke apart, both breathing hard.

"Don't do that. I have Matty to see to, and my head... Everything's jumbled."

Yes, Nico could identify with that. Although the nature of their relationship had been evolving, he didn't want to rush things, especially after this morning's revelations. And if he stuck around, they were going to end up naked.

"I'll keep it short."

"Okay. Uh, you still have glitter in your hair."

He gave her one last kiss, a chaste one this time. "I'll take a shower before I head out. You want me to skip tonight's party?"

"No, you should go. I don't want to get in the way of your business."

"You could never get in the way. Why don't you come with me?"

"What about Matty?"

"The hotel has a babysitting service, and I know the owner —she wouldn't hire anyone untrustworthy. Plus I could arrange for additional security."

"Like a bodyguard? For Matty?"

"If you want that."

"I don't want to be one of those neurotic moms."

"*Zolottse*, you're not neurotic."

"I just find it hard to trust strangers at the moment. What if Cesare sends someone else to do his dirty work?"

"I'll hire the bodyguard. Do you have something suitable to wear, or should I ask the concierge to send a personal shopper?"

"Where's the party?"

"On a yacht. We'll be there for an hour max—I'm considering investing in a yacht charter company, and I need to understand what the management team is capable of."

"I have swimwear and a coverup."

"Perfect." Nico couldn't resist another kiss. "You're perfect."

"What's up?" Emmy asked.

"Can you supply a bodyguard on a short-term basis?"

"How short-term?"

"One evening. I want to take Kaylin to a party, and she's worried about leaving Matty with a stranger."

"You're staying at my hotel. You know the entire

babysitting team is vetted, right? Vetted, first-aid trained, and loyal."

"I do. But I also know Kaylin's had a difficult time, and if hiring a bodyguard helps her to relax, then I'm going to hire a bodyguard."

"Fucking hell, you've got it bad for this woman, haven't you?"

"Is there a problem with that?"

"No problem. I'm happy for you, dude. And of course I can supply a bodyguard. If you pay me enough money, I can supply a tier-one special forces operator with childcare experience."

"Good. Do it."

"What time do you want him?"

"Six p.m."

"He'll be there. I'll send you a name and a photo by mid-afternoon."

"Any update on Cesare Cavallaro?"

"We're not monitoring him twenty-four-seven anymore, but Friday's report said he was still chasing around Queens. Plus he has a local PI watching Kaylin's grandma, so she might want to hold off contact for a while."

"She hasn't been in touch."

"Any concerning developments at your end?"

"Other than the Sara Baldwin affair? No."

"Well, let me know if you need anything more. Enjoy your date."

Emmy hung up before Nico could correct her. It wasn't a date. Was it? Things were heading in that direction, but he wanted his first date with Kaylin to be special. Cocktails, a fancy dinner, good conversation. Not nibbling on hors d'oeuvres, surrounded by drunk people as smooth-talking businessmen tried to convince him to part with half a million dollars.

There was a market for yacht charters, sure. The three-Fs crowd—if it flies, floats, or fucks, then rent it, don't buy it—would happily drop a small fortune to hire a fully crewed party boat. Nico knew that because once, he'd been a part of that group. But now, he had his own yacht, albeit one he didn't know how to sail, and he was well and truly over hookups. Hell, maybe he should just buy his own plane and be done with it?

Although in light of recent developments, he did plan to cut down on travel. Matty needed stability. A good school. Friends. Unless Kaylin wanted to homeschool him, in which case, Nico would support that decision.

One thing was for sure—he wouldn't be repeating the mistakes of his father.

36

NICO

Kaylin-the-girl had raced around the mansion in Moscow in jeans and sweaters, pigtails flying. Kaylin-the-woman had developed a sense of grace and style, and Nico's heart had flipped when she walked out of her room that evening.

She was right: this was weird, but he didn't care either.

He just wanted her.

Emmy's operator had shown up at the appointed time, a wiry man in his mid-forties with a crooked smile and hard eyes, followed by the babysitter, who reminded Nico of the cheerful grandmas you saw in movies. Matty had been laughing at a cartoon when his mom left.

And now Kaylin was at Nico's side on the upper deck of an eighty-foot super yacht, dressed in a royal-blue high-waisted bikini with a crocheted sundress over the top—an outfit Nico recognised as having come from the boutique at the Peninsula —and a pair of wedge sandals that left her only an inch shorter than him.

This was an exquisite form of torture.

Focus on the numbers. A yacht like this one could be bought for two million on the secondhand market, and the base rate for a charter would be in the region of a hundred thousand a week. Of course, that had to cover the crew's wages, maintenance costs, and fuel, but the profit margin was still reasonable as long as rental voids were kept to a minimum. Which was the biggest gamble—the company didn't have much of a track record, and Nico wasn't convinced by the company's marketing plan, which was heavy on lifestyle influencers and low on networking. But the investment would be backed by assets, and—

Damn, she was beautiful.

Nico slipped an arm around Kaylin's waist and leaned in close.

"Is it time to leave yet?" he asked.

"We've only been here for ten minutes. Have you tried one of these cheese things?"

Who cared about cheese things? Nico had already spoken to the owner of the company, and Carlos Davila hadn't impressed him. Sure, the man said all the right things, but he was too slick. Too charming.

"There's only one thing I want to eat tonight."

When Kaylin's eyes widened, Nico wondered whether he'd pushed too far, but she didn't pull away.

"What about Matty?"

"I can be very quiet."

"I'm not sure I can."

"Okay, we're definitely leaving."

"No, no, wait." She grabbed his arm and dropped her voice to a barely audible whisper. "I...we can't. Not yet. Not because I don't want to, but..."

"What's wrong, *zolottse*?"

"I'm almost sure Cesare cheated on me. I need to get tested before we can...you know."

Well, well, wasn't this a delicate subject? Nico sent silent thanks to Emmy Black and prepared to dance across the minefield once more. Before he spoke, he steered Kaylin to a quiet corner of the top deck. Only a half-dozen people were up there, mainly to take pictures of an admittedly spectacular sunset.

"Emmy's team was very thorough. As of last month, Cesare was clear of STDs."

A gasp. "How on earth did she find that out?"

"I don't know, and I wasn't going to question her methods. All I cared about was results. She also told me who he was cheating with and mentioned that during their last encounter, he used a condom."

"But...how...?"

"The operation was invasive, and I'm sorry for that. I wish there had been another way, but they were assessing every angle in order to get you out of there."

"Who was he cheating with?" Her voice had gone flat. "Tell me."

"Are you sure you want to know?"

"No, but I need to."

"It was Lyndsey."

"Lyndsey? Are you kidding me? She was, like, nineteen."

"When you went to the club on Thursdays, if he wasn't there with you, he was with her."

"I don't freaking believe this. *Lyndsey?*"

"I'm sorry."

"I don't know whether to pity her or hope she rots in hell."

"Cesare was most likely the instigator."

"Oh, I definitely hope *he* rots in hell. She was meant to be caring for my son, and instead, she was screwing my husband?" Kaylin shook her head. "I was a damn fool."

"It's over." Nico planted a soft kiss on her lips. "Done.

Finished. Focus on the future, not the past. I only told you because it's unlikely you have anything to worry about, health-wise."

"Can I have a moment? I need to digest this."

Nico didn't like leaving her alone, but he'd also promised that she made her own decisions now. And it was a promise he intended to keep. He took a step back as Kaylin sank onto a sunlounger.

"I'll be on the main deck. Take all the time you need."

"Nico..." the blonde practically purred. "I wasn't expecting to see you here."

She grabbed his shirt collar with scarlet talons and planted a kiss on his lips, then stood there expectantly. Who was she? There was a reasonable chance he'd slept with her in the dim and distant past, but he couldn't remember her name.

"Yes, it's been a long time. I'm actually here with—"

"You got so boring. Fabian said you opened a hotel in some tinpot town, and you didn't throw a single party."

"Other priorities, I'm afraid. If you'll excuse—"

"Hey, do you remember Miranda?" She waved at a redhead near the DJ. "Miranda! Look who's here."

The blonde grabbed his hand, but before she could drag him somewhere he didn't want to go, an arm snaked around his waist.

"Lost sight of you for a moment, honey." Kaylin laid her other hand on his chest. Possessive. He liked that. "Aren't you going to introduce me to your friend?"

Could be tricky.

Thankfully, the blonde liked the sound of her own voice. "I'm Cheyenne."

Ah, now Nico remembered. Cheyenne no-last-name, big on Instagram. He hadn't slept with her, thank goodness, but not from a lack of effort on her part.

"Katy." Kaylin leaned forward and the women air-kissed, European-style. "Great party."

"Isn't it? Carlos wants me to help with promoting the boat."

"Yacht," Nico said.

"Whatever. Hey, can you take a picture of me by the bar?"

Kaylin managed to refrain from rolling her eyes. "Sure."

"So, what do you do, Katy? You're real pretty. How many followers do you have?"

"Followers?"

"On social media."

"Oh, I don't do social media."

"No way! Not even Insta?"

"I used to work in events, but I'm taking time off to raise our son."

"Your...son?" Cheyenne faltered. "You and Nico?"

"That's right."

"Wow, I didn't realise."

Nico smiled at Kaylin's effortless cover story. "As I said, I have other priorities now."

"Katy, you should totally start a mommy blog. I bet your kid is real photogenic."

"I'll give it some thought."

Cheyenne smiled and pouted her way through a dozen photos, then deleted them all and made Kaylin take more. It was enough to put Nico off investing in anything, but finally, they made their escape.

"Did you get your thoughts in order?" he asked once the driver had pulled into traffic. The privacy screen was securely in place.

"I hope both of them rot in hell." Kaylin twisted sideways

on the seat and bit her lip, slowly, deliberately, in a way that shot straight to Nico's groin. "And I'll keep quiet."

Thank fuck he'd tossed a box of condoms into his luggage. He lifted her so she straddled his rapidly hardening dick and breathed her in. On several levels, this was incredibly wrong, but it felt so damn right.

"You're in control, *zolottse*. I'll follow your lead."

"I want your hands on me. All of me."

"That won't be a problem."

She suddenly stilled. "But...but I don't look like I did in my old modelling shots. I have stretch marks, and—"

He put a finger to her lips. "I have a scar on my hip where I didn't get out of the way fast enough in a knife fight."

"Oh my gosh!"

"I tell people I fell off a bicycle as a child." Nico tucked a lock of hair behind her ear. "How does that make you feel?"

"That you got hurt? I hate it."

"That I have a small physical blemish from my past. Does it change my worth as a man?"

"Of course not."

"And that's how I feel about your stretch marks. Kaylin, you pushed an entire person out of your body, and that makes you Superwoman in my eyes." Ah, fuck. He hadn't brought a handkerchief this evening. "What's wrong? What did I say?"

"N-n-nothing. Everything. Matty was six hours old when Cesare asked the doctor how long I'd have to wait for a vaginoplasty if things didn't, you know, snap back the way they should."

"I always swore I'd never get into another knife fight, but now I'm rethinking that decision."

"Make me forget him, Nico. Fuck every single memory of that man out of me."

Nico slid the crocheted dress up Kaylin's thighs and noted

the damp patch the size of Rhode Island on her bikini bottoms. Good. She was into this as much as he was.

He cupped her cheeks in his hands and kissed her.

"Cesare. Is. Gone."

37

———

KAYLIN

The lights of Los Angeles twinkled outside the windows as we glided through traffic. Then got stuck because even late at night, there were still too many cars and not enough road. Hot damn, I needed to get back to the hotel and change into dry underwear before Nico noticed the damp patch between my legs. I was a freaking mess.

"Turn it off," he murmured against my lips.

"Huh?"

"Your mind. Turn it off. You're overthinking again."

Of course I was. Staying two steps ahead was the only way I'd survived life with Cesare. If I kept topping off his wine glass, he couldn't get it up. If I reminded him about the baseball game and bought beer and nachos, he'd invite his buddies over and fall asleep on the couch. Nico presented a whole different kind of problem.

I wanted him, but I was terrified that I wouldn't be good enough.

But then he kissed me again, and my mind went blank. I might have been second-guessing every move, but my mouth knew exactly what it wanted, and that was Nico's tongue. My

266

lips parted of their own accord, welcoming him in. He kept his touch light, one hand tangling in my hair and the other skimming the curve of my breast, but the intensity of the moment made it hard to suck in air. This man took my breath away.

Heat flared inside me, the fire I hadn't felt since those early days with Cesare, although if I was honest, I'd been more turned on by the sneaking around and his dangerous reputation than the man himself.

As Nico pulled me onto his lap, I tried desperately to push the memories of Cesare and his subpar dick into hell where they belonged. Nico was the man I wanted, the man I'd *always* wanted. Now he was mine. I just had to make sure I kept him.

I had to be perfect.

He was hard already, his cock pressing between my legs as I straddled him. I wanted to rub against it, to relieve the pressure building in my belly, but his needs had to come first. I couldn't afford to screw this up.

"Show me the real Kaylin," he said, his words a caress. "I want to see all of you."

I reached for the hem of my dress, but I'd barely pulled it up to my waist when he stilled me with a hand.

"Stop," he ordered, and my heart stuttered.

"You don't want to...?"

"Stop sucking in your stomach. Relax. When I said I wanted to see the real you, I meant your mind, not your body. You think I don't notice the tension in you? We'll do what you're comfortable with and no more."

"I want...I want to do everything with you."

He pressed a kiss to the end of my nose, sweet but almost chaste. A sharp contrast to his twitching cock.

"Then why did you suddenly stiffen?"

"I...I'm scared of getting something wrong. Of doing something you don't like."

"If that happens, I'll tell you, but you have to promise to do the same."

"Okay."

"Promise me."

"I promise."

"Good." He ran a finger over the traitorous damp patch. "Fuck, you're wet."

"I'm sorry, I—"

"Why are you apologising?"

"Because...because Cesare would have called me a slut and berated me for being inappropriate."

"That's the first and last time his name gets mentioned while you're sitting on my lap."

"Sorry, I'm so—"

"Shh." Nico put a finger to my lips. "I'm just telling you how it's going to be." He leaned in closer. "So, you don't like being called a slut? A filthy, dirty little slut who's dripping all over my dick?"

My thighs clenched involuntarily, and I squirmed in his lap. Holy hell, dirty-talking Nico could make me come with nothing but words. I'd hated the insults coming from Cesare's mouth, but it wasn't the names he called me; it was the intent behind them. With Nico, they had a whole different meaning.

"I don't like it. I...I think I might love it."

"Good. Now, get yourself off."

"What?"

"You're dying to do it, I can tell. The way you start to writhe and then stop yourself. The friction feels good, doesn't it?"

"Yes," I whispered, an admission I'd never have made to any other man.

"Rub yourself against me. Use your fingers too, if you like, but I want you to fall apart in my arms before we reach the hotel." When I hesitated, he ran the tip of his tongue along my jaw. "Do you want me to help?"

Another whisper. "Yes."

He slipped his hand into my bikini bottoms and circled slowly with one finger, matching the rhythm with his tongue against mine. It was no surprise whatsoever to find out that Nico knew precisely what he was doing. The stain grew. My hips began bucking. Traffic started moving again, but I'd come before we reached the hotel. No doubt about it. When he nudged his way into me with a finger, I was gone. He swallowed his name as I gasped it, then held me close as I collapsed into a boneless heap on his lap. I was shaking, really shaking. Nico Belinsky had just given me the most earth-shattering orgasm of my life, and we were still fully clothed.

This man was going to ruin me, and I'd gladly lie back and beg for the end.

"Can you walk?" he asked.

"I'm not sure."

"Should I carry you inside?"

We were at the hotel? I glanced out the window and saw the doorman waiting a few feet away under the porte cochère, studiously looking anywhere but the car's tinted windows. Oops.

"I might just need to borrow your arm."

Nico pulled my dress down, and I checked the status of the stain. As usual, he knew exactly what I was thinking.

"Carry your purse in front of you, and nobody will notice."

"Next time, I'm going to pick out swimwear with a pattern."

"Next time?"

"Uh, if you want there to be a next time. If you don't, then—"

"Of course I want there to be a next time. I'm beyond relieved that you're thinking along the same lines."

Nico tipped the driver and doorman, then strolled across the lobby as if he hadn't just rocked my entire world. All I could think of was getting him naked. Rational thought had disappeared, and the only thing left was lizard brain.

The elevator doors closed, and we were alone again. I dropped to my knees, but Nico shook his head.

"Not here. There's a camera in the corner, *zolottse*."

"Shit, really?"

My cheeks burned as he helped me to my feet. The stupid, impulsive part of me should be thrown in a dungeon. She'd gotten me into so much trouble over the years.

Nico smoothed my dress and kissed my cheek, then wrapped an arm around my waist. Things were different now. Now, I had Nico at my side, and he was a gentleman, not an opportunist. Cesare would have let me suck his cock and then used the video to blackmail me later. Think that's an exaggeration? Think again. He used whatever threats he had to in order to keep me in line.

But Nico? Nico just thanked the babysitter and the security guard and held the door so they could leave, then led me to my room to check on a sleeping Matty. He looked so peaceful. A splodgy painting sat on the nightstand, so it seemed the sitter had kept him entertained.

Quietly, quietly, I closed the door.

Then Nico picked me up, bridal-style, and carried me to his bed.

Perhaps I should have been nervous, but everything he'd said in the car, everything he'd done, had set my mind at ease. I had nothing to fear from this man, no matter his reputation.

He peeled me out of my clothes, and the way he looked at me, the heat in his gaze, made me forget all my imperfections. After I'd returned the favour and stripped him slowly, I traced a fingertip over the scar on his hip. A thin, silvery line. A reminder of the past. Then I focused on the present. On the perfect cock jutting toward me, eight inches of deliciousness just waiting for me to taste.

He gave a low groan as I took him into my mouth, and if my years with Cesare had taught me anything, it was how to block my gag reflex. Nico cursed under his breath as I swallowed him to the root, but in a good way.

"Fuck, *zolottse. Da*, take all of it."

I'd never enjoyed sucking cock before, but Nico changed my outlook on everything. Where once there was despair, now there was hope. Where there was nausea, now there was lust. I gripped his ass as he thrust into my throat, waiting for him to come, waiting for him to fall apart the way I had. But he disappointed me by pulling out.

"Not today. The first time I come inside you, it's going to be in your pussy." He glanced toward the closed bedroom door and his lips quirked into a smile. "Quietly."

"And also quickly."

"Are you questioning my stamina?"

"No, I'm questioning my patience."

Fortunately, he took the hint and rolled on a condom. As he sank into me, inch by steely inch, I swallowed the emotions bubbling so close to the surface. Relief, desperation, ecstasy, and something deeper still. Love? A love that went further than friendship? Yes, I thought I might be falling in love with Nico Belinsky. Fuck our history. I wanted a future with this man.

He began to move in smooth, measured strokes. I wrapped my arms around him, and my legs, anything to be closer. I couldn't get enough of his hands, his tongue, his magic cock.

"Come for me, my slippery little slut," he murmured. "Can you feel your arousal running down your thighs?"

I could, but instead of embarrassment, all I felt was greed. "Give me more."

Nico picked up the pace and slammed into me, his balls slapping my ass, his cock hitting the exact right spot deep inside me. The orgasm built quickly, and when I plunged over the edge, I had to bite his shoulder to keep from crying out. He followed me with a grunt and a stream of curses, some in English and some in Russian, then gathered me against him in a sweaty tangle of limbs.

Oh. My. Gosh.

You've just ruined me for all other men.

His gaze darkened. "There won't be any other men."

I tensed because three years ago, *he'd* said that, but as the darkness in Nico's eyes gave way to concern, I relaxed. There wouldn't be any other men, but this time, that would be my choice, not anyone else's.

38

KAYLIN

"OMG! You totally did it," Addy squealed.

"Huh? Did what?"

"Did Nico."

How could she possibly know? This morning, I'd made the bed, picked up the stray clothes we'd discarded, and put the condom wrappers in the trash. If I'd been smart, I would have asked, "What makes you think that?" but I wasn't.

"What gave it away?"

"You're freaking glowing. And when we walked past Nico outside, he had a grin bigger than the Cheshire cat's."

"We all knew it was going to happen," Brooke said. "When you came over for dinner, he looked at you like you were his princess."

"Brie's an actual princess, and he doesn't look at her that way."

My cheeks burned. "It wasn't meant to happen."

Addy dismissed that with a wave of her hand. "It totally was. Don't you believe in fate?"

I wished I did, but the bad decisions I'd made were all my own. "Not really."

273

"Well, I do, and I'm telling you that you and Nico are meant to be together. Is he good with Matty?"

"He's amazing with Matty."

The flight back yesterday had been a breeze. Nico took over childcare duties from the start, leaving me to sip champagne and nibble on olives and almonds. I wasn't sure how I felt about that. On the one hand, there was the utter relief that someone capable was helping. On the other, I was a little hurt that Matty wouldn't calm down that way for me. Parenting wasn't as easy as TV lifestyle shows made out. A mommy blog? Definitely wouldn't be starting one of those.

"Then you've hit the jackpot. Knowing my luck, I'm probably destined to marry a cowboy from Idaho."

"What's wrong with that?"

"I'm not really the outdoorsy type."

"Then why are you coming hiking today?"

"Because I can't fit into my favourite jeans anymore, and a creep at the gym keeps hitting on me."

"Have you reported him?" Brooke asked.

"I tried, but he's friends with the manager, so the manager doesn't see a problem with it. *There's no rule against him using the treadmill next to you*," Addy mimicked. "I'm tied into the contract for another seven months, so hiking it is." She managed a smile. "How bad can it be?"

"We won't be going far. Matty never walked long distances before we came here."

And I couldn't carry him, not with the way my muscles ached after last night. No, today's excursion would be more of a leg stretch. A part of me wished I'd turned down the invite, but when Brooke had called to ask if I wanted to join them this morning, the joy of having friends again had overridden any fatigue.

Our first challenge was fitting everything into Brooke's Toyota compact. A car seat, four people, two dogs, and the assorted stuff a mom couldn't leave home without. A change of clothes, drinks and snacks, a blanket, baby wipes, spare pull-ups, a portable potty, hand sanitiser, toys...

Toys.

I'd paid extra for priority shipping, and Shelley 1.0 had been waiting for us when we arrived back from LA. The eBay seller would be getting excellent feedback from me. But now Matty wanted Not-Shelley. Go figure. Yesterday, he'd thrown her across the airplane again; today, they were inseparable. I'd debated which Shelley to pack and then stuffed both into the bag. Better to carry one extra toy than deal with the meltdown when I inevitably brought the wrong one.

The drive to the trailhead took just over twenty minutes, and Cricket knew we were going somewhere fun. He sat on my lap in the back seat with his paws on the door, watching the scenery go by. He most certainly approved of the move west. Leash walks around Central Park couldn't compare to the freedom of running around in the forest, not that Cricket ever went far. Once we got onto the trail, he alternated between following Vega and checking his people were still with him.

Now that I knew I was staying in Baldwin's Shore, I'd have to start thinking ahead. Matty needed to make friends his own age, and his future education was important too.

"Do you guys know if there are any mom and toddler groups nearby?" I asked.

"I think there's one at the library," Brooke said. "I'm not sure what day, though. Maybe Tuesday or Wednesday? Kiki used to go."

Addy cursed as she tripped over a tree root. "There'll be one in Coos Bay for sure. Plus there's an indoor play centre in North Bend if you want to take Matty out for the day."

"If it's indoors, Addy will go with you," Brooke joked. "Hey, Ads, you might meet a hot single dad."

Addy made a face. "What age do kids get out of diapers? No way would I want to change one of those."

"Matty's almost ready to stop using them now, but if you need a cut-off point, then four years should be safe."

"What if he was hot *and* rich?" Brooke asked. "Would you change a diaper then?"

"Nuh-uh. I'd rather go with the Idaho cowboy than deal with poop."

"You realise horses also poop?"

"Crap, I didn't think this through, did I?"

Matty toddled along happily, Shelley 1.0 in hand. Unlike Addy, he *was* the outdoorsy type. Every time he saw a bird or a squirrel, he pointed and chattered, then laughed when Vega tried to climb a tree trunk to catch one of the critters. Cesare had always laughed derisively whenever anyone mentioned small-town America, but this was my idea of paradise.

Brooke hopped over a fallen branch. "Luca said you've known Nico for a long time?"

Stick close to the truth, Nico said. "Since we were kids."

"It's so sweet that you finally ended up together. Did you know Nico's dad? I heard he was a gangster in Russia."

"He was always nice to me. Sometimes he brought me toys or candy."

"Did they live in a big house? Like a palace?"

"Yup, and I got lost there so many times."

"Was it weird living in Russia? Don't they use a different alphabet?"

"I went to the international school, so everyone spoke English, but I learned Cyrillic as well."

"OMG!" Addy shrieked. "Something just landed on my head. Is it a spider? Tell me it isn't a spider?"

I squinted at the brown thing. "It's a leaf. Here, let me get it."

"Oh, thank goodness."

That was a good moment to turn back and also to change the subject. Nico's past was his own business, and Addy and Brooke were lovely but struck me as the type to gossip.

"I think Matty's starting to get tired."

"Great, we can avoid the hill up ahead," Addy said, turning in the other direction immediately. "I think I'm getting a blister."

"I have Band-Aids in the car," Brooke told her.

"Have you both always lived in Oregon?"

"Yup. We went to school together. Brooke lived near me in Coos Bay for a while, but then she ended up in Baldwin's Shore again."

"You still live in Coos Bay?"

"Yup." Addy made a face. "Although my rent just went up again, so I might have to move."

"I need to learn more about the area. Find a preschool for Matty, meet more people, get a job."

"A job?"

"Nico might have money, but I'd feel better earning my own."

"An independent woman—I like that. What type of job do you want? Do you have a résumé? If you help with mine, I'll help with yours."

"You're looking for a job too?"

"She just got fired," Brooke said.

"I'm so sorry."

"Don't be—it was totally worth it."

"Her boss was a sleaze," Brooke explained. "He used to tell her to work late and then when she was alone, he'd make all kinds of inappropriate suggestions. So one evening, she recorded him and sent the conversation to his wife."

Addy grinned. "She emailed me a thank-you note, and now they're getting divorced."

Yes, I liked these two women. Aside from Lyndsey and

Lucia, the two backstabbers, the only female company I'd had in New York was the Divas. And I'd never been close to them. Sure, they were always friendly, but Cesare had made sure we never became friends.

My phone rang as I was strapping Matty into his car seat. Nico. Calls were still a novelty after I'd been isolated for so long.

"Is everything okay?" I asked.

"Just checking when you'll be back. I thought we could have lunch together."

"We're climbing into Brooke's car. Lunch sounds great, but could Brooke and Addy join us?"

"I'll have the staff set it up. Is frittata okay, or would you prefer something else?"

I relayed the question to the others, and they both nodded.

"Frittata's great." I almost told him that I missed him, but that might have sounded needy, and I didn't want to sound needy. "See you in twenty. Are you sure everything's okay?"

"There's nothing for you to worry about."

That wasn't a "yes," but Nico had hung up, and perhaps I was overreacting? He'd probably had a difficult meeting, that was all.

"So, what kind of job are you looking for?" Addy asked again once Vega had peed one last time and the six of us had piled into the car. The trail was quiet today, the parking lot nearly empty, but we still got stuck behind a truck driving at half the speed limit when Brooke pulled out onto the road.

"I used to be a waitress. Events, mainly, but I worked in restaurants from time to time."

"Events, huh? You should call Sara Baldwin. She just started an events company."

"Sara Baldwin? I heard the Baldwins create a lot of problems around here."

Brooke slowed for a turn, and thankfully, the truck went straight on. "Sara's one of the good guys. None of the stuff that happened was her fault. You should avoid LKB Events like the plague, though. Her cousins run it—badly—and they're impossible to work for."

"Nico said he banned them from the Peninsula."

"Yup, them and one of their brothers. I was there when he banned Easton," Brooke said. "What's that German thing? The shade thing?"

"Schadenfreude?" I suggested.

"Yes, that. He definitely deserved it."

The two of them gave me a rundown of the Baldwin family, which included far more detail than Nico had volunteered. He wasn't a chatterbox, but I'd been dead right about Brooke and Addy—they loved to ladle out the dirty details with a healthy topping of rumour.

Matty dropped Shelley 1.0 and struggled against his seat belt when he couldn't reach her. I fished her out of the footwell, absentmindedly rubbing my finger over the spot between her shell and her foot where I'd repaired a small hole. Matty had liked to chew things when he was younger, and even Shelley hadn't escaped his teeth. Thankfully, he'd grown out of—

Wait.

Wait, wait, wait.

This wasn't Matty's original Shelley. This was the replacement.

So why did it have a tight little bundle of stitches in the exact same place? I took a closer look, and the bile that rose into my throat was worse than anything I'd experienced while I was pregnant. Those *were* my stitches. This *was* Matty's Shelley. She'd been washed, but it was the same damn toy.

Which meant... Which meant... There was only one person who could have listed her for sale on the internet. Only one person who could have sent her here to Baldwin's Shore. Cesare must have realised how attached Matty was to the stupid snail—or maybe Lyndsey had told him, the traitor—and he'd known I'd look for a replacement.

He had my address.

He knew where I was.

We were so close to the Peninsula, just a few hundred yards away, but I reached for my phone anyway. I had to tell Nico how stupid I'd been, *again*. Had to warn him that Cesare would be on his way if he wasn't in Baldwin's Shore already.

Brooke braked sharply, and I was thrown forward against the seat belt. Matty let out a cry, and I shoved Not-Shelley into his hands to try and placate him.

"Get out of the way, you idiot," Brooke muttered.

The SUV was blocking the road, and I knew it wasn't going anywhere. Not until the passenger had what he came for.

"Is that a *gun*?" Addy asked. "This has to be a joke, right?"

It was no joke.

Cesare had brought Alonzo with him, the one brother who was even more sadistic than my husband. Alonzo hauled me out of the car, and when I tried to grab my phone, he twisted my arm behind my back and put his gun to my head. My knees buckled, but he held me in a vise-like grip.

"Let me go!"

"You think you can leave me, *tesorino*." Cesare spat the endearment as if it were poison as he struggled with Matty's car seat, a duplicate of the one I'd bought back in New York. He never had bothered to learn how the straps did up. "You think you can shack up with another man? Don't worry, I'll be back for him, but not until you're out of the way."

Brooke seemed to be in shock, but Addy scrambled out of the car, followed by Cricket. Vega was barking and snarling in the trunk, but the mesh dog barrier meant he couldn't do anything to help.

"You can't just take her," Addy shrieked. "What are you? A pair of psychos?"

Yes, they absolutely were.

"It's okay," I told her because the last thing I wanted was for Alonzo to decide she was disposable. "It's fine."

"The hell it is."

Alonzo aimed his gun at her face. "Shut up and get back in the car. This doesn't concern you."

Addy fell silent, but she didn't get back in the car. Instead, she glared at him, and if looks could kill, he'd have keeled right over. Alonzo backed away, pulling me with him, and Cesare was shouting at Matty to be quiet, as if that would help. We'd been so damn close to safety. So damn close, and now I was probably dead.

But at least Brooke and Addy would live.

Or so I thought.

Cricket chose that moment to sink his teeth into Alonzo's ankle, and now he was yelling too. Worse, he fired at my sweet little dog, but thankfully, Cricket ran under the car because although Cesare called him a dumb mutt, he really was quite clever.

Then Addy crumpled to the ground.

I caught sight of the blood blossoming on her shirt as Alonzo bundled me into the back of the SUV and slammed the door, heard Brooke's cry as the meathead behind the wheel gunned the engine.

And there was nothing I could do but put my seat belt on and pray.

39

NICO

"I should be able to get this finished in a week if the rain holds off." Deck stacked the last of the lumber next to the pool, dusted off his work gloves, and looked up at the sky. The black clouds didn't look hopeful. "Might be two weeks if we get those thunderstorms they were talking about on the news last night."

"There's no hurry as long as the temporary fence can stay in place in the meantime."

"Sure, I can work around it."

"While you're here, could you quote to build a playhouse? We got one from a store, but it's too small." The box said "deluxe," but there was only one room. How was that deluxe? "It would be good to run power out to it as well."

"You planning to have the kid move in there?"

"I just don't want the inside to be gloomy."

"Show me where you want it. Are we talking a cosy cottage or a full-on mansion?"

"How about something in between?"

Nico was holding the end of the tape measure and wondering whether two storeys with running water would be excessive when his phone rang. Emmy Black. One of the few people whose calls he answered rather than forwarding to his assistant.

"Is this a social call?" he asked, already knowing that it wasn't. Emmy Black didn't have time to waste on pleasantries.

"Might be something, might be nothing. Cesare Cavallaro's gone quiet. Last week, he was running around, trying to track down Kaylin's former colleagues from the events company—he even tried to hire Blackwood to help, the poor dumb fuck—but this week? Nada."

"It's not nothing. Where is he?"

"Not in the usual places. His cell phone's in his apartment, but he isn't. Alonzo went to visit Vito in the hospital on Saturday, but now he's missing too. It's possible they've headed somewhere to do the usual Mafia shit, but..."

"But?"

"My gut instincts are usually pretty good, and they're saying 'watch your back.'"

"Find them."

"We will. I'll update you later."

Nico trusted Emmy's gut, and he trusted his own. If Cesare and Alonzo Cavallaro were missing, there was nothing good about that.

"Problem?" Deck raised an eyebrow.

Nico's first instinct was to brush the question away, but he paused for a moment. Colt and Luca had two suspects when it came to the identity of the Bad Samaritan: Nico and Deck. Since Nico knew he wasn't playing vigilante in the little spare time he had, it stood to reason that Deck might be the culprit. If two of the Cavallaros really were headed for Baldwin's Shore, then it wouldn't hurt to have a trigger-happy avenger looking out for them.

"My girlfriend's been having trouble with her ex. She left him, and he's not a man who takes rejection well."

"Her ex? Do you mean Matthew's father?"

"In the loosest sense of the word. He didn't pay much attention to the boy when they shared a home. Katy's terrified of him, so my priority is to keep her safe."

"He was that kind of man?"

Nico knew exactly what Deck was asking. Was Cesare capable of harming Kaylin?

"He was that kind of man."

Deck nodded slowly. "Yeah, I see how an abusive motherfucker could get riled up if a woman ran with his kid. Try calling Annie at the hair salon—if any strangers have been asking about your girl, she'll know."

"I'll do that."

But Nico called Kaylin first. He didn't want to scare her, but he did want her back at the Peninsula and under the watchful eye of his security team. She was already on her way. Good. Nico's chest was tight as he alerted his head of security to the potential danger, and the man promised to get in touch with Brie's people too. Even when she was overseas, there was a contingent of guards present at the old paper mill to watch over her new family.

Annie hadn't heard about any strangers nosing around town but promised to keep an ear to the ground. She also fished for more details, but Nico didn't supply any. Just for good measure, he called the Craft Cabin—Paulo was the second-biggest gossip in town after Annie—but he had nothing to report. Everly was also working, and she promised to ask around discreetly in Coos Bay.

Dammit, Nico had forgotten the frittatas, and Kaylin would be here in five minutes. He called the kitchen and arranged for a server to lay the table on his terrace. No, not the terrace. Indoors would be better. There was a panic room in the bedroom, and he'd need to show Kaylin how to get in there. Should he ask Emmy Black to send a close-quarters protection team? He'd discuss the possibility with her when she called later. Maybe the wiry guy who'd watched Matty in LA would be available?

Nico paused to take a breath, to rein in the panic, and it struck him that he'd never felt this way before. This fear. Kaylin was as much a part of his heart as his left ventricle. And Matty. Fuck, he loved that boy.

Deck slammed the tailgate of his truck and ambled over. "You need anything else? A swing set? A rocking horse? Fencing for a pony?"

"How old does a kid need to be—"

The *bang* made everyone jump. Screams rang out around the main pool, glass shattered as a waiter hit the ground, and Deck reached for a gun that wasn't there. Nico's chest seized, and now he knew how Vito had felt that night in the Starlight Lounge.

"That was a gunshot," he said, as if voicing the worst would somehow make it better.

Deck was scanning the area. "Yeah, I know."

Nico's phone buzzed a second later, his head of security. "What happened?"

"Don't think it was on the grounds," the man said. "The shot came from farther away, out near the road. I've sent a team to investigate."

Who needed to investigate? Nico already knew this was related to Kaylin. He didn't believe in coincidences. Cesare had found out she was here, and he'd been lying in wait outside the hotel gates.

Nico ran.

The scene on the road outside the gates resembled a horror movie. Addy was lying on the ground in a pile of broken glass and a pool of blood. Two members of Nico's security team had gotten there first, and they were trying to stem the bleeding while Brooke sobbed into the phone. Vega was attempting to dig his way out of the trunk while Cricket snapped at the men's ankles and generally got in the way. The worst part? There was no sign of Kaylin or Matty.

"What happened?" Nico demanded, breathing hard. Adrenaline had got him to the crash site at a wild sprint, and his burning lungs were still playing catchup.

Brooke looked up, on her knees beside Addy, her eyes red. "They took them. They took them, and then they shot Addy."

"Who took them?"

"I don't know! Men. Two men with dark hair. I think one of them was her ex because he was really angry about her being here with you."

"Which way did they go?"

"Uh..."

"Which way?"

Brooke pointed south. "That way. Toward Bandon."

No, toward Medford. Cesare was heading for the airport, Nico knew it.

"Are you on the phone with Luca?"

"Y-y-yes."

"Tell him to send deputies to Rogue Valley International. That's where they're going." Nico dropped to his knees beside Addy, ignoring the sting from the glass. "How bad is it?"

"There's an ambulance on the way," one of the men told him.

But would she survive that long? Addy was naked from the waist up and struggling to breathe, blood trickling from a wound to the right side of her chest. The terror in her eyes sent another wave of fear through Nico.

"Do something," Brooke begged.

A guard pulled off his shirt, and he was about to press it over the hole when a hand stopped him.

"Looks like a pneumothorax," Deck said, sounding eerily calm. "Is there an exit wound?"

"Can't see one."

"I'm gonna need this." Deck tugged at the card attached to a lanyard around the guard's neck. "Addy, I know it hurts, but watch me and focus on breathing, okay?"

"Can't... Can't..."

"Someone get the first-aid kit from the lockbox in the back of my truck. Code's six-one-seven-four."

Nico did as instructed and when he came back, Deck had pressed the plastic ID card over the hole. Addy wasn't breathing any better, but she wasn't breathing any worse either, and Nico had to take that as a good sign.

"Here you go."

"Hold this in place."

One of the guards took over while Deck rifled through the contents of the bag. It wasn't the kind of civilian kit you'd buy in a drugstore. No, this looked more like the supplies Lev Belinsky's bodyguards used to carry in their SUV, a necessity in Russia where "accidents" were commonplace among oligarchs. Fall out of favour, and you'd soon find yourself falling out of a window.

Deck wiped the blood from Addy's skin, and in one smooth motion, he replaced the plastic card with an adhesive dressing.

"Your lung's collapsed, sweetheart. I've sealed the hole, but I need you to breathe."

Addy managed to nod, her eyes wide with fear, but she was still gasping. Nico wasn't an EMT, but even he could see that one side of her chest wasn't moving as it should.

"Any news on that ambulance?" Deck asked.

Running feet came from behind them, and Luca turned the air blue. "Fuck, fuck, fuck. How bad is it?"

"I'm thinking tension pneumothorax."

"The ambulance is still ten minutes out. You got a decompression needle in that kit?"

"Yup."

"Ever done one before?"

"Once. You?"

"Never had the pleasure."

"What's going on?" Brooke asked. "What are you talking about?"

Deck squeezed Addy's hand. "I have to put a needle in your chest, sweetheart. It's gonna hurt, I won't lie, but I need to do it. Better if you close your eyes, okay?"

Addy didn't say a word as Deck felt his way down her sternum and across her chest, but she did close her eyes as instructed. A good thing, because the needle had to be four inches long. Nico was tempted to close his eyes too. Deck found the right spot, and Luca helped to hold Addy still as the needle pierced skin and muscle. Fuck. A guard caught Brooke as she fainted, and would someone quiet those damn dogs?

There was a hiss of air, and blood sprayed across Deck's chest. Some of it settled on Addy's face too, and her tears left clean tracks through the scarlet speckles. But she began to breathe properly again, and when she opened her eyes, she only had one thing to say.

"You have to find Katy."

40

NICO

At first, Nico had been annoyed by Deck's insistence that he drive—because whose girlfriend had been abducted?—but now he realised that Deck's skills extended past lifesaving field medicine and into cornering like a maniac. Nico almost asked him to slow down, but he managed to bite his tongue.

"You might want to check your gun," Deck said.

"I didn't bring a gun."

And now Nico was kicking himself. Yes, he'd begun carrying a weapon again when he went out, but not at home. He'd felt safe at the Peninsula. Back in Moscow, he'd slept with a semi-automatic under his pillow, but he'd been out of his father's murky world for too long, convinced himself that going straight was the noble thing to do. If he survived today, he was going to buy his own shooting range and use it excessively. People thought he was the Bad Samaritan? Ha. Pretending it might be true had been fun for a while, but now he had regrets. Boy, did he have regrets.

"Look behind you."

Nico twisted to find a familiar wooden box on the back

seat. The box that held his favourite 9mm. The box that usually lived in a hidden compartment built into the baseboard beside the refrigerator in his kitchen. He was about to ask how the hell Deck had found it when he remembered who had installed his cabinets.

At least one of them was thinking straight under pressure. "Thanks."

As Deck focused on closing the distance between his truck and the Cavallaro vehicle, Nico called Emmy. She'd tried to warn him, but neither of them had realised how imminent the danger was. Nico still didn't understand how Cesare could have found Kaylin and Matty in Baldwin's Shore so fast. What had happened on Saturday? Until then, he'd still been chasing his tail in New York.

"Problem?" she asked.

"Yes, there's a fucking problem. Kaylin and Matty are gone, a friend's been shot, and I'm heading for an RTA with the local carpenter driving."

"All in the space of half an hour? Shit."

"Cesare found them here, and it happened fast. Could someone on your team have talked?"

"Absolutely not. Only a handful of people knew both Kaylin's identity and your destination, and I'd trust all of them with my life. Any idea where they're headed?"

"South. At a guess, Medford."

"I'll see what assets we have in the area."

"You'd better do it fast."

Nico felt as if he was going to throw up, and it wasn't only due to Deck's driving. In less than a month, he'd finally found the woman he wanted to settle down with, discovered he might be cut out for fatherhood after all, and lost his new family. He'd promised to keep Kaylin safe, and he'd failed.

He'd failed her again.

"Who did you call?" Deck asked.

"A contact who works in security."

"Who's Kaylin?"

"Pretend you didn't hear that part."

"They sending reinforcements?"

"If there's anyone in the area."

"Which outfit?"

Nico glanced across at Deck and figured he owed the man that much. "Blackwood."

Laughter wasn't the reaction he'd expected. "Emmy Black?"

"You know her?"

"Know of her. You got Delta, you got DEVGRU, you got 24 STS, and then you got that crazy bitch."

"You're ex-military?"

"It was another life."

"I didn't realise they taught soldiers to drive like they were in Formula One."

"They don't. I used to race go-karts when I was a kid. Try to drive like this on a sunshine posting, and you'll lose your suspension if you don't hit an IED first." Deck sucked in a breath as a deer poked its head out of the trees and quickly thought the better of crossing. "If Emmy Black's on board, she'll probably shut down the airport. That buys us time."

"You think she can do that?"

"I once heard a rumour she conjured up a tornado, and I'm only fifty percent sure it wasn't true. This could get nasty, you realise that? We got at least two men to deal with, and they have hostages."

"Hostages, money, and political leverage."

"Who is this guy? Her ex?"

"A Mob boss in New York City."

"And you're only telling me this now?"

"Nobody was intending for him to find her."

"That's what they all fucking— Aw, hell."

Tyres screeched as Deck slammed on the brakes, and Nico flew forward into the seat belt. His gun ended up in the footwell, as did his phone, and only one of them survived the impact.

Deck already had a weapon in his hand. "Duck."

Nico dove forward again as bullets zinged into the windshield. Deck leaned out and returned fire, three quick shots.

"They're running."

More shots, and then silence. Deck raised his head above the engine block again.

"You want the good news or the bad news?"

"The good news."

Above all, Nico needed hope, and right now, he didn't have much of it. The getaway vehicle, a black SUV, tilted at a steep angle in a ditch on the wrong side of the road, the front wrapped around a tree. Blood covered the bark, and a pair of elk antlers stuck out beside a wheel. Oregon wildlife: one, Mafia: nil. The driver had been thrown halfway through the windshield in the smash.

"Both of the hostages are still alive," Deck said.

Thank goodness. "And the bad news?"

"There are two males, and they've split up. One has the woman, one has the kid."

"We have to go after them."

"Yeah, I figured you'd say that. Which one d'ya want? Or do you wanna flip for it?"

Nico had made a thousand tough decisions in his life. Some were financial, some were personal, some were life or death. But this was the toughest. Nico wasn't a fool, and objectively speaking, Deck was the most likely to bring back a hostage alive. Based on his performance so far, Nico could easily imagine him being the Bad Samaritan. The ultimate vigilante. Nico gave himself a much smaller chance, both of survival and of a successful rescue.

He hated himself for the choice he was about to make.

"Go after Kaylin."

If they could only save one of them, it had to be her.

"The asshole with the kid went west. Stay safe, buddy."

Deck melted into the trees, leaving Nico on a possible suicide mission. The faint sound of breaking twigs came from the left, and he thumbed off the safety on his pistol.

Lev Belinsky had been an avid hunter. Deer, wolves, bears, leopards. Sometimes humans. From a young age, Nico had accompanied him, not by choice but out of obligation. The first time he'd killed a deer, a large buck, he'd spent hours tracking it through the forest, his footsteps quieter than his thumping heart. His father had painted its blood on his young son's cheeks, then made him drink a cupful and laughed when he vomited.

Nico had hated those trips.

But now he was grateful in a small way for his father's bloodlust because it meant he knew how to track. He could follow a man through a forest quickly and silently. His opponent? The bastard moved like a wild hog, crashing through the undergrowth in leather-soled shoes. Matty's endless sobs didn't help either. Nico heard them grow louder as he gradually closed the distance to his prey.

And there he was. Cesare. But he was carrying Matty, and there was no clear shot. The Bad Samaritan could undoubtedly hit a dime, but Nico was out of practice, and when it came to shooting, accuracy was like a muscle—use it or lose it. Nico was confident he could hit centre mass, but he didn't dare to risk a headshot.

Matty looked back over Cesare's shoulder through teary eyes, still clutching his favourite toy. So near, yet so damn far. If Nico had a working phone, he could have messaged Emmy and asked for one of her famous tornados, but he was shit out of luck and alone with a madman.

Two fast gunshots echoed through the trees, and Cesare whipped around. Nico only just had time to duck back behind a tree as Cesare stood motionless, nose in the air like a dog searching for scent.

Sweat trickled down Nico's spine, every sense heightened. Death was close. He heard a soft whistle up ahead, but it didn't sound like any bird he was familiar with. Cesare heard it too and turned, only for a black-clad figure to materialise at his side, seemingly from thin air. The whistle was followed by a *crack* as the wraith head-butted the asshole, and she caught Matty neatly as Cesare crumpled to the forest floor.

Yes, she. The wraith was a woman. She wore leather and a motorcycle helmet, but she couldn't hide her figure.

"Amateur." Nico felt rather than saw her gaze zero in on him. "You can come out now, Nicolai."

Her sing-song voice was confident, almost playful. The thought of facing Cesare had been bad enough, but Nico knew instinctively that the wraith was a hundred times more dangerous than the Mob boss. But she had Matty, which meant he had no choice. He stepped out from the safety of the tree trunk, holding his gun on her, but she had a weapon too. And probably better aim.

"Put it down." Now she spoke in Russian, which was the last thing Nico had expected to hear. "I'm not going to harm the child."

"Who are you?"

"Your friends call me the Bad Samaritan. It suits me, *da*? An oxymoron. A contradiction. I help people, but I also do things that many find distasteful."

"You're a woman?"

"What gave it away? Was it the breasts? The hips? The

voice?" Matty's sobs grew louder. "Do you know how to shut him up? This is annoying."

"Give him to me."

Nico took a chance and lowered his gun, then let out the breath he'd been holding when the Bad Samaritan followed suit with her own and stepped forward. A mirrored visor hid her features, but Nico estimated her height at five-eight or five-nine. A few stray strands of blonde hair had escaped from underneath the helmet. Her posture was a mix of regal and defiant, and after consideration, Nico was glad she'd hidden her face. If he couldn't identify her, there was no reason to kill him. And he didn't doubt that she could.

Nico took the boy in his arms, and Matty's cries subsided to quiet sniffles. The Bad Samaritan picked up the toy snail and held it out.

"Here."

Nico snatched the toy and stuffed it into his jacket pocket. "I have to get to Kaylin."

"No, you don't. Decker Langdon is more than capable of handling the situation."

Cesare was still lying motionless, and the Bad Samaritan bent to check his pulse.

"Is he alive?" Nico asked as she began rifling through Cesare's pockets with gloved hands. The man was carrying a pistol, and she released the magazine before tossing both items to the side.

"*Da*, he's alive." Next, she dropped a knife onto the ground. "This is a nice switchblade. Expensive."

"So, what happens now? You just walk away like you did all the other times?"

"That depends."

"Depends on what?"

"How much have you changed, Nicolai? In Moscow, you used to do the dirty work yourself." She offered him her gun, butt first. "The way I see it, there are three options. Either you kill him, or I kill him, or you call your friends in the sheriff's department and ask them to take him away."

She'd done her research, hadn't she? It was disconcerting, the way she knew so much, not only about Nico's life in Baldwin's Shore but about his former existence in Russia. But she was right. Two decades ago, he wouldn't have hesitated to put a bullet through Cesare Cavallaro's head.

"Would you lose sleep if you killed him?" he asked.

"Beyond the time you're wasting while you make up your mind? No."

The right thing to do, the lawful thing, would be to call Colt or Luca and let them take this motherfucker into custody. But then Kaylin would have the trauma of a trial to get through, years of legal wrangling and perhaps even a custody battle. As it was, her secret would come out. She'd still have to fight the charge for killing the cop in Virginia. Nico would hire the best lawyers money could buy, and it would be her word against Alonzo's and a pile of circumstantial evidence.

No, Kaylin had enough to deal with.

And the Bad Samaritan was right: when it was within his capabilities, Nico did his own dirty work.

"I don't need your gun. Take the boy."

"Do I have to?"

But she held out her arms, and Nico screwed the suppressor onto his pistol as she put distance between them. Cesare groaned as he began to stir. This man thought he could walk into Nico's town and turn Kaylin's life upside down again? No way. No fucking way. Nico had promised Kaylin that Cesare was gone from her life, and he didn't break his promises. Not to people he loved.

Yes, he loved Kaylin. Perhaps he always had.

"Get up."

"Fuck...you."

"That's your wife's job."

Anger fuelled Cesare's recovery. Nico gave the man a moment to roll to his knees, then shot him in the face, nothing too neat seeing as he'd claim to have acted in self-defence. Cesare crumpled onto a carpet of pine needles, his mouth gaping open and blood and chunks of brain matter spilling from the back of his head.

"Consider that a divorce."

The Bad Samaritan was waiting in a clearing fifty yards away, jiggling the snail in front of Matty as he smushed his fingers against his reflection in her visor. At least he wasn't crying again.

"Dada!"

This time, there was no need to correct the boy. It was a role Nico intended to embrace. He settled Matty onto his hip and faced the woman who both unnerved and fascinated him.

"Now you walk away?"

"Now I walk away. But first, I need to give you instructions."

"Instructions?"

"*Da*. If Alonzo Cavallaro is dead, and I suspect he is, then you will not allow Decker Langdon to be taken into custody. No questions, no fingerprints, no DNA test. Get rid of his gun and give him this one." She held out her own gun once again, and when Nico took it, she backed away. He could shoot her if he felt so inclined, but she must have known he wouldn't. "When the deputies ask, you tell them I did the deed."

"Aren't you afraid they'll catch you?"

Her laugh was oddly melodic. "Afraid? No, I'm never afraid. And if you think they'll look hard for me, then you're mistaken. They like having me around to do what they can't."

"Who is this gun registered to?"

Another laugh. "A ghost."

She headed deeper into the forest, away from the road, but Nico didn't question her sense of direction. This was a woman who knew exactly what she was doing in every facet of her life. Instead, he watched her for a moment as she strode confidently in black leather pants. Her ass wasn't as good as Kaylin's but...but there was something vaguely familiar about it. Nico had seen her somewhere before... From behind...

Holy fuck.

Could it be?

"Hey, wait. Viktoria?"

She didn't run, and she didn't slow. No, she just kept walking at the same steady pace. Had she heard him?

Was he wrong?

She gave a little wave over her shoulder.

Yes, she'd heard him.

And he was right.

He wanted to dash after her, to thank the woman who'd changed the course of his life, but he couldn't, not with Matty in his arms. And Kaylin was waiting.

His family.

They were the priority.

He let the Bad Samaritan go.

KAYLIN

I crawled away and puked into the dirt, then retched some more. I was already covered in blood and brains and who knew what else—what did a little vomit matter?

"You okay, ma'am?"

I didn't recognise the voice, but I didn't care. The man had just shot Alonzo, so as far as I was concerned, he was a hero. He offered me a hand, and I scrambled to my feet. Then I kicked my former brother-in-law in the balls. Hard. Twice. Yes, he was dead, but it was still satisfying.

Then I puked again because half of his head was missing.

"He's gone."

"I know that." I finally focused on my saviour, and although the voice was unfamiliar, the face wasn't. He'd been measuring things in Nico's yard last week. Was he some kind of undercover bodyguard Nico hadn't told me about? "My son. I need to find my son. Where's Matty?"

"I'll take you back to the road, and then I'll go after him."

"No. No! Don't take me anywhere; just find my son."

"Can't leave you out here alone. Do you have any injuries?"

"Who freaking cares? You need to get your priorities straight, mister."

"Ma'am, if I leave you here in the forest and the target circles back, we'll have two problems instead of one." Oh hell, I hadn't thought of that. "As soon as I get a phone signal, I'll call the sheriff's department." The Good Samaritan nodded toward Alonzo. "Is that the boy's father?"

"That's his uncle. His father took him."

"I doubt he'll want to harm his own son."

No, it was me they'd planned to kill. Alonzo had told me he was going to shoot me in the gut and leave me out here for the vultures, right before I'd stamped on his instep and tried to make a run for it. I'd barely gotten two steps before flesh and bone had rained down around me. Did they even have vultures in Oregon? Guess we'd soon know.

"How will you find them?" I asked.

"The same way I found you. City boys don't know how to move through a forest. This gentleman here might as well have carried a homing beacon."

Cesare wouldn't even walk in the park if the grass was damp. Soon after we'd met, I'd suggested going hiking one weekend, and he'd just laughed and taken me out to a fancy restaurant instead. In hindsight, the red flags had been waving, but I'd missed them all.

"Which way is the road?"

"Follow me, and keep your voice down."

I took one step, and my ankle threatened to buckle. Hopped up on adrenaline, I hadn't noticed the pain after I twisted it, but now it would hardly bear my weight. The Good Samaritan caught me before I fell and held me steady.

"I'll carry you."

"There's no need. I weigh quite a lot."

"It's faster this way, ma'am."

"But—"

"Trust me."

He slung me over his shoulder as if I weighed nothing, holding my wrist with one hand and his gun with the other. Ready for anything. A freaking superhero. Up close, the Good Samaritan smelled woodsy, as if he were part of the forest and not just a visitor. And he was right—this way was much faster.

Although speed was relative. Every minute took an hour as we trekked through the trees, the Good Samaritan scanning for danger and me trying to do the same upside down and not very successfully. Then he stilled.

"Shhh."

Every atom in me went on high alert as my rescuer lowered me to the ground behind a tree and put a finger to his lips.

"Stay here."

My heart threatened to jump out of my throat, but I pressed myself against the tree trunk and hoped. Hoped that if this was Cesare, he'd be joining his brother soon.

But it wasn't.

The Good Samaritan's expression suddenly relaxed, and he held out a hand.

"It's okay."

And there they were. Nico and Matty, heading in our direction, Nico with a gun in his hand and Matty still clutching that damned snail. Good Shelley or Evil Shelley—I couldn't tell which from this distance.

I tried to run toward them, but my stupid ankle gave way and I ended up on my knees in the dirt. The Good Samaritan grabbed me under the armpits and tried to help out, but it didn't matter because Nico was there. Nico and my son, but Nico didn't look happy. No, he looked horrified.

"What did he do to you? We need to get to a hospital."

"The blood isn't hers," my rescuer told him. "She just twisted her ankle, is all."

"Alonzo's?"

"He lost his head."

Nico wrapped me up in arms I never wanted to leave, and apart from a few specks of blood and the glow of sweat, he looked as if he'd been out for an afternoon stroll. Matty was okay too, and I saw now that he was carrying Good Shelley. Maybe she was his lucky charm?

"Where's Cesare?" I whispered.

"Gone. This time, he really is gone."

I couldn't hold back the tears. There was no sadness, only relief that my husband had finally shuffled off this mortal coil to meet his good friend Satan in person.

"Can we go home now?"

"Neither of the vehicles is functional," the Good Samaritan said. "We'll have to wait for a ride."

Nico helped me to stand. "There's also one small matter we have to discuss first."

"Oh yeah?"

"We're not alone out here."

Well, no, but Cesare and Alonzo were both dead, weren't they? Luigi too. When he hit the windshield, his skull had cracked like a watermelon. Someone should have told him to buckle up.

"There are more of these fuckers?" my rescuer asked.

"Not them. Our favourite neighbourhood vigilante is in the area."

"The Bad Samaritan?"

"The one and only. Funny, I always assumed it was you."

"Back atcha, but then at the Peninsula when you ran out to the road without a weapon or a plan, I knew I was wrong. So, who is it?"

"I still don't know. He was wearing a motorcycle helmet. But he seems to know you, and he said that under no circumstances should I allow you to be questioned or fingerprinted." Nico raised an eyebrow. "I'm guessing you have a history you'd rather keep quiet?"

"Something like that," the Good Samaritan admitted. "But I just killed a man. There are gonna be questions."

Now Nico smiled, and it wasn't his usual sweet smile. This one was cunning.

"No, the Bad Samaritan just killed a man. You fired one warning shot, and it went wide. Give me your gun and take this one."

"First, you had no guns, and now you have two?"

"In the Bad Samaritan's words, it's registered to a ghost. Kaylin, *zolottse*, when the police ask, you need to tell them that you didn't see who shot Alonzo."

Right now, I'd do anything for these men.

"I'll say that. I definitely will." But even if the Good Samaritan's history didn't come out, I knew mine was going to. There would be too many questions about what two NYC capos were doing in Oregon for my secrets to slide under the radar. "What will happen to me?"

"Just let me worry about that. I promise everything will work out."

Fat drops of rain began to fall as we headed for the road, and I raised my face to the sky, letting the downpour wash the blood away and cleanse my soul. The rest of my life started now.

42

NICO

"I have questions."

Emmy chuckled. "I thought you might."

"The Bad Samaritan works for Blackwood?"

"From time to time, and she'd dispute the terminology. She's not keen on working *for* anyone."

"You're behind her antics in Baldwin's Shore? The stalker she branded? The sniper shot? The Baldwin thing? Did you take my hundred bucks under false pretences?"

Emmy snorted. "No, that was all off her own bat. I merely gave her a call this afternoon and suggested that if she was in the vicinity, she might want to head in your direction sharpish."

Emmy had also grounded Cesare's jet at Medford, arranged a team of attorneys, and offered to medevac Addy to a specialist facility if that became necessary. So far, Addy was holding her own, still in surgery, but alive. Nico would cover any costs, of course, and he made sure the hospital knew she was to have the best care available. Deck had been interrogated briefly and released, sans "his" gun. As far as the cops were concerned, he was merely a bystander who'd stepped up to save Addy's life and then Kaylin's. Which was one of the few truths in this entire mess.

"The Bad Samaritan killed my father," Nico said.

"It was just a job for her, nothing personal. But she got pretty fucking twitchy when you showed up in Oregon."

"I don't know why—she seems quite capable of looking after herself."

"She is, but it was still tiring having to watch her back day in, day out. How's Kaylin doing?"

"Holding it together, but terrified of going to prison."

Thanks to the new pretrial release system in Oregon, Nico couldn't simply pay an extortionate amount of bail money and take her home. No, because the great state of Virginia had charged her with murder and claimed that she'd fled from justice, she had to stay in custody until there was a court hearing.

Right now, she was handcuffed to a hospital bed, receiving treatment for a sprained ankle that probably didn't warrant inpatient care, but it was the best Colt could do to keep her out of jail, and even that put him in a precarious position. Luca was barely speaking to Nico, blaming him for creating a situation that put Brooke in serious danger and left Addy fighting for her life. And Nico accepted that. He'd done what he thought was right, and it had backfired in a supernova of shit.

How much more was to come?

Luca hadn't wanted Nico at the hospital, and the nurses kept giving him dirty looks when he asked about Kaylin and Addy. In the end, he'd been allowed to bring Matty back to the Peninsula at Kaylin's request, but there would be questions about how much he knew. Had he aided and abetted a fugitive? The alleged crime had happened close to three thousand miles away, so he had plausible deniability—who kept track of every crime in the country?—and Kaylin would back him up on that. The attorneys would be having a great Christmas party this year.

"She won't go to prison."

"Innocent people go to prison all the time."

"Being blunt, innocent poor people go to prison all the time. When it comes to the rich, you're far more likely to find guilty people walking free. The evidence is circumstantial at best. So Kaylin's prints were in the car? Big deal—it was her damn car. She got charged because skipping town made her look guilty as hell."

"She didn't skip town."

"Yeah, and that's what the lawyers will explain. Look, the cops are gonna tread carefully on this. The authorities in Virginia are still taking flak over the Vonnie Feinstein case, and if they lock up another innocent person, especially one who's actually a victim and photographs well, the media's gonna have a field day."

"Kaylin doesn't want her face splashed across the papers."

"Trust me, the governor wants it even less. He's up for re-election in November."

"I hope you're right."

"Fifty bucks says the judge gives her house arrest with a tag while the mess gets unravelled. It'll help if she cries in court."

She undoubtedly would, and the thought tore Nico's heart in two. They should be enjoying their time with Matty in his house on the beach, not gearing up for another fight. And they'd have one, he didn't doubt that.

"I'm not losing any more money to you. And I'm waiting for the Cavallaros to put in a claim for custody."

"Daddy's dead and Grandpa's eating through a tube. Grandma's enjoying her newfound freedom by shopping at Macy's. Otello or Fausto might put in a claim out of principle, but the judge would have to be on crack to give them so much as visitation. Just relax and sit tight. Things look shit at the moment, but there's light at the end of the tunnel. Are you getting the third degree about Cesare's sad demise?"

"I've given one interview with my attorney present. He says it was a clear-cut case of self-defence."

After the Bad Samaritan walked away, Nico had put the magazine back into Cesare's gun, wrapped the man's hand around the grip, and fired a couple of rounds. When he'd told the cops that Cesare had shot at him first, no one had questioned it. The storm washed away much of the forensic evidence, and maybe someone would start a new rumour about Emmy Black's ability to control the weather.

"That's what I'm hearing too. And they've got nothing on Decker Langdon."

"Who is Deck? He's not just a humble carpenter; I know that much."

"That's his story to tell, not mine. Let's just say that he made a decision some disagreed with, and it meant his former position was untenable."

"Is he a good guy? Safe to be around Kaylin and Matty?"

"Yes."

"And the Bad Samaritan?"

"I wouldn't ask her to change a nappy, but yeah, she's fine. That was a nice touch, telling everyone she was a dude. She says thanks."

"Tell her '*pozhaluysta*.'"

"I'll pass it on."

"Are there any new leads regarding the Manassas incident?"

"One. Hallie's heading for Zimbabwe as we speak, running it down."

"Zimbabwe?"

"That's where the trail led."

"Keep me updated."

"You're on speed dial."

"I'm not supposed to be here." Brooke fidgeted on the terrace, hands in the pockets of an oversized cardigan she'd probably knitted herself. Or maybe Darla had made it? The knitting queen. "Can I come in?"

Nico opened the door wider, and Brooke slipped inside.

"How's Addy doing?" he asked.

"They said the surgery went okay, but she hasn't woken up yet. They wouldn't let me see her. Next of kin only. Her mom can't stop crying."

"Brooke, I'm so sorry. If I'd realised how fast Cesare and his brother would find Kaylin, if I'd thought for a moment that they'd show up in less than a month and start shooting at innocent bystanders, I would have handled things differently. Headed overseas, hired a team of bodyguards. I thought she'd be safe here. I thought everyone would be safe."

"Is Matty okay? When those men took them, I called Luca, but he was over toward Coos Bay, and then they drove off in the opposite direction."

"You did good, Brooke."

"I didn't." She wrapped her arms around herself, and her eyes glistened with tears. "I think...I think it's my fault that they came."

What was she talking about? Brooke had never met Kaylin before this month, and he couldn't imagine a woman like her associating with the Cavallaros. Brooke had been born and raised in Baldwin's Shore. Had she ever even travelled to New York?

"Why would you think that?"

For the life of him, Nico still couldn't understand how Cesare had arrived at the gates of the Peninsula.

"Because I heard Luca talking to Colt, and he said that

Katy—Kaylin—bought a toy snail for Matty on eBay, and it wasn't just the same as the toy he left behind, it *was* the toy he left behind. There was an AirTag inside it. And *I* was the person who said she should look on eBay for a replacement. I never thought... I just...I just didn't *think*."

That was how the motherfucker had found Kaylin? Through a damn toy? Nico felt both fury and a grudging admiration. The scheme had been so simple. So elegant. Success hadn't been guaranteed, of course, but for so little effort, what had there been to lose? For the price of mailing a package, he'd been able to go right to Matty. The biggest shock was that Cesare had known his son had a favourite toy, but perhaps Lyndsey had told him?

"The only people responsible for what happened are Cesare and Alonzo Cavallaro. Cesare was the man who abused Kaylin, and Alonzo was the man who shot Addy."

"But—"

"No buts. All you did was be a good friend."

"If I hadn't—"

"Maybe he would have found her another way. You can't blame yourself."

"Can you tell her I'm sorry?"

"Just give her a hug when she gets back. She's going to need people like you around her."

"She's coming back?"

"I'm doing everything in my power to make that happen." Nico only hoped it would be enough. How much would Emmy Black charge for a jailbreak?

"Did...did Kaylin really kill a man? There are all these rumours flying around..."

"No, she didn't. But the Cavallaro family made it look as if she was guilty and then held the charges over her head so she couldn't leave."

"When I heard the news, I didn't believe it, but the police said..."

"The legal system doesn't always lead to justice."

Brooke gave Nico a strange look. Curiosity mixed with a hint of apprehension.

"No. No, it doesn't. You're not the only person around here who thinks that way."

It dawned on Nico what she was talking about. *Who* she was talking about.

"Yes, you're right."

Brooke chewed on her bottom lip, mentally battling between fight and flight. Nico had seen people struggle with that dilemma a thousand times, usually in his father's company but occasionally in his own.

Finally, Brooke spoke. "Luca thinks it's you, you know."

Present tense? Interesting. Though it made a certain amount of sense. What better way to hide the truth about one's alter ego than to falsely accuse him of killing a man while you were busy shooting someone else? Deck would never spill the secret, and neither would Kaylin.

"And what do you think?"

"I think...I think that if you did do any of those things, then I should say thank you."

Nico could hardly say "you're welcome," could he? The Bad Samaritan didn't mind being blamed for a death she hadn't caused, but would she be as relaxed if a third party took the credit for her handiwork? Far better to let ambiguity do the heavy lifting.

"At times like this, it's hard to see a way out of the darkness, but fate works in mysterious ways." There, that sounded suitably philosophical. "Can I interest you in a drink or something to eat? I don't suppose there was much on offer at the hospital."

Nico hadn't been hungry enough to check. All he'd eaten

today was a few bites of Matty's omelette and a handful of grapes.

"I shouldn't. Honestly, I don't even know why I came here. I guess I just wanted you to find out what happened from me rather than somebody else."

"No, you came because you have a conscience." A rarity these days, but Brooke Bartlett was quite possibly the kindest woman Nico had ever met. That she should throw herself on the proverbial sword out of guilt was no surprise. "You came because you're a good person. How did you get here, anyway? Did you walk?"

Brooke nodded. "I needed to clear my head."

"Then I'll have the chef prepare a box of food to go, and my driver can drop you home. I'd do it myself, but I can't leave Matty."

"Is he okay?" Brooke face-palmed. "Duh, what a dumb question. Of course he's not okay. He must be traumatised, and confused, and missing his mom. Is there anything I can do to help?"

"There is one thing. The team of attorneys I've hired needs the assistance of a good local counsel. Could you put in a word with your brother?"

"Did you ask him already?"

"He said he had to sleep on it."

Nico understood why—Aaron's friendship with Luca and Addy went back to their childhoods—but Nico still wanted him in his corner. There was nobody sharper than Aaron Bartlett, or more familiar with the locals.

"I'll speak with him in the morning."

43

HALLIE

"Forget coming to New York," Collier said. "I'll move to Richmond. We should definitely work together more often."

"I don't always get to travel like this. Most of the time, I drive a ten-year-old Honda."

But today, we were relaxing high above the clouds on the larger of Emmy and Black's two jets, destination Zimbabwe. When Dan had asked me who I wanted to take with me, it hadn't been a difficult decision.

"Beats the subway."

We were on the trail of "Alan Thing," also known as Alain Thibault, or so we hoped. Providence had been working overtime, trawling the internet for clues. With so much uncertainty over the name, I'd asked Blackwood's digital assistant to search on Alan, Allan, Allen, Alain, Alein, Alun, Alin, and Alen, all the possible spellings plus any surname that began with T-H, combined with data that placed him in the Manassas area around the date Alonzo had run over a cop.

We'd already ruled out Allen Theroux, a junior reporter from *France Aujourd'hui*, a Paris-based news website, who'd been unlucky enough to draw the DC beat. Turned out his expense account had only covered a bargain-basement motel, but a different bargain-basement motel than the one Kaylin had been snatched from.

Next up was Alain Thibault. These days, he was an award-winning photographer with a popular travel blog, one that focused on everyday lives rather than filtered beauty. But three years ago, Thibault had been a twenty-one-year-old college dropout trying to find the meaning of life as he travelled from east to west across the United States. His old blog—where he talked about himself instead of other people—had been deleted, but Providence had found a cached copy. And during the time in question, he'd been in Virginia, staying in substandard accommodation if his comments on bedbugs were anything to go by.

Three days ago, he'd posted pictures from Victoria Falls, Zimbabwe, and despite being a digital nomad, he hadn't answered any of our messages. So now we were going to find him.

A day later, Collier wasn't feeling quite so chipper about being my partner.

"Haven't these folks heard of suspension?" he grumbled, trying to get comfortable in a seat that was fifty percent duct tape. "Or AC?"

"Want me to open a window?"

"The mosquitos are the size of pigeons."

Sifiso, our local colleague, offered a can of bug spray through the gap between the seats, and I coughed as Collier coated himself liberally. We'd just missed Thibault in Zimbabwe, but according to a post on his blog this morning, he was on his way to the Mkhaya Game Reserve in Eswatini to photograph black rhinos. Had he arrived? We had no idea because there was no electricity or internet at the camp. The brochure framed that as a good thing—venture off-grid, commune with nature—but I was clutching my satellite phone as if it were a lifeline.

"Are we nearly there yet?" I asked.

Collier chuckled. "Isn't that what kids say?"

Sifiso twisted in his seat. "Maybe thirty minutes, ma'am."

Blackwood didn't have an office in Eswatini, but it did have an alliance with a local firm, and Sifiso had been dispatched to assist us along with a driver. According to the guidebook I'd read on the plane, Eswatini was one of the safer countries in the region, but women were advised against travelling alone, and moving around after dark wasn't advisable, partly due to the lack of street lighting. The jeep ride south was terrifying—some drivers went too fast, some went too slow, and around every second corner, there was some kind of livestock standing in the road.

But the country was stunningly beautiful once we'd gotten out of the city. Rocky outcrops and rolling green hills dotted with small buildings spanned the horizon, and there was so much wildlife. I swear I spotted an elephant in the distance when we stopped for gas. Most people spoke a little English, and everyone we encountered seemed genuinely happy to see us. I only hoped Alain Thibault felt the same way when he heard we'd stalked him across two countries.

We couldn't simply drive into the Mkhaya Game Reserve. Visitors were permitted on pre-booked tours only, and our Swati contacts had taken the easiest option and booked us a one-day package, complete with three game drives, a walk among the wildlife, three meals, and a family cottage. That would give us twenty-four hours to discover whether Alain Thibault was the missing piece of the puzzle. Sneaking in was out of the question—Mkhaya was reputed to have the best anti-poaching unit in Africa, and I didn't feel like testing their capabilities.

At four p.m., a member of staff welcomed us at the

meeting point and led us to the camp. The villas were individual units set among the trees beside a winding path, open plan and rustic in style. On the plus side, the staff had hung a curtain around my single bed so I could have some privacy. On the minus side, there were no freaking doors. Or windows. And we were surrounded by wild animals.

"Is this safe?" I asked. "Everything being so open?"

The guide grinned at me. "Nobody has died yet."

Oh, that was comforting.

"Do the animals come right into the camp?"

"Sometimes you will see footprints."

I resisted the urge to shudder. Dan wouldn't shudder. No, she'd break out the snacks and stay up late for a rhino-watching party. And as for Emmy, she'd saddle up the beast and ride it into battle. *When I get home, please give me a nice, easy corporate fraud case.* Something that didn't involve claws, horns, or teeth.

"You think we'll see any rhinos?" Collier asked.

"Yes, yes, lots of rhinos. Your first game drive will start in one hour, and then we'll have dinner."

Dinner. I couldn't wait.

Probably I should have been more excited by the prospect of seeing an endangered species up close, but what I felt was guilt. Guilt that Kaylin La Rocca was facing a trial and possibly prison while I relaxed in a vacation destination. Unlike most of my fellow guests, who were chattering excitedly about rhinos by a trio of parked jeeps, I could hardly wait until dinner, and not because of the traditional local cuisine. No, I was just happy that meals were communal. If Alain Thibault was in Mkhaya, we'd see him over platters of grilled meat, cornbread, and sweet potato.

Assuming I survived any encounters with the local inhabitants, anyway.

"Are the rhinos friendly?"

"The white rhinos, yes. You can climb out of the Land Rover and take pictures."

"What about the black rhinos?"

The guide waggled his head from side to side. What did that mean?

"Not so much."

"What happens if one heads in our direction?"

"You should climb the nearest tree."

"Is that a joke?" I asked Collier as the guy moved on to speak with another guest. "It's a joke, right?"

"It is half a joke." The voice came from behind us, the accent unmistakably French. A jolt of excitement ran through me. "The black rhinos are not safe, but the guides won't put you in any danger."

I turned. Alain Thibault was handsome in a wild way, his skin tanned dark, sun-bleached hair curling around his shoulders. His cargo pants and faded blue T-shirt had seen better days, but the camera around his neck was top of the line. He offered a hand.

"I am Al. I'll be joining you on your game drive."

"Hallie, and this is Collier."

"You're here on vacation?" The question was a formality. He thought he already knew the answer, and he glanced at my hand. "You're not the couple on their honeymoon?"

I had two options—either I could go softly-softly, tell a small fib and come clean later, or I could be open with our reason for travelling halfway around the freaking world. Instinct told me Thibault would appreciate the second approach. His blog focused on people's stories, the good, the bad, and the ugly.

"Actually, we came to see you."

"To see me?" He seemed surprised but not horrified. More curious. I took that as a good sign.

"Sorry to show up unannounced. I tried sending a message, but…"

"I am bad at replying. I know this. My last assistant quit while I was trekking through Cambodia, and I haven't found a new one yet." He shrugged, apologetic. "My agent tells me I should rearrange my priorities. Is it about photographs?"

"It's about a crime."

Thibault held up both hands and took a step back. "What I did was a service to the environment. If you want the real criminals, you should be looking at the logging company. Deforestation destroys habitats, creates pollution, and ruins the planet for the next generation."

"Uh, I don't know anything about any logging."

"This isn't about the trucks?"

"No, no, no. This is about the time you spent in Virginia."

"Virginia? The United States? That was years ago."

"I appreciate that. Did you stay at a motel named the Bluebird Inn?"

"I stayed at a lot of places. Maybe one of them was called the Bluebird Inn, but I don't recall the name."

"A real run-down motel," I said. "Thirty rooms, vending machines in the lobby."

Thibault laughed. "I tend not to spend money on frivolities. All I need is a place to sleep. Life is about experiences, not material things."

"I have a picture if it would help to jog your memory."

"Sure, I will look."

I'd printed a selection of images before we left the US—the motel, Kaylin, the vehicle in question, the victim, and both of the Cavallaro brothers. I handed them to Thibault.

"Let me know if anything looks familiar."

He thumbed through the stack, pausing to study each image. "I have a vague memory of the place, but I don't recognise the people. What is this about?"

"There was a hit-and-run near the motel on the last night you stayed there. A man walking home from a family dinner was knocked down, and this lady…" I tapped Kaylin's picture. "She got blamed, but we believe she's innocent. Somebody took her car."

"I'm sorry, but I can't help you. It happened late? If I'm remembering correctly, on my last night there, I went to bed early—eight or nine o'clock—because we had to catch a bus north in the early hours. Have you ever been to New England? People say that fall is the best time to visit, or summer, but winter didn't disappoint."

Dammit. We'd travelled across two continents to the middle of freaking nowhere, and it had all been a waste. Alain Thibault wasn't a witness. He was just another piece of the puzzle that didn't quite fit. And if he'd gone to bed early, he would have missed Beatrix and her client.

"While you were at the Bluebird Inn, did you speak with a couple named Joe and Rachel Smith? They had a young baby."

"The names, they are not familiar, but I recall a couple with a baby. I asked if I could take their picture, but they didn't want that. I'm afraid I didn't speak with them further. They were…how do you say it? Cagey?"

"Right. Cagey."

Another dead end, and I hadn't even seen a rhino. Not that I was sure I wanted to, but everyone back home was gonna ask.

"We?" Collier asked.

"Pardon?" Thibault's accent was definitely easy on the ears.

"You said 'we' caught a bus north. You weren't alone?"

I quickly replayed the conversation in my head. *We.* Yes, he had said that, and I'd totally missed it. Was it important?

"Ah, *non.* I was with a friend, but she had her own room."

"At the Bluebird Inn?"

"Yes, just for one night."

"What was her name?"

A pause. "Ellen. Her name was Ellen."

Ellen? Who the heck was Ellen?

"There isn't an Ellen on the list of guests we have," Collier said.

Thibault waved a hand. "She probably used a different name. The staff weren't the type to care, I don't think. And she was worried about her boyfriend finding her."

"Beatrix? Did she ever use that name?"

"Beatrice, maybe? It's her middle name."

This trip was a real roller-coaster ride, and I wasn't yet sure whether to puke, scream, or wave my arms in the air. Thibault knew Beatrix?

"You two were friends?"

"'Acquaintances' would be a better word, but now we are friends. I met Ellen in a diner one night, and she looked as though she needed to talk. I'm a good listener. It's how I make a living, but I don't print every story on the internet. Ellen's was one that needed to stay private."

"You're still in touch with her?"

Thibault nodded. "She needed a fresh start, so I bought her a bus ticket to New Hampshire."

"A kind gesture."

"Rich men, poor men, when we die, we're all the same. We can't take our money with us, so I prefer to spend mine on doing good in this lifetime. Ellen just needed enough to get away from Virginia and find a place to stay. She insisted on repaying me later. Called it a loan, even though it was meant as a gift. But going back to your original question, she didn't mention seeing anything untoward that night. I would have remembered."

"Could we speak with her?" I asked. "She was awake later

than you, and sometimes people see things without realising they're important. Is she still in New Hampshire?"

Until then, Thibault had been open and friendly, but when his expression shuttered, I realised I'd pushed a button I shouldn't have. It was the second reminder in as many minutes that I was still relatively inexperienced when it came to investigations. Dan said I had good instincts, but Collier had spent years honing his.

"We don't mean Ellen any harm," he said. "I understand how this must look, us showing up out of the blue, but we wouldn't be here if it wasn't vitally important. A young woman who has already spent years going through hell at the hands of an abusive husband is sitting in Oregon, handcuffed to a hospital bed, and unless we can prove her innocence, her next stop is jail."

"I don't even know who you people are."

Collier produced a business card from one of the many pockets in his cargo pants. "We both work for Blackwood Security. The young woman is named Kaylin La Rocca, and a friend of hers hired us to get to the bottom of this mystery. If you want to look up the details online, much of the case is public knowledge. We have a satellite phone with access to the web."

"I have my own." Thibault grimaced. "My agent says it's a necessity. Can you spell the name for me?"

Collier did so, and when Thibault disappeared along the path to his hut, I sagged against a tree.

"I messed that up."

"We work as a team, Hallie. And we found two of our missing witnesses, so let's take that as a win."

"Thibault was asleep. We've still got zip."

"Don't write Beatrix off before we've spoken with her."

Beatrix. Beatrice. Ellen. Possibly not a lady of the night as the receptionist had thought, but rather a woman fleeing a bad situation, just as Kaylin herself had done. Thibault had been her Nico.

Finally, he returned, and this time, he was holding a phone. "She'll speak with you, but you'll have to be quick because the vehicle leaves in ten minutes. And you should find your bug spray before we go."

Thank goodness. Not about the bugs—because yikes—but that Ellen hadn't blown us off. One way or another, we'd be able to close down another avenue of investigation today. Thibault took a seat at a makeshift table, a big tree stump surrounded by logs with colourful cloths draped over them, and put the phone between us.

"They're here," he told Ellen. And to us, "Ask your questions."

Collier nudged me with a foot. He wanted me to speak.

"Uh, thank you for agreeing to talk to us. Has Alain explained what this is about?"

"A little." Her voice was soft and high-pitched, friendly but cautious. "He said there was a car accident the last night we stayed at the Bluebird Inn?"

"There was. Do you remember that night?"

"I'll never forget it. I was so freaking scared that Wyatt would find me before I managed to leave that I barely slept."

"Did you go there often?"

"Only when he was really drunk. To give him time to cool off, you know? Whenever he got hungover, his temper came from the devil himself. Oh, he still got mad when I came back, but it was fists rather than feet."

Thibault looked angry, but not at us this time. His blog painted a picture of a pacifist, but I had a feeling that if he were alone in a room with Wyatt, Ellen's ex might lose a few teeth.

"I'm so sorry that happened to you."

"Alain showed me that there are still good men in the

world. Anyhow, that night, I mixed Benadryl into Wyatt's dinner and snuck out the back door with next to nothing."

"What time did you arrive at the Bluebird Inn?"

"Nine thirty? Or ten? It took a while for Wyatt to fall asleep."

"Did you see anyone else in the parking lot? There was a dark grey Toyota parked outside room sixteen, right next to yours, and that's the vehicle that was involved in the accident."

"Maybe? I don't remember much about the car, only the man getting into it."

"You saw a man?"

"Outside the room next to mine. The parking lot was mostly empty that night, and he reminded me of Wyatt. Tall, dark hair, a goatee. I thought at first it *was* Wyatt, and I just about had a coronary. Then I wondered if he was stealing the car because he seemed kinda furtive, but he must've had a key because he drove off pretty fast."

We had a witness. We had a freaking witness, and she'd just described Alonzo Cavallaro.

"Do you think that you could pick the man out if you saw him again?"

"I-I don't think I'd want to see him. What if he's dangerous?"

"It would be a photo line-up. The main suspect actually passed away recently, so the police can't question him."

"I guess? As long as I don't need to go back to Virginia. I heard Wyatt got married, but he'll still be bitter. That man holds a grudge like no other."

"We'll be able to arrange a meeting that's convenient for you." I didn't like to take advantage of my relationship with Ford, but he'd help out if a woman's freedom was at risk. "I hope you found happiness after you left."

"I did. It took a while, but I trained as a vet tech, and my new man has four legs and a tail that never stops wagging."

"I'll bet he doesn't leave laundry all over the floor either."

Ellen giggled. "He's very well trained. Alain can give you my number if you want to arrange the photo thing."

"I appreciate your help more than you can ever know."

"That lady shouldn't be in jail. Alain told me her name, and I searched on the internet. *Kaylin.* I think I saw her too, right as I arrived. She was crossing the street toward the gas station. I remember because she looked the way I felt. Scared."

"You might be thousands of miles away, but I really want to give you a hug right now."

"If you're ever in Laconia, maybe we could get a coffee?"

"I'd like that."

We had our witness, and Kaylin was safe. Well, safe-ish. Would the Cavallaro family let her be, or would they go all out for revenge? Nico had hired extra security, I knew that much. He was Blackwood's best customer at the moment.

Thibault tucked his phone back into his pocket and handed me a can of bug spray.

"Here, use this. The guide is waiting."

44

KAYLIN

"The charges have been dropped."

Aaron Bartlett stood in my hospital room, arms folded as he delivered the news. He didn't seem particularly happy, but I couldn't blame him. I'd nearly gotten his sister killed. Brooke didn't seem to bear the same grudge, seeing as she'd convinced him to represent me, and for that I was truly grateful.

"The charges against me? In Manassas?"

"A new witness came forward. Things are moving fast and the paperwork hasn't caught up yet, but you should be out of here today."

I would have hugged him if I hadn't been cuffed to the bed frame. I'd read romance novels where women actually enjoyed that—go figure.

"No jail?" I asked, just to check.

"No jail. It's over. They'll probably let Nico in to see you soon."

Nico. At the mention of his name, my eyes went watery. He'd been my rock through all of this. The one person who'd believed in me no matter what the evidence said. The man who'd given me a home and stepped in to care for a child who wasn't even his. I'd spend the rest of my life in his debt.

"Thank you. Thank you, thank you, thank you."

"Don't thank me; thank the investigators who travelled to Africa and tangled with a rhino in pursuit of justice."

"A rhino? Are you joking?"

"One of the missing witnesses from the Bluebird Inn was staying on a game reserve."

"Oh my gosh. Is everyone okay?"

"Apparently, one of them climbed a tree pretty damn fast."

Seemed as if Nico wasn't the only person I owed a debt of gratitude. A thank-you card just wasn't going to cut it, but I had nothing else to offer. All I did was cause people problems.

"Have you seen Addy today?"

She'd been shot with a small-calibre, full-metal-jacketed bullet, which was the only reason she was still with us, according to the one doctor who'd given me any information. Even so, she faced a long road to recovery, and this was only day five.

Aaron gave a curt nod. "She's awake and asking for Mary's triple chocolate cookies."

"That's a good sign, right?"

"I doubt she'll feel quite so perky when they turn off the morphine."

"I'm so sorry."

"Colt will be along to speak with you soon."

I lay back on the pillows, not that I had a choice in the matter, and blinked away tears. Aaron had said it was over, but in my heart, I knew it never would be. Not as long as there were still Cavallaros breathing. Not as long as Matty was still with me. Vito, Otello, Fausto... They'd never stop looking for us. Their stupid family honour was at stake.

And so were the lives of everyone I cared about.

"I can't stay."

"Kaylin, *zolottse*, I understand it's been a difficult week, but if you think I'm going to drive to Portland International tonight and load you on a plane bound for Madagascar or Uruguay or some other far-flung place, think again."

Madagascar? I hadn't considered Madagascar...

I'd been back at the Peninsula for three hours. Or rather, Fort Peninsula, Oregon's newest supermax vacation resort. There were guards everywhere. Oh, they tried to look unobtrusive, but there definitely hadn't been this many muscly guys in sunglasses hanging out by the pool the last time I was here. And the bulges in their Bermuda shorts suggested they were packing entirely the wrong kind of heat.

"Fine, I'll hitch a ride if I have to."

"You're safe here."

"That's what you said last time, and now Addy's in the h-h-hospital."

Nico wrapped me up in his arms, and I melted against him. This was exactly where I wanted to be, forever, and curse the stars for aligning wrong and sending me into Cesare's path instead. Nico was my safe place, and Matty's too. My son was sleeping now, barely aware of all the drama swirling around him. Nico had kept him insulated from the worst of it.

"They'll need a few days to regroup, and that gives us time to make plans and work out where we want to go. We'll do this properly."

"We?"

"You're mine, Kaylin, and I intend to keep you. Not in a creepy, lock-you-in-the-penthouse way," he added hastily.

"But your life is here."

"Much of my business can be run remotely, and that's

what I'll do if you'd prefer to live someplace else. But we'll need to find a suitable property and arrange security, not just hop on the next plane and work things out when we get there."

"What if you have business meetings? What if you want to buy a new property?"

"The move will only be temporary."

"Will it?"

Nico kissed my hair. "The Cavallaro family can't escape justice forever."

I wanted to believe him. I *needed* to believe him. "Someday, I want to come back here. I want to come back to this place, this life, with you."

"And we will."

His lips moved to mine, and I glanced past Nico, through the kitchen window to the yard beyond. If we hadn't had an audience, I'd have hopped up on the counter and let Nico remind me exactly who I belonged to, but instinct told me these security men wouldn't miss much.

"I need you," I murmured.

"You have me."

"No, I *need* you."

As usual, he got me. A second later, I was in his arms, being carried to the bedroom. No, the bathroom. He deposited me onto the counter and pressed his forehead against mine.

"Do you want rough or sweet, *zolottse*?"

Sweet had its place, but right now, I wanted him to claim me. To fuck the demons right out of my soul.

"Rough."

"Good. We're on the same page."

He shoved my dress up my thighs and tore my panties off with one sharp tug, and my libido ratcheted from room temperature to inferno in three-point-five seconds. He kissed me hard, bit my lip, smacked my ass, and wrapped my hair around his fist.

"Are you ready, my dirty little slut?" Nico nipped at my earlobe. "Are you wet for me?"

Why was it such a turn-on when he said that? I slipped a finger between my legs and showed him the glistening evidence, then nearly came on the spot when he sucked it clean.

By the time he rolled on a condom and slammed into me, the first tendrils of an orgasm were already stirring. He promised rough, and I got borderline brutal, his hands clawing at my ass as he thrust. I raked his back with my nails, curses slipping from my lips like honey. I hadn't expected to like it this way, so wild, but with Nico, it worked. *We* worked. Sweet was good, but rough made me feel alive, and fuck only knew I needed that today. I came with a strangled cry and Nico's hand wrapped around my throat, plus the overwhelming feeling that all was finally right with the world, Addy's injuries excepted.

I finally had my dark and dangerous man, but this one *would* do anything to protect me.

"There aren't enough words to say how sorry I am."

Addy nudged a plate full of chocolate cookies across her overbed table. Brooke was in a chair beside her bed, Sara Baldwin was arranging flowers in a vase, and Deck was sitting on the other side of the room, his attention on the door, quietly alert. Nico had hired a bodyguard to sit in the hallway outside, but I knew there was no better man for the job than Decker Langdon. I'd seen him in action.

"Cookie?"

I shook my head. My appetite had deserted me. Nico hadn't wanted us to come to the hospital, but I'd worn him down over the course of two days.

"It wasn't your fault. Brooke told me what happened. Did you really marry a Mafia don?"

"He was only a capo."

"Ohmigosh! It's true?"

"Unfortunately."

"What an asshole. I've read, like, two hundred Mafia romance novels, and at no point does the guy shoot at his wife. I told Brooke to go through my bookshelf and burn all those lies." She turned to her bestie. "Did you do it?"

Brooke nodded. "In your parents' yard. Elmira Fairbanks saw the flames and called the fire department."

"Yikes. Hey, did they send any cute firefighters? Did you take pictures?"

"Uh, a couple? But they barely got out of the truck, and they were too busy laughing to pose for photos."

"Never mind. They're only second-rate heroes." She turned back to me. "I heard you saw the top dude in the forest. The Bad Samaritan? What's he like?"

"That part isn't true."

Brooke must have nudged Addy a little too hard, because Addy gasped.

"Sorry!" Brooke said. "I forgot."

"How can you forget? When Blue visited earlier, she said I looked terrible."

"She's probably jealous because she only got shot in the arm." Brooke glanced first at Deck and then at Nico. "Anyhow, we shouldn't talk about the Bad Samaritan."

"Why not? It's not as if I'm saying anything bad. He's a hero. If I had superpowers, I'd totally use them for good as well."

Nico was stifling a smirk, and I knew why. He'd come face

to face with the Bad Samaritan and lived to tell the tale, although he swore he hadn't recognised the man. The only other person to have such a close encounter was my son. Matty seemed to recall blessedly little about that day, and I wasn't going to stir up his memories with questions.

"Sometimes it's best to let sleeping dogs lie," I said.

"The Bad Samaritan isn't a dog. He's a wolf. Or possibly a lion. Or both? Do you ever read shifter romance? There's this book where the hero turns into a lion-wolf hybrid and protects the heroine from this crazy-ass cage fighter who won her as a prize. Brooke, you didn't burn that one, did you?"

"I don't think so?"

"It had a hot shirtless guy on the cover."

"Nearly all of your books have hot, shirtless guys on the cover."

"This one has a wolf-lion tattoo. I'll find it when I get home." Her smile faltered. "Although that could be a while. The doctors say I'll be here for weeks."

"Whatever help you need, I'll make sure you get it," Nico said.

"What if I need a sexy butler to bring me snacks?"

"Then I'll hire you a sexy butler. There must be an agency for that sort of thing."

"Okay, maybe getting shot wasn't so bad. I just wish it hurt less. Do you think I can get some more pain pills?"

"I'll ask the nurse."

When the nurse came, she gave Addy medication, but she also kicked the rest of us out. Ms. Crowe needed to rest, she said. Trauma took time to heal.

Addy didn't bear me a grudge, and Brooke said Luca and Aaron would come around in time. It had been a shock, that was all. And Brooke still blamed herself for Cesare finding me in Baldwin's Shore in the first place, even though Nico and I both assured her that it hadn't been her fault.

I felt like a hypocrite telling her she needed to tamp down the guilt and move on when I knew I never could. The Cavallaro family still wanted me dead. I'd spent the last two days researching potential new homes, new places to run, new places to hide. I'd ruled out mainland Europe because I wouldn't feel safe anywhere in easy reach of Italy, Nico didn't want to be near Russia, and anywhere with political instability was also in the "nope" column. We'd considered England, but the Cavallaros would expect that, seeing as Nico had a home there. Canada was a possibility, as was the Caribbean. Colt had suggested Valetia, and Australia and New Zealand had made the shortlist too.

But in truth, I didn't want to leave Baldwin's Shore. I understood why Nico had chosen the tiny town as his home. There was a real sense of community and nature's beauty right on the doorstep. As I fell asleep in Nico's arms that night, I made a silent wish.

Please, make the Cavallaro family disappear.

45

EMMY

"The Royal Suite?" I crossed my legs at the ankles and leaned back in one of the less-than-comfortable chairs in Nico's living room. "Did I just get a promotion?"

"You deserve it."

"The credit for Manassas goes to Hallie and Collier, actually. They were the ones who trekked halfway around the bloody world to find the witness."

"Is that why you billed me for a two-person safari?"

"Trust me, they didn't go for fun. Well, maybe Collier did, but Hallie isn't a big fan of wildlife."

"I heard something about a rhino?"

Yeah, so did I. Collier had barely been able to speak, he was laughing so hard, and there was a video too. Hallie swore the rhino had been ready to charge, but all it did was amble forward and she'd sprinted for the nearest tree. Credit where credit was due, she'd climbed it faster than half the SEALs I knew would have. Collier had caught the perfect shot of her peering out between the branches as the rhino stared up in bemusement.

But she'd got the job done, and that was the important thing. Dan had sent her on a spa break to recover.

Things had moved quickly after we identified Ellen Robley as the missing witness. She'd picked Alonzo Cavallaro out of a photo line-up, which tied in with Kaylin's story. And when Nico's legal team began kicking up a stink, the new police chief insisted on further forensic testing, and a strand of Alonzo's hair was found inside Kaylin's car as well. Sure, his lawyer tried to claim that she was practically his sister-in-law and she'd probably given him a ride, but that was bullshit and everyone knew it. The only loose end was the blood smear, but Kaylin had managed to get ahold of Juan, the former owner of the car, and he recalled shovelling a friend of a friend into the back seat after the guy had one too many and fell over outside a bar. It was possible Mr. Can't-Hold-His-Liquor's grazed leg was to blame. In the end, the cops had agreed to drop the charges as long as Nico and Kaylin went quietly away.

Now I was in Baldwin's Shore for another chat with Mr. Belinsky, and I was almost certain I knew what his next request would be. But as usual, he was faffing around with drinks and snacks instead of coming right out with the question.

"The rhino thing was an overreaction. How are Kaylin and the kid doing?"

I could see them on the far side of the garden, playing in a sandpit with buckets and spades. Kaylin seemed to be having as much fun as Matty, which wasn't surprising. All the people I knew who'd been held captive for any length of time had told me that they'd missed the small things. Being able to take a walk. Breathing fresh air. Feeling the sun on their faces. If I'd been stuck in a New York penthouse for three years, I'd want to make sandcastles too.

"As well as can be expected. She's concerned that the Cavallaro family will come after her again."

"Understandable."

Now we were getting somewhere.

"I want to make sure that doesn't happen."

"Also understandable."

"Any whispers?"

"Fausto's a problem," I said. He'd been talking about revenge, about family honour, about making an example of his ex-brother's former wife.

"It would be convenient if he disappeared."

"That still leaves Vito and his consigliere."

"I doubt Kaylin will send flowers for their funerals."

"Got it."

"Otello?"

"Too lazy to care and too stupid to do anything about it even if he did."

Nico nodded once. "Can I interest you in another coffee? Or a glass of wine?"

"Just coffee. Work commitments preclude me from drinking at the moment."

A smile. Yes, he understood and appreciated the job I had to do. While Nico headed to the kitchen, I rose to look out the floor-to-ceiling windows. The sea was rough today. A storm was coming. Decker Langdon—also known as Jordan Faraday—was building a fence around the pool, presumably to stop the kid from falling in. Nico appeared to be taking stepfatherhood seriously.

Faraday worked carefully, methodically, the same way as he had in his previous job. I had his file now, although I'd had to jump through hoops to get it. Damn, he was wasted here. He was another Dasha, another top-tier operator who'd chosen morals over orders and paid the ultimate price. Not death, but the loss of a job he'd lived and breathed. He'd run, and now he was burrowed in deep, making tchotchkes and waiting for his past to catch up with him.

I slid the door open. One of Blackwood's men was sitting in a lawn chair, and I threw him a salute as I crossed the terrace. He returned the gesture.

"How's the fence going?" I asked Faraday.

"Getting there. Mr. Belinksy wanted something decorative as well as functional, so the work's taking longer than it usually would."

"Attention to detail is important." I offered a hand. "Emmy Black."

There it was. The briefest flash of recognition at my name, but he recovered quickly.

"Deck Langdon."

"The sculptures in the gift shop are yours as well?"

"They are."

"You have talent. I might have some work for you myself, if you're interested."

"What kind of work?"

I gave a little shrug and tucked a business card into the pocket of his jeans. "Oh, you know. Call me if you get bored with woodwork, Faraday."

He didn't say a word as I headed back to Nico's villa, and I didn't look back. I'd shown my hand, and now I'd wait for him to play his, if he wanted to. Softly, softly catchee monkey. Faraday still had what it took. He'd proven that in the forest with Alonzo Cavallaro. Now that he'd had a taste of his old world, would he want another? Dasha hadn't been able to stay away, and neither had I.

"Double espresso, Mrs. Black," Nico said, setting a cup on the coffee table in front of me. "Disgustingly strong, just the way you like it."

"Cheers." I clinked my tiny cup against his. "Here's to the five families."

"Here's to freedom."

Nico's phone pinged twice in quick succession as he prepared Matty's breakfast. Kaylin was in the shower, recovering from an early morning orgasm. Nico's dick had never been so happy, and the rest of him was pretty fucking content too. Kaylin had confessed that she didn't want to leave Baldwin's Shore, didn't want to start over on the other side of the world, didn't want to run again. He'd asked her to hold out for just a few more weeks, but time was ticking. Could this be good news?

Yes.

Yes, it could.

The first message contained another eye-watering invoice from Blackwood Security "for services rendered." The second message came from Colt.

COLT

Did you see this?

Nico clicked on the link and scanned the news article.

New York is reeling from the deaths of three men connected to one of the city's most prominent criminal enterprises. Vito Cavallaro, best known as the boss of the sixth family, passed away in his hospital bed after a short illness. In a separate incident, his son Fausto lost his life when he plunged down the elevator shaft in his apartment building. At the time of writing, it is unclear how the incident happened, but witnesses report hearing him scream as he tumbled to the bottom.

One neighbour who did not wish to be named said he wasn't surprised, that "the maintenance team cuts every damn corner. We paid a million bucks for these apartments, and hot water comes out of the cold faucet."

Fausto Cavallaro was reputed to be among the most ruthless and cold-hearted members of the Cavallaro crime family, responsible for the deaths of numerous men in battles fought over territory in New York's underworld. There seems to be little sympathy for a man who was once accused of extorting money from a children's cancer charity.

On the same night, a long-time acquaintance of the Cavallaros, Giovanni "Carp Face" Ferrara, was found floating face-down in his hot tub by a maid. Sixty-seven-year-old Ferrara, who was often seen driving around the area in a vintage Rolls Royce, was rumoured to be Vito Cavallaro's right-hand man. The two had known each other since they were teenagers. One acquaintance said of Ferrara, "he died as he lived—quietly yet terribly."

The words warmed Nico's heart. Once again, Emmy had come through in spectacular style. An elevator shaft? That was something special, an end the Bad Samaritan would have taken pride in. Could she have been involved? Nico knew better than to ask.

But the woman's identity still bothered him. She clearly knew a lot about the residents of Baldwin's Shore, too much for comfort, and yet she never showed her face. Nico had taken to studying every female resident, careful not to stare too long or too hard, but he hadn't picked up troublesome vibes from anyone.

She was a ghost. A wraith. She'd appeared in the forest out of nowhere, and Nico had no idea how. He'd left his broken phone in the car, so she hadn't tracked him that way, and Emmy had mentioned that they didn't have the number for Cesare's burner. When Nico returned home, he'd checked his clothes for a tracking device. There was nothing. Which left satellites. Was that even possible? The tree cover would have made following by eye a futile endeavour, so maybe some type of thermal imaging? If anyone had access to that kind of technology, it would be Emerson Black.

Cesare, on the other hand, had used the KISS approach—Keep It Simple, Stupid. Blackwood's cutting-edge technology had nearly been defeated by an AirTag. Nico would have laughed if it hadn't been so horrific.

Matty toddled into the room with Not-Shelley in his arms. Thank goodness he'd taken to the new toy—Shelley 1.0 was in an evidence locker somewhere, and Kaylin said if she ever set eyes on that snail again, she'd toss it off a cliff. Not-Shelley, on the other hand, was Matty's lucky charm. He carried her everywhere.

Even through the forest.

The forest...

Fuck.

The pieces clicked together in Nico's head. Where had Not-Shelley come from? She'd been handmade by a woman in Baldwin's Shore. A woman... Darla wasn't an Oregon native. She'd moved here not long before he did.

"Here's your toast, Matty. Do you want juice?"

"Yes, juice."

Nico traded the plate for the snail. Good thing the boy

liked breakfast. He'd eat at least half a slice of toast and jelly before he lost interest, and that allowed Nico time to give Not-Shelley a once-over, checking for any sneaky little additions that shouldn't be there. But he came up blank. No lumps, no bumps, no hidden tracker.

Maybe he'd been wrong?

He filled Matty's sippy cup and focused on the toy again.

"Do you have a secret?" he asked it. "Or am I going mad?"

Unsurprisingly, there was no answer, and perhaps he *was* losing his mind? A shiny blue eye stared back at him, unblinking. The eye... He flipped the toy over and checked the other side. The eyes looked similar, but one was a shade darker. He probed the snail's face gently with his finger, and on the inside, the left eye was noticeably larger.

Well, I'll be damned.

Darla?

Holy fuck, she was hiding in plain sight. Kind of. She kept herself well-covered. He'd never actually seen her ass, thanks to the ridiculous clothes she wore, but on the surface, she was the perfect American. Never put a foot wrong. But would he really expect anything else from the Bad Samaritan? Nico closed his eyes, picturing her face. She *could* be Viktoria. Darla was pretty, even though she made an effort not to be. Memorable, but for her outfits rather than her features.

The whole Bad Samaritan thing had started with Brooke, and she was as close to Darla as anyone got. Brie's rescue had come next, and Brie was tight with the same group. Then there was the vendetta against the Baldwins...

It fit.

The pieces fit.

Nico picked up the phone and dialled the Craft Cabin. Paulo answered, as exuberant as ever.

"This is the Craft Cabin. How can I help you on this lovely day?"

"It's Nico from the Peninsula. Is Darla there? I know she's been speaking with Kaylin about cross-stitch, and I was hoping to buy more kits as a surprise."

"Darla's working at the new store in Virginia this week, but I can help. We have some fabulous new kits in. Does Kaylin like flowers?"

Darla was working at a new store in Virginia? No, she fucking wasn't. She was busy drop-kicking Fausto Cavallaro down an elevator shaft in New York; Nico would bet every cent he had on that. But nice cover story.

"Just send one of everything over."

"All of them?"

"That's right. Do you have a snail?"

"A snail?"

"Matty likes snails."

"I'm sure we can special order one."

"I look forward to receiving it."

It was over. Darla, Viktoria—although Nico was certain neither of those was her real name—had flitted into his life and fixed all his problems. He wanted to kiss her damn feet, but she'd probably kick him in the teeth. Once again, Nico took a seat at the breakfast table where Matty was stuffing pieces of banana into his mouth with his fingers. The boy still called him Dada, and Nico intended to live up to the name in every way possible.

He wanted to watch Matty become a man. He wanted to grow old with Kaylin, and he realised how very lucky he was to have the opportunity. Officer Mike Downie wouldn't see his kids turn into adults. He wouldn't teach his son to drive or walk his daughter down the aisle. Nico had ensured that both of the Downie children had healthy college funds, but it seemed so little compared with the loss of their father.

Cricket trotted into the kitchen, a squeaky toy in his mouth. According to Kaylin, the little pipsqueak had hated both Cesare and Alonzo with a passion, which only went to show that dogs were excellent judges of character. Maybe they'd take a trip to New York someday so he could piss on the walls of the Cavallaro family's mausoleum? The dog, not Nico, although he might be tempted if there were no security cameras around. It was nothing less than those monsters deserved.

"Who's a good boy?" Nico broke off a crust of Matty's abandoned toast and offered it to the dog. "*You're* a good boy."

Dogs were family too.

It was a night to celebrate. Kaylin had agreed that there was no need to move overseas now that the most problematic of the Cavallaros were out of the picture, Addy had been released from the hospital, and Aaron and Luca had thawed enough to invite Nico and his family over for dinner at Deals on Wheels again.

There was more to the Cavallaro story, but Kaylin didn't need to know that. Nico had called in a few old favours, favours from men everyone thought he'd cut ties with, and the New York Bratva was engaged in a turf war with what remained of the sixth family. Emmy had cleared the playing field, and Maxim Mikhailov and his crew were sidelining any last remaining team members.

Kaylin and Matty were free. No ties. Nico hoped that she'd agree to make things legal at some point in the future, but for now, he was just happy to have her in his bed every night, and Matty next door in the nursery. Fatherhood was an unexpected pleasure. Hell, they were going to Wonder World again next week, and Nico was already looking forward to the trip.

It was a full house at Deals on Wheels tonight. Brooke and Luca were there, as were Aaron and Romi. Blue had shown up sporting her usual scowl, the thundercloud to Addy's sunshine. Brie and Colt were there with Kiki and a full complement of bodyguards, which would at least give Nico and Kaylin's own security team some company. Yes, the danger was past, but he was taking no chances.

Sara Baldwin made an appearance with her new beau, Garrett, plus a blonde she introduced as Gracie and a quintessentially handsome but clumsy guy who tripped over one of Vega's toys as he approached to introduce himself. Lewis, an old friend of Garrett's. He was in town working on some kind of research project, and Nico didn't miss the way Addy's gaze followed him around the room. Was there something going on between the two of them?

Paulo was present, as was Everly, and Deck had swapped his usual torn jeans for a smarter pair. And there she was. Darla. This evening, her muumuu was bright pink, and she wore a matching headband. Mousy brown hair hung down her back, and were her eyes truly the colour of cornflowers, or was that fake too?

Nico found himself focusing on her throughout dinner, glancing across when it was safe, listening to every word she said when it wasn't. She gave nothing away. Absolutely nothing. When you studied her, looked beyond the drab hair and dowdy clothes, she really was beautiful, but her body was a mystery. Whoever invented the muumuu should have followed Shelley off the cliff. Darla's American accent was perfect, the dialect on point, and she was delightfully pleasant to everyone. Never raised her voice, never showed irritation, never acted bored. A Stepford hippie.

When Nico wasn't watching Darla, his attention drifted to Kaylin and Matty. *His* Kaylin and Matty. Mistakes had been made in the past, but they were together now, and that was all that mattered. She was speaking with Sara about event planning, discussing the possibility of working together in the future, and for a moment, Nico just closed his eyes and breathed.

Even with the disconcerting knowledge that Viktoria was in town, life was fucking perfect right now.

The downside of having a child was that Matty got cranky long before the evening was over, but family took priority these days. Nico picked him up while Kaylin rushed around saying goodbye to everyone, smiling, apologising for having to leave, promising to catch up later in the week.

"You forgot this." Darla held out Not-Shelley, a benign smile on her face. Her approach had been silent.

Unsettling.

"*Spasibo*," he said, almost without thinking.

Something that might have been amusement flickered in her eyes. "*Pozhaluysta*."

Fuck.

"I don't just mean for the toy," he added softly in Russian.

For the briefest of moments, Darla disappeared, and Nico saw the woman behind the mask. The sharp intelligence she usually kept hidden.

"You're not as stupid as your father, Nicolai."

"Which one was you? The elevator?"

"*Nyet*, the hospital." Then Darla came back. "You have a great evening, hun." She patted Matty on the cheek. "Such a sweetie."

She sauntered off, the muumuu billowing behind her, and Kaylin slipped an arm around Nico's waist.

"Ready to go?" she asked.

Nico's past and his future had clashed in the most unexpected of ways, but he wouldn't change a thing. He brushed his lips across Kaylin's.

"With you? Always."

My next book will be a Happy Ever After Novella, *A Very Happy Valentine...*

To go or not to go, that is the question...

School reunions suck, everyone knows this, but Serena Carlisle has put herself down as a "maybe." Maybe she'll stay home and cry into her ice cream, or maybe she'll put on her big-girl pants and show her old classmates that she's managed to make something of herself.

Marc di Gregorio is Hollywood's hottest property, and Serena's getting paid to kiss him on stage every night. A dream job, right? It would be if not for Owen Cadwallader, the man she last saw eight years ago as she was loaded into the back of a police car at the school prom. The teenage crush she's never been able to forget. He's a "maybe" too, but will Serena manage to hold her nerve and face him again? Or should she take the easy option and drown her sorrows with a handsome heartthrob instead?

For more details:

www.elise-noble.com/hv

The next Blackwood novel will be Knox's story, *The Devil and the Deep Blue Sea...*

It all started with a turtle and a pair of designer sunglasses...

A bodyguarding gig in the Caribbean? Living the dream, right? Former Navy SEAL Knox Livingston soon finds out the trip is no vacation. Pop princess Luna Maara is a pain in everyone's ass, including the local judge's. When Luna finds herself sentenced to a month of community service at a turtle sanctuary, Knox hopes she might finally rethink her behaviour, but little does he know, the nightmare is only just beginning.

Caro Menefee moved to Valentine Cay to escape her past, and the last thing she needs is a rich brat and her entourage invading the peaceful paradise. Although Knox and his equally cocky buddy sure are pretty to look at. And that's all she's going to do: look. She swore off men before she left California, and she has quite enough to worry about without adding two toned six-packs into the mix. The turtle population is declining at an alarming rate, and she's not convinced it's all down to natural causes. Will Knox help or hinder her quest to save a species? And will Caro join the turtles on the endangered list?

For more details:
www.elise-noble.com/deep-blue

If you enjoyed *Secrets from the Past*, please consider leaving a review.

For an author, every review is incredibly important. Not only do they make us feel warm and fuzzy inside, readers consider them when making their decision whether or not to buy a book. Even a line saying you enjoyed the book or what your favourite part was helps a lot.

WANT TO STALK ME?

For updates on my new releases, giveaways, and other random stuff, you can sign up for my newsletter on my website: www.elise-noble.com

If you're on Facebook, you might also like to join Team Blackwood for exclusive giveaways, sneak previews, and book-related chat. Be the first to find out about new stories, and you might even see your name or one of your suggestions make it into print!

And if you'd like to read my books for FREE, you can also find details of how to join my advance review team.

Would you like to join Team Blackwood?

www.elise-noble.com/team-blackwood

facebook.com/EliseNobleAuthor

x.com/EliseANoble

instagram.com/elise_noble

goodreads.com/elisenoble

bookbub.com/authors/elise-noble

tiktok.com/@EliseNobleWrites

The Devil and the Deep Blue Sea

Blue Moon

Blackwood Elements

Oxygen

Lithium

Carbon

Rhodium

Platinum

Lead

Copper

Bronze

Nickel

Hydrogen

Out of Their Elements (novella)

Blackwood UK

Joker in the Pack

Cherry on Top

Roses are Dead

Shallow Graves

Indigo Rain

Pass the Parcel (TBA)

Blackwood Casefiles

Stolen Hearts

Burning Love (TBA)

Baldwin's Shore

Dirty Little Secrets

Secrets, Lies, and Family Ties

Buried Secrets

A Secret to Die For

Blackwood Security vs. Baldwin's Shore

Secret Weapon

Secrets from the Past

Blackstone House

Hard Lines

Blurred Lines (novella)

Hard Tide

Hard Limits

Hard Luck (2024)

Hard Code (2025)

Hard Evidence (TBA)

The Electi

Cursed

Spooked

Possessed

Demented

Judged

The Planes

A Vampire in Vegas

A Devil in the Dark (2024)

The Trouble Series

Trouble in Paradise

Nothing but Trouble

24 Hours of Trouble

The Happy Ever After Series

A Very Happy Christmas

A Very Happy Valentine

A Very Happy Halloween (2024)

A Very Happy Easter (2025)

A Very Happy Thanksgiving (TBA)

Standalone

Life

Coco du Ciel

Twisted (short stories)

Books with clean versions available (no swearing and no on-the-page sex)

Pitch Black

Into the Black

Forever Black

Gold Rush

Gray is My Heart

Audiobooks

Black is My Heart (Diamond & Snow - Prequel)

Pitch Black

Into the Black

Forever Black

Gold Rush

Gray is My Heart

Neon (novella)

A Very Happy Christmas

A Very Happy Valentine

Dirty Little Secrets

Secrets, Lies, and Family Ties (2024)

Buried Secrets (2024)